What can twenty-first century people learn from the life of an Adirondack recluse/guide who lived a hundred years ago?

Author Charles Yaple masterfully paints a picture of nearly-forgotten Adirondack personalities interwoven with his own fascinating journey of discovery....of Foxey Brown's lost homestead in the Adirondack wilds and cold-trailing Foxey's story through the crumbling records and remains of that bygone era of legendary guides and their 'Sports.' Yaple finds much in his search to inform us today as Adirondackers seek to balance the preservation of both local culture and the natural resources giving rise to it. The story of both Yaple's deciphering of the Foxey Brown mystery as well as his re-creation of it in the words of Foxey is an extraordinary accomplishment and contribution to the lure and lore of the Adirondacks--a region well-known for yielding up its mysteries only grudgingly, if at all. And it's a whopping good tale, timeless with its themes of enduring friendship, heartbreak and redemption. *–Bruce Matthews, Executive Director, North Country Trails Association*

While researching for a new book it has been said, "If you live with your character long enough, you begin to think like he does." *Foxey Brown,* the subject of Charles Yaple's book, speaks in words that passed through the mind of the author as the story was woven together. FOXEY BROWN is a compelling story based on bits of vivid information on Foxey's life. It is a solid Adirondack novel – a welcomed addition to the body of Adirondack literature. It is the kind of narrative that captures readers and holds them fast; be wary, it is a book that is hard to put down once you start reading. As Foxey's life unfolds, exciting and unexpected events, tied to Adirondack history, tell the tale of life in a remote forest cabin. Add to this, a well-told analysis of the bond between the Adirondack guide and his client.

The historical novel based on the life of Adirondack hermit, Foxey Brown, is more than a biography. Those who love Adirondack stories will enjoy reading about the historic events of the past century and their connections to the lives of the Adirondack settlers. Known Adirondack characters such as French Louie, Floyd Ferris Lobb, Charles and Julia Preston, among others, have lives intertwined with Foxey Brown. We can but admire the extensive research carried out by author Charles Yaple that was required to flesh out the story of a somewhat little-known Adirondack character of yesteryears. *– Don Williams, Adirondack historian, newspaper columnist, author of Inside the Adirondack Blue Line.*

Charles Yaple's *Foxey Brown*...is a fact-based, woodsman informed, window into the life and times of an Adirondack hermit. The author has literally walked in Foxey's path; he rediscovered the remains of the hermit's century old homestead while doing research for the book and has spent countless hours tra[...] [...] [...] [...]f this fascinating story. You will enjoy this well-w[...] [...]ished Teaching Professor, author of The Complete Pad[...] [...]ssouri River from the Headwaters to St. Louis, Missouri.

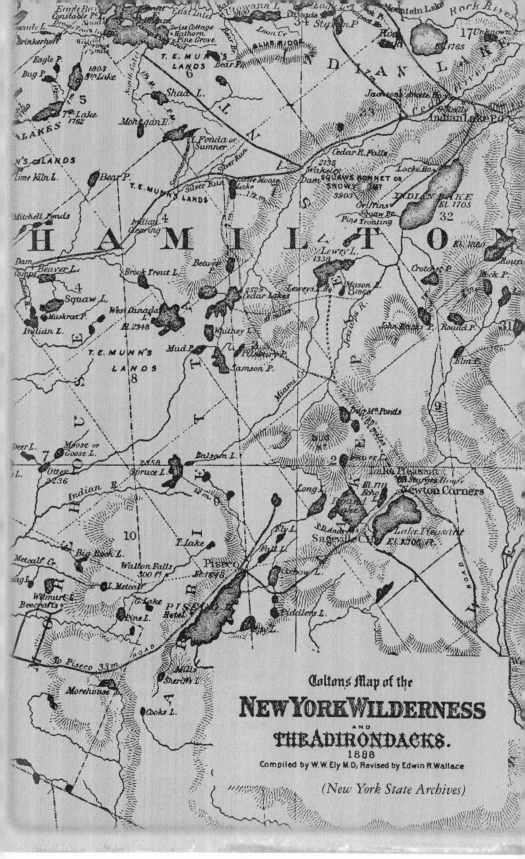

Colton's Map of the

NEW YORK WILDERNESS

AND

THE ADIRONDACKS.

1888

Compiled by W.W. Ely M.D, Revised by Edwin R.Wallace

(New York State Archives)

Foxey Brown

A Historical Novel by
Charles H. Yaple

A Story of an Adirondack outlaw,
hermit, and guide as he
might have told it

Library of Congress Cataloging-in-Publication Data
Yaple, Charles H., 1941-
Foxey Brown: A story of an Adirondack outlaw, hermit and guide as he might have
told it: a historical novel/by Charles H. Yaple

The Library of Congress has catalogued this edition as: 2011905157
ISBN-13: 978-1461042402
ISBN: 1461042402

Cover design by Angelique Bovee,
Jerome Natoli, Jessica Yaple and CreateSpace
Cover photograph: copyright 2008, Frederick T. Adcock and Cynthia E. Adcock
Text design by CreateSpace

To my grandfather Charles H. Yaple retired New York State Conservation Commission officer (1911-1932) who, beginning when I was in diapers, introduced me to the streams, fields and forests of rural Tioga County. Gramps fostered a bond with nature during those critically important formative years and, in so doing, shaped the course of my life. My dearest wish is that there were more grandfathers like him around today. They are sorely needed in this day and age of "nature deficit disorder."

NOTICE:

This book is a historical novel. Due diligence has been made to adhere to historical fact wherever reliable records were available. All named characters are known historic individuals with the exception of George Murphy, Tracy O'Grady, Neil O'Brien, Ned James, Twig Slack, Clint Neff and Sid Rogers. They were invented for purposes of telling Foxey Brown's story as he might have told it. The author assumes responsibility, and any forthcoming supernatural wrath from the historic characters, where he may have falsely attributed certain personality traits. Descendants of those historic characters are invited to correct the author's erroneous ways.

TABLE OF CONTENTS

ILLUSTRATIONS

GROUP FOUR

Introduction

The reasons for writing this book were threefold. First, it was an attempt to tell the life story of a legendary Adirondack character only briefly described in *The History of Hamilton County* and in *Tales of an Adirondack County*. Otherwise, Foxey Brown's adventurous life as a mountain hermit/guide has not been written about other than in brief newspaper articles of the early 1900's. Brown's (aka, David Brennan) brushes with the law, ingenuity creating a wilderness homestead, creativity as a hunting/fishing guide, and ultimate misfortune leading to the largest manhunt in Adirondack history make a compelling story replete with mystery, misfortune, and irony.

The second motive for writing was to describe the impact of governmental regulations that increasingly burdened traditional subsistence lifestyles of working class people in the newly created Adirondack Park during the late 1800's and early 1900's. Confronted with regulations limiting use of state forest preserve lands and prohibited from using heavily posted and guarded private estates; local people resorted to thievery, poaching, arson, and in some cases, murder. The situation has been addressed, in broad strokes, by Karl Jacoby in his book: *Crimes Against Nature – Squatters, Poachers, Thieves, and the Hidden History of American Conservation*. Otherwise, as Jacoby wrote, it is a "hidden history of American Conservation."

Unlike Jacoby's work, *Foxey Brown*...is a historical novel about a man and community faced with eking out a living in rapidly changing times. Based on five years of research, real places, names, faces, and personalities illustrate Adirondack Mountain ways of living along with a historical account of the beginning of conservation laws in New York.

Harvey Dunham's, *Adirondack French Louie: Early Life in the North Woods* also describes mountain living at the turn of the 20th century. Foxey

Brown and French Louie were contemporaries, and undoubtedly, knew each other. While they shared mountain man ways of living, their backgrounds, personalities, and life experiences were considerably different. Readers of New York history, culture, society, and environment will find both *French Louie...* and *Foxey Brown...* interesting reading.

The third, and perhaps most important, purpose for writing the book was to describe how life in the Adirondack Mountains shaped David Brennan/Foxey Brown. Initially, a college educated city dweller; Brennan fled to the mountains to hide from the law and gradually became psychologically compelled, in the pursuit of happiness, to continue living as a recluse. The influences of nature that transformed Brennan were subtle, yet profound, and are sorely needed today by millions of people who live most of their lives indoors surrounded by electronic gadgetry.

Foxey Brown Country 2006 (*Eric Davis*)

Prologue:

Finding Foxey Brown

By definition, going exploring suggests one may get into totally unanticipated things. A simple single-day kayak outing, for example, can turn into fascination and near obsession. So it was with Foxey Brown and the author's five year quest to learn about Foxey's life.

In the summer of 2005, my brother Jerry extended an invitation to go kayaking in the Adirondack Mountains. He spoke about exploring Kunjamuk Creek near Speculator and Fall Stream/Vly Lake near Piseco. It didn't take much coaxing once he described how they were small streams "off the beaten path" and we could probably have them to ourselves if we paddled on a weekday. I was hungry for some time away from teaching summer school and tree farming at our Hermit Hill home in central New York. Little did I suspect a reclusive Adirondack mountain man of the past was about to enter my life.

Kayaking Kunjamuk Creek in August provided some easy paddling, but other than a stop at Kunjamuk Cave, we encountered little spectacular scenery or much wildlife. Kayaking up Fall Stream to Vly Lake was a different experience.

To reach Vly Lake requires paddling up Fall Stream nearly five miles and negotiating around or over numerous beaver dams. The obstacles, however, are only minor nuisances as you are frequently lured on by glimpses of Vly Mountain slowly getting tantalizingly closer and closer. There is a sensation of steadily gaining altitude, of entering a world ruled by wild things, and leaving the human built world behind. Occasional human artifacts of days gone by remind the watchful observer that Fall Stream once enabled and endured a logging industry. However, for the most part, nature, using beaver engineering, has put its wild stamp back on the land.

The last finger of Fall Stream widens substantially before disappearing into Vly Lake. This gem of an Adirondack lake, while only forty or so acres in size, greets the steadfast kayaker or canoeist with all the charm of a body of water nestled between two mountains -Vly and Mud. The scene is of postcard quality and invites photographers to capture its varying moods. Fishing enthusiasts can catch hungry Northern Pike that occupy the lake in good numbers. The knowledgeable angler will, however, lament the days when native brook trout inhabited Vly Lake instead of the mistakenly introduced pike.

For curious paddlers the marshy upper end of Vly Lake offers numerous channels to explore including a hidden passage to Mud Lake. Those hoping to make it to Mud Lake may wish to opt for the kayak as opposed to a canoe due to a quarter mile narrow stretch of water choked with overhanging thickets of brush. It is a beaver's paradise, filled with a perpetually renewing supply of willow and alder – food for web footed wetland farmers but face swatters for humans trying to navigate their watery maze.

The payoff for contorting your body and boat around countless bends and switch-backs, and pulling over a beaver dam or two, is Mud Lake – perhaps more accurately called "Mud Pond." Only a hundred or so yards wide and perhaps 700 yards long, the little body of water has its own charm with Mud Mountain rising behind its western shore. Seldom fished, it offers the angler hungry pike ready to bite even in the middle of a summer day.

The grandest reward, in this writer's estimation, for venturing into Vly Lake is the sunset that can be enjoyed from an east side camping area. (There are only two established spots and the wise traveler does well to stake one out early in the day if visiting on a weekend.) After a good meal around a campfire, a day at Vly Lake ends wonderfully with the sun gradually disappearing behind Mud Mountain leaving behind streaks of light promising another day in the Adirondacks. Anyone appreciating natural landscapes will agree that such light shows are a gift to be remembered. Ironically, a few unappreciative visitors to Vly Lake sometimes bring in, and leave the remains, of their own artificially created light shows. Evidence of such a claim lay partially covered in the ashes of a previous camp fire – firecrackers and rockets used in Fourth of July celebrations. Aldo

Leopold wrote about wild places and the "still unlovely human mind" in his A *Sand County Almanac* classic.

Vowing to return soon, my brother and I headed out the next morning knowing we had found a unique place still not visited by throngs of visitors due to the work required to reach Vly Lake. We said a little prayer that the beaver would maintain their numerous dams to discourage those who would otherwise come with motor boats.

As alluded to in the opening lines of this chapter, life is a journey and one never knows where it might go next. On our way home, Jerry agreed to drive the first leg and I settled in to study my newly acquired map of the West Canada Lakes Wilderness Area. Enthused about the remoteness of Vly Lake I thought there had to be other even more solitary places to explore. After seeing a preponderance of remote small lakes and ponds that seemed to be quite inaccessible, my eyes fell onto the words "Foxey Brown Hermitage" printed across a section of wilderness just north of Vly Lake. Sharing my discovery with Jerry, a long discussion ensued as to what a Foxey Brown Hermitage could be. Somewhat familiar with celebrated Adirondack hermits like French Louie, Noah Rondeau, Alvah Dunning and others, the name Foxey Brown elicited no known stories to us. Could the Foxey Brown Hermitage have been some sort of wilderness retreat, a place started by a church group, or to the other extreme, a house of prostitution? As the miles clicked by we threw out all sorts of wild theories to explain how someone could gain the name, Foxey. Perhaps the person had been an outlaw who "outfoxed" authorities or started a fox farm back in the "heyday" of the fur trade.

Arriving home I did what any modern day researcher would do – execute a "Google" internet search. Thoroughly curious now, I entered the term "Foxey Brown" and clicked the search button. Sure enough up came Foxy Brown, not quite the same spelling but close enough. Clicking the first entry on the Google list of possibilities up flashed an image and information about a modern day Rap musician. Seeing a pretty and attractively shaped young lady singing in a music studio sent me back to the other hits conjured up by my Google search. The singer Foxy Brown occupied every listing before my eyes. No Foxey Browns with Adirondack connections were found. Where next to search? Perhaps some of my Adirondack colleagues at the SUNY Cortland Outdoor Education Center at Raquette Lake would know about Foxey Brown and his hermitage.

My Adirondack friends knew nothing about Foxey Brown, hadn't even heard the name. OK, another cold trail. Let's see, this Foxey Brown Hermitage existed somewhere near the Piseco/Speculator area in Hamilton County. How about the local historical society? Executing another Google search got me to a Hamilton County listing and telephone number for the county historian. Lady luck was now smiling; the telephone rang and was answered by a kindly man named Paul Wilber, a retired SUNY Oswego professor. Sure, he knew about Foxey Brown – "a man of the 1890's who hid out in the mountains near Piseco Lake because he thought he had killed a fellow in a barroom fight back in Boston. And later on, serving as a hunting guide, Foxey lost a rich railroad man named Carlton Banker in the mountains. You can read all about it in *The History of Hamilton County*." My Foxey Brown saga and pilgrimage had begun.

Armed with the basic Foxey Brown story appearing in the *History of Hamilton County* and in Ted Aber/Stella King's *Tales of an Adirondack County*, I hungered to learn more about this mysterious man of the Adirondacks. Did he really kill a man in a barroom fight? What happened to him after he lost a hunting client? What was it like to live as a reclusive mountain man six miles from civilization? Why was he known as a feisty fellow who shot at people? What does his homestead look like today? I was hooked and proceeded to bait my brother for another foray into Vly Lake country. The map suggested we could kayak to the lake, work through the marsh maze, pick up where Fall Stream entered and simply hike upstream until we found Foxey Brown Hermitage. According to the map it could only be a mile or two upstream. No need to involve other people in our quest. It would be our secret adventure.

A late June afternoon in 2006 found Jerry and me facing the water and brush maze at the north end of Vly Lake. We were now positioned to find where Fall Stream entered the lake and visit Foxey Brown's homestead. Knowing which passage led to Mud Lake didn't protect us from entering two other channels that promised to lead to the mouth of Fall Stream. They were dead ends. The third attempt was a charm of sorts as after twenty minutes or so of navigating through overhanging brush and over a beaver dam we entered a large pool in the stream. Glancing to the west bank, we saw the remains of an old brick fireplace and part of its chimney. Had we found Foxey Brown? We quickly docked the boats and began to explore. At our feet lay a large concrete pad nearly thirty by thirty feet wide with the fireplace located near the stream side. Covered with plastic were a wood and a propane fired cook stove. An abundant supply of cut and stacked firewood lay nearby. It, too, was covered in plastic. Had someone already discovered Foxey's old place and was using it as a hunting camp? Gloom and disappointment began to set in as we thought Foxey Brown's homestead might be frequented by many local people. Our appetite for exploration was renewed, however, after consulting the map. This place was much too close to Vly Lake to have been Foxey's lair. Whatever its history we would make it our camp for the evening and move further upstream the next morning.

Sitting around a campfire in the remains of the old fireplace that evening we sensed the place had a long history. How did someone get so much cement in here? Certainly it was not hauled in by backpack or boat. We agreed, "If this place could talk, what stories it might tell." Indeed, it could. We would later learn that our campsite had hosted weary searchers after a long day of looking for Carlton Banker in November 1916 and that a frantic Foxey Brown had visited to inquire if any new clues regarding his friend had surfaced.

Back in our kayaks early the next morning we continued up Fall Stream. The wide pool quickly disappeared and the watery landscape once again became beaver paradise with winding brush choked channels everywhere. After an hour of paddling, pushing through brush, and ducking under fallen trees across the stream we could paddle no farther – the water was too shallow. Not to be deterred, we waded and pulled the kayaks behind lured on by Fall Stream's transition from a placid channel to a fast moving mountain waterway. Rocks and boulders began to stamp their ownership on the watery landscape. It soon dictated beaching the boats and proceeding on foot upstream towards our goal. Surely, we would make contact today. *The History of Hamilton County* said Foxey had lived right on the stream bank where it had been dammed to create Brown's pond.

We had easy going at first with flat, sparsely wooded glades characterizing the stream corridor. Soon, however, large boulders in the stream and steep and heavily wooded banks dominated stream surroundings forcing us to wade and sometimes jump from stone to stone. The cool water was refreshing and revealed a darting brook trout now and then as we waded.

Now travel was slow as we avoided slippery rocks and strong currents by returning to the stream bank. Even the best of beaver engineers couldn't tame this section of Fall Stream.

Lunch time found us approaching a clearing and a tamer piece of water. Expectantly, we rushed ahead thinking "this must be it." Alas, despite the beauty of the site, we had encountered another false alarm. No evidence of a human-made dam or building foundation was to be found. Serious consideration of the area suggested it was a natural clearing most likely kept that way by occasional flooding. Not to be discouraged we embraced our discovery with lunch enjoying the company of a wild and free mountain oasis. The sunlight dancing between trees in the glade, wild flowers sharing their colors and fragrances, and cool air rising off the water provided atmosphere no restaurant can create.

The little clearing was soon behind us and now blown down trees, and steep hillsides surrounding the stream, forced more wading and rock to rock travel. Deep pools sometimes eliminated any choice except to exit and climb over and around fallen trees in the forest. Doing so underscored in my mind the difficulty trees had growing in such thin soil. It also was a testament to the tenacity of life as we encountered trees eight to twelve inches in diameter (breast height) seemingly growing out of boulders.

It had taken us until 3:00 p.m. to travel another mile. Looking ahead on a straight stretch we saw only more mountain stream disappearing into the hills. Deeming it wise to allow plenty of time to return to the Abrams Camp before dark, we agreed to hike one more hour before giving up.

A short time later we began to hear a roar louder than the normal rumble of Fall Stream. Was it water coming over the remains of Foxey Brown's dam? It did look brighter up ahead as if a clearing might also exist there. Traversing from boulder to boulder became easier as their numbers and size increased. Rounding a bend the sound of falling water increased tremendously. Fifty yards later, around another bend, we were greeted by a series of waterfalls with large pools sure to host sizeable brook trout. Rising some forty to fifty feet above us in three levels the falls had created an enchanting forest scene. Seeing them alone would have made our struggles up Fall Stream worthwhile. Despite our desire to find Foxey's hideout we dallied to thoroughly enjoy the waterfalls and its charms. The country boys remaining in our sixty year old bodies delighted in exploring the pools, crevices, and singing waters of that aquatic wonderland.

Following photographing one another posed on different rock outcroppings, we climbed to the top of the falls. Once again, no sign of human habitation or past landscape alterations were visible - only a long corridor of stream and dark forest. Fall Stream had shared some of its treasures but still possessed the remains of the Foxey Brown Hermitage. Sticking to our plan we turned and headed down stream at 4:00 p.m.

We had planned a celebration back at base camp to honor finding Foxey's place. While we had failed in that regard our disappointment was tempered knowing we had visited a special place that day.

Beaten but not defeated, we schemed over the West Canada Lakes Wilderness Area map and vowed to attack the Foxey Brown Hermitage from the upstream side next trip.

Work and other circumstances delayed that next trip until late August 2007. The hike up Fall Stream had "whetted" my appetite to learn all I could about Foxey Brown. The winter of 2006-07 was spent researching the history of the Piseco area, thoroughly reading *The History of Hamilton County*, *French Louie*, and an array of other Adirondack books and old newspapers.

Tantalizing pieces about Brown's life surfaced. To my surprise, I learned he had completed some college studies and was known as a well read and informed man. He also lived at a unique time in Adirondack and American history as his tenure (1890-1921) in the mountains coincided with the second phase of the Industrial Revolution and advent of the American conservation movement. Brown witnessed and had time to reflect on the over harvesting of forests, wholesale slaughter of wildlife for sport and market, the beginning of hunting and fishing laws, and the ejection of squatters, like him, living on public lands. He also lived through a rather brief period when people rapidly changed ways of living transitioning from using horses and buggies to automobiles, from kerosene lanterns to electric lights, and iceboxes to refrigerators. And, of personal concern to Brown, executioners went from using gallows to electric chairs.

Armed with many new revelations about the history of Piseco and the Foxey Brown/Carlton Banker case; my brother and I struck out on a Fall Stream backpacking trip once again in late August, 2007. The plan was to hike the Spruce Lake section of the Northville/Lake Placid trail to where it crossed Fall Stream and then head downstream to find the remains of the Foxey Brown Hermitage.

Before starting up the trail we visited the Piseco Post Office hoping the clerk could suggest a village elder that might know something about Foxey Brown's place. She said, "Why aren't you the lucky ones, here comes Bill Abrams. He's a walking history book of past times in Piseco." Bill was friendly but a little bit guarded talking to two strangers from downstate. We began to chat and, sensing we meant no harm, Bill shared some stories about his grandfather (Floyd W. Abrams) "taking care of Foxey when the old hermit came to town, got drunk, and shot off his revolvers." Floyd did this by shepherding Foxey up to the Abrams Sportsman House and giving him a room for the night until he sobered up – no booze was allowed at the Abram's place.

We also learned the place we had camped on Fall Stream the previous year had been the Abrams family hunting and fishing camp for many years. It had, indeed, been a search headquarters in 1916 when Carlton Banker disappeared. Foxey Brown had surely been there.

After talking for a half hour or so, we asked Bill for directions to Foxey's homestead. He said, "We used to go there when I was a kid, but it has been a long while. You go out the Spruce Lake trail about three miles to where it first gets steep and bends to the left. Then head down over the mountain to Fall Stream. Follow the stream and you'll find the remains of an old foundation Brown used for a barn. Stone work from the dam also should be fairly easy to spot." Barely able to restrain my excitement, I hauled out our map and asked Bill to point out where he would "head down over the mountain." Without hesitating he did so. Not thinking to ask more questions then, I inquired if Bill would allow me to interview him later in the fall. Gaining his approval, we bid farewell and hustled to the trail head. Now Foxey Brown's camp was in our sights! Equipped with map, compass, and a GPS unit my brother had recently acquired, we could not fail. Come what may, we would camp at Foxey's homestead tonight or tomorrow at the latest.

Confidence and a positive outlook are good things. Unfortunately the rigors of back country travel can quickly change an enjoyable outing into an ordeal. The first indicator that all might not go well came from my feet. I had recently purchased a fairly expensive pair of brand name hiking boots. Following good procedure for breaking in new boots I had worn them for nearly a month while cutting firewood and doing various other chores at Hermit Hill tree farm. The difference now was a thirty-five pound pack on my back. About a half mile up the trail, one boot began to cause severe pain in my foot as if the lug sole didn't want to bend. Soon both feet were getting the same cramped treatment. Taking them off, stretching, bending and adjusting the laces did no good. The boots had to go, there was no choice.

Thankfully, I had brought along the same mesh sneakers used the year before to wade Fall Stream. After changing footwear we headed on up the trail. While my feet felt normal for a while, it was increasingly evident the sneakers did not provide the same level of support as the hiking boots. The weight of the backpack on poorly supported feet was taking its toll.

More trouble surfaced as Jerry tried to calculate the distance we had traveled. We had a somewhat cloudy day and the tree canopy along the trail was dense in places. Consequently, he kept losing the satellite signal and soon lost track of where we were mileage wise. And, of course, trying to find by guess and observation where Bill Abrams had meant "the trail gets steep and bends to the left" was difficult at best. The only safe option was to find the ford in Fall Stream up ahead. From there we could know our location for certain and chart a course downstream towards Foxey Brown's homestead knowing full well extra travel time along the stream would be necessary.

Bad luck was still our companion as we approached the Fall Stream ford and camping area. About thirty yards out we began to hear barking dogs. There in the camping area were three large Mastiff breeds tied to trees while their two owners slept in hammocks seemingly totally un-aware the dogs were announcing our presence. We stopped expecting to exchange greetings with the pet lovers. Nothing, no movement at all, came from the hammocks. Had we stumbled upon a murder, suicide or drug overdose scene? Clearing my throat, I yelled "Hello the camp." Mo-mentarily, an arm flopped over the side of one hammock and, then, a heavily bearded head slowly rose above the edge of the other. It slowly said, with a mouth missing two front teeth, "Hey man, how ya doing?"

Being old enough to remember the "Hippie" days, I was transported back in time to an encounter with a group of them in the mountains of Oregon. That time it was at a hot springs full of naked folks smoking marijuana. Right or wrong, this seemed all too similar and I quickly responded, "Good, just passing through on to Spruce Lake. Have a good day." Jerry, similarly assessing the situation, waved a hello salute and began wading across Fall Stream.

Without comment to one another, Jerry and I quickly put several hundred yards between us and our fellow wilderness trekkers. Even my tired feet didn't complain. Stopping and looking back we saw no pursuers but could still faintly hear the dogs barking. Going a ways farther, and getting on the downside of a knoll, returned us to the natural sounds of the forest. Jerry said, "What in the hell was that all about? I thought I had already seen all variations of human carbon-based units." Laughing in agreement, I countered with, "And who carried in the dog food for those three canines? No wonder the guys in the hammocks were tired and needed a nap!" "They probably have enough grass to smoke and don't mind eating whatever the dogs like," said Jerry. Pausing, he added, "Now there's a way to economize weight in one's backpack – dried dog food."

The trail forked away from Fall Stream putting a ridge between it and any hikers. We were now on our way to Spruce Lake and definitely going away from Foxey Brown Hermitage. It was approaching five o'clock, we were tired having left home early in the morning, and didn't want to turn around and go back past our Hippie friends. Checking our map we noted that Fall Stream, on the other side of the ridge, meandered and finally disappeared into the mountains a mile or so away from the trail. We decided to follow the stream a short distance and make camp for the night. That was the best decision we made all day.

We selected a campsite on a rise 100 feet or so from the stream. The ridge between us and the trail would make it very unlikely anyone would discover our site – especially people traveling the North Country/Lake Placid trail with Mastiffs – not good tracking dogs. After a hearty meal, and soaking of tired feet in the cool stream, we analyzed our day. Disappointed in not getting closer to Foxey's place we made a plan of attack for the next day. We would rise early, leave our camp, and skirt the Hippies and dogs, head down Fall Stream with day packs. The map suggested it could only be two miles or so back to the water falls we had discovered last year. Traveling lightly we ought to find success before noon tomorrow. Everything seemed in order. Even Fall Stream seemed to agree as the sound of water gently tinkling over rocks blended with the patter of light rain on our tents.

Morning sun, the promise of a clear day and a good breakfast quickened our spirits. Approaching the Fall Stream ford and the hippie camp, we sneaked a peek from behind some large trees. No barking, no dogs, no hammocks, nothing. Perhaps our hippie friends had been day hikers and headed back to Piseco late yesterday afternoon. Maybe we had jumped to erroneous conclusions and they were simply pet lovers giving their large dogs some exercise.

Free now to begin exploring Fall Stream anywhere, we opted to travel back toward Piseco closer to where Bill Abrams said to just "Head down over the mountain." The map revealed a feeder stream crossing the trail and emptying into Fall Stream. We would go to it and use it as a guide to reach Fall Stream. Doing so, we wouldn't have to trust our ailing GPS device and could use the stream to easily find our way back to the trail.

Following the feeder stream was easy going through mixed hard woods. Our light day packs were a blessing compared to what we carried in yesterday and our tributary soon led to Fall Stream. The way back would be easy to spot as a large and distinctive boulder marked the confluence. To be double safe we tied a red marker on a stick beside the boulder. With great expectations we followed Fall Stream. In a short time, however, its appearance began to change. What had been a singing mountain stream tumbling over rocks and boulders became a still, silent, and deep channel.

Yep, we were headed into beaver territory and they had their own ideas as to what was beautiful and functional. We were now forced to follow the stream bank; which in itself became increasingly difficult to follow. Willow and alder thickets choked the stream banks, and to remind us this was their home, the beavers had chiseled sharp little tree stumps about knee high every so often. Not to be deterred we decided Foxey would not have lived along low lying, beaver dominated ground but up where it was high and dry. We would keep the stream in sight and move up the hill somewhat. Another plan nature would shoot down.

We gained elevation and kept in contact with Fall Stream. The trouble now was blow down! Hardwood trees don't like wet feet and the forest cover now was predominately fir and spruce — shallow rooted ones that couldn't stand much wind or frost action. They seemed to reach twelve to sixteen inches in diameter and then drop like flies leaving their bodies piled every which way. Indeed, we would need wings to travel far in the coniferous jungle before us. It was time for lunch and re-evaluation of mission strategy.

Our wrist watches now read 1:00 p.m. and we had struggled to cover perhaps half to three-quarters of a mile. True, we were now near the vly that Foxey had used to raise cattle but the map showed it was extensive and the stream snaked back and forth adding considerable distance if its entirety was to be explored. It made no sense that he would have built a home in the low lying (flood prone) vly. Somehow we had to skirt the vly and find places along Fall Stream where he might have lived. However, to explore the remaining stretch of Fall Stream in the time remaining to us meant moving a considerable distance away from the stream bank and up into the deciduous forest. Otherwise, we would only continue to struggle with the tangle of alder, willow, spruce and fir trees along the stream that snaked through the vly.

Having made a decision to move upland, we relished being in the hardwood forest and having an increased line of sight between the maple, beech, ash, and black cherry trees. Several times we passed an old stump that showed signs of a saw having ended the tree's life. Lured by such clues we poked ahead.

As the old adage goes, "Time flies when you are having fun." Before we knew it, a time check revealed the afternoon had worn on to four o'clock. Wishing we had somehow lugged all our camping gear on this bushwhacking expedition, wisdom dictated heading back to where we had left our camping gear. The never ending reclamation powers of nature had won again. The actual home of Foxey Brown remained hidden from us. All evidence suggested we were close. However, once again there would be no celebration at camp tonight.

Jerry and I discussed our two failed attempts to find Foxey Brown for hours. Jerry was genuinely interested in Foxey Brown but he and his wife were moving to the mountains of North Carolina so sharing further quests would be difficult. Besides, I needed to find Foxey's place soon to help write up his story. It was time to seek professional assistance. And I had just the person in mind – enter Dr. David Miller.

Dave is a "Distinguished Teaching" Geography Department professor and colleague at SUNY Cortland. It didn't take Dave long to recognize an interesting way to help. Why not make finding Foxey Brown's homestead an assignment for students in his Global Positioning Systems (GPS) class? The scheme was for me to tell them about Foxey Brown. The students would then analyze computer generated maps and predict the most likely spots that might have once held Foxey's homestead. A culminating experience would occur the following spring with Dave, his students and me going into the West Canada Lakes Wilderness Area to find Foxey Brown's place. What an assignment – students participating in direct, hands-on, real world learning! It had the makings of experiential education at its best with students taking initiative, making decisions, and dealing with the consequences of their work.

Dave's students fully embraced the assignment. Questions poured forth during the school year. We met several times to reflect on student progress and to assess potential sites and zero-in on the best possibilities. May 2008 came and it was time to put two semesters worth of work to the test. The students had come up with a map and five potential spots to investigate. Sadly, weather and other circumstances caused postponement of an early May outing and we couldn't start until May 20th. Graduation had come and gone leaving only two students able to go Foxey Brown hunting.

Joining Dave and me that spring morning were Tim Armbuster and Nate Speiro. Flush with the enthusiasm of our young companions we arrived at the Northville/Lake Placid trailhead in Piseco around noon. It was a pleasant, low seventy degree day with little black fly activity – at least to start. Equipped with good GPS equipment we started up the trail with Dave making us stop fairly often to record location points on his machine.

The first three miles up the trail went well with rest stops and time for a lunch break. We arrived at the determined "jumping off" spot around 2:30 p.m. From here on it would be bushwhacking down over the mountain toward Fall Stream. This was a cue for the black flies to come on stage. They descended on us in swarms making quick donning of head nets mandatory. Needless to say, this slowed our pace considerably as we went around downed trees and through thick brush. Most troublesome were the dense clumps of Witch-hazel. Perhaps native people and pioneers welcomed the shrub-like vegetation for its branches and their supposed ability to divine hidden underground sources of water, but for us it was more like something an evil witch had thrown in our way. Thank goodness it was a sunny day allowing Dave to maintain good satellite connections with his GPS units. Actually, we all carried a GPS unit and regularly coordinated with Dave.

Difficulty in navigating the shrub-choked woods forced a dilemma around four o'clock. By our calculations we were nearing Fall Stream and could now head towards any one of six previously identified locations that might hold the remains of Foxey Brown's homestead. The trouble was that each site was at least a quarter mile apart. With heavy backpacks starting to sap our energies we agreed it impossible to visit all six locations. We had to choose one and make it our camp for the night.

An even number of voters can make a majority decision impossible. Thus it was that Dave and I favored site five and the two students voted for site two. Now, of course, professors always have to set good examples, so tired as we all were, it was time to rest a while and discuss the pros and cons of each site. This we did and Nate indicated he was now uncertain as to the best choice. He would trust luck to settle the matter by tossing a coin. Heads he would go with site five that Dave and I favored and tails he would stick with site two. Flipping the coin into the air, Nate deftly caught and slapped it on his forearm. Heads it was – matter settled and lady luck would be with us that day.

Lifting our backpacks on to tired bodies we set out for site five. In less than 150 yards the first positive sign appeared showing we were nearing what was once cultivated land. There among the trees in nearly overgrown clearings were numerous piles of field stones made by someone to allow room for crops and pasturing of animals. Soon we were descending a hillside with small patches of blueberry bushes here and there. Another 100 yards through thick stands of balsam fir brought us to Fall Steam and an expansive vly area. Leaving our backpacks by the stream we began to explore. Forty yards later it was time to shout, "Hallelujah!"

There before us were the remains of a human-made dam. Huge boulders, dynamited from the hillside and rolled into the stream bed, formed a dike extending high up on each bank of Fall Stream. Only a sluice way opening allowed the water to pass through. Getting closer to the spillway, old boards and beams were visible under the water. Looking downstream from the dam, iron spikes were still sticking into large beams that had served to support the base of the dam. It was easy to visualize how at one time a substantial body of water had been backed up causing local people of the early 1900's to refer to this place as Brown's Pond.

Old professors like to study and contemplate. Young men often look and go. Eager to see what else was around this place, Nate and Tim disappeared back up the hillside. Soon a shout rang forth urging Dave and me to come see what had been found. Following the direction from where our students spoke, we stepped through a clump of balsam fir trees to find our young companions standing in a small clearing that once overlooked the dam and vly. Stone piles on the edges and a suspicious mound in the center of the clearing suggested where a building had once stood. This had to be Foxey's cabin site. Everything fit the old photograph I had of Foxey's cabin! Despite our excitement we agreed it best to pitch tents and make camp before exploring further.

Dave was first to ready his tent so he began looking for firewood. Two minutes later he shouted, "Gentlemen you need to come see this." Tracing his voice back toward the stream we stepped through a stand of sizeable spruce trees. There stood Dave in the remains of an old stone walled cellar hole. Just as the newspapers said at the time of Carlton Banker's disappearance in 1916, Foxey had a barn with an underground basement.

On the slope of a steep bank we found the discards of human habitation – parts of old wood stoves, pieces of glass and crockery, and other iron items unidentifiable to us. This had to be the Foxey Brown Hermitage. Unfortunately, it had been used by hunting and fishing groups long after Foxey's day as sheets of plastic and assorted camp cooking utensils littered various spots around his original home. In Foxey's day such behavior would have warranted a rifle warning shot and an expletive saying, "Get out of here or I'll send you lead for sinkers."

Lengthening shadows on the hillside suggested we best forgo further exploration and tend to fixing dinner. We selected Foxey's barn foundation for our kitchen/cooking area and built a campfire in the center of the cellar floor. Wanting to sleep as close to where Foxey did for so many years I pitched my tent on the mound in the clearing thinking it had to be the remains of his cabin which had fallen or been shoved in when the State declared this a wilderness area.

Having played on some championship athletic teams, and more not of championship caliber, I understand the meaning of "the thrill of victory and the agony of defeat." Sitting around the campfire that evening, I could sense we all shared in the satisfaction of having worked hard to find success. There was excitement in the air and Dave and the students were full of questions about my research on the life and times of Foxey Brown. And, of course, I was perfectly willing to expound profusely. As are many folks, they were intrigued that an educated man like Foxey Brown/David Brennan could live alone in this wild place for so many years. The disappearance of Carlton Banker also filled their imaginations causing a great deal of speculation about what happened to him. And they wanted to know what happened to Foxey – something I didn't know much about in May of 2008. We talked a long while after dark despite being very tired from the day's long hike.

I never sleep well the first night or two in a strange place and this one was no exception. What seemed like a million thoughts about Foxey and this place roamed through my mind. Was this really his place or perhaps it was just another old hunting camp? If, indeed this was his home, what do I do tomorrow? Do I go north, south, east, or west of the site? How is it best to utilize the efforts of my fellow campers? How did Foxey get in here – certainly not the way we came? On and on my mind rambled and sleep eluded me. With much gratefulness I welcomed five o'clock – my normal wake up hour.

Trying to be quiet as possible, I rose and stoked the campfire hoping the others would not wake. I selfishly wanted some alone time with Foxey's Place. In the cool, gray dawn I made my way to the dam and sat on the boulders which once had made Brown's Pond possible. As sunrise first announced itself I imagined Foxey sitting here or casting a line for a brook trout breakfast. Did he reflect and give thanks for the opportunity to live in such a special place? I thought he might have just as I do for my life at Hermit Hill.

I began to stroll along the south side of what I imagined to be the border of Foxey's pond pretending that water stretched several hundred yards to the opposite shore. Stepping into a stand of balsam firs, there before me lay the remains of a large wood cook stove. Had it been Foxey's? Sure looked old enough. Scanning the area a bit more, my eyes fell on a partially buried one bottom plow – just the kind one would hitch behind a horse or ox and walk behind to turn over the soil. Amazed at its good condition, I began to dig it free from the earth and vegetation slowly swallowing it. With some grunting and tugging I rolled it free and up onto a hummock. Stepping back for a full view, I could see it was a fully intact plow ready to go to work. All it needed was some ox or horse power and a good man to steer it! No one else according to recorded history had ever farmed here. It was Foxey's plow!

I was elated and now knew, without a doubt, this was the Foxey Brown Hermitage. The plow verified (just as the history books said) that Foxey (David Brennan) Brown had raised cattle and farmed the Fall Stream vly for twenty-five years. Hunting and fishing camp operators don't farm their lands. The size and weight of the plow also suggested that, at one time, a primitive road of some sort came into Foxey's place – it certainly wasn't backpacked in.

Returning to the campfire, I was happy to see Dave making his breakfast. Telling him there was a big surprise to share after he had eaten, piqued his curiosity and he looked at me as if to say, "Well?" I held back revealing my discovery, savoring the pleasure of actually showing him the plow. Instead, I playfully asked what he believed would be a significant artifact to find. Catching on to my little game, he replied, "Foxey's diary" and leisurely continued eating and sipping his first cup of coffee. "Nope, but if this thing talked many a story could be entered into one's diary," I countered. Sensing my excitement, Dave grabbed his camera and said, "Let's go photograph you and this thing."

We found additional artifacts that day at Foxey Brown's including the remains of several woodstoves of varying types and brands. Cracks and warps in the metal testified to the many cold nights they had warded off. It was easy to imagine cold and weary hunters warming hands and feet while sharing adventures of the day. And what did they drink?

Being an antique bottle collector, I had dreamed of finding Foxey's trash dump and discarded beer, whiskey, and patent medicine bottles. A few broken shards here and there but nary a one came into our possession. Had Foxey, really stuck to French Louie's rule of not drinking in camp? Was Foxey too clever to fall for the false claims of patent medicine hawkers? Aside from the debris of the post Foxey Brown years, artifacts we found suggested my man lived a simple existence. Either that or someone had carried off or deeply buried a lot of things.

The day passed all too quickly for my liking and a farewell campfire soon drew us together. Our student friends presented me with an old frying pan found during their jaunts around Foxey's place. Indeed, rust holes and all, it could date to his day.

Like the night before, sleep did not come quickly. Still too many things to think about, more trips into this place to plan, this discovery being just the beginning of piecing together Foxey's life. What was it about this man that captivated my thoughts so strongly? Had I found him or had he found me?

Finding the remains of the Foxey Brown Hermitage was, indeed, historical research full of false starts, twists, turns, and dead-ends. In 1890, Foxey sought to hide in the wilds of Fall Stream. He had succeeded then and continued to be a mysterious character. Could sleeping on the same ground where he lived for so many years somehow provide clues? Drowsiness began to compete with my consciousness and I drifted to sleep wondering what Foxey's life had been like here on Fall Stream. If only he had left a diary or memoir. How would he have told his story?

1

RUN FOR THE HILLS

Local Pub near Boston, October 1, 1889

Damn! That George Murphy wouldn't stay down. Why did the big jerk always look for a fight when he was drunk? I went over to O'Hara's Place that night planning to have a drink or two, play some pool and go home. But, George Murphy hung out at the bar too. The trouble with big George was that he didn't like to lose at pool and got meaner than usual the more he drank. Usually, I managed to talk my way around George's bad nature, two hundred and fifty pound body, and avoid a fight. I'm not sure what happened just after I had won three straight pool games from George. I tried not to gloat or irritate him further in any way. But he was furious, grabbed me, swatted my face and sat me up on the pool table like a little boy not worthy of a regular fist fight. Maybe I had drunk too much or was just plain tired of George's bullying but, I think it was the insult to my manhood that caused me to rap him in the head with a cue stick. Down he went, and I figured I finally had him licked.

My problems, and poor luck, would have remained small if George Murphy had only stayed down. But he didn't. George got up and charged like a bull after a cow in heat – George, however, didn't have love making in mind. I hit him hard again. Hard enough so the cue stick quivered like a fishing rod might when you set the hook on a big fish. Poor George slumped forward, went face down on the floor and laid perfectly still. That's when my life as David Brennan ended and one as Foxey Brown began to take shape – a life that cast me as a murderer, outlaw, mountain man, Adirondack guide, and unfortunate soul sometimes in the wrong place at the wrong time.

Right then, in my life story, I was twenty-nine years old, had taken some college courses, read a lot, and was trying to mind my own business working on the railroad. I'd grown up on a poor farm in Benedicta, Maine, where my dad had died from too much work when I was about fifteen. Looking back to those early days, I guess I couldn't stay out of trouble, not real bad stuff, but, well, I just got bored easily, drank too much at times, ran with friends and other sorts cut from the same cloth, and somehow seemed to wind up fighting more often than I should. My family thought it best for me to go somewhere else to finish growing up. So, I came here to Boston.

Work on the railroad was all right. I did most any kind of track maintenance they needed and it got me free rides out into the country. Having grown up on a potato farm, I liked the fresh country air and quiet places to read and do my college studies. I'd been able to save up a few dollars and hoped to finish my studies and find more interesting work. But, there I was in that bar, and the next thing I knew the guys were telling me something about George Murphy.

They were saying Murphy wasn't breathing, was turning blue, and had started to look like he was dead. Then, someone hollered that the police were on the way...which was about when I decided not to stick around and get hung for killing Murphy. Sometimes in life you have to run like a rabbit or stand and fight like a bear. I decided to be a rabbit and not stick around and get hung for killing Murphy. George's dad and uncles were on the police force and, being a tight family, weren't people I could fight. Besides that, I had once seen a botched public execution in Boston. The executioner didn't tie the hangman's knot right and the poor prisoner slowly strangled to death instead of having his neck broken quickly. I sometimes had lingering nightmares recalling the man's body twitching for minutes at the end of the rope.

Anyway, I ran full stride for home grabbed my blankets, a change of clothes, and the sixty-six dollars I had saved up. Didn't leave word for anyone as to where I was going mainly because I had no idea. And, what my relatives and friends didn't know couldn't hurt me or them when the police came asking questions.

Right then working on the railroad saved my hide. My buddy Tracy O'Grady worked the night shift as a night watchman down at the terminal. Not liking George Murphy or the police much, he was sympathetic when I told him my troubles and needed a quick ride out of town. After thinking a minute or so, Tracy said, "knowing you work on the railroad, a box car will be the first place cops will look for you. We have to outsmart them. Say, there's a train heading out soon and my cousin Neil O'Brien is the engineer, I'll get him to put you on the locomotive as an extra hand stoking the boiler. Let's go find him!"

Sure enough, just up the tracks a bit sat the locomotive puffing away with twenty or so boxcars hooked up to it. Tracy jumped onto the locomotive and started talking with a man. After three or four minutes, Tracy waved me on board. "You're in luck Neil's got no use for the Murphy's either and he's willing to help you out. Stay back in the firewood storage area and act like a worker. Let Neil do the talking if anybody comes around before the train gets started." Tracy gave me his dinner pail and said the train was going straight through to Albany where the New York Central would take it on to Syracuse, New York to unload and bring back a big load of salt among other things. Shaking my hand, Tracy said, "If the cops come around asking about you, I'll say I saw you jump on boxcar headed up to Augusta, Maine. With that he grinned and jumped to the ground. So, there I was in the middle of the night headed for Albany and on to Syracuse, if I completed my train ride.

After we had traveled an hour or so, Neil came back to the wood storage area and said he believed we were in the clear, at least for now. He figured my next obstacle would come when we reached Albany, because his job was to unhook the boxcars, hook on to new ones and head back to Boston. The New York Central would take our present load onto Syracuse. So I would have to decide where to go after Albany. He knew the watchmen for the New York Central and could probably arrange a boxcar ride. I didn't have to decide until tomorrow when we reached Albany.

As the train chugged into the night I considered my options. One possibility was to hide in Albany, or better yet, a big city like New York. However, big cities meant lots of police to always avoid especially if the Murphy's got word around about me. Then I thought about a country place of some sort. People from the country always seemed a lot friendlier than city folk. Country people look you right in the eye and say, "How you doing or good morning." Besides, moving to a totally different way of life would throw the police off my trail. But I had no idea where to go – certainly not back to Maine. I decided to ride on toward Syracuse and take my chances there.

As we neared Albany, Neil asked what I wanted to do. "Guess I'll take that boxcar ride on to Syracuse if you can arrange it." "No problem," shrugged Neil. "I'll talk to the New York Central watchman and you won't be bothered on the boxcar." Neil did just as he said when we got to Albany and escorted me to a boxcar about a dozen or so back from the Central New York locomotive. The watchman told me to stay in the back of the car behind some freight until the train got up to full speed. Neil gave me a jug of water and a couple of apples saying, "I'll tell the other workers you headed for New York City. Good luck and stay away from bars."

In an hour or so, the train was underway taking me toward a new chapter in my life. Who would have thought twenty-four hours earlier that things might change so drastically, so quickly? While it wasn't good to have the law after me, I thought a change of scenery might be beneficial. I would miss my college studies but not the boring railroad work. I didn't intend to work like my father and wear out before my time. There had to be opportunities around Syracuse.

Shortly after leaving Albany, the train slowed and labored to make it up a long hill. A man had been waiting near the tracks for such an opportunity and jumped aboard my boxcar. His quick arrival startled me, but he seemed harmless. Drifters or hobos, as we railroad workers were starting to call them, were common. This guy was an especially sad looking case with dirty clothing, scruffy beard, cuts on his face, and a black eye. He also smelled terrible! Of course, I probably didn't look much better considering the punches I had taken from George Murphy and a night on the run. After warily looking each other over, there was an unspoken understanding that we were two guys on the lam. He spoke first asking, "Do you know where this train is heading?" I told him, "West, going to end up in Syracuse." "Shoot," he responded, "I'm going the wrong way!" He proceeded to explain how he had hopped a train in Gloversville, three days ago, got caught near Johnstown by some railroad cops, also known as "Bulls," who proceeded to pound him up. Afterwards, they took him to some woods near the edge of the city, threw him down, and said, "Start running and don't come back!" Taking their advice, he ran a long ways before stopping. Not knowing his location, my new companion walked until finding some train tracks, waited, and jumped on my boxcar. I could tell this fellow wasn't the "swiftest boat in the harbor," as we said back in Boston. Seemed like he could have figured out which way was east. Anyway, this drifter had been places unknown to me. So I kept the talk going.

Curious about Gloversville, I asked what he had been doing there. "Just passing through, was up Lake Pleasant way in the Adirondacks before that." "Doing what?" I queried. He explained that mostly he had worked in logging camps as a "chopper" cutting down trees from October until thaw out the following spring. Logging companies were cutting hard on State land all over the mountains. Desperate for help, they paid up to a dollar per day plus free room and board. But my fellow traveler had grown tired of all the hard work and long (twelve hour) days that started before daylight and ended after dark. The bosses expected cutters to drop at least sixty trees per day. Too much chopping for him so he headed back to Gloversville, worked in a hide tanning factory for a while, drank away his money, and started living on the streets. I could see he was real nervous and kept walking back and forth toward the boxcar door. As the train slowed and chugged up another long hill, he said, "I got to go, can't go back to Johnstown or Gloversville cause those bulls will kill me." He wished me good luck, and jumped out the door. Last I saw of him he was rolling down a grassy knoll towards a creek. I wondered if he could swim.

His departure got me thinking what I would do if different railroad bulls caught me on the boxcar. They wouldn't know Neil or Tracy out here and would assume I was just another drifter hitching a free ride. I had no railroad identification from my job in Boston and, if I did, it wouldn't be something smart to show authorities. I would have to lay low and get off as close to Gloversville as possible. Heck, working in an Adirondack logging camp couldn't be much tougher than laying and fixing train track. Swinging a maul and driving railroad tie spikes had to be harder than chopping trees with an axe. And, hiding out in the mountains with a bunch of loggers ought to make it difficult for police to find me. Who ever heard of Lake Pleasant anyway?

My problem then was to keep laying low in the boxcar and figure out when I was somewhere near this Gloversville place. Now that was no easy task. During the daytime I could tell direction by the sun and knew this old train could make 15-20 miles an hour on level ground. But how many miles was it to Johnstown and Gloversville? During the day I could watch for signs on buildings, but what about after dark? It seemed best to guess when I was getting close, jump the train, walk, meet people and ask directions. I had some money and could find a place to eat, clean up and rest.

Well, my sense of direction was good, but my estimation of miles traveled was a bit short. I jumped off near a good road when it seemed like Albany was a long ways back. After a bit, along came a man about my age, driving a good-looking horse and wagon. He was headed west so I waved and asked, "how far to Gloversville?" After spitting some juice from his chew, and flashing a little grin, he said, "Stranger you got a far piece to travel. It's nigh on twenty-five miles to Gloversville. Hope you're not planning to get supper there because you haven't even got to Fonda or Johnstown yet. Going to Johnstown, can ride if you want." The fellow seemed a decent sort so I climbed aboard. He spit again, flicked the reins, and away we went.

Not much was said for a mile or so until he declared, "Just got off the train I reckon." There was no sense denying it. Most people on foot would have an idea where they were. I replied, "Yes, got sick of riding that noisy contraption and figured my legs needed stretching." Again, there was silence before my new companion stuck out his hand saying, "My name's Ned James, live up in Johnstown. What do you go by?" "David," I stammered almost blurting out Brennan also. "David Brown, come from down near New York City," I lied. Thinking a minute, Ned said, "Funny you remind me of a fellow from Boston that I once met. His name was Brown too." Trying to act casual, I countered by saying, "You have a good ear for accents; I lived there until my late teens." "Me too," said Ned "Moved away when I was ten." Not wanting to continue this line of conversation, I asked if there was a good place to eat and stay in Johnstown. "Yep," blurted Ned. "Next to the local jail the best cooking is at the old Wayside Inn – my wife cooks for the jail," he laughed. I responded with my own laughter knowing for certain it sounded nervous. Ned continued, "Can drop you off there if you wish." To this day, I'm not sure how I nonchalantly responded, "Are you talking about the jail or the Wayside Inn, Ned?" Maybe, I was already learning to be "Foxey" Brown. Anyway, Ned let out a roar saying, "Good one Mr. David Brown," and he laughed again, even harder.

I could see Ned James was an inquisitive man and it might be best if I chose the topics of discussion. "Yep," I declared. "Lost my folks and am headed to Gloversville to meet up with my brother. He's been up there a while working in a tannery. Kind of smelly work but it's steady he tells me." "Sure can agree with that, we got some of those places in Johnstown too. I'd rather be on the other end of working with those hides though," said Ned. "Rather be catching the critters and selling the hides to the tannery." Not knowing much about trapping, I asked if someone could still make a living these days as a trapper. Ned began to explain that lots of men in the Adirondacks made a living hunting, fishing, trapping, farming a little, and working off and on for logging companies. Some of them also make fair wages serving as guides for sportsmen visiting the mountains. Not wanting to seem too interested, I asked how a guy with no experience gets work with a logging company. Ned laughed and said, "Man, all you got to do is visit a local pub in Gloversville and ask who is hiring. The jobbers, logging companies, are always looking for help this time of year. Come first snowfall they want to be in the woods getting their camps ready for winter and do some serious cutting." Trying to seem disinterested, I replied, "It sounds like too much work for me." "Yep, but it sure beats working in a stinky, smoky tannery" retorted Ned as he sent his mouthful of tobacco chew flying.

Not being a man who liked long, drawn out talk about nothing in particular, I was pleased when Ned seemed in the same frame of mind. He appeared to drift off in thought being conscious only of the horse and fairly frequent bumps in the road. Of course, my mind kept racing from one thing to another. Unlike Ned, I was a man on the run for murder.

After a while, Ned indicated we would soon see Fonda and about five miles after that the Wayside Inn near Johnstown. Fonda didn't impress me much and we finally approached what I took to be the outskirts of Johnstown. Up ahead I could see what looked like a hotel or inn. Stopping at the inn, Ned once again stuck out his hand and said, "You seem like a decent sort, Mr. David Brown. You take care, and if you ever need work in Johnstown, just stop by and ask anyone for Ned James, Sheriff Ned James." With that, he smiled, spoke to the horse and drove off.

Talk about being between a rock and a hard place, I was stumped as to my next move! If I stayed at the inn Mr. James just might check at his office and see if the telegraph had sent any messages to be on the lookout for a murderer named David Brennan out of Boston. The inn would be an easy place to pick me up. If I ran, and he checked at the Wayside, my absence would be a sure sign that I could be Brennan. Not knowing the local territory, my chances of evading him would be slim. I couldn't get back on a train because that would be a logical place for him to check. What to do?

Sometimes, in poker and life, it is best to just hold your cards. That's what I decided to do, besides I hadn't had much sleep, was dirty, and very hungry. If Sheriff Ned James took me to jail, there would be chances to escape and really go on the run if need be. One thing was for certain; I wasn't going back to Boston and dance on the end of a rope for the likes of George Murphy.

At daybreak I headed to the dining room for a good breakfast. The food was ready around 6:15 and I began to eat pancakes and eggs when the front door opened and in walked Ned James – Sheriff Ned James. I tried not to choke on my mouthful of pancakes as Ned walked straight to my table and sat down. "Good morning, Mr. Brown," he said. "Hope you are enjoying the food here." Looking him in the eye, and somehow without stammering, I managed to say "Yep, good stuff." "You're probably wondering what I'm doing here this morning, Mr. Brown," went Ned. Knowing I had to come up with something light hearted, I said, "Well I can't believe you like the food better here than what Mrs. James puts together for you." Laughing loudly, Ned blurted out, "Another good one Mr. Brown! No, you see I've got to deliver a prisoner to Gloversville this morning and remembered you were headed that way to see your brother. Wondered if you would like a ride?" Once again, it was a moment of making a big decision. How in the heck could I turn down his offer of a ride? So, I didn't.

A few minutes later I found myself sitting beside Ned on his wagon. In the back was a prisoner named Twig Slack, and he was just that – skinny as a broom handle, but equipped with some wiry looking arm muscles. Twig was going to trial in Gloversville for robbing a store. I noted a holster and revolver on Ned's belt as he undid the handcuffs on Slack's hand so the prisoner could visit the outhouse. Slack never acknowledged my presence and said to Ned, "It's about damn time," along with some other choice cuss words. In a strange way, Twig Slack's eyes reminded me of George Murphy. He definitely had the mouth to go with the resemblance.

In short order, we headed for Gloversville. Traveling a few miles with some small talk here and there, we reached a creek where the bridge had washed out forcing Ned to ford the stream. As we were about half way across, the horse stumbled, lost its balance, spooked and reared up on its hind legs. To my, and Ned's, complete surprise Twig Slack rose up, cupped his hands together and hit Ned over the head. He swung at me, missed, jumped into the creek, bounced up and ran through the shallow waters toward the shore from whence we came.

Slack's blow to Ned's head was not a knockout punch, but it did daze him making me fear he would fall into the stream. Grabbing Ned and the reins, I was able to get the horse settled down. Glancing back at the far shore I saw Slack heading into a patch of woods.

Catching his breath and sizing up the situation, Ned said, "Well, David Brown looks like I won't be going to G-ville today. I best head back to Johnstown and get some deputies to chase down Mr. Slack. He sure has more troubles now than just robbing a store!"

Someone wise once said something about "one man's troubles being another man's opportunity." Well, this sure was my opportunity! After getting back across the stream, I asked Ned if he was all right. Confirming he wasn't hurt, Ned thanked me, said he knew I was a good man and hoped our paths would cross again. Well, I liked the "good man" part but wasn't real keen on crossing paths with a sheriff anytime again in the near future. Waving good-bye, Ned headed for Johnstown and I was afoot on my way to Gloversville. Walking along, I kept pondering what I would have told Ned when he got around to asking where my brother worked and lived. That sure would have put me in a difficult position because I had no idea about names of tanneries or streets in Gloversville. As one of my railroad buddies said about using dynamite, "Play around with it, and sooner or later, it will get you."

I completed the remaining miles to Gloversville at a steady pace arriving about noon. Smoke hung thick over the city as factory and home chimneys billowed large clouds of the stuff. A sickening odor of dead flesh surrounding the tanneries added to the smoke's bite. And, of course, the numerous horse drawn wagons and buggies contributed their share of stink and sticky substance to the roads. The stench of dead flesh got stronger as I approached a large tannery, then a slaughterhouse, and in the city business district, a butcher shop using a vacant lot next door to discard animal inners, heads, feet, and hooves in open barrels. Once again, I was reminded of my growing passion to breathe country air.

Drawing on my hobo acquaintance's advice, I sought out the nearest tavern and entered one called the Annex. Noting that the place was not very busy, I walked to the bar, caught the bartender's eye and ordered a beer. My long walk had worked up a considerable thirst and I soon was ordering another. The bartender was a friendly sort so when he brought the beer I said, "Heard that the logging companies up north are looking for workers this time of year." "They sure are, but they don't come to this small place much," he replied. "You need to go up a couple of blocks to the Alvord House. I bet a hiring boss is there right now since it's late in October." Pausing a moment, he volunteered some advice, "Whatever outfit you sign up with, ask lots of questions about pay, number of hours per week you're expected to work, and living conditions. Some of those camps are pretty unhealthy places." Tipping my hat, I downed the last of my beer and headed out the door.

Sure enough, the Alvord House was booming. Signs touting logging camp work hung here and there. In a side room, I found three different tables with men lined up waiting to talk to company representatives (or "jobbers" as I heard the men call them). I picked the table with the shortest line and got in. As I worked my way toward the front, I could hear the jobbers saying what they needed were "choppers, road monkeys, and river drivers for next spring." Seeing as I had no idea what a road monkey or log driver was, and the boxcar drifter had mentioned choppers were tree cutters, I decided my experiences on the railroad had best prepared me to be a chopper. Axes were not a strange tool to railroad line workers like me.

When I got where I could see the table clearly there was a large map and sign reading Aird Logging Company. On the map I could see this was near the Lake Pleasant and Piseco Lake places mentioned by the hobo. As my turn to talk came, the jobber said, "What kind of work can you do and how much experience do you have?" Wanting to sound experienced, I replied, "Chopper, I've cut lots of trees, worked for the railroad going on eleven years." Looking me over the jobber said, "You look rugged enough, let me see your hands." Checking my hands, he indicated his company pays ninety cents a day plus room and board to start. Expectations are that choppers can put down at least sixty trees in a twelve-hour day. You pay your train and stage fare into camp and if you stay the whole season you get reimbursed. He finished saying, "Any questions?" Not heeding the Annex tavern bartender's advice about asking lots of questions, I shook my head and asked, "Where do I sign up?" The jobber looked me over once again and handed over a roster with places on it to print and sign your name. He had already checked off the chopper category for me. As I wrote David Brown on the roster, he said, "Be here tomorrow morning at seven sharp to catch the train to Northville. Find a store and get yourself an extra wool shirt, several pairs of wool gloves and some good boots that will keep your feet dry. The company provides all the tools but clothes are your business."

I was nervous about having taken the logging job so abruptly but it was important to quickly put as much distance as possible between Boston, railroads, Sheriff Ned James, and me. Right then, it was best to let the Adirondack woods swallow David Brennan and give birth to David Brown, the logger.

2

LUMBERJACK DAYS

I enjoyed the Fonda, Johnston and Gloversville (F. J. & G.) train ride to Northville even though the small locomotive had to slowly "puff and wheeze" its way into the mountains. It felt good not to be hiding out in a boxcar – a pleasure I should have savored more fully because my manner of travel was about to change drastically.

Waiting at Northville were stagecoaches to take us the rest of the way. Simply stated, stagecoaches were ridiculous machines. Riding one made my trip to Wells and over to Sageville a jolting, bone-shaking experience. First off, a stagecoach was not much more than some seats and a few boards bolted to four wheels pulled by four horses. Although you could see springs on the contraption, it's a mystery as to how they served any useful purpose other than to let passengers bounce up and down. All anyone needed to get seasick was some water! Playing into this primitive machine's hands were road surfaces that got progressively worse the closer we got to our destination. It came as no surprise when folks walking along our path turned down offers of a stagecoach ride. Several bluntly stated they could make a heck of a lot better time on foot and "feel better at the end." I took their use of the word "end" to have a double meaning referring both to their mental outlook and the feel of their butt.

It took two stagecoaches to haul regular passengers and transport eleven of us to Wells. After quick introductions (David Brown of course), I pretty much kept out of the conversations. From what I could tell, except for the man I took to be a foreman, we were all pretty much new to the logging business. Most of us had probably handled an axe before, but not to the extent that would fill our days in the near future. Clint Neff, the man I suspected might be the foreman, didn't volunteer a whole lot of information. Seemed to me he was sizing us up by letting loose tongues wag and thus get a feel for each man's personality. I remembered Abraham Lincoln once said, "It is better to be thought a fool, than to open your mouth and remove all doubt." So, I decided to be "quiet Dave" the lumberjack. I needed to succeed at this new job and avoid sitting in a Boston jail or meeting the hangman.

After several hours on the road we approached a place, around midday, called Wells. To my pleasant surprise there was a big hotel run and a sign that read "Hosley Hotel." But before we could get off the stages, Clint Neff jumped down and identified himself as one of Asa Aird's lumber camp foremen. He advised us there wouldn't be time for lunch – we were at Wells just to change horses. We could grab something quick to eat but the stage would leave within a half hour. Soon we were all crammed into the stagecoaches again and on our way to Sageville/Lake Pleasant. Passengers said the place kept changing its name back and forth and right now it was Sageville – the county seat. It happened to be located on Lake Pleasant.

Like the rest of the men, I was curious about logging camp life and still didn't know what a river driver or road monkey was or much else about a logging camp for that matter. I didn't give in to my curiosity and remained patient hoping someone else would ask questions. Sure enough, a short time later a young lad by the name of Hoyt asked Clint Neff to tell us what things were like in the camp. Clint was a man short in stature and similar in speech. "Food is good and plenty of it. Get up around three in the morning, work until eight or so, get some more chow, go till lunch about two in the afternoon and finish up around dark or so. More you chop, more you get paid. You get Sundays off but many of us work all seven days, not much else to do back in the woods anyway. The highest pay goes to the river drivers in the spring when they ride the logs downstream. Trouble is many of them don't live long enough to enjoy the extra money. Me, I'll stay a high banker up and out of log jams and fast water." That was a lot of information in a hurry and put sort of a hush on the talk.

After we left Wells the mountains got bigger and there was increasing evidence of logging. Many areas along the road were skinned back considerably from logging and where people were trying to carve out farmland. The farms we saw were small, rough looking and poor compared to those downstate. It appeared most people were struggling to get along with five or so cows, some pigs and chickens. I learned later that most Adirondack farmers had to work in the logging camps during the winter to make ends meet leaving women and children to tend the animals. Everyone relied on year-round hunting and fishing to supplement their food supplies.

Near five o'clock or so we started to catch glimpses of a large lake as evening shadows began to fall. Clint volunteered that it was Lake Pleasant known for its good lake and brook trout fishing. He said, "Won't be long now before we get to Sageville and closer to the camp at Willis Mountain. Lots of spruce there that need cutting."

We bounded into Sageville around 6:00 p.m. and stopped at the Lake Pleasant Hotel. I was surprised at its size and all of the accommodations it offered. Once again, Clint had advice for us. We could stay in the hotel at our own expense or bunk in the stable haymow at no cost. It would be warm there and Clint had extra blankets for those who hadn't brought one.

Three of the men chose to sleep in the hotel. With nightly rates ranging from $2.50-$3.00, I figured it best not to appear flush with money and elected to stay in the barn. My dad had been a quiet man and once told me that "Speech is silver and silence is golden." Experience had also taught me that if you had some silver or gold it was best to be silent about it.

I did decide to take advantage of the hotel dining room. The menu listed typical things, like ham and chicken, but also brook trout and venison. Remembering their sweet taste from boyhood catches made back in Benedicta streams, I chose the trout. Soon the waitress brought out my meal with six fish (heads on) averaging nine to ten inches in length. The first succulent bite confirmed the accurateness of my memory. Fresh baked apple pie was an easy choice for dessert!

Clint rousted us out next morning at 5:30 a.m. We all ate breakfast in the hotel and assembled outside to begin our trip into the logging camp. Around seven o'clock a bearded man approached and said, "My name's Asa Aird, supposed to be a decent day and we're going to head on in to Willis Mountain soon. If you need any last minute supplies the general store down the street is the place to go. We pull out of here in one hour." With that, he turned and went back to the stable. As some of the men headed for the store, I decided that Clint Neff was someone I needed to get to know if my days as a logger were to be somewhat bearable. So, I simply said, "Clint, I followed the recruiter's advice back in Utica and bought a rain slicker, an extra wool shirt, wool gloves and socks and a pair of one size too large rubber bottomed/leather upper boots. Is there anything else you would recommend?" "Yep," he replied, "An extra pair of boots. Wet boots usually don't dry overnight and pulling on wet, partly frozen boots in the morning ain't no way to start the day. Besides if you rip or ruin your only pair, it makes life pretty tough. Taking care of your feet in the woods is important." Thanking him, I headed for the store and paid half again more than for the pair I got in Gloversville.

True to his word, an hour later Asa Aird returned with drivers and three teams of horses pulling buckboard wagons. The last wagon was loaded with supplies securely tied together and covered with an oilcloth tarp. "Hop aboard boys, this is your ride back to the camp," Aird bellowed and motioned toward the first two buckboards. We all did as he suggested.

We hadn't gone far before it became very apparent that walking, indeed, might be the better choice. Boulders were everywhere and the drivers often had no choice but to get off and lead the horses between, half way up the sides, and right over boulders. There were few straight stretches of road without obstacles. Every hill climbed and then descended led to wet spots in the terrain. Being the Adirondack Mountains, there was water almost everywhere. Wet spots were crossed on something called a corduroy road which were just a few logs thrown in perpendicular to the roadway and covered with some dirt. There were no bridges so streams were forded at the shallowest spot possible. Needless to say, not many miles per hour were gained as we plodded toward Willis Mountain. Many of us did choose to walk.

We reached the logging camp just after midday. While I hadn't expected to find anything like the hotels in Wells, or Sageville, the stark and primitive building that was to be home did come as a surprise. I could see two or three outbuildings, and one long structure with a low-lying roof. The walls were logs about ten to twelve inches thick and the roof had been made out of tree bark cut in wide strips about six or so feet long. Smoke rose from two makeshift chimneys. It was cold enough that day, however, to make getting inside any warm place a welcome prospect.

The interior of the building was laid out with the dining hall in the middle, the kitchen on one end and the sleeping quarters on the other.

Not knowing Aird had sent a messenger ahead we were surprised to find a hearty meal ready and waiting for us inside the building. The menu consisted of pork, beans, and potatoes and some sort of apple cobbler. Noticing the serious look in the cook's eye, I guessed maybe he wasn't happy to be cooking for a bunch of new men who might be fussy. The way he stood and looked at us, I guessed his policy was "Take it or leave it." We all caught on quickly, dove in, took seconds and said, "Good chow." In a logging camp no straight thinking man makes the cook or the foreman an enemy.

Altogether, there were twenty-eight workers including the cook. After eating with us Asa Aird headed out the door saying, "Boys, since it's Sunday afternoon and it'll be dark in a few hours, Clint is going to show you around the camp. After that, do what you like, but remember there's no drinking done here! Breakfast is at three in the morning." With that, he left and didn't come back. Some of the men looked at each other and said, "Did he really say breakfast at three o'clock?"

Clint showed us to the sleeping area indicating any empty bunk was up for grabs. Surprisingly, there wasn't much squabbling over who would sleep where or on top or lower bunk. I headed for the far end where there was a door and grabbed a bottom bunk. I could see my spot was a considerable ways from the only stove but figured that wasn't a factor in October and, if there was fire in the building, I could get outside fast.

After the men stowed their gear, Clint walked us around the camp. My impression of the camp earlier in the day was fairly accurate. Everything was constructed in primitive fashion using nothing but logs to keep costs down. According to Clint, the logging companies looked at their camps as temporary places to house men and animals until all marketable trees had been cut. After that, camps were usually abandoned and deteriorated quickly by the harsh Adirondack weather. Sill logs for a building were mounted on a few stones to get the log walls started. There was no sawed lumber anywhere except for door and window frames. The floors were made from split balsam fir logs. Wide cracks in the floor were common. And I guessed this would make all sorts of critters under the floors in the kitchen and dining hall well fed. My education about logging camp critters would be dramatically continued once the winter season came into full swing.

Nearby the main building was a fairly decent barn for horses and equipment. Again, it was a log building with hemlock bark slabs for a roof. On the end there were sleeping quarters for six men known as team-sters. They had to be up extra early to ready the horses for a day's work and were bunked separately to avoid disturbing the sleep of the choppers. Clint kidded that the real reason was their strong body odor gained from constant work with the horses! Off to the side about thirty yards was a small building used by the camp blacksmith. A six-hole outhouse stood between the bunkhouse/dining hall and Asa's small cabin. Wagons, large sleds, with runners instead of wheels, and parts of sleds, filled the camp yard. A contraption of special interest was a huge water tank mounted on a large sled. One of the jobs road monkeys performed was to water the roads in winter and create a hard icy surface so log sleds could more easily haul their heavy loads.

Walking around more we noticed a structure down near the creek that had been built into the earth. A stone foundation formed the inner walls and a split log wall, with a door, closed off the side facing the creek. A low-lying roof covered the partially underground building. We were told this was the root cellar used to store perishable foodstuffs. Again, this was off limits to everyone except the cook.

At the end of our look at the camp, Clint told us to do what we pleased. Some of the men played cards while others slept or swapped stories. Since it was a pleasant late October day, with no snow yet on the ground, I opted out of playing cards and instead walked a large circle around the camp to get acquainted with the lay of the land. Not being an Adirondack wilderness woodsman, I always kept the camp in sight. My little hike revealed that many acres of land had already been cleared of marketable timber. I could see how our work would entail traveling a mile or more along the sides and up the mountain to reach uncut timber. Seeing how far the remaining cutting sites were from camp explained why dinner would be brought to us in the woods each day.

The heavy cutting of trees around Willis Mountain had created many clearings filled with dead tree tops. In the distance where axes had not yet done their work, I could see long stretches of hardwood and evergreen forested mountains and open land in the low-lying areas. Streams flowed off all the major mountains filling the lakes and ponds below. The views, smell of clean mountain air, and the quietness were relaxing making memories of life in Boston already seem less attractive. This place could fill a man's mind without him really noticing. I began to wonder, given a choice, if I would return to my former life.

New surroundings make getting a sound sleep difficult the first night. All the snoring, belching, and loud exits of gas from twenty some buttocks didn't help matters. My mind wandered widely from curiosity about what tomorrow held to George Murphy lying dead on the barroom floor in Boston. It had never been my intention to kill the man but only to make him stop beating on me. I began to contemplate the wisdom of frequenting places where people consumed alcohol and finally drifted off to sleep.

Morning came sooner than I would have liked. As Asa had forewarned yesterday, the breakfast bell rang at 3:00 a.m. Sitting up in bed, I noticed Clint Neff had taken a bunk next to me. He was already dressed. As I got up he said, "This is a good end of the bunkhouse to be on if you like to turn in early. Some of the boys tend to hang around the stove at night and gab about things. They also use the door near the stove to visit the outhouse which is often especially when we work late and don't eat till seven or so." I told him that sounded good to me and we headed for the dining hall.

More new lessons about logging camp life came with breakfast. The fare consisted of pancakes and maple syrup, eggs, venison, beans and all the coffee you could drink. I wasn't quite sure about the cook's love for beans considering my experience in the bunkhouse last night. I assumed they were probably good for hard workingmen and didn't cost much. Those who had postponed going to bed early were slow to rise and came to the table a bit bleary eyed. Their pace picked up when Asa entered the room and said, "Boys, you've got fifteen minutes to eat and then we're going to get organized for work." With that he sat down, ate, and on the fifteen minute mark stood to speak again. "We're going to break up into three tree chopping teams of five men with one man supervising the other four in each team. I'll have your supervisors stand as I call out your names." With that he introduced Tug Thomas, Bruno Jones and, of course, Clint Neff. Thomas and Jones had already been at camp when we arrived. I knew for sure then that Asa had planted Clint on the trip up from Wells to size us up. Seemed to me like a pretty smart thing to do. Anyway, I was hoping to end up on Clint's team and, to my great delight, he did choose me. However, thinking about it afterwards, I wasn't quite sure if he did so because I needed watching or if he saw that I had some good skills and qualities. Either way, I was determined to prove to be a good worker. This was my new life.

A full moon that morning provided sufficient light to enable horses and wagons to navigate the still darkened forest. I learned later that the road monkeys would drive torches into the ground once snow fell so work could start at 4:00 a.m. and go after dark when necessary in the evenings. Somehow cutting by moonlight or candle (torch) light didn't seem romantic. Of course, I kept such thoughts to myself.

Clint assembled our team and demonstrated the preferred method of felling trees. Pulling a three and half pound, single bit, axe from our wagon, he approached a spruce tree about twenty inches in diameter. Checking to see which way it would fall best, he pointed to an old stump and began chopping until reaching a point halfway into the tree. He then laid his axe head into the notch with the handle pointing out. Looking to see that the handle pointed toward the old stump, he walked around, without taking his eyes off the tree, 180 degrees to the backside. Retrieving his axe, he took five or six more swings slightly above the front notch and made the tree fall and bounce precisely off the old stump. Displaying no signs of pride or satisfaction, Clint said, "Don't get the wrong impression boys, it doesn't always work out that way exactly. Show me a man who says he never hangs up a tree and I'll show you a liar. Best advice I can give you is to treat every tree like it is able to kill you – cause it can! That is especially true for any tree that's hung up; they aren't called widow makers for nothing. Boys, we are on our own out here, you get hurt, we patch you up best we can cause no doctor is going to reach you in less than a day's time." I had liked Clint since our trip on the stagecoach. He was an easy-going, no nonsense sort of man, with a lot of common sense. I could see things in him that would be good for me to copy, especially his lack of a bad temper.

Following his safety-first approach, Clint went to a leaning tree and pulled out a quarter pound felling wedge from his back pocket. We learned how the wedge could be used to make a tree seemingly bent on going one direction end up where the chopper desired it to finally lay. There was an art to this and Clint demonstrated it perfectly. A boyhood of cutting firewood had acquainted me with felling wedges and methods of getting stubborn trees on the ground. It occurred to me not to assume that all my tree-chopping associates would be similarly experienced.

Clint gave each man an axe and placed us far enough apart so a falling tree couldn't reach the next cutter. Directions were given to cut nothing smaller than a sixteen-inch tree. For a while he watched a man, gave some advice and moved on to the next. I was last to come under his gaze and, had by that time, felled three trees with butts facing downhill to make skidding easier for the horses. "Looks like you've handled an axe before David." "Yes," I replied. "Maine farm boys learn the ways of axe at a tender age. Winters are long, snowy, and cold – boys get firewood responsibilities before age ten. Of course, then we didn't have to worry much about where trees fell." Clint thought for a moment, grinned and said, "Maniac farm boys usually make good choppers." He laughed again at his joke, went to the wagon, took an axe and began chopping a short distance away. From time to time he would stop chopping and go check on the other men.

After a while a wagon pulled up loaded with food. Checking my watch, it was only 8:30 a.m. but I sure felt hungry enough for it to be dinnertime. Clint called to the other men and encouraged them to eat. "Boy's you best keep your strength up, it's a long day out here and you've got several months to go before spring. Keep something in your stomach and drink lots of water." Always being a little hungry, I needed no further encouragement. Watching all of us eat, I was glad not to pay Asa's weekly grocery bill.

I figured it wasn't good lumberjack manners to ask how many trees a man had felled, but noted I had ten down to this point and Clint already had seven even with his time outs to check on the other men. At my present rate, I was averaging close to five an hour. In a twelve-hour day I would get the required sixty trees. However, it was a good thing we started around six this morning. I was dying to ask how the other men were doing, but didn't. As they use to say, sometimes it is best to let the chips fall where they may.

When the dinner wagon showed up around 2:00, I had thirty-seven trees on the ground. That left me about four and a half-hours, assuming we would quit at 7:00, to fell twenty-three more trees. Six trees per hour would do it. That is, if I could keep up my pace and didn't run into many big diameter trees. My years of hard work on the railroad held me in good stead because sixty trees lay on the ground at seven o'clock; two others had gotten hung up. As the camp wagon picked us up Clint said, "That's a pretty good day's work for the first day, boys. But, we'll have to pick up the pace tomorrow. The five of us felled 280 trees." A bit of quick arithmetic in my head added the sixty I had cut and sixty Clint had felled to be 120. That meant the three other guys had downed only 158 trees – twenty-two less than they should have managed. Without divulging who had cut less than the quota, Clint suggested tomorrow would be a better day. He said, "Why over on West Creek there's a fellow named Pat Whelan who can drop seventy trees in a day, working just as fast toward night as in the morning. Let him be your hero!"

We got back to camp for supper around seven-thirty. Some of the men were so tired they nodded off as they ate. There wasn't much talk before bed, as everyone knew 3:00 a.m. would come all too soon. I asked Clint how long most men remained lumberjacks in the North Woods. "A man forty and still working in the woods is pretty uncommon. It's best to make plans for a different sort of work if you can." Thinking about the day just passed, I could see his point. But, happy to be safe from the law, and confident I could handle lumberjacking for a few years, I quickly fell asleep giving no more thought to the subject.

The next morning we were a man short on our crew. Evidently, the man decided a chopper's life was not his cup of tea and headed out during the night. It turned out he had cut only thirty-eight trees the day before while the other men had, indeed, cut their quota of sixty each. Every man has his motivations, and in a free country, can pursue those that work best for him. Sometimes, however, life presents more "have to do" things than "want to do" tasks, especially if you are a guy on the run from the law.

Snow came during the next few days accumulating to nearly a foot on the ground. It made life a bit easier for horses skidding logs out of the woods. And, other than making things a little slippery, the cooler weather accompanying the snow, took less energy out of us. Nonetheless, cutting sixty or so trees each day was still very hard work. Having lost the enthusiasm from the first few days of proving myself, life turned into a routine of eating a great deal of food and sleeping as much as time would allow.

There was one more down side of working in the snow and getting wet on a regular basis. Now, we had a new smell in the bunkhouse each night as several dozen wet and dirty socks dried near the wood stove. Fortunately my bunk close to the side door was blessed with a small, but steady, draft of fresh air.

Other bunkhouse resident activities mixed with the sounds and smells of living with twenty or so lumberjacks. Now, I was no stranger to mice and rats, but some creepy, crawly critters make poor bunkmates. Never before had I encountered such things as bed bugs and lice. My mother had always kept a clean house, but evidently many of the men came from different circumstances. Clint was quick to pick up on the problem and got the boss to get something called anguinum. It was a remedy used in those days to get rid of lice. The stuff did help some but it was best to keep a constant lookout for the nasty invaders. Always up for a little sport, the men made a contest to see who could come up with the biggest louse. I didn't see it, but the winner they said was a louse almost as long as a man's fingernail.

Despite the hard work and primitive living conditions, the camp had other lighter moments. One man in particular, Bruno Jones, seemed to constantly complain to his supervisor, Tug Thomas, about the hard work and short nights. Tug had a way of laughing off this sort of complaint and would say something like, "And the days are mere nothings." Not to be out done, Bruno fired back, "Well by Judas, I hang up my pants on the bedpost when I turn in an' when I get up in the morning they're still swingin'." Tug let out a roaring laugh and said, "Well, by gosh Bruno I guess you'll just have to keep those pants on."

Asa Aird was a hard man but not without common sense as to how to keep the men motivated to work hard. Many days he would chop along-side us and never failed to cut the most trees. He also liked to surprise the men at mealtime with hard to come by treats like chocolate, fresh apples, and once, real Havana cigars all the way from Cuba. Of course, everyone had to light up at the same time making the bunkhouse air thicker than any fog I had ever seen. Again, I was glad to have my drafty bunk location.

Most nights the men were too tired to do much except eat, gab a while and go to bed. Saturday nights were a different story. Some of the men would walk the whole seven miles out to Lake Pleasant to get their alcohol and find a woman. For me, staying away from alcohol was a good option that I usually took. As for women, I'd had my fill. You see one of the rubs between George Murphy and me was a woman named Gloria. Gloria and I had been serious for a while, even talked about getting married. But, then I caught her cheating with another man and ended the affair. She ran around with several guys after that, and was with George the night that I killed him in the barroom fight. Actually, I think she instigated the trouble because George mumbled something about "talking down his woman" when he started pushing me around. A good woman is like a royal flush in poker – very hard to come by.

Most men would stay at camp and play poker on Sunday or just eat and sleep. I kept out of the poker games. I had reasons for my reluctance. First, I was a very good poker player. Second, sooner or later in poker someone will lose more money than they can afford. This leads to resentment towards the bigger winners, especially if they win consistently. As the saying goes, "The winners sit back and joke, while the losers say deal-em." The last thing I needed was trouble with people who shared my new home in these mountains.

As Christmas approached many of the men, who lived within twenty miles or so of the camp, asked for the day off. Since Christmas was on a Wednesday, they also wanted a half-day before and after to travel. Continuing to demonstrate his wise ways, Asa agreed. To my surprise just about everybody took advantage of the holiday. Those who weren't going home, including Clint, decided to visit a village known as Newton's Corners or the Four Corners where there was a special place called the Brooks Hotel. Knowing there would be no other vacations before spring, I decided a break from camp life would be good and accepted Clint's invitation to join him and the others. Once again, my life was going to have a significant change.

Clint was right about the Brooks Hotel being special in this part of the country. It was a grand, three story building with covered porches wrapping around the first two stories. Owned and operated by Ernest Brooks and his wife, the hotel attracted large numbers of patrons from faraway places during the summer months. It also served local folks including farmers, lumberjacks, and others of various livelihoods. We arrived around 7:00 p.m., enjoyed a steak dinner and "retired" to the bar for a drink. Being Christmas Eve there were only ten men, I presumed without families, enjoying various beverages.

Around 9:00 p.m., there was a commotion in the entrance way as Mr. Brooks enthusiastically greeted a new guest who we could hear say, "By the da holy feesh, Ernest, ah tink eet cold out dah." Right away some of men exclaimed, "It's French Louie!" From the tone in their voices, I could tell it was someone they enjoyed seeing. Ernest entered the barroom with a ruggedly built man who stood only about five foot six tall. I guessed he was in his late forties and noted there was a special twinkle in his blue-black eyes. As the bartender poured a double shot of whiskey, Louie said, "Yo giv ones to da boys as yo me." Crowding around, the men began to ask him all sorts of questions mostly about deer, bears, wolves, trout, and other critters.

Clint could see I was confused about the celebrity who had joined us. "French Louie," he said, "is a local legend. He's a fisherman, hunter, trapper, and sort of hermit who lives back on the West Canada Lakes, maybe twelve, fourteen miles from our camp at Willis Mountain. There aren't any woodsmen better than Louie. Everybody admires his resourcefulness and ability to live off the land. Besides that, he's also a great guy. I suspect he's taken advantage of the small amount of snow on the ground right now to make a special trip into the Corners to get more supplies for winter. Come on over and I'll introduce you."

Picking up quickly on my Boston accent, Louie laughed and said, "Yo tak funny lak me." This response caught me off guard as the men at camp had gotten used to me and, like most people, I didn't think much about the sound of my voice. Not wanting to disagree, I replied, "Yep, but the difference is the men here want to hear what you have to say, they aren't much interested in Boston." This got a big laugh out of Louie, Clint, and the others. "Louie, da boy," exclaimed Louie, "Give da boys anoder drink." With that everybody saluted Louie and he left with some old friends to visit a barroom down the street. "That's his pattern," said Ernest. "He'll bring in a bunch of furs, get paid, leave enough for food and supplies with me, buy candy for all the neighborhood kids, and drink up the rest with anybody and everybody till he's broke. I'd better go keep an eye on him."

It might have been best if the night had ended just by meeting French Louie, but fate had another game to play. After Louie left, four men started a poker game and let the rest of us know they could use a couple more players. The whiskey was doing its work on me, and I hadn't played back at camp, so I suggested to Clint we try some poker. "Nope, don't play, but will watch if you want to join in." Three of the men at the table looked like local fellows from the Corners area. The last man definitely wasn't a woodsman. Tall, skinny, and with delicate, almost feminine hands, he hadn't worked with shovels or axes. Supposedly, he was a land buyer for a large timber company grabbing up land north of us. For some reason he reminded me of an undertaker. The man went by the name of Sidney Rogers.

Now there are several basic rules of good poker playing. One is to always cut the cards before they are dealt. Others are to watch how much you drink, keep a close eye on all the players, and never draw to an inside straight. There are times to take chances, but mostly it is best to play the odds. It also helps to have a good memory. That's why I always liked either five card or seven-card stud where you can see many of the cards already played. However, this night we were playing five-card draw.

The game, like most, started out being somewhat friendly with stakes set at five and ten cents - five cents to ante, and a ten-cent limit on bets. The first hour went well for me while the local men also won some. Rogers won only a single hand. It was Rogers' turn to deal and he suggested we up the ante to twenty-five and fifty cents. Now, this is pretty big money when most men earned less than a dollar a day. However, with winnings already in front of them, and more drinks in their bellies, the local men agreed. With a growing tension in my belly, I went along with Rogers' suggestion.

Rogers became very talkative and dealt the hand without offering to have the deck cut. This aroused my suspicions somewhat since he had dropped out of the previous hand and played with the discards as the rest of us finished. He won that hand with three kings to my three jacks. It was a sizeable pot of twenty dollars or so. I became less suspicious when he won the next pot dealt by a local man.

However, a pattern began to emerge where he would win big pots every other time he dealt. Each time someone would have a good enough hand to think they could win. But, Rogers would have cards just a bit better. Again, I noted he would drop out of the hand, just before his turn to deal, play with the discards, and then deal without offering to have the man to his right cut the cards. Sitting with men between us, it would be awkward for me to ask to cut the cards. Soon Rogers had regained all the money he had lost and much more. A man dropped out of the game having lost all his money. That left four of us for a while. Now that no one was sitting between Rogers and me, I asked to cut the cards each time before he dealt. He obliged but I could see a vein in his neck throbbing and his face getting a little red. He lost that hand and the next two before it was his turn to deal again. Continuing his pattern, he dropped out of the previous hand and played with the discards. Shuffling the deck quickly, he began to deal without offering a cut of the cards. I had seen enough and objected saying his poker manners were slipping. I then tossed my cards into the center of the table without looking at them. Perhaps catching on also, the two other men did the same. Giving me a dirty look, Rogers raked in his take - three antes of twenty-five cents from each player. Nearly broke, and sensing trouble was brewing, the two remaining local men said they had had enough and went back to the bar leaving just me and Rogers sitting across from each other at the table. Clint had been watching, about ten feet away, from the bar end closest to our poker game. Rogers glared at me for several moments and blurted out, "OK, Mr. Foxey man, how about you and me play head to head, cut the cards all you want, and let's see who comes out on top." A little voice in my head said, "You won some money, don't get into trouble and call attention to yourself." Unfortunately, I had enough whiskey in me to bring out my Irish temper and I glared back saying, "Let's do it!"

It's hard for a man to concentrate well just after having done something he knows is plain wrong. Somehow, it changes the flow of things for a person. It didn't take long before I had won all the money Rogers had accumulated in front of him. Pulling his wallet from an inside coat pocket, he grabbed a few dollars of what looked like his remaining money, and took the cards for his deal. Offering a cut, which I accepted, he dealt the cards and lost again.

Clearly down to a last dollar, and close to the point of rage, as measured by cherry red ears and a rapidly pulsating vein in his neck, Rogers, in a loud but cracking voice, bellowed, "Tell you what, Mr. Foxey, let's play one last hand for fifty dollars." His words brought a hush to the barroom and several watchers back to the table. By this time I thoroughly disliked this poor excuse for a man and was ready to go anywhere he wanted to settle matters. I replied, "Mr. Rogers it doesn't appear you have

the funds to cover a fifty dollar bet." Rogers stared at me as he slowly
pulled back his coat and delicately pulled a large revolver from a holster.
Gripping the gun only by the tip of its handle, he carefully placed it on
the table so the barrel was pointed directly toward me. He then reached
into the side pocket of his coat and slowly placed a small revolver next to
the big one.

Like many dangerous moments in life, time stood still as I looked at
the business ends of those two handguns. I barely heard the men gasp and
chairs scrape the floor as they stood and backed away from the surrounding tables. My eyes focused on the fully loaded cylinders of each revolver.
I could tell one was a big bore weapon, maybe a .45 caliber. The other was
smaller, most likely a .32 caliber. I knew .32 caliber revolvers were said to
have killed more men at poker tables than any other gun. When fired, the
slow moving bullet tends to tumble causing considerable damage when it
hits human flesh... Clint broke my trance as he eased into the chair next
to Sidney Rogers saying, "Now Mr. Rogers do you really want to wage
that fine looking pair of revolvers for a fifty dollar bet?" "I do for a fact,"
replied Rogers as his trembling fingers shuffled the cards. "All right sir,
but you better consider all the possible consequences of your actions,"
advised Clint as he looked Rogers squarely in the eyes and directed his
attention down towards Clint's lap. I couldn't see what Clint had, but
noted a shudder go through Sid Rogers' body.

Like life, poker is an uncertain business. I had been dealt a pair of
sixes. Since this was a prearranged wager, there was no additional betting.
I drew three cards. Rogers drew one making me think he probably had
two pair of some kind. Looking at my three new cards, I had a jack, an
eight, a deuce, and the two sixes. Thinking to myself, I said, "OK, Let
the man have his guns and fifty dollars. I'm still ahead by four hundred
or so." But, again, just like in life, you just never know. Coming back to
the moment, I laid my cards down face up. Rogers groaned, tipped back
in his chair, slumped, snorted softly like an exhausted bull, and dropped
his cards face down on the table. Looking at Clint, he slowly stood up,
turned, and shuffled out the door.

Whispers began to fill the room as Clint stood, sheathed a seven-inch
Bowie knife, and, one by one turned over Rogers' cards. Rogers had held
a deuce, three, four, five and another five. The man had tried to hit the
ends of a little straight and came up short. One of my sixes would have

done the trick for him. Later, I wondered why he tried to hit a straight knowing I had drawn three cards and couldn't have had more than a pair. Right then, a great swell of relief overcame me as the room filled with men's voices recounting to each other what had just happened.

A few minutes later Ernest Brooks returned with a very drunk French Louie. As was his custom, Louie had visited every bar in town celebrating and buying drinks for everyone. "By da holy feesh, les hab anoder dink!" he shouted. However, having just heard down the street about some "foxy" poker player and Sidney Rogers, Ernest was in no mood for more drinking in his hotel that night. Brooks ran a very respectable place and didn't want the hotel's reputation tarnished. He closed the bar and hustled Louie off to bed. Passing Clint and me, he said, "I expect you boys will be gone in the morning at first light – don't stay for breakfast!" Knowing there was no sense trying to explain our innocence, Clint and I nodded and headed for our room.

My head was spinning from the events that had unfolded in the last three hours or so. Here I was a fugitive on the run for murder, away from home and family on Christmas for the first time ever, narrowly escaped from getting shot, and drew attention to myself as some sort of card shark. The whole episode could have easily attracted the local sheriff. And, while I didn't know it yet, I had gained a new name, Foxey Brown that would go along with my reputation. As usual, most every time I drank, trouble came my way.

As Clint shut and locked the door to our room, I realized I hadn't thanked him for backing me up against Sid Rogers. I said, "Clint you sure bailed me out of a bad situation downstairs. I think that no good card cheat would have shot me if you and your Bowie knife hadn't got involved." "No problem," he replied. "I used to play a lot of poker myself and could see what that Rogers fellow was up to, playing with the discards and all. I figured it best to keep matters even handed and just a poker game if possible."

In the excitement of all that had just taken place, I had barely looked at the revolvers won from Sid Rogers. As I placed them on a bed Clint said, "The big one looks like a Colt Thunderer model, probably a double action in a .41 caliber." I hadn't seen a handgun like it and asked how he could tell so quickly. "Saw a picture of one in a story about Billy the Kid. Seems like it was Billy's favorite, even had one on him when Sheriff Pat

Garrett killed him back in 1881." Checking the Colt over we found Clint had identified it correctly. I had been right about the smaller revolver. It was an Iver Johnson double action, five shot model in a .32 caliber.

"Quite a deadly combination of weapons," said Clint. "That Rogers was definitely a bad character; might be best if we each slept with a revolver under our pillow in case Rogers comes looking for revenge." I agreed and handed Clint the Colt.

I couldn't sleep and my thoughts turned to the local card players in tonight's game. Two of them had lost all their money and I had over 850 dollars from my gambling with Rogers. Thinking he was still awake, I said, "Clint, got any idea how much those local fellows lost in that card game." Making a little snort like he had just fallen asleep, Clint said he had been watching and guessed they each lost somewhere around fifty dollars. "Doesn't seem right does it," I said. Sitting up in his bed, Clint looked over and said, "Poker is poker, you put in your money and take your chances, but lady luck ought to decide who wins and who loses. Course, you can do anything you want with the winnings. Those men know you weren't the cheater." "All the same, Clint would you take $150 down to Mr. Brooks in the morning for those fellows," I asked. "Yep, would be my pleasure, we best get some sleep now though."

Taking Mr. Brooks' advice, Clint and I were on the road for Lake Pleasant by 3:30 AM. Clint had slipped an envelope, with note and money, under Mr. Brook's office door We left our logging campmates to find their way back alone hoping they wouldn't blab to everyone the name and location of our logging camp.

Once again, I was on the run from someone who would like to cause me bodily harm. Maybe someday I would learn to stay away from drinking whiskey and playing poker. People involved with those activities usually have problems of one kind or another sooner or later. Now, I also had to worry about Asa firing me for bringing trouble to his camp.

3
SHORT TERM LOGGER

Without new snow to hinder us, Clint and I made it back to camp just before noon. The other men, minus two who decided to call it quits, returned later. Knowing those who had been with us at the Brooks Hotel would lose no time telling everyone about "Foxey" Brown's exploits, Clint thought it best to go straight to Asa and give him the details. This we did, and to my surprise and relief, Asa wasn't much concerned about the poker game and Sid Rogers. He did emphatically remind me about the rule of no drinking at camp.

To stem an endless flow of questions from my campmates, I made it clear right away that I didn't want to talk about the matter. The men were good about honoring my wishes and left me alone, but of course whispered behind my back.

The card game adventure had left me with an immediate problem to solve. I now had two revolvers and over 800 dollars in my wallet, counting my savings and poker game winnings. The guns and money could not safely be left in the bunkhouse or carried into the woods each day. Clint, once again, came to the rescue suggesting the guns and money could go in a safe Asa kept in his cabin. Asa wrote a receipt and thanked me for turning over the guns. Smiling ever so slightly, he said after thinking about my Brooks Hotel adventure, it would be best if I played no poker while at camp. That was advice I had no trouble taking.

By midafternoon we all were headed for the woods. Renewed from the little Christmas vacation everyone got engrossed in their work and we hacked away by torch light until eight o'clock or so that night. Asa was mighty pleased to see nearly thirty or more trees per man on the ground in a shortened workday.

The days after Christmas disappeared quickly, almost as fast as the accumulation of several feet of snow. Snowshoes were now necessary to get around in the woods. While the snowshoes let us move more easily, they also reduced hourly production levels. In addition to walking slower, we had to dig snow from around the trees to cut somewhere near their butt ends. To maintain the forty trees per day quota, we simply had to work more hours, making fourteen to fifteen hour days commonplace. Toward the end of winter that tiring pace would lead to a big problem.

It is no wonder lumberjacks are known to be hell-raisers when they get to town. Life in a lumber camp is demanding and pretty routine day after day, week to week, and month after month. It consists mainly of working, eating tons of food to maintain energy levels, and sleep. Sensing the monotony and hard work was undermining the men's morale, Asa loosened his rule about alcohol and provided a few bottles of whiskey on Saturday nights – it was to be the only way booze was allowed. This kept some of the men in camp and helped relax tensions. Asa also understood the value of music as a release. He and Clint could play a pretty good fiddle and sing a little. It was pleasantly surprising to see a bunch of hardened, whiskey drinking, cussing lumberjacks sing. While none of us could really carry a tune, the volume of thirty men singing at the top of their lungs served to shake the camp walls. The louder the fiddlers played, the louder the men sang.

Most of the songs pertained to the logger life. One simple song, in particular, seemed to be a favorite. I'm sure it was borrowed from another camp, but the men sang as if it were their very own. It went...

A is for axes, I suppose you all know;
B is for boys that choose them so;
C is for chopping we first did begin;
D is for danger we ofttimes were in.

So merry, so merry, so merry were we,
No mortals on earth were as happy as we;
Hi derry, ho derry, hi derry down,
Give a shantyboy whiskey and nothing goes wrong.

E is for the echoes that through the woods rang;
F is for the foreman, the head of our gang;
G is for the grindstone, so swiftly turned round,
And *H* is for the handles, so smoothly worn down.

I is for the iron that stamped our pine;
J is for the jobbers that all fell for wine;
K is for keen edges our axes did keep;
L is for the ladies kept everything neat.

M is for the moss that chinked our camps;
N is for the needles that mended our pants;
O is for the owls that hooted all night,
And *P* is for the pine that always fell right.

Q is for the quarreling we'd never allow;
R is for the river our timber did plow;
S is for the sleds so stout and strong,
And *T* is for the teams that hauled them along.

U is for usage we put ourselves to;
V is for the valleys we cut our roads through;
W is for the woods that we left in the spring,
And now I have sung all I'm going to sing.

So merry, so merry, so merry were we,
No mortals on earth were as happy as we;
Hi derry, ho derry, hi derry down,
Give a shantyboy whiskey and nothing goes wrong.

The first time I heard that song I thought it could very easily be altered to fit my former railroad life. *A* is for all aboard, I suppose you all know. *B* is for boys who ride them so. *C* is for caboose coming at the end. *D* is for dicks who beat your brains in... I didn't finish my version thinking railroad life was a thing of the past for David "Foxey" Brown, lumberjack of the North Woods.

Having picked up on the men's favorite tune, Asa usually ended breakfast each day with "Boys, Hi derry, ho derry, hi derry let's get those trees down." To which we would reply in unison: "Give a shanty boy whiskey and nothing goes wrong." I wish that last verse had remained true.

Because of the continued buildup of snow we had to remain on snow-shoes much of the time. To increase productivity, we began to "drive trees." This was different than driving logs in a stream, river or lake. Driving trees involved notching standing trees almost to the point of making them fall over. But, instead of dropping trees one at a time, men stayed in a line and worked their way up a slope until twenty or so trees below tottered in a row below them. Then, when everyone was alerted the uppermost tree would be felled into the one just below it. Just like dominos, when they work properly, the trees would take each other down one after another. Whoever thought of this trick was a smart man. But, it requires teams of smart men to make it work safely.

Every so often a tree down the row would miss its neighbor and someone would have to go down the hill to get the notched trees doing their domino thing again. Since it was dangerous work and took extra energy we took turns with this duty. My turn came up on a day in late March. About three in the afternoon, the fifth tree or so down the hill lodged in the sixth without knocking it over. As was his practice, Clint called a halt to all chopping by the other men. To be on the safe side, Clint would also go down the hill with a chopper and serve as lookout in case a tree decided to fall on its own. The men at the hilltop were to watch for any trees in neighboring rows that might decide to fall and, if so, warn us. Everything looked fine as we approached the tree needing attention. It still stood straight and didn't weave back and forth. Just before lifting my axe, I glanced at Clint noticing he nodded his head indicating approval to start. I had made only three or four chops when Clint yelled, "Look out!" I remembered nothing after those words until waking up in my bunk two days later.

It must have been late afternoon because the sun was shining through a west-facing window near my bed and the room was empty of people. I laid there a few minutes trying to get my bearings when Old John the cook came to check on me. "By gosh, Mr. Foxey it's good to see you awake. We thought maybe you were a goner. That old tree whacked you pretty hard," he said. Trying to sit up, I fell back when a sharp pain streaked up my spine. All I could reply was, "what tree?" "Well sir, I don't know all the details but as the boys tell it, the top broke out of a tree next to the one you were working on causing it to spin off the stump. Lucky you jumped when Clint yelled cause the top of that old tree came straight down and stuck in the snow right between the two of you. Guess a branch hit you alongside the head and you been out since." When Old John mentioned my head, I felt a bump near my hairline. It didn't hurt much compared to my back. With a big grin, Old John said, "You rest some more. Clint and the boys will fill you in on the details later on. I got to get back to the kitchen. Glad you're back with us, Mr. Foxey."

By the time Clint and the men returned from their day's work I had managed to roll out of bed onto the floor, and using the upper bunk support, get myself into a standing position. Then I could slowly walk around. Standing near the wood stove helped warm my back muscles and eased the pain some. I was there when Clint and the men entered the building.

"Well look who's up and at it," said Clint. Most of the others chimed in with similar words of encouragement including something to the effect of, "You can't keep an old fox down." But I noted several men including Bruno Jones were silent. Entering last, Asa looked me over and exclaimed, "Hi Derry, ho derry, hi derry this boy is up and around!" Shaking my hand, he whispered, "Let's talk after we've had some supper. You must be hungry, come and sit by me and Clint." I did so although the sitting down and getting up afterwards was not pleasant.

The meal passed with Asa and Clint making small talk and telling me several times how happy they were that I was on the mend. Finishing his pie, Asa said, "If you feel up to it, let's you, me and Clint go over to my cabin and talk." Anxious to find out more about what had happened I managed the short trip with considerable pain expressing itself in my back.

Stoking up his wood stove and offering me a chair that I declined, Asa pulled out his pipe and tobacco. Passing the tobacco to Clint and me, he said, "Dave, I want you to know we debated about hauling you out to Lake Pleasant, but your vital signs were good and there was concern about maybe you having a broken back. So, we decided it was less risky to give you some time to come around." That sounded reasonable to me and I nodded my head in agreement telling him I thought a few days rest would make me good as new. "Sure hope so," Clint said, "I'm missing my best man out in the woods." "That's a fact Clint," agreed Asa. "But we've got to tell Dave here that the whole damn thing never should have happened. I'm part to blame for relaxing my policy about no alcohol in camp. From questioning the men, it appears when you and Clint went down the hill to take care of the lodged tree Bruno pulled a whiskey flask from his pocket and they all took a swig. No one was watching when the top of a tree from another row snapped off and fell into the two you guys were working on. Its amazing Clint caught a glimpse of the falling tree and could tell you to look out. Otherwise you might have gotten the full brunt of its weight." Hearing this, I thought to myself that once again booze and the company of foolish men had almost done me in. Noting my silence, Asa continued to tell us Bruno is on notice that any other screw up will get him fired. "I'd like to fire him right now, but we're too close to the end of the season and I need him to finish getting our logs out."

Taking a long draw on his pipe, Asa looked directly at me and said, "Dave, there's more bad news. Evidently when the men were hauling you out of the woods, your wallet fell out. The finder left it on Clint's bunk a day later. Not knowing if you were going to live or die, Clint turned it over to me. From the way things were stuffed back into it, I'd say someone went through its contents. There's also talk in the bunkhouse that your last name is Brennan not Brown and that you used to work on the railroad back near Boston. Now, Clint and I don't really care about your past; you've been a good worker here; but we thought you should know what happened." At first, I couldn't think what was found in my wallet that would provide so much information. Then, I remembered the old payroll stub I had hidden away in case of a run in with railroad dicks on the way out from Albany. How could I have been so stupid to leave that in my wallet? There would never have been a need for such proof out here in the woods.

Asa cut me off as I started to speak. "Dave, there's more. You were a little delirious while you were unconscious and rambled on about a fight, a man dying and you had to go hide. Several of the men overheard this. Clint told them you were just dreaming. But they are speculating you changed your name because you are on the run from the law." Again, Asa interrupted as I started to speak. "Dave, you can explain if you want but you aren't the first man to come to these mountains to escape some troubles from the past. Clint told me what you did for those poker players that got cheated back at the Brooks Hotel. A bad man doesn't do something like that. So, if you want to get healed up and come back to work we'll just ignore any rumors going around." Hearing all this so quickly hit about as hard as the tree that had recently knocked me low. Forgetting all pain, I slowly lowered myself into the chair thinking I had to say something or my silence would serve to justify what the men were saying.

This was another time when the simple truth was the best approach. So, sparing a lot of detail, I told Asa and Clint about my fight back in Boston with George Murphy. And that, even though it had been self-defense, his family was connected to the police and would make sure I hung if they caught me. Looking over at Clint, Asa said, "Sounds like it was a fair fight to me what do you say Clint?" Clint paused, rubbed his head, and responded, "You can tell a lot about a man from the way he talks, works and plays cards. I'd bet things happened just the way Dave has told it." "OK, that's the end of the matter then," said Asa. "Dave, you can rest easy knowing your secret won't leave this room and that there really isn't much organized law up this way yet. The closest Sheriff is down in Northville." I wasn't sure it would be possible to ever rest easy again, but Asa and Clint's words were a welcome relief. After saying thanks and shaking hands, Clint and I headed for the bunkhouse.

An aching body said sleep, but my mind wouldn't shut off. While I believed Asa and Clint could be trusted to keep my secret, it appeared quite a few other men had suspicions about my past. Stories involving a man on the run for murder are just too good for people to forget. My best bet was to heal up, finish the season, and move on to another logging camp. Events occurring during the next three weeks threw that plan onto the scrap heap.

Several days passed and I still couldn't move without pain and swinging an axe was out of the question. After a full week, things remained the same. Noticing my lack of progress and growing restlessness Asa asked if I could help out in the kitchen. Anxious to earn my keep, I agreed thinking it had to be only a temporary thing.

While I didn't know much about cooking, Old John was patient and allowed me to do basic things like peeling potatoes and cutting up vegetables. And, of course, there were the dirty dishes, pots and pans.

The only good thing I could see about dish washing was that it kept fingernails clean. However, with the right attitude, a fellow can get by and learn new things no matter the situation. And so it was that Old John taught me to cut meat and to bake.

Pork and beef were hauled into camp once a week but freshly killed deer were relied on also. Winter and heavy snow cover made deer hunting much easier when the animals herded together in sheltered spots. Knowing this, local folk took the opportunity to make extra income by supplying logging camps with venison for a price of five to ten dollars per deer. It seemed no one cared how many deer were taken and some people practically made deer hunting their profession. Talk was that a local Indian by the name of Johnny Leaf would sometimes bring in an animal for a bottle of whiskey and that he had killed nearly 200 deer one year.

To my complete surprise, French Louie sauntered into our kitchen on a Monday morning in late March. It was evident from the warm greetings that he and Old John had done business before. "Louie, how the heck are you doing, sit down and have some coffee," shouted Old John. "Louie da boy be doin good," replied Louie. "I be needin some fluor and beens. Me give yo venison." Old John told him that would be fine and poured Louie some coffee. Looking over at me Old John said, "Have you ever met Dave here?" Louie glanced at me and said, "Yo be da poka guy up da Books Hotal who caugh da cheeter. I her yo goot mun." I was amazed at his memory since we had met only very briefly that night and Lou had gotten dead drunk. "Yes, I'm the guy you said talks funny but not like you." Showing a full set of good looking teeth and twinkling blue/black eyes, Louie laughed loudly. "Louie da boy no fogets."

Packing up several pounds of beans and a big bag of flour, Old John asked Louie what he was doing here at Willis Mountain. "I be comin out wid ma furs to da Corn'rs and did som trappin ober on Fall Stream ne'r da ol lumba camp." "That place still standing," asked Old John? "Yep, good nuff for Louie da boy. I gots ta be going, yo boys stop and see me if yo up Wes Canada way." With that Louie shook our hands, gathered his supplies and opened the door. Looking back with a big grin on his face, he said, "Da venison, be hangin behin yo food shed."

Shaking his head and laughing, Old John said, "What a guy! Everybody loves Louie. He just has a way about him that people admire. Why the man practically lives on nothing except what he catches or raises off the land. Those furs he mentioned probably weigh more than 200 pounds and he'll pull them out on a sled he rigged up. No horse, no ox, just Louie. They say he is unbelievably strong, can set a bear trap with his bare hands. He'll go on into Newton Corners, sell the furs, pay anything he owes, give old man Brooks enough for new supplies and go on a binge for several days. It'll be drinks for everybody, candy for the town kids, and big meals till his money is gone. After that, it will back into West Canada Lake country until he needs supplies or just feels like coming out."

Coming from a big family and now surrounded by lots of fellow loggers, it puzzled me how someone could live alone for such long periods of time. Old John explained that most of all Louie loved his freedom. He had been briefly married once and couldn't stand being stuck in one place all the time. Back in West Canada country, Louie was lord and master of his surroundings. Deer, bear, fish and other critters supplied all the meat he could eat and a small garden grew most everything else he wanted. "But, what does he do with the rest of his time," I asked. "Well sir, said Old John. "Louie keeps busy all the time constantly building camps along his trap lines – they say he's got fifteen or so stay-overnight places hidden away. Besides that he's always inventing and building something. If it's not a better chicken house then it's a cooler that will keep things from spoiling all summer. He goes to sleep when it gets dark and gets up at first light in the morning. "But, what about people company," I started to ask.

"Some folks don't need lots of people around them," said Old John. "Quite a few of the local guides stop and see Louie from time to time and he does some occasional guiding of his own. But, even then, Louie's need for company doesn't last long. The boys say Louie tires of people quickly and has been known to leave his own cabin when folks stay too long. The men that come to hunt or fish with Louie learn quickly that he isn't going to tend to their every need. Summing Louie up, I guess you would say he is his own man." Glancing at his pocket watch, Old John indicated that we had to stop talking and get busy fixing the next meal for our men in the woods. The talk had stopped but my mind continued to mull over the remarkable French Louie.

That night Clint and I had a chat about my future as a lumberjack. From what I could see my back was going to take a long time to heal and I sure didn't want to be a camp cook on a permanent basis. Clint shared some news that helped confirm my growing reservations about logging camp life. First, it looked very certain that Asa wasn't going to set up another logging camp next year. This site was pretty much cut over and

Asa was considering going back to being a lumber mill operator/owner down near his family place on Airdwood Lake. And, Clint himself had pretty much decided not to continue as a lumberjack. "I'm pushing 50 years of age," said Clint and "My body is beginning to remind me of that fact. Asa's offered me work back at his mill, but that too is pretty hard for an old man. I've got family downstate that could use help on their farm. I'm thinking that would be a good place to be for an old man when he needs looking after."

Hearing this, it was pretty clear I was back at another crossroads in my life. I couldn't go downstate with Clint even if he asked. Too many lawmen were down there. Going to work at Asa's mill wasn't a good bet either – bad back and all. Besides, like Clint said, it was tough work for older men and it wouldn't provide a paycheck every week all year round

I'd been thinking about French Louie and the way he lived. An option was to copy his lifestyle somewhat. Louie lived a long ways from the law and people who could tattle on him. Now, I didn't want to live quite as primitive as old Louie and considered trying to homestead a little closer to a settlement where a man could more easily get supplies. I was curious about the abandoned lumber camp over on Fall Stream that Louie mentioned. It was five miles or so north of Piseco Lake and Old John had said the lumber company would probably follow standard practice, now that the woods had been timbered, and let ownership go back to the state. And, the talk around camp was that the State didn't pay any attention to forest lands that had already been heavily timbered. A man could pretty much settle there without anybody giving a darn. I asked Clint what he thought about my idea. "Funny you brought this up Dave, I've been thinking the same thing," he said. "You've got enough money and experience to get started with a cow or two and make a small farm there. There's enough open land for hay and plenty of water near the old camp." He paused a moment and then, to my great luck, said, "Dave, I would be willing to stick around during April and May to help get you started. If you want we can hike over to Fall Stream on Sunday and take a look at that old camp." That clinched the deal for me. In a span of a few years I had gone from farm boy to railroad worker, college student, logger and then back to being a farmer. But, my next life turned out to be a lot different than farming potatoes back in Benedicta, Maine.

Foxey Brown/David Brennan at Fall Stream, circa 1900.
(Copyright 2008, Frederick T. Adcock and Cynthia E. Adcock)

French Louie with snake. (Courtesy Adirondack
Museum, Blue Mountain Lake, NY)

Piseco Lake Hotel (Copyright, 2008, Frederick T. Adcock and Cynthia E. Adcock)

*William P. Courtney
(Joann Dunham Estes)*

Abrams' Piseco Lake, Adirondacks

Abrams Sportsman's Home (Joann Dunham Estes)

Floyd W. and Mary Abrams , circa 1900. (Joann Dunham Estes)

Judway Brothers' Store & Post Office, Piseco, N.Y. 1905

(*Joann Dunham Estes*)

4
FALL STREAM

When sober, most woodsmen were short on words and long on getting things done. Neither Clint nor French Louie had described the old Fall Stream logging camp in any detail. Perhaps men like them tended to cautiously share things they valued. Unlike the loggers who had left the buildings after chopping the trees and floating the logs downstream, Clint and Louie recognized this place could be a home for someone. Thinking it was strange how something one man discards can become another's treasure, I too felt the old camp could be a good place to live.

The old camp sat along Fall Stream on a hillside looking northeast, across a large pond and beaver meadow, into the backside of Willis Mountain. I could see the meadow had once been much larger before all the beavers were trapped out. Clint said Adirondack Mountain people called the meadows, vlys. Smaller streams just above and below the pond meandered down from the mountains feeding Fall Stream and the vly. Nestled into surrounding mountains the camp felt isolated from the outside world. That feeling frightened and comforted me at the same time.

The logging camp owners had recognized the site's potential for backing up water and created a dam and fifteen to twenty acre pond. They had taken advantage of the land's natural features where Willis Mountain sloped down to bottle neck Fall Stream against a hillside that led up to the Spruce Lake trail. Building the dam had not been easy. My guess, based on my railroad work, was that it had taken dynamite, many men and lots of horses and oxen to get the job done. Huge boulders, weighing a ton or more each, had been blown loose and dragged into place to make a dam several feet in height. Altogether the dam stretched close to

100 feet across the stream and had been fitted with a sluiceway to control water flow. Smaller pool digger dams, just like beavers built, had been constructed below the main dam to protect its base. Despite lack of care for a few years, the dam was solid and held back several feet of water – deep enough for trout according to Clint.

The loggers had also spent a good deal of time digging into a hillside just above the stream to create a cool storage area for food supplies. Rocks, smaller than those in the dam, had been hauled in to make a stone foundation about twenty feet wide and thirty feet long. The building was made so three sides, about seven feet deep, were underground. A log wall and door provided a walk-in entrance from the outdoors. Clint suggested a fellow could quite easily remove the sagging roof, add a floor, new walls and new roof to create a two-story barn that would shelter several cows and hold hay. It was obvious he had been thinking about this place for himself, but was more strongly drawn to kinfolk downstate. Louie, of course, used the place only as a one or two night camp along his trap line.

The camp mess hall and bunkhouse was in bad shape due to neglect and the never ending work of nature. Rain, snow, along with the freezing and thawing of several winters had collapsed the roof causing the log walls to sag and the floor to rot. However, the logger boss' cabin, about twenty four by forty feet, had been constructed from sawed lumber and still stood straight despite a few leaks in the roof. The floor plan was open with a loft above the main area – plenty big enough for one man. The cabin site offered a great view of the pond and mountains to the northeast as well as providing a short trip to the storage area that would become my barn. Clint pointed out that a short walk to one's barn was important during cold and snowy Adirondack winters. "No sense shoveling snow wherever you don't have to," he quipped. A guy, who had grown up with Maine winters, and now with a bad back, couldn't argue with that. I liked Clint's advice and even considered connecting the cabin and barn like many farmers did back in Benedicta.

Walking around, we determined the loggers had cleared about fifteen acres. That and the nearby vly made a total open area of nearly fifty acres. Blackberry bushes and various other plants had worked their way back into the open hillside areas. The adjacent forest offered a variety of mixed hard woods, spruce, and pine that had escaped the axe. "Yep," declared

Clint, "everything's here to get a farming man going – lots of water, pasture area and grass on the vly, shelter for critters, wood to burn, and a road of sorts to get to town for supplies. Piseco Lake is only four miles or so to the south." Thinking for a minute, Clint added, "With deer almost as thick as flies, a guy wouldn't have to rely on farm animals for meat right away either."

We spent the remainder of the afternoon looking over the site and at odds and ends of equipment left by the logging company. Discussing possibilities, we enjoyed a leisurely hike back over Willis Mountain. I went to sleep that night thankful to have a friend like Clint and some options despite nagging worries that I was unsuited to live alone as some sort of hermit/farmer. Events of the next few days pushed those uncertainties to the side and forced a course of action.

News from the outside world usually came to a logging camp through the kitchen. Once a week or so supplies arrived from the nearest village and, with them, word (newspaper) about what was happening outside the forest. This week we learned some fellow in Saratoga County had killed a panther – supposedly the last one in these mountains. Another sign of changing times was the Governor's order for the state Forest Commission to map out official Adirondack wilderness areas. While having any sort of law regulate my potential home on Fall Stream made me uneasy, even more discomforting news came from reading about an electric chair being installed at Clinton Prison. Seemed some poor guy named Joseph Chapleau was going to be the first guest to try it out!

I never really learned how the month of March got its name, but to me it had always been the month when we start to "march" out of winter and into spring. Things in the natural world start to change in March and you can look forward to warmer weather and April thaws. So, March is usually sort of a hopeful month. Not this year, however.

Feeling much stronger and no longer being needed by Old John, I decided to go with Clint and test my ability to once again swing an axe. It was a fine day with sunshine and above freezing temperatures. Loosening up and getting used to the axe again took a while. But, the sun's warmth relaxed my back muscles and it pleased me to be doing some physical work again. Around nine or so that morning we were taking our break when someone shouted fire! Looking back towards camp, two or so miles away, a large black cloud billowed upwards several hundred feet in the air.

That much smoke could only come from the main building. Without a word, we all ran to the wagons and headed for camp.

Traveling two miles in a horse drawn lumber wagon on an icy logging road takes more than a few minutes. This ride seemed like an eternity with hell waiting at the destination. Well, if hell has lots of big fires we got a glimpse of it as we neared the camp. Rounding a bend the camp came into view pulling our eyes to the mess hall/bunkhouse in total flames. Old John and two men from the blacksmith shop, empty water pails in hand, were looking on. Their blackened faces and sweat-drenched bodies proved they had made great efforts to save the building. Asa ran to them asking if they were all right and what had happened. "Don't know," replied Old John. "I was in the kitchen and smelled smoke but didn't pay too much attention as the wind sometimes brings a little smell back into the kitchen. Then I heard a roaring sound coming from the bunkhouse area. Went to look and the whole room was filling with smoke because the stovepipe was lying on the floor. I went to grab a pail of water and to yell for Jeb and Josh in the blacksmith shop. By the time I got back flames were all over the place. And, of all the damn luck, to make matters worse, the wind picked up."

Asa just stood, not saying a word, and stared into the fire. After several minutes he kicked at the ground and said, "Boys let's meet in front of my cabin in twenty minutes." With that he spun around and marched off like a man on a mission. The rest of us remained watching the blaze that was consuming everything we owned aside from what we were wearing.

It wasn't long before the men began offering opinions about the fire's origin and what to do now. After a bit we headed for Asa's cabin. When Asa came out he had a Winchester 30/30 lever action rifle in hand. Working the lever and chambering a cartridge, he asked, "Anyone seen Bruno this morning?" Everyone sort of looked at each other and either shook their head sideways or murmured "No." Clint approached Asa and said, "I wondered why Bruno wasn't in the woods, thought maybe you gave him some other duties." Pondering the situation for a minute, Asa declared, "Boys we've got two sets of problems here. The mess hall and bunkhouse are lost, someone unsuccessfully tried to open my safe, and Bruno is gone. Second, you men have lost everything and we've got no place to feed and bunk everyone." Lifting his rifle, Asa began, "Part of me wants to head out and find Bruno, see what he has to say for himself. But, it's going down to zero or below tonight and I think we are done in terms of logging business here. So, it's best if most of you head for town to find food and shelter. I'm going to keep Clint and a few others here to wrap things up with the logs that are down in the woods. Fortunately, most everything else got hauled out last week. Give me a few minutes to meet with Clint and I will pay up what is owed to each of you. You are all good men and I am damn sorry this thing happened. Life stinks sometimes. Meet me in the blacksmith shop in a half hour at least there's some heat over there."

As Asa and Clint entered the cabin, the men began to shuffle off – some silently and others murmuring about the situation they were in, and where Bruno might be. Some would go home a few weeks short of the pay a full season in the woods could have got them. Others would find a hotel in town, drink away their troubles and find some new work when they were broke. The good news for me was that Asa still had my money and pistols in his safe. Eight hundred dollars would get me through the winter somewhere.

At the appointed time, Asa and Clint returned to the blacksmith shop. Asa began to read off names of men he needed to keep in camp – Clint, Old John, Tug Thomas … and finally, Dave Brown. Hearing my name called caught me off guard. Counting Asa, Clint, Tug, and me made only fourteen men – Old John to cook and the remaining ten to finish up the logging operation. But, why me? I had just got back to work in the woods, didn't know how my back might hold up… Asa's reason came to light later, but right then he was shaking each departing man's hand and giving them a pat on the back as he handed over their pay. I learned later, cash strapped as he was Asa gave every man an extra fifteen dollars to help cover their fire losses.

Those of us who remained in camp split up with five sharing Asa's cabin and the others in the blacksmith's shop huddled close to the hearth. Fortunately, Asa had extra blankets stashed away and the food storage building had enough meat, potatoes and carrots so Old John fed us after salvaging some pots and pans from the burned out mess hall. Other than discussing an appropriate punishment for Bruno if he ever got caught, the mood was somber and conversation sparse. I found out the next morning why Asa had chosen me to remain in camp.

After a breakfast of beef stew, Clint and the rest of us headed for the woods to bring in downed logs. Asa and another worker went to town to fetch enough supplies so we could get through for a few days. During our ride to the woods, Clint explained why Asa had decided to keep me on. Clint had mentioned my interest in settling over on Fall Stream and how it would be to Asa's advantage to have the two of us look after his camp until all the equipment and whatever else he wanted to salvage could be hauled out. That would allow Clint and me to finish out the winter here instead of moving to some hotel in town until spring. Being near to Fall Stream, we could look after Asa's camp and get an early start preparing my new home. All things considered, I couldn't argue with Clint's logic or come up with a better plan, and Asa liked the idea. Fate seemed to be drawing me deeper into these mountains.

The remaining days of March and April at Willis Mountain were spent helping Asa wrap up his logging operation. On weekends, Clint and I made several day trips to Fall Stream planning out what would be necessary to get my little farm in the mountains up and running. We drafted several lists of necessary items knowing my money could quickly disappear if we weren't careful. Asa once again proved to be a generous man. Not needing items like pots, pans, dishes, silver ware and other kitchen items salvaged from the burned out mess hall, he sold things at bargain prices. One of the best deals was an ox and wagon for twenty-five dollars. Asa also sold the contents of his personal cabin enabling me to head to Fall Stream with a good wood stove, bed, kitchen sink, table, chairs and other household things. Altogether my payment to Asa came to $195. With my last pay I had about $650 to fix up the Fall Stream cabin, build a barn and buy necessary equipment including a plow and other tools to work the land. I also had to invest in some new clothing to replace everything lost in the fire. Supplies to get through next winter would "chew up" the remaining money.

Getting in and out of Fall Stream was another hurdle to overcome. The trail over Willis Mountain, across Willis Vly and around the end of Fawn Lake was long and difficult. The village at Piseco Lake was closer than Lake Pleasant and a mile or so of road through the woods would connect my Fall Stream homestead to the Piseco/Spruce Lake Trail that was already open to wagon traffic. So Clint and I roughed out a road of sorts from my place on Fall Stream up to the Spruce Lake Trail. Those using a horse and wagon might find my road very difficult but a slow moving and powerful ox could handle the task. Besides, I wasn't interested in having a major highway lead to my hideaway in the mountains. There was no sense making it easy for the law to find me.

We started by making the cabin weather tight once again to prevent perishable items from getting ruined. This meant getting a leaky roof repaired right away. To accomplish this, Clint showed me how to make roof shingles. We thought of borrowing necessary tools from Asa, but Clint pointed out that a man could always earn a few dollars making shingles for other folks. Sometimes a "bundle," that will cover 50 square feet, can be worth a dollar. "Besides," he said, "all we need are a froe and wooden maul to split the chunks. I can make a shaving horse to hold the pieces, and using a draw knife we can flatten the shingles so they are all pretty much the same thickness." We began by bucking up a few ash logs into pieces eighteen inches long. Using the froe and maul, Clint split off the bark and green sapwood to expose the strong inner heartwood. He pointed out that shingles made from the heartwood don't twist and warp and they can last a good twenty-five to thirty years. "Yep, ash is got a nice straight grain and splits easy, it's also a great firewood – but ash wet or ash dry, a king shall warm his slippers by." I had never heard that wood wisdom before and asked him to repeat it. He did, and began to recite a whole poem/story about firewood.

> Beechwood fires are bright and clear if the logs are kept a year.
> Chestnut's only good, they say, if for long tis laid way.
> But ash new or ash old is fit for queen with crown of gold.
> Birch and fir logs burn too fast, blaze up bright and do not last.
> It is by the Irish said, Hawthorn bakes the sweetest bread.
> Elmwood burns like churchyard mold,
> E'en the very flames are cold.
> But ash green or ash brown is fit for queen with golden crown.
> Poplar gives a bitter smoke, fills your eyes and makes you choke.
> Apple wood will scent your room with an incense like perfume.
> Oaken logs, if dry and old, keep away the winter's cold.
> But ash wet or ash dry, a king shall warm his slippers by.

"Clint, you never cease to amaze me. Who wrote that poem?" "Got me," he shrugged, "just heard my father repeat it many times. Can tell you from experience though that it's solid advice. Just like mixing your firewood for different needs and occasions. My job as a boy was to get Momma seasoned apple tree roots for her stove when she wanted to bake bread. She said apple tree roots made very hot and long-lasting coals to warm the oven. We'll talk some more when we go to work on next winter's firewood pile." Working with Clint was always enjoyable because I never knew what might come out of him next. A day later we had produced twenty bundles of shingles to make the roof watertight once again. Many more were needed for the barn project.

Strong barns are essential to farmers who try to make a living in heavy snowfall country. Without a good barn it's difficult to properly protect and care for animals and, if nature cooperates, store bounties of the harvest. Hemlock boards were ordered from Asa over at his Lake Pleasant saw mill. Buying these meant laying out extra money, but the uniform boards made building go quicker, easier and created a more weather tight and long lasting barn. While waiting for the boards, we fortunately found some nearby cedar trees of sufficient size to make sill logs for the barn. After felling the trees, logs were hewn to make fairly square sill beams that were laid up on a foot high stone foundation. Matching the underground portion of the barn to the exposed section took some engineering but Clint came up with a design that provided strength and a good seal from the outdoors. We then cut and shaped hemlock logs to make joists for the barn floor.

Once the sawn lumber arrived, we were able to finish our unique little barn. A crowning touch came as we made a ground level entrance to the upper floor of the barn. That feature made hay storage much easier for a one-man farm operation. A large door on the lower level provided easy access to the outdoors for the animals. A few windows from Asa's camp gave the barn good light and ample ventilation especially when upper and lower level doors were open – all the better for curing hay.

All together repairs to the cabin and construction of the barn took $320 of my savings leaving $330 to buy a cow, food supplies and other necessities. We decided purchasing a plow to till the soil could wait until next year. The vly had more than enough grass and hay to feed the ox and a cow. A good vegetable garden with lots of potatoes and critter meat (deer, squirrels, grouse, rabbit, fish…) from the forest and pond would make up my basic foodstuffs. Flour and some canned fruits from Piseco had to be hauled in before winter.

A month or more had disappeared quickly and in late April I realized the time for Clint to head south was rapidly approaching. I dreaded his departure but knew, sooner or later, I had to fend for myself. We spent most of Clint's remaining days getting my woodpile started. Considerable quantities were necessary to get me through the winter and I didn't want to be cutting and hauling wood through deep snow. In a week or so we cut and split close to twenty face cords. We figured if I pecked away, a little each day, by fall I should have the twenty-five to thirty face cords necessary for winter and the following spring – maybe even some left over for the next year. Growing up in Maine taught me it was always good to have extra firewood.

At the end of the third week in May, Clint decided to hike out to Piseco Lake and send word downstate to his family indicating he was heading home soon. Clint and I had talked several times about trying to contact friends back in Boston. It had been nearly seven months since I had disappeared after tangling with George Murphy. I was feeling guilty about leaving my family and friends guessing what had happened to me. For all they knew, some of George's family and cronies had caught up with me, evened the score, and provided a secret burial spot. Clint and I hatched a plan.

After getting downstate, Clint would mail a letter from me explaining to my mother back in Benedicta, Maine that I was well. My letter would not provide details as to where I was now living. Mother could let family members know I was all right but would have no details to give them. The plan was for mother to respond to Clint at his central New York address and he would send her letter on up to me. Not a foolproof plan but hopefully one good enough to keep the law off my trail. If the authorities did catch up with Clint, he would stall and get word to me quickly so I could move elsewhere. As is often the case, fate intervened to create an ending I hadn't considered.

Clint returned from Piseco later that afternoon. He had picked up enough supplies to fill every square inch of his pack basket. He quickly removed his pack, handed it to me, and asked if I would unload it as he had to make a quick trip to the outhouse. Five minutes or so later, he came back into the cabin with a bulge under his shirt – one that gave out some whimpering sounds. Sounds I knew were not his belly rumbling from eating too much. Quick as you could say, "Boston baked beans" out from his shirt came a furry, floppy eared head. The puppy was jet black and had a white patch around one eye and another white mark on its chest. Its ears suggested there was a lot of Labrador retriever in its blood. "Couldn't resist," said Clint. "They were giving these pups away down at the post office." The dog's markings reminded me of a boyhood dog, called Spook 'cause he barked at most anything his nose caught a whiff of. Besides, Clint continued, "I figured you needed a companion out here. He'll probably scare more game than he catches, but Labs make faithful friends!" I didn't disagree and figured if Spook were a barker it would help keep varmints away from the garden and let me know if visitors of the human type were headed my way! Seeing me thinking it over, Clint laughed and said, "Sure hope you don't want to name him Clint." "No way," I exclaimed, "Although, if he's as good a friend as you, I'll be a lucky man." Not one to show emotion, Clint slapped me on the shoulder and declared, "By gosh that hike to Piseco made me hungry, let's eat."

The meal turned out to be the last one for us. Clint thought it best to head south early the next morning. The family would be heavy into planting time and doing first cutting of hay soon. The reality of being alone in these mountains was now looming squarely in front of me.

We talked long into the night about many things including Clint's family. His great- great- grandfather (Jacob) had been a Revolutionary War soldier and fought at the battle of Saratoga in 1777 and actually was present when Burgoyne, the British general surrendered. Seems Jacob was a sharpshooter and the family still had the flintlock rifle he carried. After the war, in 1788, Jacob received a tract of land in what is now Ithaca, New York instead of pay from the new, and nearly broke, United States government. Central New York in 1788, was pretty much all wilderness causing Jacob and his family many hardships to get there and start a farm. But they succeeded and Clint's great grandfather, grandfather, and father had farmed the same land ever since. Deep roots were calling Clint back to that land. The wanderlust that grabbed him as a younger man had run its course and now he wanted to finish his days surrounded by family and places where he had played as a boy. I wondered if I would ever get back to Benedicta.

Mulling Clint's story over some more, I could see where Clint had learned so many farming skills and how he had become a creative, patient, and self-reliant man. Working the land for a living demands these things from a man, or from a woman for that matter – as visions of my mother tending the garden, cooking, cleaning, doing barn chores… flashed through my mind.

We talked more about the importance of having a dog out here. Clint began by reminding me I had come to the Adirondacks to escape the law. "Now the absence of lawmen is good and bad," he said. "Good because you get second chances without going to jail, bad because they aren't here to protect you from bad folks. Plenty of men come up here and just disappear. Sometimes they get murdered for whatever they have – furs, money, just their gun and basic supplies. There's a family gang, the Wadsworths, over near Wells that you want to steer clear of if they ever show up. Word is French Louie had to chase them off once over at his place on West Canada Lake."

Clint went on to share rules to keep in mind when meeting strangers in the woods. "First, whenever possible, it's always good to see the other guy first! This provides time to look the fellow over quickly and make sure there's a tree or rock for you to step behind. Most men in these woods will be armed so don't assume you alone have a gun. Sizing up men can be tricky. Trappers are probably good folks, as is a man with a fishing pole, but a man with a gun can be hunting for food or for money to put in his pocket. If a man sees you first and hides, either he is afraid of you or is setting up an ambush – either way he's dangerous. Best rule is to spot strangers first and simply avoid them." Considering my experience in bars with people like George Murphy and Sid Rogers, I listened to Clint's advice about life in the woods very carefully. People are somewhat like apples – rarely is one perfect, most have blemishes, and some are plain rotten to the core.

Next morning, we yoked the ox and loaded Clint's belongings on the wagon. Our ride to Piseco Lake allowed more time to talk between Spook's frequent barking and seeking of our attention. Did he know Clint was leaving or was it just puppy behavior?

Clint and I promised to keep in touch especially when he received word back from my mother. We also made plans for him to come back next fall to do some deer hunting with me. The deer were smaller in size, and in numbers, downstate due to over hunting and less forest cover. A couple of hours later we arrived at the Piseco Hotel where the stage would stop. Like most days, it was behind schedule so we went inside for some food and a farewell drink.

The bartender was a friendly and talkative sort named William P. Courtney. We quickly learned Courtney had been the hotel proprietor since 1876, and "knew everyone in these parts" since he was also the postmaster and owned the local blacksmith shop. Courtney wasted little time asking, in a polite way, who we were and what our business was in Piseco. Of course it didn't matter much to Clint, going home and all, if Courtney knew his name. But, there I was trying to hide out up on Fall Stream and being obliged to share my name with a prominent man of the Piseco community. "Ah, Clint Neff," repeated Courtney. "Worked for Asa Aird over in Lake Pleasant for quite a while didn't you. And, David Brown, you must be the one got into that card game up at the Brooks Hotel – heard the boys nicknamed you Foxey. Yes sir, guess you boys are all right." Clint took this opportunity to pave the way for me to have a friend in Piseco. "Dave here is settling up at the old logging camp on Fall Stream. Going to do a little farming to get by." Catching on, I asked Courtney if he could suggest someone who might have a milk cow for sale. It didn't take but a moment for him to say, "Go over and see Floyd Abrams at the Sportsman's Home, he or his brother may have an extra animal."

A huge mounted lake trout hung above a mirror behind Courtney's bar. Noticing I was studying the creature, Courtney said, "Yep, caught that several years ago on one of old man Lobb's spoons a ways off of Pine Island," as he pointed out the window. Anticipating a story, I asked, "What's a Lobb's spoon?" Courtney began by telling us how Floyd Lobb may have been the greatest lake trout fisherman of all time and Piseco's most famous person. Turns out Lobb was an avid fisherman and invented a fishing lure that proved to be very effective in catching lake trout. It got so famous fishermen from all over began using his lure. "Yes sir, old man Lobb was a one of kind guy," said Courtney. "He died recently and, at his request, they buried him with a good deal of his fishing equipment – grave's unmarked though. Matter of fact, he was so fascinated with fishing that on his dying day, sick as he was, Lobb fished and caught two trout as friends rowed him across the lake. He caught those fish from a mattress they laid in the bottom of the boat. If there's fishing in heaven, Old Lobb will truly be in his glory."

Courtney moved down the bar to serve other customers and Clint whispered, "Don't be fooled, there's a story suggesting Courtney and Lobb weren't always on the best of terms."

As the tale went, Courtney and Lobb were neighbors. Courtney raised geese and Lobb had turkeys. Unfortunately for Lobb's turkeys, they had the habit of wandering onto Courtney's lawn. This irritated William P. considerably. After a few very direct discussions, Courtney warned Lobb next time his turkeys trespassed they would be shot. Lobb ignored the threat.

Not long afterwards, one of Lobb's turkeys took some fatal steps and found bird paradise at the end of Courtney's gun. Hearing the gunshot, Lobb surveyed the situation, grabbed his gun and promptly blasted one of Courtney's geese that had been dusting itself in the road. Turning to Courtney, he barked, "An eye for an eye and a tooth for a tooth, you killed my turkey, and I killed your goose."

The sound of horses neighing outside interrupted our laughter. "Stage is here," shouted Courtney as he headed for the door. Clint turned to me and said, "Might as well say good bye here, Dave. I've enjoyed our adventures and working with you. I'll get your letter sent back to Maine and let you know what I hear. And I'm looking forward to chasing some white tails next fall. Pick out a big buck for me, will you?" By biting the inside of my cheek, I fought back tears, and told Clint I would be forever grateful for his friendship and all he had taught me. "Don't mention it," he said. "By next fall you will probably have some things to teach me. Living in the woods is like going to school for those willing to learn." We shook hands and Clint headed for the door. Not wanting to prolong the uneasiness in my stomach, I turned to the bar and ordered another drink from the bartender covering for Courtney. There was a temptation to spend the rest of the day at the Piseco Lake Hotel bar. But, that would be no way to honor all the time and effort Clint had invested in helping me start a new life.

Four o'clock that afternoon found me headed up the trail towards Fall Stream leading a cow purchased from Floyd Abrams. I had also stopped at the Judway Brothers grocery store (needed some tobacco and canned fruit) and at the post office to alert the clerk that mail might come for a David Brown now and then. He could just hold whatever arrived until I came to town – something I didn't intend to do very often.

It took a while longer to cover the five miles or so home with the cow in tow. I was really going to be alone in the wilds of Fall Stream and my mind raced considering all the things needing to be done before winter.

Approaching the cabin fifty yards or so away, something didn't feel right and Spook began to bark loudly. A gentle breeze was making the cabin door swing slowly back and forth. I knew we had shut the door securely. Drawing my Colt revolver, I slid sideways along the porch wall to a window and took a quick peek inside.

5

FEARSOME FOXEY

The cabin had been ransacked. My belongings were scattered here and there, not destroyed but thrown about as if the intruders were looking for something of special value – like my money stash hidden inside the barn's stone wall foundation. A quick trip to the barn brought relief as the money was safely there along with my shotgun and rifle. For some reason, I had hidden them also before Clint and I went to Piseco. Who and the hell would wreck a man's camp and take, as it turned out, only some food? This reminded me of young punks back in Boston who vandalized places just for fun.

Nothing seemed out of order in the barn, so I decided to use what little daylight remained to further investigate matters and headed for the pond. Sure enough, fresh human footprints were in the mud near the dam – two sets of them. Nearby, I found the innards of eight trout. Next to them laid the tobacco ashes from someone's pipe. I couldn't imagine local people breaking into my cabin and suspected the culprits were vacationing near Piseco. In recent years, more and more "Sports" – city people from downstate were visiting the Adirondacks to hunt and fish. I figured if that was going to be a problem, I'd best come with a plan to deal with such people. I needed the fish in my pond and wasn't going to put up with people breaking into my place!

My emotions hadn't brought me to tears since I was a small boy. However, that night all the things that had happened since my fight with George Murphy overwhelmed me. Maybe it was triggered by Clint's departure and the break-in at my camp, but the realization that I was totally on my own to live or die shook me. I bawled like a baby. Spook was quick to sense my pain and came to lie quietly at my feet – head on his paws gazing up at me as if to say, "What's going on?" Some folks believed crying once in a while was good for the body and soul. They may have been right because I could feel troubling things stored inside loosen and leave. As my body relaxed, a deep sleep embraced me until way past my normal morning wake up time. Only bright sunshine streaming through the cabin window interrupted my coma-like slumber. The light, however, didn't seem to trigger any wakeup call in Spook as he continued snoring and twitching as if he was dreaming about chasing a rabbit.

I began the day cleaning up the cabin and, while doing so, recalled when my father, Owen, had died in 1870. My mother had cried a good deal up until the funeral. I remembered her there, looking straight ahead almost without emotion. I sensed she was thinking, "OK, what's next?" The next day she told me the best way to get past your pain is to get busy. Busy she got, because she alone had me and my younger brother and sister to rear. My situation was a bit different, but like hers, my past had died and now choices lay ahead of me. Sometimes those choices are planned out and sometimes they just present themselves.

I threw myself into cutting hay off the vly and working the firewood pile. A week or two later a Saturday morning found me, at the barn, sharpening my scythe and getting ready to cut hay. I still needed a good deal more. Spook began to bark and ran toward the dam causing me to notice two men fishing on the far side of the pond. I don't know what possessed me but I grabbed my rifle and ran toward them shouting at the top of my lungs, "Get out of here or I'll send lead for sinkers!" They just looked at me so I fired three rounds – one in the air and two so they landed about twenty feet in the water from where the men were fishing. The two Sports jumped back shouting something about their right to fish. I replied by placing another bullet in the water a little closer to them. They forgot about their rights and ran at full sprint, as best they could in their hip boots, into the woods and on up Willis Mountain. I guess they decided it was best to be right and gone instead of dead right there in the pond. Self-impressed with my little play on words, I had my first chuckle in weeks.

Most days in a man's life are not memorable, but that Saturday in May 1890, I later learned, marked the beginning of my reputation as some sort of wild man who lived along Fall Stream. I had never shot at a human before and certainly hadn't tried to hit the fishermen. However, a man's reputation is often made for him based on someone else's impression and needs. Evidently, those Sports headed back to Piseco and William P. Courtney's hotel where they had been staying. And, of course, they had a story to tell. Mix in some alcohol and shake it with people hungry for a good tale and you'll get something considerably different than what really happened. By the end of the weekend, it was going around Piseco that a guy named Foxey Brown up on Fall Stream had shot ten or fifteen times at some fishermen with bullets kicking up the dirt at their feet and striking tree branches near their heads. Getting quickly into the woods was the only thing that saved them from certain death.

This situation bothered me at first, but a smart man turns adversity into opportunity. If it took the reputation of a wild man to keep people away from my homestead, so be it. I decided to play the part to the best of my ability. Thereafter, any one approaching "Brown's Pond" got acknowledged by my gruff, "I'll send you lead for sinkers," greeting and a gunshot or two. I decided it might help to look the part of a wild man also. So I grew a full beard and let my hair get long. The trick was not to overdo my performance to the point that a lawman was brought in to round me up.

A month or so passed and I was anxious to learn if Clint had heard from my family. I hadn't been to Piseco since he left and needed a few supplies. Surely, enough time had lapsed for Clint to get word from Benedicta and forward it to me. Not needing the ox and wagon, I decided a brisk walk could get me to town in considerably less than two hours. After getting on the main trail, I met two or three people headed towards Spruce Lake. While they acknowledged me, no one stopped to chat but merely touched their cap or said, "Howdy" and kept walking. It didn't occur to me that my appearance might be unnerving folks until I reached the edge of town. There, on three separate occasions, women working in their gardens or hanging clothes out to dry, moved quickly into their house and closed the door as I approached. Not thinking too much about it, I hastened my pace to the Piseco Hotel and post office.

A glance in the glass of the hotel main door gave me a clue as to my appearance. I did look somewhat fearsome with beard and long hair. Thinking things were progressing according to plan, I entered the building and went over to the post office area. I identified myself and asked for my mail. An obviously nervous clerk said, "I don't think there is any mail for you Mr. Brown, but I'll double check." After looking through several bins, she shook her head and said there was nothing for me. Dejected, I turned and left to go visit Judway's Store for my supplies.

The few men and women at the store stepped aside pretending to have important conversation with one another as I entered. Mr. Judway waited on me politely but made no conversation as he entered my name and items purchased in his logbook. This puzzled me somewhat as I paid in cash for the tobacco, tea and some canned fruit. However, I decided not to ask why my name had to be recorded. Maybe it was his way of keeping inventory and knowing who might want what.

I nearly had got off the porch when William Courtney walked up the steps. "Howdy, Dave I heard you were in town. Say, I want you to know that I didn't send those fishermen up to your pond. Seems like some of the Sports have been going up there each spring for the last three or four years. Beats me how they found out about the good fishing up there." I didn't know whether to believe him or not, but asked if he would spread the word that the pond was part of my homestead and I needed to protect it from being overfished. And, of course, breaking into my camp was grounds for getting shot. He emphatically agreed and told me to see him next time I was in town so we could talk some more about protecting "Brown's Pond." With a sly grin on his face, he turned and headed inside the store leaving me greatly puzzled about what Mr. William P. Courtney was up to.

My return to camp was greeted by Spook's joyful barking and the cow's mooing to be let loose. Here was my family. They didn't give a dam about my appearance only that I would provide for their care. Whoever came up with the term, "dumb animals" got it wrong. I would learn over the years that animals have individual personalities and can communicate what's on their minds if a man learns their lingo and body movements. Knowing these things makes for good companionship with animals and success when hunting those needed for food.

I put the disappointment of not hearing from Clint out of my mind thinking that surely next month will bring good news. I spent the rest of July building partitions in the barn, hauling in hay off the vly, cutting and splitting firewood, tending to my small garden, picking berries, and hunting for meat as needed.

No visitors had showed up since my encounter with the sport fishermen. But just after breakfast on the first day of August, Spook began to bark, and there was a shout from the edge of my woods – "Hello the camp and Dave Brown, this is your neighbor Tim Crowley." Hearing this I edged to the door rifle ready just in case. Clint had said that Crowley had a camp up at Spruce Lake where he made a living picking spruce gum and catering to the Sports during hunting and fishing seasons. "Dave, I've got a letter here for you. Lucy Abrams at the post office said you were waiting for some mail and wondered if I might drop it off to you." I hadn't met Tim Crowley, but his story made sense so I went out to chat with him. Giving me the letter, he apologized for not stopping by sooner to offer any assistance I might need. Old man Courtney had said I should meet Crowley as he was a good man. Right off, from the way he spoke and looked you in the eye, I sensed he was a straight shooter. Despite me being desperate to open the letter, we chatted for a half hour or so about life in the woods. Turned out Crowley had a large two story log cabin and family up at Spruce Lake. He did pretty well picking the sticky gum off spruce trees and selling it to a company downstate that made it into chewing gum. "If you're interested Dave, I pay fifty cents a pound to people like French Louie when I pick it up at his place on West Canada Lake." That sounded pretty good to me. I said I would keep it in mind and thanked Crowley for bringing the letter. Tipping his hat, he headed up the trail.

Opening that envelope brought devastating news. I could barely believe what my eyes were reading. Inside were my letter and a note explaining Clint was dead. He had never made it home. He had taken a room at a hotel in Syracuse that caught fire during the night. Most of Clint's belongings had survived the fire. Smoke, however, had killed him and several other guests. His family had mailed my letter to my mother but it came back sometime later marked "Undeliverable." Knowing Clint had been living near Piseco Lake, and had a friend named David Brown, they took a chance and mailed the letter back to me.

At first I wanted to cry, but an overwhelming sense of anger took hold of me. What kind of god lets this happen and people like Bruno Jones continue to walk the earth? I vowed never to let anyone get close to me again – it hurts too damn much to care about people. I would live out my life here on Fall Stream away from that crazy world out there full of pain and misery. This little camp and pond would become Brownsville and I will be the mayor and sole resident. Woe be it to anyone who dare tread on my property!

Pain, grief, and remorse are strange things. The more you think about the underlying situation, the more it can hurt the body, mind and spirit. Some people seek relief by getting drunk and letting the stupor and forced sleep dull the pain. Others seek out friends and cry on their shoulders. A third remedy, as my mother advised, was to throw yourself totally into work. I chose the first and last options.

After writing a letter to Clint's family expressing my sympathies and what a great person he was, I headed for town. It was convenient that both the post office and Courtney's Hotel were in the same building – not that there were any shortage of saloons near Piseco Lake. Twelve alone lined the road from Piseco to Lake Pleasant. Lumberjacks and other hardworking laborers were thirsty people, especially on Saturday nights.

Anyway, Lucy Abrams took care of mailing my letter and old man Courtney poured the whiskey. I don't remember much except telling William P. to keep my shot glass full. My next recollection was waking up in a room totally unfamiliar to me. Walking outside I recognized the building as Floyd Abrams Sportsmen Home on the Haskell Road that led back toward the mountains and Fall Stream. Seems I had gotten drunk to the point of passing out and Courtney had carted me over to Abrams' place to sober up – no booze was sold there. After letting the fresh outdoor air clear my head, I went back in to the desk to find Floyd. "Well, Dave. You sure tied on a good one. According to Courtney you got real sad, then silly, and scared the heck out of everybody by shooting your pistols off into the air. He thought it best to get you out of there." There wasn't much I could say except to mutter that I sometimes was a damn fool. I offered to pay for my room, but Abrams said he owed Courtney a favor or two and there would be no charge. Perplexed as to Courtney's generosity toward me, I thanked Floyd and headed up the trail toward home with hat in hand. My head hurt way too much to wear it. Even the sounds of crows calling and my clothes rustling as I walked caused me severe pain.

With option one for curing my loss of Clint and disappointment of not being able to contact my family behind me, I busied myself getting Brownsville ready for winter. But lingering guilt about not getting word to my mother bothered me at night. I had to figure some way to tell mother I wasn't dead. With Clint gone, Asa Aird was the one man remaining that I could fully trust. I considered hiking over to Asa's place to see if he might be heading to Gloversville, Johnstown, Fonda or another city. But on second thought, those three cities were too darn close to Sheriff Ned James' jurisdiction. I wanted to avoid that man and his sharp memory. Maybe Asa would know someone headed farther away who might mail a letter to my mother. Then it would have a postmark far from my Piseco hideout.

My resolve to contact mother grew weaker as one day vanished into another that fall. I fell into a schedule of getting up at first light and going to bed at dark. The long hours of physical labor, plenty of fresh air and a diet of wholesome food and spring water made sleep come easily. An uneasy peace came over me and there was little hunger for human company.

Hunting season interrupted my daily routine with the arrival of an occasional sport hunter. Local folks seemed to prefer avoiding my place, but some outsiders evidently had not heard about the fearsome hermit of Brown's Pond. Perhaps, William P. Courtney was having fun letting an occasional Sport learn about me first hand. At any rate, those who did show up promptly got the Foxey Brown treatment – angry words and bullets. It was an effective remedy – they didn't return. I learned later my success in driving unwanted company away was, indeed, beholden to some skullduggery on the part of William P. Courtney.

I hunted alone taking a deer whenever one was needed for meat. The deer were plentiful, and as colder weather set in, I kept one hanging to cure most of the time. Just after the official hunting season ended, and a dusting of snow arrived, I had a visitor of the three-legged kind! A hunter of questionable judgment and poor marksmanship had shot a yearling doe in the hind leg blowing it off from the knee down. This sort of thing usually happened when a Sport hunter shot at a running deer and failed to lead properly with his rifle. There will also always be some hunters "Who can't hit the broad side of a barn." Whether the deer is standing or running, they will aim at the head and hit it in the ass!

I was tempted to put the poor critter out of its misery with a bullet. Being near the barn, I grabbed my rifle and took aim. I paused when noting how well the deer moved along on three legs. A closer look revealed that its injured leg was healing and showing no signs of bleeding. The bullet had somehow made a clean amputation. I speculated she'd been able to lick the wound and stem the flow of blood. So far this animal had defied the odds and was surviving. I had always liked "the underdog" and lowered my rifle. Like me, this deer was trying its best to get by in these mountains.

Spook's behavior also puzzled me. Normally he relished and earned his keep by chasing any deer crossing his path. Spook's skills helped immensely whether he was guarding our garden or assisting on a deer hunt. Somehow, this deer presented a different situation for him. As Spook approached the young deer, it made no attempt to run or face him. It just kept browsing along as if to say, "I'm just passing by neighbor." Spook appeared to respect the deer's response to his presence and he merely sniffed it over and trotted back to the barn.

I thought, "This deer won't be around long." I surely couldn't afford to feed her precious hay from the barn throughout the winter, even if it might eat hay. As it turned out the animal was a companion, of sorts, until the following spring. I suppose, like people, there are dumb and smart animals. I won't say it figured out that my and Spook's constant presence discouraged predators from hanging around, but that did work in the deer's favor. It learned to glean some nourishment from the soiled ox and cow bedding I pitched out of the stable and helped itself to pond water where I kept a hole in the ice open for my animals. It also benefited by being able to browse the ample supply of young trees and brush that were reestablishing themselves in the cleared forest and vly edges. Depressions in the snow near the barn testified to it spending nights near us. I couldn't imagine that, other than a break from the wind, it was enjoying any heat or shelter from the barn. But, my senses weren't as sharp as Spook's or a wild deer. Again, maybe, she found comfort in the lack of bear or wolf sign near the barn. Whatever the case, her determination to live was reassuring to me that first Fall Stream winter.

A woodstove and well-stocked woodshed are also reassuring in these mountains. Utilizing a woodstove and woodlot, like planting a garden, is a declaration of independence. The stove and firewood provide freedom from depending on someone else to deliver something essential for your survival. One's "life, liberty and pursuit of happiness" are also enhanced as the firewood cutter gets to decide how warm to keep his cabin in direct proportion to how much and often he feeds the stove. There is no tax on a man's firewood pile.

The act of cutting, splitting, and stacking firewood has a special aspect of independence. No company boss or committee of any sort told me when, where, what, and how much wood to cut in a day. Breaks from my task were entirely of my own choosing. And at the end of the day, the rewards of my labor stood directly before me in the amount of wood I had cut, split, and stacked. And, I knew exactly how it would benefit me come winter. This was a considerably different way of living compared to some poor soul scraping hides all day in a tannery simply for sake of a paycheck. The paycheck, which the factory worker usually had spent before the next one arrived, kept him going temporarily – but the need for it enslaved him week after week. I often thought most people live like flies trapped on a window. They follow the light back and forth seeking escape in the same small stretch of space but never quite find it. Perhaps lifetimes of such frustration is what inspires poor human souls to put "Free at Last" epitaphs on their gravestones. Life at Fall Stream allowed me to live free as long as I was smart enough to make it happen.

Sitting near a woodstove during a howling snowstorm also provides a man satisfaction and a sense of independence knowing what could be happening to you outside. It is similar to standing on high ground come flood time in the spring. I should say, "Partial independence" because none of us are ever independent from nature's blessings of sun, rain and the fertile soil that make trees and gardens grow. I tried to keep these things in mind as the sweat poured down my brow when cutting wood in early May or September. Black flies inhibited my independence come June. But that's a story better told later on.

Learning how a wood fire burns, and about the stove that holds it, are essential when your survival and comfort are directly tied to them. In addition to knowing the burning behavior of different woods, successful cooking and keeping cabin temperature where you want it requires experience in mixing them. First off, having seasoned wood is important to making it do what you want in the stove. Some, as the firewood poem taught, take longer than others to season.

Hard (sugar maple), ash, or beech alone makes a nice bed of coals to bake with or grill fish and steak over; but when a just roaring fire is needed, mixing a little seasoned hemlock, fir, pine or spruce keeps the fire burning brightly. Never try to grill meat over a fire of black cherry unless you want sparks on the floor and in your face. Hemlock too, has a snap, crackle, and pop characteristic. Many a forest fire got its start from a novice camper who didn't properly tend a black cherry or hemlock campfire.

A sufficient fire to make a quick meal can be obtained from dry aspen, pine, fir or hemlock. These woods don't make a lasting bed of coals so you have to add hardwood soon after the meal to obtain a good heating fire. Mixing the right combination of split and round chunk wood determines how quickly a fire burns or holds throughout the night. The combinations chosen also influence how much or little creosote gets produced. Creosote buildup in a chimney has brought about the doom of many a poor soul. Once ignited the black caked or tar like material burns at high temperatures and is difficult to put out. A neglectful chimney caretaker often learns the evils of creosote on a cold wintery night as his place burns down.

When selecting wood easy to split and start fires quickly, I chose ash and soft (red) maple. Rounds with no knots will split straight and true with little effort. The firs, hemlock, and pines, because of their knots, require a little more effort, but when well-seasoned make good kindling.

A woodstove's design is another thing to consider. Whenever possible, it's best to have one stove for cooking and another just for heating. Cook stoves are designed to hold pots and pans, heat water, and provide an oven for baking purposes. But cook stoves don't have enough firewood capacity to comfortably heat a cabin or hold a fire overnight. Combination stoves offer some cooking surface but hold much smaller amounts of wood. Large chunk stoves that hold big pieces of wood provide the longest burn times and give off the most heat. I liked stoves with a round burning chamber because they provide a better draft and burn cleaner having no corners where creosote can build up.

I always enjoyed watching a wood fire in the evening and appreciated finding a good bed of coals on chilly mornings. Somehow the fire at night relaxed me before bed and the coals in the morning promised another day of comfort. I didn't know much about my ancestors, them being buried back in Ireland, but tending my wood fire gave me a sense of connection with their lives. Like them, I ate, stayed warm and dreamed around a wood fire. Dreaming and contemplating the mysteries of life come more easily around a wood fire.

However, problems can come about from spending too much time around a wood stove, especially in the winter. It's called "cabin fever." Too much warm and dry air is not good for the mind or body. It causes a man to become lethargic and, in extreme cases, subject to wild thoughts and behaviors. I learned the remedy for cabin fever was to get outside into the fresh air every day and exercise. Anticipating the negative effects of cabin fever, I made it a point to take long walks despite weather conditions. Spook was a willing companion and anxiously waited for me to dress and open the door. He even understood what hour and minute we normally went outdoors and would begin to pester if I was a bit behind the appointed time.

With confidence comes complacency followed by carelessness. Becoming comfortable with my winter walks, I decided one thirty degree, bright sky, February morning to snowshoe into Piseco for a few extra supplies. I had also noticed that William P. Courtney kept a small library of sorts in his hotel and would loan books out. Spook as usual was my escort. He bounded along on a snow crust that was strong enough to bear his weight, but not mine. Spook was thoroughly enjoying some new scenery. Watching his shenanigans boosted my spirits and I looked forward to seeing what was happening in the outside world.

My first stop was at Courtney's hotel and the post office. I anticipated having no mail and that was the case. My main objective was to find out how long the post office would hold a journal if one arrived for me. It had been a year or so since I had read a copy of *Colliers Weekly*. Reading had been one of my favorite activities back in Boston. *Colliers* helped keep me informed of news and I liked its use of photographs. Besides, the founder Peter Collier was an Irish immigrant who had achieved success by working hard and saving his money. Clint had also mentioned how much his father enjoyed reading *Farm Journal* finding many of its "how to farm" articles helpful. The price to get these journals was $1.50 each for a one-year subscription. The clerk said holding my mail for a month or so wouldn't be a problem so I ordered the journals.

William P. was off on business in Lake Pleasant and I wasn't comfortable asking those left in charge about borrowing reading material. It didn't take a genius to sense they were uncomfortable with my appearance and presence. I resisted the temptation to have "just one" drink and headed over to Judway's store. To my delight he had a recent copy of the *Daily Leader* newspaper out of Gloversville. Copies of it had found their way into Asa's lumber camp making a way for the men to keep up with news in Hamilton County and the outside world. I inquired about some considerably older copies of the *Daily Leader* lying in a corner and Judway threw them into the total price for my supplies.

I carefully loaded the items purchased into my pack basket, shouldered it, and opened the door. Greeting me was a strong gust of wind, a darkening sky and the promise of snow. I dismissed fleeting thoughts about staying the night in town knowing animals had to be fed and that remaining here would probably lead to the consumption of alcohol. Memory of my last drinking bout, throbbing headache and all, was fresh and I headed for home.

Reaching the trailhead, I mounted my snowshoes and Spook and I were off on a double time pace. The looming storm changed both my and Spook's mood. He now chose to keep just a few steps ahead, nose to ground for the most part. We made good time the first mile or so as the sky grew darker and darker and the first snowflakes began to dust my cap and Spook's back. Soon, the snow was driving itself into our faces. Hoping we were merely into a squall, I ignored it, and plunged ahead at a quicker pace. A break in the snow's intensity brightened my spirit causing me to think we would make it home. It was not to be, this storm was only taking a break like a mountain lion relaxing its muscles just before pouncing on an unwary deer. It was as if an "Old Man Winter" really existed and was blowing his lungs out directly at me. The driving snow became so heavy and intense I could barely see Spook four steps ahead. In a matter of three or so minutes the trail and my snowshoe tracks from this morning were obliterated. There was no going ahead or back. Traveling in the blinding snow would soon get us lost or injured from a fall. Once lost, we would have little knowledge of our whereabouts after the storm let up. I had to wait it out, however long it took, right where we were. An age-old conflict for humans is that nature's plans often are different than ours and we become losers.

At least two, maybe three, inches of snow fell around and on us in the next half hour. The squall had become a major storm showing no sign of letting up. Good fortune had left us near a large boulder and some hemlock trees. Unsheathing my belt axe, I quickly cut some hemlock boughs and four sapling poles. Brushing the snow away from the boulder, I leaned the poles against it to make a lean-to frame and layered on the hemlock boughs. Brushing the snow away again, some more boughs were placed on the ground until I had a good six inches of depth. If Spook and I had to spend the night in this makeshift lean-to, I had to stay as dry as possible and not let our escaping body heat melt the snow. Spook's hair and hide would let him get away with a night in the snow – I might not be so lucky. Trying to get a fire going under this hastily constructed shelter was out of the question – even if I got a fire started there was no way to find enough food to feed it.

Thinking about what else would keep me dry, I remembered the newspapers in my pack. As reluctant as I was to give up precious reading material, the newspapers could make an additional barrier between the frozen earth and us. Spreading the newspapers, and some more boughs, I climbed into the lean-to and pulled Spook in with me. Placing boughs against the open ends, Spook and I were at last away from the pelting snow. We wanted to remain snug in our storm shelter, but not too snug! This meant getting air and a way to vent (get rid of stale air and moisture) as the snow buried us. I had saved one pole and used it to poke a hole in our hemlock bough ceiling. It was our chimney absent a fire to warm us.

The night in the quickly improvised shelter was far from "being as snug as a bug in a rug." I had worked up some sweat in the hasty process of building the shelter causing me to experience some chills as my inner clothing dried. Fortunately, I had Spook's body to help warm first my hands, then my feet, and the rest of me as we curled closed together. There was no sleeping for me as the hours dragged by. My mind would not relax to the point of dosing off.

The closeness and silence in our little tomb got me thinking about George Murphy lying in his grave. No dog there to warm his bones. Would Spook and I join him this long winter's night? If we died, when would someone find us and make a proper burial? Perhaps my fate was to have wild animals clean my bones and spread them around the forest. Was a death of this sort my punishment for having taken another man's life? Should I peacefully accept whatever came tonight? I wrestled with the thought for a short while and then shouted, "The hell with that!" My angry outburst made Spook jump up and begin barking. I laughed thinking we both disagreed with the notion of just giving up easily.

As the snow buried us deeper and deeper the silence grew to the point where no wind noise was audible. Nothing but Spook's breathing, and bad breath, provided evidence of our continued existence. I began to count out loud to five hundred and then thrust the vent pole upwards to keep our chimney clear. It would not be good if the pole froze in place.

Between thrusts, I returned to thoughts and memories about my life before coming to these mountains.

It struck me that somehow I was different from most folks. From boyhood I had been rebellious, never content with things staying the same, always wanting to be somewhere else, seeing things differently from my family and school chums. My frustrations got me into trouble with my dad and fights with neighborhood boys. Sometimes I got thrashed but usually gave more than I received. But either way, I always felt bad after the fights. In the end, fighting solves nothing. If you win, the other guy is always going to hold it against you and will most likely seek revenge – sooner or later! So you can't rest easy or turn your back. If you lose, then you are left to play the other role. It is probably best to observe and fight like bears. When bears do brawl, the fight is mostly bluff and snarl, knowing if they get wounded making a living will become increasingly difficult.

Like other young people, I wanted things that only money could buy. Most of them drifted into monotonous jobs to get some basic things (a mate, house, kids) and a little extra from time to time. I wasn't willing to pay the price, however, and left Benedicta. I had read a story once about a hungry wolf that came upon a dog traveling with settlers headed west in search of new farmland. The dog was well fed and invited the wolf to sneak in and see if he might like living with the people also – the people wouldn't notice since the wolf closely resembled the dog. After a good meal from dinner leftovers, the dog and wolf lay under a wagon watching the humans seated around a campfire. The wolf noticed a leather collar around the dog's neck and inquired as to what it was. The dog replied, "The collar lets the people tie me up so I don't wander off and neglect my duties." The wolf asked what these duties might be. "Well," replied the dog. "If I am tied up, I can warn the people when danger is near or be here if they want to play with me." The wolf observed that the dog must then spend a great deal of time tied up. "Yes, but it is the price for always being well fed," answered the dog. Thinking this over briefly, the wolf thanked the dog for her hospitality and loped over the nearest hill.

My thoughts were interrupted by Spook's snoring. Evidently he wasn't too concerned about his life with me – I seldom kept him tied. Once again, I cleared the vent and received a dusting of snow and view of a still very dark night. Settling back beside Spook, I began counting to five hundred again, and despite my unwillingness to sleep began to nod, abruptly wake up, nod again and wake up. Although determined not to sleep, sometime later I awoke to my own loud snort. I guessed considerable time had passed and once again pushed and wiggled the vent pole upwards. Snow, and then, a beam of daylight invaded our shelter. Aside from some pretty cold feet, I had come through the night in good shape. Kicking away one side of the lean-to, I crawled out to be greeted by bright sunshine and two feet or more of newly fallen snow. Despite large snowdrifts everywhere and bent trees, bearing heavy snow loads, I recognized where on the trail we had arrived before the storm. Our shelter had worked! Luckily I had cut poles of substantial enough size to bear the snow load. Spook liked his den so much that he reluctantly stood, stretched, and finally came out to my beckoning.

It took a good bit of time and effort to snowshoe back to Brownsville in the soft, newly fallen snow. Spook, although well rested, was content to follow in my tracks as I broke trail. He too, was learning that life is like a dance – sometimes you lead and sometimes you follow.

Reaching the last knoll just above my cabin, I rejoiced in having safely gotten home. After building a fire and tending the cow and ox, I made some food for Spook and me. Relaxed and warmed beside the roaring stove, grateful for its heat and a good supply of food, I took momentary pride in my decision to build a shelter instead of plunging forward into the storm. More, and better, thinking chased that prideful notion from my mind. There was still a great deal to learn if I wanted to live in harmony with the quickly changeable elements that rule in these mountains – or anywhere for that matter. Few of us are prepared to weather the sudden storms of life whether they come from natural disasters or unpredictable humans.

6

MOUNTAIN LIFE

"He lo de camp, dis be Louie de man!" There was no mistaking that voice and use of the English language – there was only one French Louie. "Fox-eye, ah ben tinking mybe yo lik know tings 1 lern bout living in dese woods." Funny how good luck can follow bad turns in life. I lost Clint recently and here was a local hero showing up to help me out. Or, had my friend, "Old Man" Courtney asked Louie to stop by?

There was a story going around that Louie mysteriously had gained possession of Courtney's best deer dog a few years back causing Courtney to go way out to West Canada Lake to fetch her. When Courtney asked about the dog, Louie professed to know nothing about its whereabouts. Unknown to Louie, Courtney and his dog had a signal where William would fire a rifle shot and she would bark in response. Courtney touched off his rifle and, sure enough, a bark immediately came from an island off shore from Louie's camp. Louie grinned and said, "must be doze darn Frenchman must ta stool err. I gal yo fin err."

I didn't care if Louie "found a dog" once in a while. There are always two sides to a story and here was Louie offering me his help. I learned later he was paying Courtney back for stealing his dog. They had known each other for a long time back when Courtney had a camp at Spruce Lake before Tim Crowley. It was my good fortune that Courtney had taken a liking to me and was having great fun telling his hotel guests about "Foxey Brown" the fearsome hermit of Fall Stream. Courtney even concocted a story about me shooting a hole in his hat when he ventured too close to my camp. His stories were good for business and also suited my needs in keeping people away.

It was clear that Louie was familiar with "Brown's Pond." There weren't many places teeming with trout that Louie didn't know about. First thing he shared was where to find trout in my pond during the heat of summer. "Fin de cool wader s de key," he said. He went on to tell me the way to find that out was by knowing where the springs under the pond lie – the trout will be attracted to that area and stay active enough to be hungry for a juicy worm. Now, not all ponds/lakes are spring fed so to start you've got to have such a place. I did, according to Louie and he proceeded to show me the spots. I would learn over the course of the next few summers that he was absolutely right. What he wouldn't tell me is how he figured this out. All he would say is, "Yo go be lik de feesh." I didn't blame him for not sharing his secret. After all, he didn't know me that well and Louie's knowledge gave him an advantage over other guides when it came to finding fish for city visitors in the summer.

I had always loved a mystery and Louie's words – got to be "lik de feesh" kept reeling through my head. I had spent more than a few boyhood summer days back in Benedicta wading in the streams. Your bare feet quickly sense cold water bubbling up from the streambed or shallow pond. So finding cool spots in them wasn't too difficult a task. But, how do you get to the bottom of a pond or lake that's thirty or more feet deep? Louie was no swimmer/diver, that's for sure, because he nearly drowned once when a preacher man told him everyone could naturally swim – like all the animals. Believing this Louie went off alone, jumped in twenty or so feet of water, and promptly sank despite flailing his arms. A coughing and hacking Louie had to claw his way up the side of a big rock to avoid a watery grave. So how was he being like "de feesh?"

I figured he had to be using a thermometer. But when I asked him about using one, he just laughed and said, "Me no nee dat ting." He never would reveal his secret. Perhaps living free in the mountains for so many years he just learned by trial and error where the best fishing spots were. Louie also had some pretty smelly concoctions he used for bait. Every critter he killed, including their brains and innards, had a use. Maybe, he had developed a secret bait trout couldn't resist.

Louie loved snakes and went out of his way to keep them around his garden. He would collect them from miles around always looking for big ones to carry home inside his shirt. At home he built shelters for the snakes and made sure they were somewhat well fed. Snakes kept insects, especially potato bugs, and mice numbers down in his garden. So, they were his pets as much as Spook was mine. Louie showed me how to make snake shelters using rocks and a hole in the ground. We found a couple of garter snakes in the vly and put them into their new homes. Then it was time for crickets. Louie caught several, placed them inside the shelter and closed off the entrance with a rock. The snake could now dine in privacy. And thanks to Louie, I got to dine on plenty of fresh, unblemished, potatoes and vegetables for many years.

I learned more from Louie during his brief visit that spring. And, at his invitation, my education continued later that summer at his camp. Louie's place on West Canada Lake was a good twenty miles or so in from Piseco Lake. It was an amazing place when one considered it had been constructed by Louie's efforts alone. His cabin was a two-story log building with a third floor/attic in the peak. It stood about one hundred feet from the lake and provided an inspiring view of the mountains. The building, especially the main level, enjoyed considerable natural lighting due to a dozen nicely spaced six and nine pane windows. The cabin doors were paneled as opposed to have been put together with rough sawn lumber or split logs. All floors and partitions were made of two inch thick hand split planks. Everything inside, including a wood cook stove, had been carried in on Louie's back or on his one-man sled. Louie did have some assistance with the cook stove getting a lumber camp some four miles away to bring it that far when they were hauling in supplies via horse and wagon. He hauled it the rest of the way when the snow crust made sledding easier.

Reminding me of how farms were built back in Benedicta, Louie had connected his woodshed and chicken house to the cabin to avoid shoveling after heavy snowfalls. It also eased the efforts of stoking his stove and allowed him to hear any critters trying to snatch a chicken or two. Louie pretty much lived in the back corner of the cabin's first floor. It was his kitchen and bedroom combined. His bed was positioned so he could tend the woodstove without getting out. On cold nights he would open the stove door and shove in some pre-arranged pieces without shedding his blankets. In similar fashion, he would cook his breakfast from the same position. The rest of the cabin was used for storage and Louie's hunting/fishing party guests – which sometimes numbered ten to twelve men and their guides.

Louie's chicken house was like a little fort. The house itself was made with eight to ten inch logs and included a small loft for hay storage. The chicken yard was cleverly created using upright poles stuck deeply in the ground and rising nearly twenty feet into the air. Split rails were interspersed horizontally to increase the structure's stability. Additional poles interspaced across the pen's top made it difficult, but not impossible, for any flying predator to gain access. Owls and hawks have their place in the natural way of things but not when they deprive a mountain man of eggs.

The chicken yard was fairly large, encompassing more than one hundred square feet. Louie had wanted it to be even larger. Knowing something about chickens from my parent's farm, I agreed with Louie that people and chickens are somewhat alike. If you keep too many chickens crowded together they almost certainly will begin picking at each other. And, one poor bird always ends up receiving punishment from all the others. This makes for bad plumage on chickens and trouble between people.

Successfully raising chickens deep in the Adirondack forest is not an easy task. In addition to predators, tending to their dietary needs and keeping them healthy is challenging. Louie had a special, pretty much homemade, recipe that helped his birds flourish to the point where he often had excess eggs to trade at local logging camps. His blend consisted of dried venison, pulverized bones, cornmeal, and potatoes. He often ate a similar hash seasoned up a little with onions and other spices.

Another feature of Louie's place that I admired and copied was his "ice hole." Keeping things cool during hot summers was a constant problem especially since I had a cow. I could turn extra milk into butter with my churn, but after that had no way to save it for trade in town or up at Tim Crowley's place. Louie had dug a deep square hole in the ground and lined the sides with poles and split balsam fir. He would fill the hole with soft late spring "sugar snow," stomp it down as hard as possible, and let it freeze. A cover for his ice hole consisted of some old planks and a thick layering of spruce boughs. Ice was never taken from the hole ensuring that things would stay cool even in August.

One thing about Louie that I couldn't copy was the way he ate venison. His method of cooking, using the term very loosely, was to put some bear lard in a frying pan or "stir," drop in the meat just enough to sear both sides and quickly eat it. Sometimes, he would skip the stir and just eat it raw with a little salt, blood running down his whiskers. You could say Louie wasn't squeamish as nosey visitors sometimes discovered to their surprise. One Sport noticed Louie dumping a pan into a small hole in the earth. Wondering what Louie was up to, the Sport waited until Louie went fishing and investigated the hole. Lifting the cover, he was greeted with an unbearable stench and a gooey mess of fish and animal body parts Louie was saving to fertilize his garden. Or, was it ingredients for his secret fish bait?

Another snoopy visitor snuck his way into Louie's locked cabin one day while Louie was off on a trip. Being hungry, the uninvited guest went to Louie's flour barrel in hopes of making up some pancakes. Removing the lid, he was greeted by a rather large snake eager to get out of that flour barrel. The snake hadn't gotten into the barrel by accident. Seems Louie had discovered snakes would eat any worms or critters contaminating the flour during his absence. Stories like this about Louie's resourcefulness made him the living legend that he was. And I, too, became a snake fan always keeping a pet and a few of its friends around.

Louie looked forward to having an occasional guest, but he "talked out" in a day or so, and would sometimes just leave visitors in his cabin and head for the company of forest and stream. He was a secretive person and wasn't one to gossip much about his business or that of other people. Louie, however, did let loose from time to time when visiting the outside world. Some of his drinking binges added to his fame. Like me, Louie once clobbered a guy during a bar room brawl – he used a shovel instead of a cue stick. Unlike George Murphy his opponent lived. Considering my situation with the law, our common experience created a bond making me comfortable Louie wouldn't be one to broadcast the location of my place to every Sport who came along.

Louie's secretiveness took many forms. He literally had dozens of boats hidden on the lakes and ponds of the West Canada Lakes region – all of them either hand built or hauled in on his back. The boats made access to the best fishing spots easier and increased the size of Louie's catches. Since he depended on trout for food, fertilizer, and income, Louie wasn't fond of other folks using his boats. It was rare when an outsider would stumble upon one of his clever hiding places.

The old Frenchman was also possessed with never having enough camps. Tim Crowley guessed Louie had as many as two-dozen different little hideaways in the mountains. Considering the amount of time he spent away from home during the winter this made a lot of sense. The main source of Louie's cash income came from trapping so he needed a long trap line and places to safely spend the night. He often sought out a large boulder and constructed a lean-to facing the side of the rock. Just enough space was left between the boulder and lean-to so Louie could squeeze through. A campfire built against the boulder's face enjoyed a natural draft and kept Louie snug and warm for the night on a thick mattress of fir boughs. Other camps were made under rock ledges, caves, and uprooted trees. In some ways, he was like the bears he trapped and occasionally hunted – totally free to range widely in pursuit of daily business and resting wherever the end of the day left him. Times were changing, however, and the complete freedom Louie had enjoyed for nearly twenty years was starting to get pinched.

Limitations on Louie's freedom began once the lumbering industry found its way into the inner reaches of the West Canada Lake country. While, for the most part, the lumber company bosses and workers admired Louie and helped him out, he now had to share his wilderness with them. Their clear cutting, creation of tree top jungles, and damming of rivers and streams changed the landscape causing Louie to adjust his trapping and hunting routines. Greater restriction and changes in Louie's, and all of our ways of life, also came from other outsiders who sought the same fish, wildlife, trees and plants that had supported Adirondack people for generations.

Trouble for year round Adirondack folks actually got started back in 1885. Before then, the State had not paid much attention to the money value of the Adirondack woods and let lumber companies cut trees for little, and sometimes, no fees. Slowly the State caught on and in 1885, after many years of establishing do nothing investigation committees, the legislature passed regulations that put all Adirondack State lands into what they called a Forest Preserve. They also created a Forest Commission to protect and supervise what went on in the state forests. Supposedly, those lands were to be kept wild forever and not be sold, leased, or taken by any company or person.

However, rich men like William Rockefeller and William West Durant had already created private estates in the Forest Preserves. Unwilling or unable to find money to enforce the law, the State turned around and allowed more individuals and organizations to buy preserve lands. Around 1890 a group called the Adirondack League Club bought 100,000 acres in Hamilton and surrounding counties. Soon a growing pattern set in where private owners controlled more and more of what had been merely wild land neglected by the State. In a way, I was like some of those private estate owners when I chased people away from Brownsville. The difference was I didn't control much land and the State still owned what I lived on.

I learned the situation with private parks was a hot topic in Piseco when I went for supplies one day in 1893. Floyd Abrams and William P. were at the post office talking about a story in an Albany newspaper that had just arrived. According to the story there were more than sixty private parks totaling some 940,000 acres compared to only 730,000 acres in the state owned forest preserve. They said this situation was going to make life difficult for local people because the best hunting and fishing lands were often in the private parks and the owners didn't welcome trespassers. Floyd predicted it was only going to be a matter of time until trouble broke out between local folks and the out of town private park owners. I couldn't say much considering my habit of chasing folks away from Brownsville. It seemed certain I would become even more unpopular.

Meanwhile other forces were shaping up that would also limit free use of the Adirondack woods. In 1890, a group of doctors in New York City formed an Adirondack Park Association and began lobbying the state to create a park for what they called the free use of all the people and as forest lands necessary to preserve the headwaters of the State's rivers and for future timber supply. The legislature obliged and in May of 1892 placed the Forest Preserve and all adjacent private lands within the boundaries of the new Adirondack Park. Altogether, the new park contained more than three million acres. And, the State continued to strengthen its grip on the mountains in 1894 when the Forest Preserve's forever wild classification got put into the state constitution.

These developments were the beginning of the end for "squatters" like Louie and me who had settled on, and freely used, state forest land. At the time, however, we thought the regulations were aimed at the lumber companies and large sport clubs trying to buy up state land. So we, and most local folks, went merrily on our way using the state forest to hunt, fish, trap, and cut firewood. And, to be truthful, some of us made a little income by turning a state tree or two into boards or shingles.

It wasn't long, however, before we began to realize the State was serious about its new laws. Forest, Fish and Game protectors began to visit even the remote places where Louie and I lived. In 1895, Louie and John Leaf got caught killing and selling venison to local hotels. Louie had to pay $35.00 and poor John a whopping $100.00. It was one of the first times a local jury convicted some of its own citizens. Despite the fines, the income was good enough so Louie and John continued poaching – and got caught again along with quite a few Piseco residents.

Recognizing that the State was going to increase regulating use of the Forest Preserve, people began to understand the need to live differently. They could no longer get along with a little farming and lots of hunting and fishing. Gradually more and more residents were forced to become laborers and wage earners. Many men tried laboring jobs but preferred being in the woods and along the streams serving as guides for increasing numbers of hunters and fisherman visiting the Adirondacks. Besides being more soothing to their spirits, guiding also paid better. The number of guides grew rapidly and in 1891 an Adirondack Guides Association was formed to protect the interests of those practicing the trade. But not everyone could become a guide – especially not a fugitive from the law like me.

By 1898, Adirondack people were being squeezed harder and harder between the private park owners and the State of New York. Many of the private parks were heavily fenced in and patrolled by armed guards to keep poachers out. Meanwhile, the state continued to hire more game protectors and forest rangers to arrest unauthorized users of forest preserve land. These trends left local people with fewer places to hunt, fish, and cut trees. Those who didn't own woodlots were often left without places to harvest firewood. Shortages of firewood and high prices soon occurred threatening to lead to violence.

The firewood situation got so bad in Piseco that William Dunham wrote to the state requesting an exemption from the firewood restrictions. In a well-written letter, Dunham said, "As a good many of the people here have no woodland of their own and cannot buy any of their neighbors, it becomes quite necessary for them to cut what wood they want to burn – which does not exceed twenty-five cords for each family for a whole year – on the State [lands]." His letter didn't sway the State and they stuck to their ruling that any taking of wood from State lands amounted to thievery. Treated as thieves, local folks found ways including night time logging and tracking the whereabouts of forest rangers so people could collect firewood and not get caught.

Thanks to some good growing seasons, things I had learned from Louie, and hard work my little farm improved a great deal during the next two years. I wasn't guiding or selling Forest Preserve logs and no one knew if I took an extra deer for food. And in a way, Foxey Brown, the wild man of Fall Stream, was a game protector much to the dislike of those who got shot at when trying to hunt or fish around my place.

I built a chicken house and pen just like Louie's. I bought six chickens and a rooster in Piseco and hauled them into Brownsville. Soon our new feathered companions were laying eggs and, if I slept a little past daylight, there was a rooster-powered alarm clock to roust me out of bed. All was good until an unwelcome visitor showed up one night. Now, the arrival of a fox, bobcat or other predator would set Spook to barking in a hurry and quickly get my attention. But this hungry guest didn't walk in and announce itself to Spook or me.

As was our usual chore we fed the chickens just after daylight. Arriving at their coop, we opened the door to find two dead chickens on the floor. One had been almost totally eaten and the other had merely been decapitated – head nowhere to be seen. Looking up at the roost we saw the rest of the chickens sound asleep. Sharing their slumber, like some sort of houseguest, was a large great-horned owl!

Now, normally a bird of prey will kill and haul (fly) its victim away to be eaten at its nest. But, if the meal is too big to carry, they will eat their fill and then fly away. Usually an owl can carry a chicken away, but I guessed it had trouble getting itself and the chicken out of my coop as I had constructed a pretty good enclosure like Louie's. Putting speculation aside, I now had to deal with a dozing great horned owl before it woke up.

The easy thing would have been to kill it. Never having been this close to a living owl, I decided to learn more about them and grabbed a stick. Remembering the last time I used a stick to handle trouble and saw George Murphy's body on the floor, I gently tapped the owl behind the head. Stunned, it toppled to the floor where I quickly pulled its legs together and threw my jacket over its head. Scooping it up in a bundle, I headed for the barn where I kept a cage used to isolate chickens. Putting the owl inside, Spook and I stepped back to see what would happen.

After a minute or two the owl fluttered and stood up blinking and adjusting its large orange eyes in the poorly lighted barn. Noticing my presence, it jumped on the cage perch and sat there motionlessly staring at me. It seemed alert and to be functioning normally as it tracked my movements turning only its head from side to side.

Observing the bird more closely, its eyes were of particular interest – very large for the size of its head and mounted in front, above its beak. I knew then why experts claimed an owl could see (and hear) a mouse more than one hundred yards away on the darkest of nights. When the bird stretched its broad wings, I understood how it flew/glided so silently through the air. I had been startled many times along Fall Stream or in the woods when one, out of nowhere, flew past me.

Working nicely with the owl's eyes and broad wings were a set of sharp talons and a hooked beak that could quickly cut muscle, tendons and bone. I sure didn't want to experience those tools in operation and suspected the owl had some other attributes and skills to help keep itself fed. On several occasions in the past, I had seen an owl take a skunk. How was it that no other animal seemed to put skunks on their dinner list? Could it be that owls have a lousy sense of smell? Thank goodness for the creator's wisdom in making owls. Too many skunks meant nothing but trouble for dog owners. To my good fortune it had taken only one time for Spook to learn the skunk lesson. But even that was once too much because nothing but time really reduces the stench of skunk spray.

I was curious if the owl could stand being held in captivity. I could provide water, but what would it eat? Certainly, I would not feed it chicken!

Later that day, Spook killed a woodchuck that had gotten too close to the garden and too far from its hole. As was his habit to share prizes, Spook brought the dead woodchuck up to the cabin door. I had eaten woodchuck before and found it quite tasty especially if it had been a young chuck. If you think about it, woodchucks eat mainly tender grass shoots like a deer during the summer – so there's nothing wrong with woodchuck stew. I did, however, prefer freshly killing my own woodchucks.

It struck me the owl might eat the woodchuck. Thinking, they can't be that much different from a mouse, and I'd bet, if woodchucks were out at night, a hungry owl wouldn't hesitate making a meal out of one.

My prisoner didn't move as I placed the woodchuck on the cage floor. I waited a good twenty minutes or so to see what would happen with my experiment and got nothing for my time. Checking every half hour or so throughout the remainder of the day, nothing changed – owl on perch, dead woodchuck on floor. I went to bed thinking owls don't accept handouts.

Going to the barn for morning chores gave me quite a surprise. The owl was still on its perch, but the woodchuck was missing. That is, the woodchuck as I had left it. In one corner of the cage lay the woodchuck's head, hide and entrails. In the opposite corner, stacked neatly as stew meat in a butcher shop showcase, were twelve or so bite size chunks of woodchuck meat. Motionless still, the owl blinked its eyes as if to say, "What do you think about that?" I did think about it and decided owls are pretty adaptable critters. I also decided my chicken house should be owl proofed a bit better and there was no point in killing or holding this remarkable creature captive. Perhaps, I was subconsciously giving this winged culprit a second chance because living at Fall Stream was doing that for me. Whatever my motivations, the chicken house got renovated and the chicken thief went free. Thereafter, I always wondered when a great horned owl let loose with a "hoo, hoohoo, hoo, hoo" if it was my former guest.

Carlton Banker, front row in light-colored suit, with F. J. & G. Railroad staff. (Used with permission of Fulton-Montgomery Community College Evans Library)

Carlton and Ada Banker home in Gloversville, NY, circa 1910. (T. Samuel Hoye)

Foxey Brown/David Brennan homestead on Fall Stream.
(Gloversville Morning Herald, November 17, 1916)

7

CARLTON BANKER

Falling into the routines of hunting, fishing and working my homestead made the seasons, except for winter, come and go quickly and a new century greeted me on January 1, 1900. I didn't feel any different but somehow I had now spent nearly ten years hiding out on Fall Stream. My reputation of being a wild and eccentric mountain man was working to keep away unwanted visitors and I was getting along better than most local folks who had to pay taxes and suffer through tough economic times.

It struck me one day that these mountains have always had three types of human visitors – those who come to live and take what they need to survive; those who come to rape, get rich and leave; and those who come to hunt, fish, and fill their spirits with mountain wildness. Those in the first and third group will most likely work to protect the mountains. The second type, having no spirit, has to be restrained. I classify all as visitors because even those who stay are only visitors in the grand scheme of things.

Circumstances initially forced me to become one of those who came to stay. But after a while, however, I remained by choice believing life here far richer than what most people experience. Although lonely at times, I was immensely freer than most men. Free to experience life guided only by the rhythms of nature and what I wanted to do each day. I say free, but there is a price for everything in this world. Nature, for example, has no mercy on those unprepared for her changing moods. Many have paid a deadly price for not having an adequately stocked pantry and woodpile come winter.

Having paid nature's basic rate, I was free to come and go as I pleased. How many other men can decide to go fishing, hunting, berry picking, swimming or whatever pretty much whenever they desire? I reported to no foreman, manager, or town board as I was the mayor of Brownsville and manager of all land my axe and plow could tame. As for need of conversation, there was Spook, the animals and occasional visitors or a trip to town for supplies. Those trips sometimes got me into trouble when I forgot my basic beliefs and drank too much. What is it about alcohol that leads many a good man into foolish conversation and onto paths of madness? Why is it memory of a terrible hangover headache, and a vow never to bring another one on, is so short?

I had no use for those who come to rape, get rich, and run. Those who lived here and sought nothing but fortune were not much better. Those who particularly bothered me were the ones who overharvested things of the forest, lakes, and streams. No longer did loggers mainly cut to supply local building needs. Each year increasing millions of board feet of logs were floated down streams like the West Canada to feed hungry mills downstate and beyond. Deer got shot by the hundreds and small trout were gathered by the wagonload to feed fancy resort restaurants. I suspected local folks who supported such activities might one day find nature's cupboard bare and pay her price. Common sense and only a small reverence for things we didn't create dictate better behavior. Painful as new state regulations were, I knew in the long run they would protect the forest. But it was certain local people wouldn't support regulations that denied them reasonable access to food, shelter, and warmth.

Adding to these problems was a new breed of people coming to the mountains. Improved transportation was bringing not only the "Sports" who came to hunt and fish, but summer-long residents who lined the shores of lakes and ponds with their cottages or demanded more hotels to accommodate them – men, women, children and their pets! Piseco Lake hotels, for example, were usually booked months ahead of the summer season. Many of these seasonal guests thought they wanted some mountain wildness but only if it included all the comforts enjoyed back home.

The Sports were an interesting sort. Mostly they were men who came up our way seeking connection with the woods through hunting and fishing. Somehow it was important for them to hunt, shoot, and cart a deer back to the city. Maybe it had something to do with re-establishing a sense of manhood, showing the neighbors that city men were capable of living off the land even though more and more necessities of life got purchased at nearby stores. Maybe it was a reaction to working indoors most of the time back in the city or doing jobs that provided little satisfaction other than a paycheck.

I thought others came to the mountains because of the stress that work, family and community life lay on them. Most of the Sports had pretty good incomes. Some were good men and some were spoiled and lazy just looking for diversion and a good time away from home. The last type seemed fascinated by their guns and equipment but spent most of their mountain time indoors playing poker and drinking. I never had much use for most of them and often refused offers to serve as a guide. One Sport came along, however, and changed my life.

I first met Carlton Banker in 1902, up at Tim Crowley's camp when I was delivering some spruce gum. Carlton and one of his relatives, Ira Wooster, had been hunting out of Tim's place without a guide and were having no luck. Most of the local men knew I had deer around my farm and pond, but my "fearsome" reputation kept hunters away. And most of the local guides respected my right not to have every Tom, Dick and Harry trespassing where I was trying to make a living. Anyway, Tim mentioned that Banker was a good guy who loved deer hunting. "Don't get me wrong," Tim said. "Banker isn't one of these shoot everything in sight guys. He really likes being in the mountains – been coming here since he was a young man back in 1893. He's happy, just seeing wildlife, even if he doesn't shoot a deer. I was just thinking you might like to consider another source of income now that the market for hides, shingles, and even spruce gum is down. And, to top it off, Banker is a railroad man back in Gloversville. I thought your railroad background might also let you guys hit it off." Tim had a good point. My money stash was getting low and winter meant having to buy some supplies. So, I agreed to talk with Banker and hung around until he and his friend came out of the woods.

The first thing most people would notice about Carlton Banker, especially without his fedora hat, was a lack of height. He stood maybe five foot four and had noticeably small feet. Short men sometimes make up for lack of size with very boisterous speech and aggressive behavior. This wasn't the case with Carlton. He spoke in a steady and thoughtful manner that somewhat hid, at least to start, even his passion for hunting. After introductions, Banker began by telling me about the fine buck he got up here in 1900, but this year the most they had seen were deer out of shooting range. And none of those had antlers. I told him I was pretty sure hunting with me on my little preserve at Fall Stream could produce better results, but there were no guarantees. With that, we settled into discussing my ways of operation – which I was mostly making up as we spoke.

I made it clear that camp outs away from my cabin wouldn't be possible due to having animals to feed. I also wouldn't be able to provide fancy foods and cooking like they might get back home. Lots of simple fare such as meat, potatoes, beans, and biscuits would be the best I could do. And, they would have to sleep in my cabin and put up with my snoring and Spook's bad breath. If they shot deer, I would transport them back to Piseco on my wagon. This seemed acceptable, as did my fee of $4.00 per day plus expenses. The plan was for them to show up at my place the next day with their gear.

Carlton and Ira arrived in the morning as agreed and after stowing Carlton and Ira's gear, we hunted the backside of Willis Mountain where it bordered my pond. The deer liked to bed down there during the day and Carlton and Ira's hike in that morning might have pushed deer between my place and the Spruce Lake trail toward Willis Mountain. I put my two guests on watch near a deer trail and headed straight up the mountain at a steady pace so as not to cause any nearby deer to feel they were being stalked. Once up the mountain a quarter mile or so I began a slow circle back down hoping to keep any deer between my watchers and me. This time I made more noise but varied my pace as if I might be stalking game. Sure enough after a few minutes there was one shot, a pause and then three more shots in rapid succession. I held my position for a half hour or so in case something came back towards me and then made my way down to Carlton and Ira. From a good distance I could see Carlton stooped over something and Ira holding two rifles. Carlton had shot a nice twelve-point buck and was busy dressing out the animal. Lifting the deer, we guessed it had weighed close to 200 pounds. He had shot the deer once in the chest sending his 30/30 bullet through the outer edge of its heart. Carlton accomplished this at a distance of eighty yards or so – a good shot for most any rifleman. Ira had fired at another smaller buck as it ran away. A search of the area where the fleeing deer disappeared turned up no sign of blood or hair.

That night we enjoyed a hearty supper of venison I had already hanging, along with potatoes, carrots, biscuits, coffee and some rice pudding. It was a cold night and the warmth of my wood stove, a good meal, and the success of the day gave us a sense of being secure. Talk flowed freely. I learned Carlton was an official with the Fonda, Johnstown, and Gloversville (F.J. & G.) Railroad – the same one I had taken to Northville nearly thirteen years ago when fleeing from Boston. The railroad was planning to open an electric division in a year or so and Carlton would become the superintendent of it. Electric railroad cars were a whole new concept for an old steamer locomotive fellow like me and I listened intently as Carlton explained how the electric trolley worked. As he talked, the subject changed to electric lights for homes, street lights, refrigeration and other new inventions including a solar motor that could power a steam engine. It seemed some fellow named Aubrey Eneas back in Boston had already got one working out in Arizona to help irrigate crops.

All these inventions sounded like they could make life easier for people, but caused me to wonder how folks would pay for so many things bought from the store. More and more families were even buying meat instead of raising their own chickens, pigs, and cows. I thought soon they'll be buying vegetables from the store too. And, if folks stay up later at night with their electric lights and telephones, how will they get enough sleep to work the next day? Seemed like people would just be going faster and faster.

Carlton lived in Gloversville with his wife (Ada) and two young daughters (Helen and Marian). Ira Wooster was Ada's (Wooster Banker) brother and a frequent companion of Carlton's. They had discovered Piseco Lake in 1900 staying at Leamon Foote's hotel in Rudeston and then at Floyd Abrams Sportsman's Home near the trail to Spruce Lake. The Bankers fell in love with the area. So much so, that Carlton's wife told the children "if they ever got to Heaven, which she sometimes doubted, they wouldn't like it as well as Piseco." Hearing this, reminded me that it is easy to live someplace, work hard every day and go blind to its beauty.

The subject of our conversation turned to hunting and the decline in the population of deer and bear. Knowing I had lived at Fall Stream since 1890, my guests asked to hear my thoughts about the situation. I had to confess that like others who lived in the mountains, it once seemed the numbers of deer and bear were limitless and I took a deer anytime need for meat arose. It had been nothing for someone to kill a dozen or more deer per year. Until recently, use of dogs (hounding) was common as was floating up on deer in a boat or getting them in the winter when they yarded up together. In the old days, we didn't think too much about a hunter like Johnny Leaf killing so many deer each year. But that was before the fancy restaurants down state started featuring venison on their menus. And, of course, more Sport hunters meant that some would be game hogs and take way more deer than a man could eat.

So by 1892 we were down to a legal limit of two deer per hunter for the season and people like Johnny and French Louie were getting arrested more often. It was still difficult, however, to get a local jury to convict someone they knew needed meat to feed a family. Various tricks were also used to get around game protectors trying to catch hunters in the first place. One ruse was to ring the school bell when a protector stopped at a hotel for supper and to spend the night. Anyone out in the woods knew then that it was an "all is clear" signal to commence hunting.

Bear, like beaver in the old days, were once so plentiful (and pesky) that a ten-dollar bounty was paid for killing one in 1892. This changed within a year, however, as hundreds of bear got killed. Ten dollars, in the eyes of local people, bought a lot of bullets and a pretty darn good rifle. Carlton said some experts worried the bear may go the way of beaver and moose that no longer existed in New York State. A magazine he read called *Woods and Waters* had even begun a campaign to save New York black bear. And there were other efforts to reestablish beaver, moose, and elk in the mountains. All these animal populations had declined in a period of approximately twenty years.

Missing also from the Adirondacks was the howl of wolves on a cold, full moon night. When I came to these mountains wolves were still around and could be heard regularly or even trapped occasionally. But supposedly, around 1893, a hunter near Brandreth Lake shot and killed the last Adirondack wolf. They say the man had the wolf stuffed and it now sits in a museum someplace. Common wisdom in the mountains had been that fewer wolves meant more deer, but some of us sensed the wolf's demise had interrupted the natural flow of things – perhaps greater than just their voice being lost from the evening chorus. But missing the wolf and its howl, there was no one to carry the forest melody at night. Coyotes lived too far to the west. Only the solitary yip of a fox or hoots and screeches of owls remained to break the silence of a winter night.

The mention of winter brought questions from my guests about how I survived the cold and heavy snowfalls – especially like the blizzard of 1900 when more than five feet of snow fell on February 28th. I pointed to the wood stove saying it takes care of the cold if well fed. As for the snow, I had nowhere to go. So, there was no problem. I tried to prepare for each season just like my animal neighbors – store food and figure out how to stay warm.

As talk continued, it became clear Carlton was pretty convinced we had to save wild places and things. He had read a book written by some Marsh fellow called *Man and Nature*. Written back in the 1860's, the book made a strong case that humans had to protect forests because they stabilize the soil and slow down the bad effects of flooding. Forests even influence the weather and help avoid droughts and prevent the land from turning into deserts like it had over in the Mediterranean. So, while he had concerns, Carlton also thought the Adirondack Preserve and Adirondack Park laws were probably good things.

In 1902, there was still considerable confusion about the Adirondack Preserve and Adirondack Park. Some local people didn't understand that the Preserve consisted of state owned lands within the Adirondack Park. And the Park, itself, was much bigger holding both state and private land. Either way they were suffering as the State played with such designations. In my case it didn't matter either. Brownsville was inside both the preserve and the park. And, "Forever Wild" meant no camps, farms, businesses, or signs of permanent human habitation should exist in the Preserve unless it was a State operation of some sort. Places like Tim Crowley's hunting camp at Spruce Lake and the Abrams Camp below me on Fall Stream were all living on borrowed time. Likewise, my farm at Brownsville would also be on the chopping block one day.

Carlton and Ira agreed that was a legitimate concern, but believed since I was a homesteader/farmer a "grandfather clause" would be part of any final legislation. The State would have to do something to protect long-time permanent residents. Hearing that was somewhat reassuring but, with my luck most anything could happen.

Carlton had great faith that our new president, Theodore Roosevelt, being a champion of the common man would work all this out. That,

along with Roosevelt's deep interest in all things outdoors, would lead to
laws good for wildlife and people. Just the mention of Roosevelt's name
uncorked Carlton's great enthusiasm for the man who now led our nation.
He proceeded to tell the story of how close I lived to the beginning of a
new chapter in American history. Although I had read about McKinley's
assassination in 1901 and Roosevelt's journey out of our mountains to
accept his new office, I let Carlton tell the story about the special night of
September 12, 1901.

Convinced a rapidly recovering McKinley would recover from his
wounds, Roosevelt followed advice from other Cabinet officers and joined
his family on September 11th for a planned Adirondack vacation at the
Tahawus Club near Mt. Marcy. The goal for September 12th was to hike
to some cabins located at the foot of Mount Colden, spend the night, and
ascend Mt. Marcy the next day.

The morning of the 13th brought a steady rain, but characteristically,
Roosevelt insisted the party push ahead despite steep and rain-slicked
trails. Thick cloud cover limiting vision to only ten feet or so complicated matters. Determined, Roosevelt and friends trudged on and reached
the Mt. Marcy summit around noon. As if announcing Roosevelt's presence on New York's tallest mountain, the clouds briefly cleared out providing the visitors with a spectacular sun-filled, blue-sky view. When
cloud cover returned the party descended to Lake Tear of the Clouds to
eat lunch. There, the guide Harrison Hall caught up with Roosevelt's
party and handed Theodore a telegraph indicating McKinley was close
to death. Marching non-stop Roosevelt led the group some twelve miles
back to the Tahawus Club. Intending to spend the night, a second telegraph convinced Roosevelt to leave at once. And, so at 10:30 p.m. he
climbed aboard a one-seat wagon driven by David Hunter and raced
off into the fog – the only light being a lantern tied to the end of the
wagon. Much like my trip from Northville years ago, these evening travelers experienced the joys of uneven corduroy roads and mud holes large
enough to swallow wagons. Reaching the outskirts of Tahawus property
near Minerva, Roosevelt transferred to a two-seater buckboard pulled by
a fresh team of horses. Carrying just a small bag, Roosevelt got in the
back and covered up with a raincoat to ward off water from the splashing
wheels. With a snap of the reins, the new driver, Orrin Kellogg, headed

them back into the night towards a third relay waiting at Aiden Lair Lodge.

Although he didn't know it, somewhere between Minerva and Aiden Lair Lodge, Theodore Roosevelt had become the 26th president of the United States. William McKinley had died that evening in Buffalo.

Arriving at Aiden Lair Lodge around 3 a.m., Roosevelt was met by innkeeper and new driver Mike Cronin. Cronin had been asked by authorities not to tell Roosevelt about McKinley's death. He would be informed by an official telegraph waiting at North Creek. Cronin and hotel visitors, sneaking a look at Roosevelt, honored that request.

The final sixteen miles to North Creek was a hair-raising ride. Holding a lantern for Cronin, Roosevelt was off to meet his destiny on a misty and very dark early morning. Never one to flinch in the face of danger, Roosevelt urged Cronin to go faster despite slippery hills and narrow passages where one misstep by the horses could send them to a sure death over steep embankments. Cronin suggested it might be best if they slowed down but Roosevelt coaxed him to go faster saying, "If you are not afraid, I am not. Push ahead!"

Their hazardous ride took one hour and forty-one minutes – supposedly the quickest trip ever between Aiden Lair and the North Creek train station. Arriving at the day's first light, Roosevelt leaped off the wagon and was handed a telegram indicating McKinley had died. Reading it without comment, he bounded up the train platform stairs, two at a time, rushed past a waiting crowd and stopped before a special train waiting to transport him to Buffalo for a private inauguration ceremony. Waving to the crowd, he boarded the train and was off via Saratoga and Albany to meet his destiny as the 26th president of the United States of America.

Focusing on Roosevelt's ride, I thought this world has many realities. There I was sound asleep on the night of September 13, 1901, my world consisting of living off the land at Fall Stream; Carlton had his railroad and was tucked in bed with family at Gloversville; and another man, a mere twenty-five miles from me, rushed by on his way to becoming president of the United States. Only three men and three very separate realities, yet somehow our lives, and the separate lives of so many others, make a whole – at least for a time on this planet.

Listening to Carlton recount Roosevelt's Adirondack Mountain adventure was fascinating. Not so much because of what happened to Roosevelt, but due to Carlton's enthusiasm and genuine affection for his hero. I had almost applauded when Carlton had recited Roosevelt's words to Cronin about not being afraid and to "Push ahead!" For a moment it was like being in a theater back in Boston and hearing a professional actor do his lines.

I too, admired our new president. What wasn't there to like? Roosevelt was a national figure who espoused the outdoor life and needs of the workingman. He understood the importance of protecting wild things and places so future generations of hunters and fishermen could have the same opportunities that had shaped his life. This was all good from my perspective as a hunting and fishing guide.

But, I think it was Roosevelt's energy that made him so attractive to Carlton and others who had sedentary jobs in the so-called civilized world. As if reading my thoughts, Carlton began to speak again saying, "Yes sir, I think Roosevelt gets reinvigorated by frequently connecting with nature. Reading about his younger life it's easy to see how strenuous outdoor work strengthened the frail body he was born with. But now, I believe hiking, hunting and fishing clear his mind and provide time in wild places that help him identify purpose for his life. I think that is what he meant in one of his speeches –'I *wish to preach, not the doctrine of ignoble ease, but the doctrine of the strenuous life.'*"

Carlton was on a roll about his hero. "Yes sir, Mr. Roosevelt practices what he preaches. Did you hear about the Frenchman who came to visit him recently? T.R. invited the man to join him in a little exercise. They began with two sets of tennis and then went jogging. A workout with a medicine ball followed the run. Sensing his companion's enthusiasm was dwindling, Roosevelt asked, 'What would you like to do now?' The exhausted Frenchman replied, 'If it is all the same to you – just lie down and die!'" Carlton, so humored by his story, barely got the last line out before giggling like a schoolgirl causing Ira and me to laugh even louder. With a sly grin, Ira remarked, "And Carlton, that's how you make me feel sometimes – like just laying down and dying." Evidently, Carlton's energy level was a bit larger than Ira's.

Unlike Carlton, I had never seen Theodore Roosevelt in person. From what I had read and seen in pictures, however, I sensed they both possessed high energy levels that constantly sought outlets. I couldn't be sure about Carlton's prospects for applying that energy, but it appeared Roosevelt was on a path to do very special things. All men leave earth having cast a shadow, some leave a footprint; very few create permanent reminders of having been here. I suspected Theodore Roosevelt was one of those very few. I didn't share those thoughts with Carlton and Ira thinking it best to wait a bit and see how our new president fared.

Being a railroad man Carlton checked his watch frequently. Doing so, he exclaimed, "My goodness, it is half past eleven already! Dave, it's probably way past your normal bedtime." He was correct; it was way past my eight o'clock and "hit the hay" routine. Carlton had given me a cue, but instead of jumping on the opportunity, I said something about the beautiful gold watch he sported. Mentioning the word "gold" extended my bedtime another hour.

Other than his comment about Carlton's energy level, Ira hadn't been very active in the conversation up to now. But, despite the late hour, the opportunity to talk about gold prodded his mind and mouth. Chuckling, he said, "Dave, you know there are all sorts of stories being told about you back in Piseco. One of them is that you have a secret source of gold back here in the mountains." This caught me way off guard since I had not heard that tale before. Not sure how to react, I just shook my head sideways and laughed. "Yep, and when I get short on gold, I just go on over to my secret diamond mine." Well, Carlton began to howl, rocking back and forth with glee. Enthusiastic in everything he did, Carlton's hysterics got Ira and me going. Soon the whole cabin shook from our merriment. Not to be left out, Spook, at first startled, began to howl. And, to our amazement, a dog way off on a distant mountain returned Spook's overtures. We were providing late night entertainment for the whole of Brownsville and beyond!

When calm returned to the cabin, Carlton said, "Seriously Dave, the story is that you and Tim Crowley found the remains of the old Belden brothers mine up at Spruce Lake and made a new strike. That's how Tim affords a large place and keeps his family in such fine fashion. People also say that explains how you get along nicely here at Fall Stream with only a cow, an ox, trapping a little, and making shingles from time to time as revenue. Talk is that Tim's spruce gum business is just a ruse to get the gold out." This was news to me. I hesitated and started to respond about the ridiculousness of such stories but Carlton cut me off. "Don't worry Dave, Ira and I know that story is pure fantasy, the same pie in the sky thinking that has gone on for years. We did some research on gold in the Adirondacks including the Belden story. It's true the Belden brothers came to Spruce Lake around 1824 in search of gold. They sank a mineshaft about fifty feet into the side of a mountain. Supposedly they secretly worked the mine for years and took out the minerals in sealed barrels and boxes in the middle of the night all the way to the nearest railway station in Amsterdam. After a while one of the brothers got sick and moved back to Connecticut. The remaining brother worked for another year or so and then moved out also. It is said that he convinced his neighbors one early spring to help him move out quite a few head of cattle. There was still a good amount of snow on the ground, and despite some hard shoveling, most of the cattle died before reaching Piseco. So Belden left Piseco without much to show for his efforts and never returned."

"Yes," I interrupted. "And today the old mine shaft is filled with water and brush. Large birch trees thicker than a man's body also cover the mining site. Where in the heck is there any evidence of Tim and me mining gold?" "Exactly," said Carlton as he continued.

"Here's another reason why we believe there is no quantity of gold in these mountains. Back in 1874, the Fulton County Marble Company organized in Lake Pleasant to mine silver, iron, marble and any other minerals found while digging. There was a good deal of excitement and our F.J. & G. Railroad was approached about building a branch from Northville to Lake Pleasant to haul the materials. Since that involved a large investment the F.J. & G. decided to seriously study what quantities of precious materials could be won from the earth. This took some time, and as luck would have it, the marble turned out to be too soft for commercial use and the small amounts of iron and silver petered out. That has been the pattern every time someone finds a little speck of silver or gold dust."

It was evident Carlton knew what he was talking about but that didn't eliminate my problem. I surely didn't need stories about gold prompting more people to come prospecting here in Brownsville. If someone found even a trace here there would be a rush and my hideout would be announced to the world. Besides, the lure of gold makes people do crazy things and take unnecessary chances. My own brothers, Hugh and Martin, had caught "gold fever" back in the late 1880's and went off to

Colorado seeking their fortunes. What they got was a permanent burial spot when the rickety mine they were working collapsed.

After offering condolences about my brothers, Carlton and Ira's advice about the rumors of me finding gold was not to worry. They suggested rumors like these get started from time to time and soon subside. They both knew William P. Courtney, the Abrams family, and other innkeepers whose best interests were to keep the hunters and fishermen coming not prospectors. Carlton and Ira promised to have a chat with them about squelching gold rumors and point out the real treasures in these mountains lie in their solitude and wildlife. Their words were comforting but I now knew that I had real enemies in Piseco who, for whatever reasons, wished me no peace.

We had now talked ourselves into a new day – Carlton's watch vouched that it was past midnight. As evidenced by their snoring, sleep came quickly for Carlton and Ira. Somewhat over tired, my mind kept rambling from one thought to another. To my frustration, I repeatedly focused on my fight with George Murphy and what I would do if the long arm of the law came knocking on my door. Mother used to say, "There is no rest for the wicked or the weary." Children should always listen to their mothers.

Little did we know that night as we delighted in conversation that a tragedy had unfolded in Piseco on November 3rd. There had been a hunting accident near T-Lake and young Fred Abrams had been killed by his older brother, William. Somehow the two hunters had lost contact with each other. A deer appeared a hundred yards or so away from William (who had to wear eye glasses) and he shot at it and thought it fell down. As smart hunters do, he waited a few minutes to let the animal die. When William later approached the spot expecting to find a dead deer; he found instead, to his horror, Fred lying there. The teenager had died instantly from a gunshot wound to the neck. Apparently Fred had been crouched over looking at the same deer and stood up just as poor William pulled the trigger.

All of us knew the Abrams family and their Sportsman Home. Carlton and his family had stayed there often; as had I on occasions when Floyd took me there to sober up. Floyd Abrams was well known and highly respected for his hard work as a farmer, guide, inn keeper, and fire warden for the State. My heart ached for them all – but most for William.

For the family, time would scar over the loss of Fred; but William would always carry an open wound. And unlike me, running and hiding after killing George Murphy, William had to bear the daily presence of family and community members who knew what had happened. I wondered if my mother and family back in Benedicta had learned about me killing George Murphy. I prayed maybe they didn't have to live with the gossip that follows such news.

Carlton, Ira and I continued our deer hunting the next morning. It was one of those sunny, warm, dry fall days when everything in the world seemed in order. We hunted along Fall Stream with no luck, had some lunch and went on individual deer watches at the base of Willis Mountain. About 3:00 PM, I began walking a big circle to move deer toward my guests and around 4:30 met Ira and then Carlton at their spots. Carlton was grinning like a schoolboy who had just stolen his first kiss. "What happened," Ira said. "Couldn't be another big buck, we didn't hear you shoot." "Nope, something a lot more memorable," replied Carlton. "I was standing on watch kind of nestled into some small trees and along come two, then three and finally six deer – all does. Somehow the wind was just right and they hadn't hit my track so they couldn't smell me. I froze in my spot so they couldn't see me and remained perfectly quiet. Now those deer knew something wasn't just right, but didn't know where the trouble was located. So, two of them started snorting making that sharp high-pitched whistle-like sound made when they sense danger. Well, they couldn't make me budge, so next they started pawing the ground with their front legs, kind of stomping and scraping to make me move. I didn't go for that tactic either and then the fun began. I don't know why, but I started talking to those deer in a low, steady, monotone voice saying, 'Hope you're having a good day. Where you been? How do you like the weather?' And they would perk up their ears, look straight at me but couldn't pick my shape out from the trees. So, I continued just talking nonsense to them for about three minutes with the same results. Hunting season and all, these deer were just curious about the forest talking to them. Finally, I said, 'Where's your big brother, you know, the one with the large antlers?' While I don't think that particular question bothered them, it was the end of our conversation because they snorted one last time and just ambled off into the woods. Now, how often does someone get that close to living deer in their natural surroundings? Ada and the girls will sure like this story!"

Stories a man treasures say a lot about his viewpoints and character. Observing what stories he chooses to tell reveals his true values. I knew now that Carlton would enjoy hearing my experience with the three-legged deer and not find it silly or juvenile. Carlton Banker was someone I could totally respect just as I had Clint Neff.

Carlton became my closest friend over the course of the next four-teen years. That friendship would become bitter sweet and intertwine our destinies in deadly ways. A routine began where Carlton and Ira, or sometimes another friend of Carlton's, would come to my place to hunt in the fall, fish in the spring, and explore in the summer. Brownsville continued to be a resident community of one but its mayor Foxey Brown now looked forward to the return of seasonal friends. I remained a recluse but was no longer the wild man of Fall Stream. However, a serious blun-der a few days later almost caused me to become the dead man of Fall Stream.

Every day has its own personality and this one began with promise of being especially good. Sunrise revealed a mist lazily hanging only a few feet above the pond surface. There was no fog elsewhere and sunlight glistened off the autumn foliage highlighting a mix of red, orange, and yellow hardwood leaf colors along with the always present green of the spruces and firs. The air was dry and pleasantly mixed with end of season odors coming from fallen leaves, goldenrod, and other decaying plants. All this brightened my spirits and filled me with energy. It was a good day to be alive.

After chores, Ox, Spook and I headed for the woods to pull logs. The morning hours disappeared quickly as we made several trips to the cabin and back to the woods. My labor had stoked my appetite and I hungered for some dinner. Against my better judgment, I had been saving one large hard maple log for chunk wood – some pieces once split that would help bank a fire overnight. The log was about twenty inches across and around eighteen feet long. By itself, Ox could easily haul it down to the cabin after the limbs were taken off. Being hungry and getting a little weary, I hurried to cut off the numerous limbs. I went to the wagon, grabbed a chain and my cant hook (some people called it a peavey) to roll the log and fasten the chain – something I had done thousands of times.

The log lay on a slight slope. The arrangement of knots left from where the limbs had been suggested it would roll over easier if rolled up hill. Using the cant hook I tried to pull from uphill side but found the log too heavy. Without thinking much, I went to the downhill side, attached my tool, turned my back and hunched under its handle. Using my legs and back, I nearly rolled the log before the cant hook slipped causing the log to come back and pin my right foot between it and the forest floor. There I was standing on one leg, facing downhill, with the log on the back of my heel and ankle. I felt no pain only pressure from the weight of the log. I didn't know whether to laugh or swear from having done such a stupid thing. Not quite believing this had actually happened, I looked for my cant hook.

The tool laid beside me, not two feet away, pinned flat under the same log that was holding me prisoner. Even if I could wiggle my fingers under the cant hook, there was no way to muster enough strength from my trapped position to roll the log or free the tool. I looked around for sticks or stones within reach that might serve to get me free. There were no stones and the few sticks I could grab were rotten and quickly broke from the slightest pressure put on them. Trying to simply pull my foot free seemed to only increase the log's pressure as it settled more firmly into the ground. I tried twisting and turning my body in every direction imaginable to gain advantage over the log. It didn't take long to figure out something in my foot or ankle would have to dislocate or break before I could face the log. Hearing me cuss loudly, Spook came over to see what was going on.

Now dogs are good diggers and I had seen Spook dig out more than one woodchuck. It struck me perhaps he could free my foot. This was, however, not a situation that Spook had trained for. There was no wood-chuck, and in Spook's realm of experience, no reason to dig around my trapped foot. Despite all kinds of encouragement, the best I got out of Spook were numerous affectionate licks on my hands, face, and boot. Ox, as he was prone to do, just stood and looked giving no expression of understanding what was going on. After a bit, he wandered off back toward the barn and Spook lay nearby patiently waiting for me to quit fooling around with the log and go home too.

To that point the situation hadn't struck me as being too serious. But my confidence in quickly getting free began to wane. There I was caught in a leg trap just like one of the hundreds of critters that French Louie took every year. The difference was Louie, or no one else, would come along to check on me in a day or two. And this trap belonged to nature and my own foolishness. I had broken two rules for working safely in the forest – don't hurry and don't get careless.

I began to consider my options. Even if I had my rifle that lay in the wagon, firing signal shots wouldn't bring help. Even though it was hunting season the chances of anyone being nearby were pretty unlikely. Who would come near fearsome Foxey Brown's place when there was shooting going on?

Having worked up a sweat and thrown off my coat, I was down to my shirt and pants. Checking my belt, I found the four inch hunting knife that always hung there. Despite its small size, perhaps the knife could help me dig my way out of this mess. Looking at the knife's keen edge, I tried not to think about how muskrats sometimes are forced to free themselves from leg traps.

8

WITNESS ROCK

After an hour of digging I had removed enough dirt to expose one side of my trapped foot, but not nearly enough to pull it free. It was hard work as I had to bend forward and then try to reach back under my body to where my foot was pinned under the log. Even removing a small stone required considerable effort and, of course, there were troublesome tree roots to cut through. I tried again to get Spook digging but he still didn't catch on to the game I was playing. He knew there was no woodchuck or squirrel to be had under the log. It was only his master involved in some monkey business not part of a dog's world. Of course, right then I was thinking of myself being more like the ass end of a dim-witted horse, or worse yet, a dead one.

Another hour of digging got the other side of my boot exposed. Still, I couldn't pull free from the log. Somehow, when the log had rolled, the toe of my boot and its sole get pinched under a tree limb stub. My toe was free, but the shoe still held fast and the pressure of the log was causing considerable pain to my foot. Stretching beyond what I thought possible for my body, I managed to get the knife into the laces of my boot. Despite having dulled its edge after using it as a shovel, the blade cut through the laces and with some wiggling I got my foot out of the boot. Free and grateful to no longer be a trapped man, I retrieved my cant hook, lifted the log and propped it up enough to pull out my boot. A sense of disgust and anger about my careless behavior overwhelmed me as I limped home in the late afternoon shadows. What should have been a joyous day had turned into a near disaster. The good news was that I had no broken bones, and suffered only some swelling and a strongly renewed sense of humility.

That evening, safe and sound in the cabin, I mulled over the events of the day. It struck me that I had encountered another brush with death. Getting hit by a falling tree back at Asa Aird's lumber camp had brought me close to an earthly departure in a hurry. But today, I had escaped what could have been a slow and lingering death from cold and starvation. I decided it was preferable to go the quick route. Even a rope seemed better than being caught like a poor animal left to starvation in an unchecked trap. I vowed to check my small winter trap line every day.

Thinking about leaving this world caused me to reflect on the next life if there was any to be had. I had never considered myself a religious person. Perhaps it had something to do with being brought up in a strict Irish Catholic family back in Benedicta. Like it or not, we children went to church most every Sunday with our mother and father. The whole town had gotten its start as some sort of experiment by the Catholic Church and it was kind of expected that families would be faithful parishioners. During services, after chanting the Latin liturgy, the priest would deliver a short sermon in English. Doing so, he often spoke about the "Spirit of God" being with us. This always seemed strange to me. I couldn't figure out why God's spirit would want to be inside any building, fancy or otherwise, when all his creations had taken place outside. Besides, it seemed to me, most men I knew where happiest outdoors and didn't really want to be in church on Sunday listening to a bunch of words they mostly couldn't understand. Words are only sounds or marks in a book describing real things. Why wouldn't God's spirit be outdoors where the men wanted to be and where he, himself, had done his work? Of course, I didn't dare ask knowing I would get my ears cuffed, or worse, for being disrespectful to the church.

Then there was the foul, choking, smell of burning incense during the church service. Why would God create the earth and clean fresh air and then want people to worship him inside while choking? First of all, there is something different about forest air compared to indoor air. Even when not burning incense, a man indoors is surrounded by all kinds of dead things (tables, chairs, stove, firewood, boots, clothing, food…) each giving off their own gases. Together, these things make up the air he breathes. Now, during the warmer months this isn't a real problem as outside air gets mixed in from open windows and doors. But being closed up in winter, air gets stale and ugly and can lead to that cabin fever sickness.

In the forest, even in the middle of winter, a man is surrounded by all kinds of living things. Trees, especially spruces, firs, and pines are growing year round mixing their odors into the forest air. In the warmer months fallen leaves and other decaying things on the forest floor help new plants grow to create odors far different from the smells of cultivated fields or the vly.

I sometimes thought maybe forest air influences how we feel and think even though we most often are unaware of it. It never failed that I felt better, regardless of ailment, after getting into the forest. My head cleared, muscles loosened, and problems dwelled upon indoors seemed much smaller as I worked or went on a hike. It was as if the natural world was baptizing me each time by simply carrying on its everyday work.

If a man takes the time to look, energy can be seen constantly flowing everywhere – insects, birds, wind, sunlight, the flow of the stream. I was most conscious of this energy or power when light, sound, temperature, and the things (leaves, trees, rock, water) of a place occasionally blended together in a special way. It fed me and made my "cup runneth over" as the priest used to say.

Cutting firewood in the forest can open pathways that let a man connect to the "Spirit of God." The chopping and sawing loosens up muscles, joints and the mind. After breaking a sweat and getting into a rhythm your work begins to blend into the scene and becomes part of the forest. Animals, for example, can sense when a man is engrossed in his work and poses no danger to them. Often times deer, squirrels, chipmunks, and birds of all sorts come close by to observe what the human is up to. Their presence, the air, sunlight, clouds, breezes, smell of split wood (each tree having its own particular odor), sounds of the forest, knowing you will be warm in winter ... combine to create a sense of peace, tranquility, and connection to a higher power. To me, that was the Spirit of God – a god seeing things living together in age old ways just as he created them. Even though I wasn't always aware of it, my connection with the Creator increased each day as I went about life in his mountains. After all, mountains were his first places of worship according to the Bible.

Not long after moving into Fall Stream I discovered a big rock, about a quarter mile upstream, at the base of Willis Mountain. When I say, "big rock" I am referring to a boulder half the size of a railroad locomotive. The boulder's shape reminded me of a locomotive because it is wide at the rear where wood or coal fuel got stored. Moving forward, the boulder narrowed some like locomotive engines do. And at the very front, a large chunk of boulder had split off creating sort of a prow or pointed area that I imagined to be the locomotive's V-shaped snow plow. I suppose some people might liken the boulder to a ship. But, it was my boulder, for a while, to call what I wanted.

Anyway, it stood alone, apart from other boulders, at the edge of the forest next to a small rivulet that feeds the nearby main course of Fall Stream. I read somewhere that huge boulders like this were left behind when glaciers receded after the Ice Age. For that I was thankful. The location was a special place due to the large boulder's presence. To me, it had many merits including the power to heal – at least things that ailed my mind. I named it Witness Rock for several reasons. First, I knew it had been part of this landscape before critters of any sort lived on Fall Stream. It had seen countless numbers of plants and animals come and go like the beavers, wolves, mountain lions, and moose that once were here in large numbers. Perhaps, it had even offered shelter to the mammoth and saber toothed tiger some say once roamed North America. Mainly, the rock inspired me to witness or consider many things about the life of David Brennan – Foxey Brown if you will.

Getting on top of Witness Rock without assistance required some physical strength because its relatively smooth face left little for hands and feet to grab onto. By himself, a man had to grasp the rock's face wherever little projections were located and pull up foot by foot to its top. After two such trips, I constructed a make-shift ladder and hid it in the brush for future use.

Witness Rock's flat top offered a comfortable surface whether my stay was an hour, part of a day, or an evening assuming I was willing to haul up some firewood from below. The temptation to stay long was strong because the old rock provided a wide view of Fall Stream, the vly, mountains, and the tops of surrounding trees. The stream bubbling along next to its base made a music that added another spirit soothing aspect to Witness Rock. Each visit caused me to wonder if other humans had enjoyed it. I suspected very few did because of its remote setting in the mountains. The history books said Indians visited the north woods mainly for fishing and hunting and that Piseco Lake got its name from an ancient Indian word meaning fish. Whatever the case, perhaps some young Indian boy used my boulder for a vision quest as he prepared to enter manhood. While I didn't sit in a sweat lodge or go without food for days as the Indians did to prepare their minds for visions, Witness Rock became a powerful and sanctuary kind of place for me.

It was easy to imagine untold numbers of mountain lions or bears, over the centuries, lying in wait on top of Witness Rock for an unsuspecting deer to stop and drink from the stream below. My hunting success from Witness Rock suggested those critters ate well. But Witness Rock was more than a great spot for a hunter to ambush his dinner. Like Foxey Brown it stood alone amidst millions of trees miles from other human beings and the activities that consume them. It provided a vantage point to see all that made my life possible on Fall Stream – my cabin, barn, pond, fields, crops, animals, and the vly. Seeing these things in their entirety caused me to give thanks for the way they were sustaining my life. Without the rock I could not witness these things as a whole. I wondered if more people would be happier if they could occasionally see the bigger picture of their lives. And maybe a special place, and its power, might help them come to understand that possessions are not the important things in life. You can't take possessions into the next world. But memories and experiences might go along for the ride. If so, perhaps life is about building a tapestry of experiences. Many of the tapestry's threads would suggest labor as most men and women have to work. But we also laugh, lament and love to some degree before leaving. I thought we ought to mix in a good deal of laughter because it lets you live longer. I never heard of a man who died from laughing. Besides, it creates a brighter tapestry. Maybe that's why so many men loved guiding. The labor was seasonal and varied with different tasks. There was also a whole lot of laughter around the camp fire and about the only lamenting was over the "big one" that got away!

My favorite times on Witness Rock were at the ends of hot summer days when the cabin filled with warm and stuffy air. At such times, I developed the habit of cooling off in the pond, grabbing some food, a blanket, and a sailcloth tarp before heading to the rock. Evening breezes lifted cool air off the pond and Fall Stream making the top of Witness Rock pleasant above the working level of most insects. A small fire and a star-filled sky made the struggles of the day fade away and opened my mind to wonder about the powers of whatever or whoever created this place. Knowing that, for a time, I was manager of all I could see brought a sense of accomplishment. Perhaps this was the place destiny had picked for me. Truth be told, I bet many men would have loved to be as free as me. And I was not alone, night sounds from owls and other critters provided assurance that life, and some death, was going on around me.

Other seasons were also special at Witness Rock. A silence came in the late fall on certain days as if a long anticipated rest was coming with the arrival of winter. Not a total silence but an almost undetectable sound of some creature breathing peacefully. It was difficult to hear clearly staying just beyond the range of my full reception. At first, I reasoned it was merely a slight breeze flowing through some hemlock trees. But observation of nearby tree branches and dead grasses showed no air movement of any sort. Yet, the sound continued in a slow rhythmic fashion like a man might make when in a deep sleep. Somehow I felt in the presence of a friendly spirit or invisible creature. It relaxed and comforted me. Most men are rarely at ease long enough to enjoy such benefit of nature. Witness Rock was my fortress, asylum, and church. I always slept well there. Somehow, I sensed a higher power liked the place too.

Looking into a clear night sky and watching the stars always overwhelmed me. I tried to wrap my mind around how it all started and how it could all have an end someplace. After a while frustration would always set in when I couldn't imagine an end to it all. The best notion I could come up with was that there was no end; just endless universes with stars and planets on some voyage unknowable to me. And, maybe, the curse of being a human (or blessing depending on how you look at it) is that we must wander from one existence to another trying to make sense out of it all. And might God himself be caught up in some sort of grand adventure involving the ongoing creation of new things? I never could understand the concept of heaven taught by the many religions. How could a God capable of creating all the wondrous things on earth and, throughout the universe, be satisfied to have millions of souls sitting around in "heaven" just worshipping him all the time? It seemed to me God is a restless being and easily bored without new things to do. Perhaps that restless characteristic can be seen in the creative energy found in some people.

I shared Witness Rock with Carlton and my views about God, religion and the meaning of life. We had many talks there and around the woodstove at night. He agreed my Witness Rock was a unique place and that the view, indeed, inspired thoughts about spiritual matters. Carlton also believed regular contact with nature could refresh and reinvigorate a man for his work. Unlike me, however, he thought organized religion and formal places to worship were important to society as ways to guide people and instill good values and behaviors. He admitted this opinion was probably based on his upbringing in a Protestant Church (Methodist Episcopal) and the practices and philosophies of his family and hero, Theodore Roosevelt (TR). Carlton said Roosevelt's view of Christianity was one that focused strongly on service and the premise of Christ having come to serve God and humankind. Carlton liked to quote what TR said when stepping down as governor of New York. "When death comes..." a man's life can be measured in how "mankind is in some degree better because he has lived."

This made sense to me but it still didn't reconcile Bible tales about Christ preaching to people in the fields, on hillsides and along streams and that he told stories about birds and animals to make his points. It seemed to me Christ avoided the temples and synagogues and didn't get along with people who ran such places. If Christ was interested in organized religion and fancy buildings, why didn't he give specific instructions as to how such places should be built and operated? Wasn't that the stuff of Old Testament teachings? Hadn't Christ come to teach about love, forgiveness, and compassion for all creatures? Why didn't he dress in fancy robes, sport gold jewelry and sleep and eat in the best inns? And, if fancy buildings were so important, why did he go to wild places to sort out his problems? These and other questions about religion sometimes caused Carlton and me to talk into the midnight hours. We never did totally agree on the importance of organized religion. I couldn't understand how in the name of Christ, churches and religious leaders, supposedly following Christ's teachings about love and forgiveness, could have been involved in so many blood baths in the past ranging from the Crusades, to the Inquisition to people being burned at the stake as witches because they acted a little strangely. Foxey Brown the eccentric man of

Fall Stream would have been a candidate for such treatment two hundred years ago near Salem, Massachusetts.

In the end, Carlton was comfortable seeing the Church, despite its flaws, as doing more good than harm. Without it, he thought people wouldn't have a constant reminder about something bigger than themselves operating behind the scenes. He maintained a sense of humility, and kinder human behavior, could flow from church attendance especially since not everyone could have their own individual Witness Rock.

I asked what drove his passion for fishing, hunting and spending so much time in these mountains. Carlton was quick to see where my question would lead the conversation and admitted church attendance alone was not sufficient to keep him connected to a higher power. He suspected many men were drawn to the woods thinking the attraction was catching fish and shooting deer while the real incentive was to visit wild places and somehow connect, at least partially, with the great mystery that created the heavens and earth. We thought, on a much smaller level than God plays at, hunters are displaying a similar affinity for adventure and use of creativity in unknown places. We recalled adventure stories about men, including Theodore Roosevelt, feeling most fully alive when they were at risk in uncertain situations. We ended our conversation about religion and spiritual matters recalling how such adventures in the Adirondacks resulted in more than few hunters getting shot by other hunters every year. I let Carlton have the last word when he remarked, "Yes, that's the big difference between God and we mortals – he doesn't die if one of his adventures gets messed up!"

While I was now mayor and pastor of Brownsville, my term of office was being defined by the outside world. Backers of the Adirondack Park were increasingly pressuring the State to purchase and make land swaps to increase the size of the public preserve within the "Blue Line" shown on a map of the mountains. Even my little place on Fall Stream was going to show up on a map one day as the State's head map maker, Verplanck Colvin, was relentlessly surveying most every nook and cranny of the mountains.

Transportation in, out, and across the mountains was increasing rapidly as railroads continued laying track to haul cargo and passengers. And a fellow named George Selden out in Rochester had patented a gasoline driven automobile. The most troubling was news in 1898 that a telephone line had been run from Speculator (the Four Corners) through Lake Pleasant and on into a tannery at Piseco. If Piseco got a regular lawman, the telephone device would make it easy to check on a possible (David Brennan) fugitive from Boston living under the assumed name of Foxey Brown.

Many people and lumber companies, who had stripped the forest of marketable timber were leaving and sold their property for as little as $.50 per acre. It was clear the State intended to increase and strictly regulate use of its holdings. But once again, people like me, French Louie, Tim Crowley, William Courtney, the Abrams family and others with hunting and fishing camps figured we would be "grand-fathered" out of the law and allowed to remain in our long-standing forest homes. We thought the state was after the large corporations who continued to fatten their profit margins at the expense of the people and State of New York.

Our assumptions were reinforced with the election of a new governor in 1898. In our eyes, Theodore Roosevelt was a "man's man" who, despite coming from a wealthy family had the common man's interest at heart. Besides, he was a hunter, fisherman and Spanish American War hero who had personally led his men in battle. And, as reported in *Collier's Weekly*, he had stated his opposition to corporations becoming too powerful – "A corporation is simply a collection of men, who may do well or who may do ill. The thing to do is to make them understand that if they do well you are with them, but if they do ill you are ever and always against them." We took this to mean Mr. Roosevelt wouldn't be concerned about a few long standing mountain men simply making a living in these woods.

The only disturbing thing about Roosevelt from my point of view was his position on applying the death penalty. Denying a stay of execution for convicted husband murderer, Martha Place, he allowed the first woman to be executed by electrocution in New York State. Seems Place was a particularly blood thirsty woman who unsuccessfully tried to kill her stepdaughter using sulfuric acid and strangulation. Failing to do so, she had better luck taking an axe to her husband and chopping him to death. Martha's bad luck was that Theodore Roosevelt would have the last say about her execution. During a recent speech at Grant's Tomb, he had proclaimed, "There is a time to be just and there is a time to be merciful, there is a time for unyielding resolution and a time for the hand of fellowship and brotherly love. The great man is the man who knows the time for one and the time for the other." It probably wasn't much consolation for Martha Place to be the beneficiary of Roosevelt's resolve. She did, however, make history as the first woman to earn a seat in the "Empire State's" new electric chair.

Mulling Roosevelt's words over, I was pretty sure the Murphy family wouldn't show David Brennan "the hand of fellowship and brotherly love" either. That is, unless the fellowship was between them standing around watching me dance at the end of a rope or fry in an electric chair. I wasn't particularly motivated to see which form of execution the state of Massachusetts was then using or to be the first to demonstrate the effectiveness of any other new device. For me, consideration of life and death issues seemed best kept to Brownsville from my court atop Witness Rock.

9
SECOND CHANCES

Unbeknown to me, Carlton and Ira had told their Gloversville friends about their good times at Dave Brown's camp. Soon, letters of inquiry started to arrive about possibilities of fishing or hunting at my secluded camp. Because of my troubles with the law, I wasn't sure about opening Brownsville up to numerous people fearing sooner or later some lawman might figure out David Brown was really David Brennan – a fugitive from justice back in Boston. While guiding could provide some sorely needed extra income, it was safest to scrape along with my animals and living off the land. I didn't respond to the inquiries despite reminders from Carlton that the folks who had written were reputable and able to pay above average guiding fees.

Spring came early to the mountains in 1903. Severe drought and warm winds quickly cleared the snow and dried the forest floor. Such favorable conditions prompted early arrival of sport fisherman. And, according to plan, Carlton and Ira were due the first week in April. Needing supplies, I agreed to meet them on Saturday in Piseco.

I enjoyed a leisurely ride in the warm spring air as Ox trudged along ahead of the wagon. Spook preferred following at his own pace occasionally disappearing to investigate things only a dog's nose and ears detect. It was another great day to be alive and guests coming into Brownsville promised to make it even more special.

We reached Courtney's Hotel and Piseco Post Office an hour or so before the stage normally arrived. William P. had gotten elected postmaster again and I found him sorting mail. Looking up, he greeted me, "Hey Dave, hear you're doing some guiding these days. Sounds like you got along pretty well with Carlton Banker and his brother-in law from Glov-ersville." Thinking a moment, I replied, "Yes, I guess he didn't mind being with a gruff and wild looking mountain man like me." Laughing, Courtney said, "For sure, all he could talk about last fall when he brought that big buck out was what a great guide you were." A sly smile came over his face and he waved a hand saying, "Come on over to the dining room, have a cup of coffee with me." Unsure of what my friend William P. was up to, I followed him over to a table. "Want something to eat with your coffee, Dave?" I declined knowing Courtney wanted to talk more than eat. Adding a good deal of sugar to his coffee, Courtney began encouraging me to take on more jobs guiding Sports. He figured it would be good for me and Piseco if more wealthy people like Carlton Banker came to hunt and fish. They were already coming in increasing numbers for summer vacations and it would help local folks if the spring and fall months provided a steady source of income.

Sensing my reluctance, Courtney continued by telling me not to worry about my past. "Local folks don't care much about a man's past as long as he causes no trouble here. You've been here going on thirteen years and keep pretty much to yourself up on Fall Stream. No one's going to take the time to find out what might have happened to you back in Boston many years ago." This sounded good to me except for one thing – the stories going around about Tim Crowley and me having a gold strike up at Spruce Lake.

"Oh, that," chuckled Courtney. Some city dude got all liquored up over at Rude's Tavern last summer during a poker game. He was short covering a bet and wanted to trade a map showing where there was gold up at the old Belden mine. Turned out all he had was a regular map of the Spruce Lake trail and an X on it. Well, no one would let him cover the bet with such a thing and he left mumbling about how sorry they would be. Seems after the game was over, the boys got talking about the old Belden gold mine story and all the other unsuccessful attempts to find gold or silver. They all had a good laugh and figured if you or Tim had gold, you sure were doing a great job of disguising your wealth. That was pretty much it." Courtney's explanation made sense, particularly to a man of my experience knowing the strange things that happen when you mix booze and poker.

Slapping his knee, Courtney said, "I better get back to work or I'll lose my postmaster job. Good jobs are hard to come by in these parts.

Come on, Dave, you didn't pick up your mail." I took my mail and went to the front porch to wait for the stage and my guests.

Almost on time a little after noon, the stage rolled to a stop in a cloud of dust. Carlton was first to jump out and brush himself off. Ira was nowhere to be seen. Sticking out his hand to shake, Carlton said Ira had gotten sick yesterday and wasn't up to coming. "You will have to put up with my stories all by yourself, Dave. That damn stagecoach ride has made me hungry as a bear; let's get some lunch!" he exclaimed.

One thing I always had to keep in mind about Carlton was how much he could eat for such a small man. Where he put it all never ceased to amaze me. He ordered up a batch of six trout, fried potatoes, and green beans. Not having pork often, I went for the ham and scalloped potatoes. Liking the look of my choice, Carlton asked for a side order of the ham. We topped the meal off with apple pie and second cups of coffee.

Thoroughly stuffed, we loaded the wagon, with what seemed like a great amount of equipment and baggage for one man, and headed for Brownsville. It didn't take long for Carlton to start catching me up on news from the outside world. And, of course, the topic of conversation soon turned to Theodore Roosevelt. Events were unfolding that were sure to directly influence Carlton's line of work.

For years railroad companies had followed the practice of giving preferred companies rebates on the published freight rates. This gave some shippers and certain market areas advantages over their competition. Congress and Roosevelt saw the unfairness of this practice and had recently passed the Elkins Anti-Rebate Act to combat it. It meant the beginning of government railroad regulation. While Carlton understood the need for this law, implementation meant more documentation of business practices for the F.J. & G. railroad and increased workload for Carlton as a superintendent. He was very happy to get away from this fray and spend a week with me in the Adirondack wild.

Continuing with his Roosevelt tales, Carlton shared news closer to his heart. On March 14th, the President signed an executive order creating the first federal wildlife bird reservation. Pelican Island in Florida, although only three acres in size, was the beginning of Roosevelt's vision to create a national system of wildlife refuges. Something had to be done to stop an expanding market for bird feathers for the fashion industry. The plume feathers of some birds like herons, egrets, spoonbills and pelican were sometimes worth more than gold. Authorities had actually caught market hunters using cannons to harvest dozens of birds with one shot. Carlton's words reminded me of stories about brook trout coming out of these mountains by the barrel. At one time, some people actually used them for garden fertilizer.

Our talk made time pass quickly, and before we knew it, Ox was pulling us down the hill into Brownsville. I noticed Spook was limping some. Going on thirteen years of age, the round trip to Piseco and back was a bit much for him. Despite having general good health, Spook had begun to have hip problems and too much running caused him some lameness. The time was near when Spook would have to share the wagon with me or stay home. It occurred to me the same options wouldn't be available when I grew old. Life as a recluse in the mountains demands a body capable of hard work.

Carlton and I had an unforgettable week. The warm and dry weather made comfortable days and cool nights – still cool enough that we didn't have to deal with black flies. We fished and caught our limit of trout every day; often so early that the remainder of the day was spent catching and releasing them. This necessitated that we stop using worms to avoid killing the greedy little brookies that quickly swallowed and stomached the bait. Like starving deer the trout put any food stuff available in their empty stomachs. Some even chased bare hooks we dropped into the water. Carlton remarked he had heard about fish in the Amazon River of South America that can, in minutes, strip the flesh off a man. We agreed it is always best for a man to consider carefully where he bathes or has his pants down lest he be relieved of life, possessions and reputation.

Our fishing expeditions took us the full length of Fall Stream from where it dumps into Vly Lake up to its beginnings below the Belden Vly. We also explored many of its little tributaries delighted to find brook trout everywhere. One place where a feeder brook joined Fall Stream presented a mystery for us to unravel.

The heavily shaded pool still held a floating ice paddy. Remarking about how long snow and ice could remain in north facing portions of the mountains, I looked into the stream and spotted the fully submerged carcass of a very large deer. Head up, its antlers and wide-open eyes riveted my attention. It was as if the animal was making one last lunge hoping to see daylight and breathe. The animal's antlers were massive and had numerous points. Calling Carlton, to come witness my discovery and help me, we were able to secure a rope around a portion of the antlers and, with considerable effort, pulled its lead-like, waterlogged body to shore.

The number of points on the buck's antlers totaled eighteen, all but two at least six to twelve inches long. The spread between the front two tines measured twenty-three inches. Most spectacular was the thickness of the webbing that held all the antler points together. The webbing reminded us of moose antlers. I teased Carlton that our good President Roosevelt, and the Boone and Crocket Club he started, might like to see this beauty.

Examining the deer's body revealed no wounds of any sort eliminating suspicions of a hunter's poor aim or death from the fangs of wolves or mountain lion – who no longer lived in these mountains. It appeared to have been a very healthy animal easily weighing two hundred pounds. Perfectly preserved by the icy cold water, the animal probably could have still been safely eaten. It remained a long way from deteriorating to the point where fish and other stream critters could enjoy its flesh. Our curiosity was aroused. What manner of death had the mountain imposed on this magnificent animal?

Could this great buck have broken through the ice and drowned? The water was deep enough at around eight feet in the center of the stream. But the stream itself was only twenty feet or so wide. Surely, a strong deer could thrash its way to shore and survive a good soaking. We stood there in silence at a loss for answers. Carlton asked if animals died from heart attacks or strokes. Noticing a good deal of gray hair on the deer's muzzle we agreed that could be a possibility. Had the extremely cold water and stress of trying to escape brought on a human like demise? Only the mountain and the stream knew for sure and they weren't talking.

We cut off the unfortunate deer's head. The skull and antlers would make great conversation for many who had yet to visit Brownsville. Paying last respects to our discovery, we agreed its remains would either feed some four-legged critters or the fishes. We debated briefly, decided the waters had claimed its life and deserved the rewards, and pushed the deer's carcass into the stream. Always thinking and ready to apply his wit, Carlton asked if I would enjoy a drink downstream once warmer waters had begun to decompose the deer's flesh? I responded that sometimes a man could think too much.

Hiking back to camp in the dwindling light of the day, we talked about the number of deaths, human and deer alike, these mountains had witnessed. None of the deaths were mysteries to them – they had seen all first hand. How many people, since the first visited here, came and never left, their bodies hidden by the earth? We humans like to keep historical records about our past. However, such scholarship probably doesn't matter much from the mountains' point of view. They simply host the various forms of life that come along from time to time. I suggested the mountains didn't need any of us two legged, four legged, creepy, crawly, or finned critters to exist. Thinking for a moment, Carlton agreed but said its existence would be a whole lot less colorful and mysterious without those things. "Finding good company every once in a while makes life richer." Not knowing how mountains think, I suggested we settle on the notion that it was best to err on the side of being very cautious around our wilderness host. Hearing my words, a sly grin filled Carlton's face; "By gosh Dave, you took the words right out of my mouth. Sounds like you've read John Burroughs essay on the Adirondacks where he said, 'It is something to press the pulse of our old mother by the mountain lakes and streams, and know what health and vigor are in her veins,' But he also cautioned to remember, 'how regardless of observation she deports herself.'" I hadn't read the book but Carlton was going to fix that situation.

On Saturday night we began to get ready for Carlton's departure the next morning. I had forgotten about one fairly large and heavy box Carlton hadn't opened. Smiling like a child grabbing a present from under a Christmas tree; he pulled the box out from under his bunk. Next he decided to play the "guess what's in the box" game. To have a little fun, I answered, "A case of ammunition for all those times you miss when shooting at deer!" Feigning deep hurt, Carlton said he would take the box back home if it wasn't so damned heavy. With that, he opened the box and began tossing books to me. One of which struck me solidly in the midsection. It was John Burroughs' *Wake-Robin* containing the quote he had laid on me a day ago.

"Dave, I know how much you like to read. I thought these might appeal to your interests." Of course, the next ones out of the box were books written by T.R. Included was, according to Carlton, most everything the president had written and published. Glancing at the titles as I stacked them were: *Hunting Trips of a Ranchman, Ranch Life and the*

Hunting Trail, The Winning of the West, New York, The Wilderness Hunter,
Hero Tales from American History, American Ideals, The Rough Riders, The
Strenuous Life, and even Roosevelt's first book, *The Naval War of 1812.* I
could see Carlton was waiting for me to respond, so I admitted to having
read none of them. "Great," he replied. "We will have lots to talk about
in the future."

I had read others that Carlton pulled from the box, including Mel-
ville's Moby *Dick,* and Cooper's, *The Path Finder.* The last two books Carlton presented were written back in the 1850's by a man named Henry
David Thoreau. The first was titled *Walden.* The other was *The Maine*
Woods. Carlton remarked that Thoreau was a relatively unknown author
but thought I would like them because of Thoreau's strong beliefs about
the importance of living simply. He was surprised to learn that I had read
parts of Thoreau's *Walden* in one of my college courses. Without thinking,
I joked that Thoreau had gone to the woods to live simply and I had come
to the mountains simply to live!

Carlton didn't react to my little play on words. I sensed he didn't
know whether to laugh or express sympathy for my plight. Carlton had,
of course, heard rumors about my past, but being a friend and gentleman
he had never brought the subject up. Believing I could trust Carlton with
most any secret, I decided to tell him about George Murphy and how I
had come to live in the Adirondacks.

Carlton listened carefully to my story about the fight with Murphy.
Pausing for a moment when I stopped, he asked if I had ever made inquiries about the case with authorities back in Boston. I hadn't, other than
the plan Clint and I devised many years ago, due to my fear of giving the
police a lead as to my whereabouts. Pausing for a few moments, Carlton asked if I would trust him to do some checking for me. He had a
close friend back in Gloversville who happened to be the sheriff there.
He would tell his sheriff friend that a fellow named David Brennan had
applied for a job with the F. J. &G. railroad and he wanted some checking
done on Brennan's background. That way if Brennan was wanted for killing George Murphy, the sheriff would come back to Carlton looking for
Brennan. Carlton would then just give him some fictitious address that
Brennan has supposedly provided. So far, this sounded like a smart plan.

I don't know why, but I asked Carlton the sheriff's name. Carlton's
answer nearly caused me to tip over backwards in my chair. "He's a good

man, named Ned James," replied Carlton. Noticing me wince and kind of shudder, Carlton asked why mention of Ned James' name shook me so. I explained my encounter with Sheriff Ned James years ago and the lasting impression of how smart he was. Carlton laughed and said, "But you didn't tell him you were David Brennan back then did you? I doubt he is going to connect, even if he remembers after so many years, the names David Brown and David Brennan. David is a pretty common name." Putting my fears aside, I agreed the odds were pretty small that Ned James would think Brown and Brennan were the same man. It was worth a gamble to see where I stood with the law.

So, it was with a sense of great anticipation that Carlton and I finished his vacation at Brownsville. He promised to contact Ned James when he got back to Gloversville. We both figured it would take a month or so to get things checked out in Boston regarding the David Brennan/George Murphy case of 1889. I anticipated continuing to be a "wanted" man come summer.

I was tidying up the cabin on a Saturday morning a week later when Spook began to bark. Looking out the window, I was surprised to see a horse and wagon with two men approaching. Soon it was apparent that one man was Carlton. There was no mistaking Carlton's fedora hat and small body size. Getting closer, I saw the other man was Tim Crowley. Opening the door, I exclaimed, "Carlton, Tim what in the heck are you doing here?" Jumping off the wagon before it fully stopped, Carlton bounced up the porch steps saying Tim had been in Piseco and offered him a ride. With a wink of the eye he continued, "Thought you might want your mail and the supplies you ordered." I didn't know what the devil he was talking about but caught on that he was making small talk until Tim left.

The three of us chatted a few minutes mostly about how dry things were getting and hoping fisherman would be careful with campfires. Tim had Sports coming in to Spruce Lake and soon left us alone. Carlton pushed me inside and closed the door.

"I couldn't wait to tell you – George Murphy didn't die! There never was any warrant for your arrest. Ned James had checked up on any wanted people from Boston in 1889, right after the two of you met near Fonda. He made another inquiry for me last week just to learn more about George Murphy. Murphy fully recovered, opened his own bar and often jokes about how you straightened him out with that cue stick. Neither he nor the family has any hard feelings toward you."

Hearing this left me lost for words. Several emotions and a dozen thoughts were going through my head all at once. Finally, I stammered, "I'll be dammed, I'll be dammed! I don't know whether to shout for joy or cry." Carlton laughed and said, "Well while you are deciding I'm starving, haven't had a thing to eat since six this morning."

Carlton and I talked for hours over biscuits, honey, a whole pot of coffee – right on through normal time for a midday meal. Carlton didn't have many details about how Murphy had survived my whack in the head with a cue stick. He woke up an hour or so later and didn't remember much about our fight. Turns out he shied away from trouble after that and became a pretty good citizen.

My mind was swirling with "what might have been" if I had known about Murphy's recovery all these years. Would I have worked on the railroad for another twenty-five or thirty years like so many other men back in Boston ending up with a gold watch and small pension? Would I have married and had a family? Would I have gone back to Maine to be near my brothers and sisters? Sensing what I was probably thinking, Carlton came right out and asked, "What do you think you would have done knowing Murphy didn't die?" I shared all the things that were going through my mind.

Like usual, Carlton got right to the heart matters, "The important question now is what will you do with the rest of your life?" I couldn't answer that question. Before Carlton's revelation about Murphy, the situation had limited choices and my mind had focused on making the best out of what had been handed to me. Now I was almost like the teenage David Brennan who had to choose between a Benedicta farm life or find his future in the outside world. Part of me fretted about now having to make choices.

I had put a lot of work into Brownsville – my place here on Fall Stream. Despite the loneness and hard work, this was home. The stream, pond, fields, and woods provided most all my needs. Most importantly, I was free to do as I pleased without consulting other people. How would I fare in the outside world being around lots of other people all the time?

"Dave, here's a thought," said Carlton. How about taking a vacation? Go back to Boston and Maine, if you want. See how you like your old world. I can get Ira to come and stay here with me. It's still early spring; we can care for your animals, cut some wood, fish a little...it would be fun for us."

Carlton was giving me good advice. But, the thought of leaving my comfortable situation scared me. What if the Murphys were setting a trap? Maybe George was really still filled with hate and this was a way to lure me back to Boston and get his hands on me.

It was now time to do afternoon chores and make our supper. We agreed not to talk more about my big decision until morning. That night I tossed and turned trying to fall asleep, wrestling with one thought after another. Sitting up in bed, I realized it was now safe to contact my family. I had to write to mother so Carlton could take the letter out to Piseco.

It was well past midnight when I returned to bed. Sleep still did not come quickly. But the next morning I awoke from the most restful sleep I could remember – David Brennan was now a free man with no need to wonder when a lawman might come to haul him away to the gallows or electric chair.

I took Carlton up on his offer to be the temporary mayor of Brownsville. He and Ira would come in on April 29th; and spend a couple days before I went to Boston. Unfortunately, fire would once again alter my plans.

The inevitable happened on April 20, 1903. Seventy-two days of wind and drought created conditions for the worst forest fires in recorded Adirondack history. For decades loggers had habitually cut trees and left the tops, limbs and all, where the tree fell. Millions of hemlock and fir treetops, propped up by their numerous limbs, lay waiting for a spark to turn them into torches. While no one knows for sure, that spark probably came from the smokestack of a wood fired railroad locomotive that the logging companies continued to use for transport. Following the railroad tracks to find saw timber saved time and money as did leaving the branches on the tree tops. It was also possible some farmer had been burning a field prior to spring planting or that a careless fisherman had neglected his campfire.

The center of the fires was to the north at Lake Placid. But fires soon also raged around Schroon Lake, Lake George, Olmsteadville, Newcomb, Ausable Forks, Saranac Lake and Clintonville. Thankfully, the fires themselves didn't reach the Piseco/Lake Pleasant areas. The smoke and falling cinders, however, were another matter.

No warning came to Brownsville on the 20th other than the arrival of smoke late in the day. We had had some forest fires back in 1899, but they burned out after causing only minor damage. The Piseco area had been logged hard so many years ago that any remaining tree tops had long since rotted away. My farming and firewood cutting activities had also pushed the tree line back a good distance from my camp. I decided to stay put and take care of my animals – a trip to Boston would have to wait. At first, my situation seemed good. The smoke made sleeping a little difficult but tolerable when I moved my mattress to the cabin floor to find more breathable air. Spook was also restless but found his new bunkmate reassuring.

The following morning greeted us with even thicker smoke and falling cinders. I had now resorted to wearing a handkerchief mask wetting it from time to time. Fortunately the cinders were not hot enough to ignite the cabin or barn roofs and I didn't have to fight fire. I later learned the fires were so numerous that cinders fell in Albany, 150 miles south of Lake Placid. Smoke was even detected, and cause for concern, in Washington, DC.

There was no need to notify Carlton about a change of plans. He obviously knew what was happening – our region of New York State was making national news. Fortunately for Carlton, his work was with the electric division of the F. J. & G. and not with a spark belching steam locomotive portion of the company.

Fires in various locations continued some fifty days until heavy and steady rains began to douse them on June 7th. When finished the fires had destroyed 600,000 acres of Adirondack Park lands. By June 10th or so the winds had cleared out the lingering smoke odors and fresh air once again dominated at Brownsville. Small things we take for granted shape our approach to everyday life. My trip to Boston would underscore how much I enjoyed fresh mountain air.

Carlton and Ira arrived June 20th and we spent the weekend going over care of the animals and preparing for my departure. Carlton's family had come up from Gloversville to stay at the Abram's Sportsman Hotel. That way, Carlton could have them up to Brownsville for a day or go visit in Piseco.

Monday morning came and I was off to catch the stage in Piseco. I carried only a small suitcase loaned by Carlton with some clean clothing and personal items. I shaved and Ira gave me a haircut of sorts thinking a professional barber along the way to Boston could spruce me up some more.

I was nervous about my trip. I hadn't been any further than Piseco or Lake Pleasant in thirteen years. True, I had kept up on current events through my reading and discussions with Carlton and William P. But, that was not the same as actually mingling in the real world.

The stagecoach's arrival at Courtney's Piseco Hotel was following its normal pattern of being late. William P. and I talked for an hour or so while I waited. I told him what was going on, how Carlton found out George Murphy had never died. "Well there you go," he said slapping his knee as was his usual habit when he got excited. I could see he was genuinely happy. But he made sure to encourage me to return for good after visiting in Boston. "You're an excellent guide, Dave, and now you can openly work with the best of them."

I took a seat inside the stage with three other men I didn't know. From the looks of them I guessed they were Sports who had come in to fish. Just as the driver got aboard William P. came running out – "Here, Dave some mail just came in for you." With that the driver snapped his whip and we were off. Without thinking I stuffed the letters in my pocket as the stage lurched into motion.

I hadn't been on a stage since my ride into Lake Pleasant and Asa Aird's lumber camp in 1889. The present ride over to Wells and on down to the Northville train station verified my earlier impression of stagecoaches. The seats were padded a bit more and the roads some-what improved, but the ride was still far from comfortable. After a bit, I settled into the uneven bounding and bouncing of the stagecoach and remembered the mail Courtney had given me. Glancing at the return address, I noticed two were from Gloversville and the third was a larger envelope from Benedicta – oddly the return address was not from my mother but from my sister Mary Brown Cummings. Mary's letter explained our mother, Catherine, had died on January 17, 1901. Broth-ers Hugh and Martin had both been killed in Aspen, Colorado on Feb-ruary 18, 1890. My older brother John and sister Bridget had married and were doing well. And, brother James was living in Oregon, address unknown. I wondered if he too had caught gold fever like Hugh and Martin.

It took a few minutes to absorb this information and realize how much had happened during my recluse days on Fall Stream. Hugh and Martin had been killed, probably in a mining accident, while I was spending my first winter at Fall Stream. Fortunately, my fellow stagecoach passengers were not the talkative sort and I didn't have to make a lot of small talk – although it might have eased my pain and the terrible jostling we were receiving as the driver tried to make up for lost time. He would have an easier time making up his losses than I would mine.

Carlton had arranged free round trip tickets to Boston – courtesy of some trading between the F. J. & G. and the other railroads I would travel. Riding on the new electric division train once I got to Gloversville was a stark contrast to the stagecoach and old steam powered trains I had known in the past. Quiet, fast, and quite comfortable a passenger could even read a newspaper during his journey.

Gloversville, Fonda, and Johnstown had grown considerably in thirteen years, but my perspective from the train showed little improvement in the scenery. Dirt, dust, rough looking buildings and choking smells still filled my senses. Perhaps Boston would have done better to clean up during my absence.

I arrived in Boston the next day around 8:00 a.m. Approaching the outskirts, I could see it had not changed much except having grown a lot bigger. It seemed to have the same problems I noted back in Gloversville only on a larger scale.

I had written to Tracy McGrady after Carlton found about George Murphy's miraculous recovery. There had been no response leaving me to wonder how he was doing. I figured he could have moved, not received the letter in time to respond, or had some misfortune fall on him. I decided to check at the railroad yard where he worked.

Arriving there, I asked a worker if he knew Tracy McGrady. To my mild amazement, the man said, "Sure" he's a supervisor and pointed to a nearby building. A heavy set man was seated behind a desk as I entered the building. He didn't look up as I asked where to find Tracy McGrady. "Who's asking," he said, still not raising his eyes. "David Brown," I softly told him. "Who," responded the man? Stammering a bit, I said "David Brennan is what I meant to say." Quickly looking up at me, he stood and studied me for a moment before saying, "Damn it is you Dave!" Hearing that I knew he was the same Tracy, despite being fifty pounds heavier and nearly bald, who had helped me hop a train many years ago.

Tracy had received my letter just two days ago and had immediately responded. Yes, George Murphy was alive and well, had his own restaurant/bar, and held no bad feelings towards me. Shaking hands, Tracy repeated two or three times how I hadn't aged, looked the same as the night I hid on that late night train to Boston. I thanked him and pretended he looked great too. "Nah Dave, I got fat and lazy – too much time behind a desk for my own good. But, damn it's good to see you." We talked for a half hour or so before Tracy suggested we go over to Murphy's place for lunch, see George, shake hands and let "bygones be bygones." Still unsure about Murphy, I agreed and off we went.

Murphy, too, had gained a great deal of weight and looked considerably older than I remembered him. Tracy didn't have to make introductions, as George also recognized me right away. I got very nervous, almost in a defensive position as Murphy quickly came from behind the bar and approached me. "Son of a gun, it is you Dave. You look good. I'm real glad you've come back." Sticking out his hand, he said, "No hard feelings. Let's have a drink." Tracy, said, "See I told you Dave, George considers the fight with you a learning experience, maybe even turned his life around." Shaking his head in agreement and laughing, George replied, "You bet, but it's a good thing I have a hard noggin!"

We spent a couple hours eating lunch with George. He had never finished college opting instead to open his own business and start a family. He had six kids, a good wife, went to church on Sundays, and took a drink only on special occasions like today. Both George and Tracy seemed awed learning about my life in the Adirondack wilds. They couldn't hear enough about my adventures, people like French Louie, and how I lived pretty much off the land. In their eyes, I seemed to be the lucky one for escaping a "one day is the same as another" existence in the world of job, family, and responsibilities.

George had to get back to work preparing for the evening meal crowd and Tracy also needed to return to his railroad office. We agreed to meet again later that night and finish catching up on old times. Leaving with Tracy, I asked if my cousin Ellen and family still lived at our old address. Grimacing, Tracy told me Ellen and her husband George Johnson had both passed on. The kids, Andrew and Jane, grew up and moved some-place over in Rhode Island.

I found a hotel and stashed my gear. Since it was still early afternoon, I decided to visit some of my old haunts. Until now I had been focused on the reunion with Tracy and George and getting a room. Having settled those matters, my attention switched to surroundings I hadn't seen in more than a decade. Weaving through crowds of people and the street noise unnerved me. Boston was always a busy place but now there were more people of many colors and races and a harsh mixture of sounds as they spoke their native languages. It was as if I was in the middle of a thousand crows chasing one poor owl that had made an unfortunate visit to their neighborhood.

I bought a newspaper and read the headlines. The Chinese were the newest immigrants to the city and were being accused of criminal behavior. To make matters worse, youth gangs were causing severe problems for authorities. Continuing my walk, I encountered large numbers of poor children playing games in the filthy and congested streets while older youth lingered in groups on street corners. Adults walked hurriedly past me, looking every which way, but never making eye contact with anyone. It was easy to see how these conditions provided good breeding grounds for gangs and lawlessness. Plops of horse dung here and there in the streets also made the situation ripe for other critters to breed and make people sick.

Despite the appearance of no one being interested in my presence, I had the feeling of being watched. Not quite the sensation as a man's neck hair rising when an unseen bear was nearby, but still one making me feel apprehensive. It struck me that in terms of a hunter/prey situation in the woods; I might now be getting sized up as prey. I was a stranger here, outnumbered, and armed only with my pocket pistol. I thought it best to keep moving and not present myself as an opportunity for a city hunter.

I met Tracy at six o'clock and we went on over to Murphy's for supper. George joined us and we talked through the meal. Around eight George had to excuse himself to help move tables and chairs around and get ready for some musicians to show up. Soon Tracy and I were watching people dance – something else I hadn't seen in a very long time. Observing the antics of the dancers caused me to think how people and wild animals have a great deal in common – especially in the realm of mating rituals.

Now I had seen lots of Irish jigs where men would compete to see who could dance most cleverly and the longest. Mother used to tell a story about a family member back in Ireland who had danced so hard to please a young lady that he dropped over dead right after being proclaimed the dance champion. And at a German festival I had once seen two men dressed in suspendered shorts, stockings up to their knees, striped long sleeved shirts, and little bow ties. They faced off and danced in odd ways as if they were two ruffed grouse sparring for a hen's affection.

Two men in particular reminded me of the male ruffed grouse. Warming to the music, they slicked back their hair, rolled up shirt sleeves to expose forearms, and thrust out their chests before approaching the ladies and asking for a dance. Out on the dance floor they pranced and gyrated while gazing into their gal's eyes looking for a sign of approval. I kept waiting for them to totally mimic the grouse by drumming on their chests. Falling short of this, they did make detectable grunts and moans as they danced.

Then there was the woodcock tactic used to gain female attention and approval. Back home on Fall Stream I had observed male woodcocks (sometimes called timber doodles) on late April full moon nights. About the size of a robin, with longer legs and a slender six inch beak, the woodcock probes for earthworms in soft earth along streams, ponds and other wet areas. During mating season the male will fly a hundred feet of more into the air, fold its wings, and free fall to the earth, stopping just short of a collision, and fly off to repeat the maneuver. Sure enough, a man on the dance floor was dancing on his toes, rising as high as he could stand, doing a little jump, landing and squatting close to the floor in front of his lady, rising and then repeating the same pattern.

Other birds and insects have courtship rituals too. The blue jay, for example, will tempt a potential mate by offering a seed or other blue jay delicacy. The offer provides opportunity to touch beaks, and perhaps open the door for more intimate body contact. Watching the men buying drinks at Murphy's bar and hand delivering them to a favored lady supported my theory. It was heavily reinforced as I observed sufficiently aroused men and women feeding each other little chunks of cheese Murphy had made available. George had become a good business man knowing people drink more when they eat and dance.

Determined not to let overdrinking, in some strange twist of fate, bring about a repeat of my troubles thirteen years ago, I excused myself a little after ten o'clock. I thanked George for his hospitality, forgiveness regarding our fight, and promised to stop and see him next time I was in Boston. He shook my hand several times, patted me on the back, and made me repeat the promise to visit again. After telling Tracy I would see him tomorrow, I headed for my hotel and a sleepless night.

My greatly anticipated trip to Boston and long list of things to do were going to get abbreviated. A man does not sleep in the woods for more than ten years, with almost total silence, and easily adjust to continuous night time noise. Accustomed only to Spook's breathing/snoring and an occasional owl hoot, the night sounds of Boston were overwhelming. The clopping of horse hooves on brick streets, constant sounds of human voices, occasional shouting, singing of drunks, fire alarms, and what I took for gunshots, prevented any sort of rest coming my way.

Then there was the air – or lack of it. A warm June night at Brown's Pond is one thing. A warm June night in a Boston hotel is close to hell – if hell is a terribly hot place. Back home at Fall Stream, a cool breeze will work its way up around eleven or so at night. Not in Boston, or any other large city I suspected. There was no point in trying to sleep – the noise, heat, and unpleasant smells coming through my hotel window were too much to ignore. Frustrated, I made my way to the hotel roof top.

I had anticipated finding other people unable to sleep on the roof top, but it was all mine. I sat for a long time overlooking a good portion of Boston sensing the flow of life that went on there. I didn't fit, not even years ago when this had been my home. I was born and raised a country boy. That was what made living in New York's Adirondack Mountains possible. Most men need, or can at least tolerate, constant interaction with other human beings. Others need wild places and considerable alone time to function best. Conditioned by my instincts, upbringing, and the hand of fate, I belonged where wild things made their home. They, Spook, my friends Carlton and William P. were my family.

At 5:00 a.m., I went to the hotel room, packed, and headed for the train station. I caught Tracy coming to work at 6:00 a.m., said good bye and was on my way back to Brownsville via Albany, Gloversville, Northville and another damned stagecoach ride. Or, maybe I would walk from Wells to Piseco.

10

ADIRONDACK GUIDE

Spook's barking, and charge to greet me, prevented a complete surprise return to Brownsville. Reaching the knoll above camp, I could see Carlton and Ira standing on the cabin porch. Ira had a look of bewilderment on his face, but Carlton was giggling like a schoolboy. "Didn't like it out there did you," he shouted before I had gotten halfway to the cabin. I said something about him being a smart ass and sat with them on the porch for a long time explaining what happened. In the end, we agreed the trip out was the only way to make a good decision about where to live and how to make a living. Carlton suggested the fight that night in Boston with George Murphy might have been destiny beckoning me to a life in the forest. I wasn't sure why all these things had happened. But, I could now be David Brennan again when the census taker took roll. However, again as fate one day dictated, I would always best be known as that Adirondack guide, Foxey Brown – an eccentric recluse who lived for many years in the wilds along Fall Stream.

Adirondack mountain farming has always been a difficult and risky business. Even in good years most farmers barely got by from harvest to harvest. Such circumstances led to the rapid decline of farming as a way of life. A farming man with family is doomed to endless hard work and a short lifespan. However, there was often little choice since the lumbering and tanning industries had pretty much disappeared around Piseco. Living alone in the woods made my needs different and my workload a little easier. However, weather and natural calamities cause trouble for all who till the earth, plant seeds, and hope.

What started out looking like a bad year turned into a decent growing season. The vly produced ample hay, and the pond, water, for my two cows and an ox farm. The garden supplied vegetables; the stream and pond fish; the forest edge raspberries, blackberries, and blueberries; and the forest itself gave meat for the table. Two cows were suitable for milking and extra milk turned into butter provided something to barter with William P. at the Piseco Hotel or Floyd Abrams at his Sportsman's Home. Each year I sold a cow before winter and bought a new calf come spring – making it necessary to winter over only Ox and one cow. Extra cash came occasionally from shingle production. But thanks to Carlton, guiding became my main, and best, source of dollars. I lived simply, saving money for those storms of life that might come my way again.

My needs from the stores in town remained very small consisting of purchases of salt, a little sugar, some flour, tobacco for my pipe, and reading material – supplemented by Carlton's generous supply of good books. During my infrequent trips I continued to be puzzled by the increasing number of basic food stuffs being sold at the stores. And they were not just for the Sports coming in for the season. Year-round residents were purchasing things that just a few years ago would have been made at home or done without – ready-made shirts, pants, dresses, fancy soaps, patent medicines, butter, candy and toys among other things. The number of fruits and vegetables available in tin cans was most surprising. Considering the dirty conditions I had seen years ago in cities, I wondered about the safety of eating things produced "how and who knows where" and if it was good for people to become dependent on faraway places to produce the basic things of life. I suspected such dependency created weaker rather than stronger people.

It appeared people believed they needed more and more money to buy things instead of doing for themselves. Almost as if, subconsciously, they thought accumulating things might ward off an appointment with death. I thought it foolhardy for a man to gloss over his mortality by collecting an endless array of material things. Opening up a dead man's casket years after burial will show he took nothing anyone buried with him. The Egyptian pharaohs, with all their gold, surely know this – their final resting spots having been disturbed by thieves in search of treasures left behind.

Living close to the land keeps a man mindful of life and death issues. Tending to the needs of plants and animals on a farm provides a constant reminder of the fragileness of life. Too much sun withers things up and too much water rots them out. As my old potato farmer father used to say, "A drought will scare you to death, but a rainy season will ruin you."

A man can try to invent ways of making things from faraway places grow in the mountains, but it takes a lot less time to stick with what is already there. That's one reason I liked making shingles. The trees grew here, I made the shingles, local folks used them, the shingles wore out, and nature provided new materials allowing me to make more shingles – a neat cycle all happening in our community. Making and sharing hand-made things also brought people together and they sometimes became friends. That's how I met Cy Dunham and Bill Gallagher.

Cy (Cyrus) was a farmer near Piseco who served in the Civil War. He was getting up in age when we met, but for someone approaching sixty years, he could still do most everything on his farm. He needed shingles and ordered several squares. To save some expense Cy agreed to come up to Brown's Pond and haul them home. This created an opportunity for him to see Brownsville. He was impressed with my cozy camp in the mountains and especially liked my barn with its upper story for hay and lower earth-sheltered area for the cattle. Being older and more experienced Cy had acquired much knowledge about cattle. He was quick to understand health issues I described and always shared good home remedies. As the years passed we traded many things back and forth. One of my best guns came in a trade, for a cow, with Cy.

I also got to be friends with Cy's son William David. William was a bit younger than me, but we shared a love of reading and words. Like many of us he worked as a guide; but William also served as a store keeper, machinist, Piseco postmaster and, later, forester for the State. The thing I liked most about William was his poetry writing especially one that dealt with his relationship with his Dad. He called it *A Lodging for the Night*. It spoke to me in a sad way because I never really got to know my own father and had been away from home for so many years.

The night was dark, no stars were out
The ground was wet and cold.
I saw a light shine through the night,
From a building that was old.

I staggered up to the front door,
I knocked both long and loud.
Unless I'm sheltered from the night,
The grass will be my shroud.

My knock was heard, I thank the Lord.
The door was opened wide.
And soon a man with feeble steps,
Was standing by my side.
Come in, my lad, I welcome you.
The fire shines warm and bright.
You are welcome to my humble cot,
From a cold and stormy night.

I went inside, by his request,
I stood before the fire.
I thought to meet a stranger here,
But this man was my sire.
My thoughts went to long ago,
When in anger I left his door,
And I made a vow as I tramped the world,
That I'd go back no more.

Now here I was once more again
In the cot where I was born.
And a welcome home greets me tonight,
That I once left in scorn.
Now those of you, who chance to hear,
What I have had to say.
No matter what your home may be,
It's better than to stray.

Bill Gallagher over near Oxbow Lake also got to be a friend I could trust. Bill was a young farmer around age twenty-two trying to raise a family. As I did in the past, Bill worked for the Aird family in their lumber business. Like a lot of young men he had to work two or more jobs to make ends meet and keep his farm going. Bill's energy was contagious and helped an old mountain man like me stay focused. Bill also became a steady outlet for my shingles after he opened his own lumber supply business.

Actually, I was kind of a cross between Cy, Bill Dunham and French Louie. Louie was probably best called a hunter/gatherer who did a little gardening and guiding. His life was very dependent on wild things of forest, field, and stream. To make trapping and hunting successful Louie had to travel scores of miles throughout the West Canada Lakes region often spending many days and nights on the trail. I did all right as a hunter/gatherer and guide, but French Louie was the master outdoorsman. I always enjoyed his infrequent and brief visits. What happened to me in the fall of 1903, made him chuckle.

Early September brought a spell of wet weather and along with it periods of fog. One evening I decided to hunt deer the next morning. A while before daybreak I headed for Witness Rock. First light from my perch promised a clear day and great view of the vly and intersecting game trails that came down from the mountain. Sure enough there was a brilliant sunrise, but around 7:30 it grew overcast and a fog started to roll in reducing visibility to forty yards or so. No deer had come along so I decided to head up the mountain a little ways. I hadn't gone far when I heard movement up ahead and found fresh deer tracks and droppings steaming on the moist forest floor. I noted which direction the deer had headed and decided to go up the mountain perpendicular to their line of travel and then walk briskly parallel to them. Guides call this a "benching" technique that, done right, can get the hunter ahead of the deer where they can be ambushed. The trick is to get the wind in your favor and not make much noise while walking along at steady pace. Deer know the difference between a stalking walk, if they hear it, and when something is just passing through. Often they will hold and let things just walk by and later continue their own business.

Again, I found a good vantage point and stood next to a large tree. An hour later the fog had cut visibility to less than twenty yards. It was now a waste of time trying to hunt deer as they would have to practically be on top you for any shooting to take place. I decided to go home and headed down the mountain confident I would come out close to Witness Rock. I had lived and worked here almost every day for thirteen years. What happened next made me feel as if I had somehow been transported, without my consent, to another world.

Walking down the mountain for fifteen minutes I still hadn't arrived at my rock. What was wrong? I just came down the same hill that I had climbed earlier! Several times I noted a certain tree causing me to think Witness Rock was just ahead. After another fifteen minutes of travel nothing looked familiar and visibility decreased more as the fog's moisture caused leaves on the trees to droop. I knew in this situation it is best to stop, build a fire, get comfortable and wait the fog out. However, I continued to walk – my confidence and stubborn Irish streak shaking off this long-standing woodsman's wisdom. Time passed quickly and I knew it was way past noon from the rumblings in my stomach. I had long since eaten the biscuit taken from my kitchen this morning. It was time to stop, build a fire and wait this thing out.

At first, the damp wood struggled to burn and only added smoke to the fog. After a few minutes the bigger and dryer wood reached kindling temperature and I had a comforting fire. I sat and snacked on a few raw Beechnuts thinking no sensible squirrel would get itself into a situation like this.

After a bit, I started to relax. A feeling of peace and snugness came over me. This predicament had taken me away from all those possessions and obligations normally surrounding me. The land, cabin, animals and tools back at Brownsville, in an unspoken way, ruled my life. They were constant reminders of work that needed to be done and focused my thinking every day. Somehow the fog and warmness of the fire brought back early childhood memories of being held on my mother's lap in her rocking chair – a time when I was safe, carefree, and cared for. Maybe this is the way it felt when I lived in her womb. There were no worries snug in that small and nourishing world. Relaxing and reflecting on these things caused me to doze off.

I awoke and realized it was now late afternoon. With fog still very dense, I thought spending the night here might be necessary. I began to accumulate firewood and rig up a brush and fir bough lean-to next to a large fallen tree. Puddles of water were nearby to provide drink even if food was sparse.

Part way through my shelter construction the fog began to weaken its hold on my shrunken world. In a short while visibility became good for nearly fifty yards. I decided to explore a short distance from my make-shift camp and after traveling no more than fifty yards found, to my amazement, that I had camped almost next to Witness Rock – exactly where I had started from early this morning! At first, my mind would not concede it was the same place, but there was no mistaking my special rock. There in the soft earth were my tracks from the morning! I had walked a large circle, or perhaps several, during that foggy day in the woods.

Later, sitting with Spook by the comfort of my woodstove, I reflected on the day's experience in the fog. I wondered how many men in the past had succumbed to overconfidence and stubbornness in the woods, paying for it with their lives. I had had the good fortune to undergo this humbling experience during a reasonably warm season not during finger numbing winter weather. Indian people would probably say that Wendigo, the forest spirit who took unwary people, just wasn't around that day.

I had also heard that American Indians believe nature has power places that serve as portals or viewing posts into other worlds where a person can gain understanding of life's mysteries. I was uncertain about such things but sensed they were on to something every time I visited Witness Rock. On some days, in late fall, when the wind was just right and no critters were to be heard; I could hear the place breathing – a sound of an easy inhaling and exhaling like listening to a man fast asleep. I knew it most likely was the wind moving through a nearby stand of hemlock and white pine trees. But the persistent rhythm unnerved me as if I was being patiently watched by a force hidden from my eyes. Anyway, I resolved to be better prepared next time lest, whatever the forces may be, I got permanently sent into another world before my time was up.

Getting sent into a new world is exactly what happened to wealthy private park owner Orrando P. Dexter on September 19th. Neither money nor fame can stop a carefully aimed Savage .303 caliber bullet.

Hard feelings between local residents and private estate owners had been escalating ever since the State encouraged wealthy non-resident individuals to create large parks within the Adirondack Park. Seems the State didn't have the money to buy back abandoned timber company lands to protect trees and wildlife, or to hire sufficient numbers of forest rangers, so authorities came to believe rich estate owners could help do the job. Eager to protect their properties and private game preserves people like

William Rockefeller, William Whitney, William West Durant, and Dexter actually fenced off the land to keep local residents and Sport hunters and fisherman out. In addition, they hired armed guards to patrol the preserves to catch and prosecute trespassers. Faced with fewer or no places to hunt, fish and gather firewood tensions and confrontations increased between local residents and the land barons. Some likened the situation to medieval times in Europe when barons controlled the lands and forests. Others pointed out that the situation was one in which the rich had taken over the land just as they had come to monopolize business and industry in the United States.

At first local people welcomed the private estate owners thinking they would be more reasonable to deal with than State officials and regulations forbidding traditional uses of the forests and streams. But soon the private parks became the most despised aspect of the evolving conservation movement. Armed guards, barbed wire, lighted estate compounds, and no trespassing signs became targets for local residents to vent their anger. The anger was first expressed with threats, vandalism, bullet holes in estate structures, suspicious fires, and an occasional rifle blast in the air or bullet bouncing off trees in the general direction of estate guards. Reciprocation came from estate owners by hauling more and more trespassers into court. At first no local jury would side with the estate owners. Blessed with seemingly unlimited monetary resources the estate owners used expensive lawyers, the court system and friends in "high places" to prosecute and convict trespassers.

Being a lawyer by profession, Orrando Dexter was especially astute at acquiring large quantities of land and barring access to local residents. He owned approximately 7,000 acres near the Malone/Santa Clara area including a body of water named "Dexter Lake." For years Dexter had taken people to court for trespass and damages causing neighbors to hate him. He also used his wealth to force out local people whose properties he desired and even fired a long time employee when the man accidently mentioned he was a Democrat and not a Republication. In short, Dexter was an arrogant man of nasty disposition.

Despite having received threats of personal harm, Dexter left his summer home alone in a buggy around noon on September 19th. He was preceded in a separate buggy by his farm manager Azro Giles. Following behind Dexter in another buggy was a hired hand. Somehow, the three

individual buggies got separated by sufficient distance so they were sometimes not in sight of each other. After they had traveled a short distance,
Giles looked back and noticed that Dexter's buggy was empty. Hurrying
back to see what had happened he found Dexter lying dead beside the
road. Dexter had been shot in the back, the bullet entering below his left
shoulder and coming out just over the heart. The bullet continued and
eventually lodged in the horse's back.

Giles testified later that he had never heard a shot. The hired man
did recall hearing shots but neither of them could find any trace of the
murder. Subsequent investigation by authorities turned up only several
footprints made by a "coarse shoe or boot such as is worn a great deal by
workmen, woodsmen and hunters of the Adirondacks."

Despite a $10,000 reward posted by his father and the efforts of
highly paid Pinkerton detectives, in the end Orrando P. Dexter's murderer was never apprehended. Suspicious circumstances and rumors
surrounding the case (Giles hearing no shots) persisted for years. One
thing for certain is that local residents were not forthcoming with good
leads for detectives to follow. While murder is an evil act, so too is shut-
ting off a man's ability to feed his family. As the old saw goes "desperate men do desperate things." I was anxious to hear what Carlton had
to say about the anger people were expressing toward private park
owners.

Hunting season officially opened in October and I guided for a couple
of groups. They got their deer but I don't think they liked my "do for
yourself" style of guiding the hunt. I figured if a man shoots a deer ethics
obligate him to properly dress out the animal and respectfully care for it.
Of course some of them would probably have had a heart attack from the
exercise. I based this opinion on the size of belly many Sports carried and
from the hacking and coughing they suffered after any sort of exertion.
They also wanted to stay up late at night expecting me to play cards or
entertain them with stories. They seemed to have no conception that, in
addition to guiding them, I had animals and a farm to tend each day. I
looked forward to Carlton's arrival the next week.

As became their custom, Carlton and Ira packed in something special
for the mayor of Brownsville. This time it was a new wool shirt, some
socks, and clams from Boston. Yep, clams were now packed in ice and
brought by train to Northville. They had kept them packed in ice all

the way up to Piseco in the stagecoach. They figured an old New England like me would relish a change of diet. It took a while to get my basic cooking utensils on the woodstove to steam the clams, but the wait was worthwhile when we dipped the little critters in melted butter and savored their unique taste. Later I would grind up the shells and add them to my garden soil.

Carlton also bought me a new hat – a fedora just like his. Well, this kicked off a whole bunch of kidding between the three of us. I had often picked on Carlton about his fedora being a "limb catcher" in the woods and that his lack of height didn't matter out here – so the fedora wasn't helping him on two counts. Brownsville wasn't concerned about fashionable styles for men either. And, of course he retaliated by calling my flat cap a poor looking pancake that couldn't shed water when it rained. I countered that it didn't need to because it was 100% wool and simply had to be wrung out when wet and wore again as the wool retained its warmth. Ira's head wear made the joking-around session even more interesting because his choice was a hunter's cap, constructed of pure wool, complete with brim and ear flaps. He tried to end the debate pointing out Indian cold weather headwear consisted of a wolf's head/hide skinned out to provide complete coverage for the wearer's head, ears, and neck. Not to be denied the last word, Carlton observed that was smart on the Indian's part but one could be mistaken for a wolf and get shot! We all laughed, but did understand the woods these days were full of greenhorn hunters who would shoot at most anything. I thanked Carlton for the fedora and promised to wear it when venturing into Piseco or Lake Pleasant.

The mention of greenhorn hunters got us onto the subject of ways they try to combat black flies and mosquitoes in the mountains. Smoke is very effective, but one can't always stand in or near a campfire. Then there is just staying in motion so the critters can't light and bite. Of course, there are also all kinds of lotions available in stores – most of which only have short periods of effectiveness before a man has to rub on another dose. And when the insects are really thick and hungry, they just ignore most anything one can rub on.

The most disturbing thing about black flies is their inclination to hang around a man's eyes. This habit bothered one fisherman new to the mountains so much that he concocted a scheme to keep the flies out of his eyes. Being a heavily bearded man, he theorized that attracting them to his whiskers would be the thing to do. But, what could he use as an attractant? Spying a jug of maple syrup nearby he figured its sweet smell and stickiness would do the trick. Well, it worked – sort of. The trouble was wasps and bees liked the maple syrup too.

William Dunham also had some ideas about dealing with black flies and mosquitos. He came up with a poem about them. He called it *Skeeter Creek*.

I got a little camp, you know
Way down on skeeter creek
There's lots of bugs and bats around
And skeeters mighty thick.
They are buzzing morning, noon and night
And as you go to bed,
You grease yourself with oil-of-tar,
And cover up your head.
And then you lay and wonder
Where the next one you will feel.
For you know by now, the "gang's all here"
And are bound to have a meal.
They are sneaking down the back of your neck,
Crawling up your sleeve
So there's no use of getting mad
For the skeeters will not leave
So up you jump and poke around
And finally build a smoke.
And then you sit and wonder
Which one first is going to croak.
Then you lay down flat upon the ground
Stick your nose down in the boughs
And try to get a little air
And make some solemn vows.
That if this old body is still intact
When the dawn begins to show
That you'll be moving down the trail
And the moving won't be slow.
And when you meet your friends next day
With lies so smooth and sleek,

You will tell them all what fun you had
Down on skeeter creek.

Unlike my other Sports, Carlton and Ira volunteered to help with chores so we could spend more time hunting. I think they liked being around the animals and the smell of hay coming down from the mow. Even the manure shoveling didn't deter them. It was obvious, however, from their attempts to milk the cow that their fingers were unaccustomed to that art. As much milk ended up on the floor as in the pail. Of course, Spook didn't mind their poor aim.

After supper I shared my "lost in the fog" experience with Carlton and Ira. They had heard about the Windego legend and Carlton knew a story concerning a fellow named Gideon Prince who had frozen to death after getting lost on a hunt. The man's mind got so twisted that he was found nearly naked. We all agreed strange things can happen in the forest – especially when a man is alone. I sure could vouch for that after my encounter with Adirondack fog.

The recent Dexter murder and situation with rich people owning and controlling so much Adirondack land was on my mind so I asked Carlton for his thoughts. This was like inviting a bear to discuss the merits of honey. As usual, Carlton was full of news about his hero, President Theodore Roosevelt, "who would do something about the situation and needs of the working man." Carlton had traveled to Syracuse on September 7th when Roosevelt (TR) visited the city and made a public speech called "A Square Deal." TR was taking on big corporations he believed had become too powerful and were unfairly exploiting the common man. Despite his personal wealth and position, Roosevelt considered himself a champion of the people especially those who worked hard with what they had. As would become his regular practice, Carlton shared a quote from TR: "Finally, we must keep ever in mind that a republic such as ours can exist only by virtue of the orderly liberty which comes through the equal domination of the law over all men alike, and through its administration in such resolute and fearless fashion as shall teach all that no man is above it and no man below it." In Carlton's view, this statement captured the essence of the problem facing Roosevelt and others trying to preserve wild things and places. It must be done fairly and without destroying the livelihood of working class residents in those areas.I agreed and pointed out that it is one thing, for example, to limit Sport hunters to a yearly take of two deer during fall hunting season but it's a hardship for a poor mountain man trying to feed his family in March. And relying on the good will of wealthy land barons to serve the needs of mountain people will have no better result than does reliance on corporate philanthropy to help working class city folk.

Carlton continued saying, "If traditional ways of making a living in the mountains must change, then somehow government must help develop decent paying jobs for local residents so forests, fields, streams, and wildlife don't get destroyed. If the Adirondacks are to be a giant playground for wealthy downstate folk, they and public tax dollars must fund such usage without impoverishing year-round residents. The State needs to follow Roosevelt's advice and help Adirondack residents start businesses for which they have a passion and can earn more than just a subsistence wage."

This made a lot of sense to me as I reflected on my guiding business and how it paid me more handsomely than the poor laborer slaving away in a lumber mill. The five dollars a day plus meals I was now receiving let me save a few dollars each month for "a rainy day." But not everyone can be a hunting/fishing guide. "Exactly," said Carlton. "And if people can't find jobs that let them get ahead financially they will resort to drastic measures including thievery, arson, and murder."

Looking to get into the conversation, Ira chuckled and said "I don't mean to make light of a very serious situation but it reminds me of a new story I heard about William P. Courtney." Thinking there couldn't be one unknown to me I asked, "Which one is that?"

Ira began to tell us about the time Courtney had taken his son hunting near Spruce Lake one winter. Moose had been pretty much gone from the mountains for a long time. But, to the hunter's surprise, they came across a small moose apparently trapped in the snow. Moose being rare, Courtney decided it was worth some money if he could get it out alive. He had heard owners of a park in Saratoga would pay twenty-five dollars for such a prize. That is, if the animal was delivered.

Well, the snow was too deep to bring the moose out right then. So, father and son felled some trees and made a corral around the trapped animal. Motivated by notions of making a good sum of money, they alternated staying there the rest of the winter to feed and tend the animal. After a bit, the moose became quite tame and would even allow the Courtneys to lead it around by a rope.

When spring arrived they began the long journey to Saratoga nearly eighty miles away. It was an arduous trip full of difficulties and repetitive explanations to passer-byes as to what they were doing with a live moose. Finally, Saratoga was nearly in sight – they soon would reap the rewards of hard work.

Nearing the park, they were first greeted by several dogs running free. Not having seen a moose before they began to bark and circle Courtney's antlered pet. The poor moose panicked, reared up, broke its leash, and bolted for the woods – dogs on its heels. Courtney and son, of course, ran after the frightened creature and its canine pursuers only to be quickly left far behind. Hours later they located what remained of their prize – a bloody and heavily chewed corpse. Needless to say, it was a long trip back to Piseco Lake for the two entrepreneurs. They say, Courtney still grins sheepishly and shrugs his shoulders when the story comes up.

After we had a good laugh, I said, "Well, son of gun, Ira that is one I've never heard before. Doesn't surprise me though, William P. is like most of us – he'd rather tell funny stories about someone else than on himself." I made a note to have the moose story ready next time Courtney got picking on "Foxey Brown," the fearsome hermit of Fall Stream.

Overall, 1903 had been a very good year for me. David Brennan was now a free man and could use his given name. I had a couple of good friends and several ways to keep "the wolf away from the door." There were still gaps in my life, however, having no family with the exception of older brother James way out in Oregon someplace, I decided to write back to the Benedicta postmaster and ask if he would kindly inquire around the community as to James' whereabouts.

The winter of 1903-04 made life difficult for all Adirondack residents especially January 7, 1904. The day brought record breaking forty-seven below zero temperatures straining the efforts of the best wood stoves. Heavy snow falls compounded the situation trapping people in poorly heated houses. Hundreds of deer died trying to herd together in their wintering grounds – so many that people stacked them up like cordwood the following spring. It was a good bet also that many of the few remaining bears died in poorly chosen dens.

As if punishing me for boasting about my wood stove, old man winter tested my ability to stay warm. Despite keeping the woodstove fire roaring, I was forced to adopt French Louie's scheme of pulling his bed next to the wood stove. Keeping a supply of firewood nearby enabled stoking the fire every couple of hours without getting out of bed. Louie told the story of Frank Baker, the caretaker at Chapin's camp up on Beaver Lake, who wouldn't take the job unless Chapin provided him with six alarm clocks. When asked why he needed so many clocks, Frank said, "I'm a heavy sleeper and by setting each alarm to ring at a different hour I can tend the stove throughout the night." That may sound a bit extreme, but allowing one's food supply to freeze up is serious business in the woods.

The exceedingly low temperatures and deep snow also tested my ability to care for the animals. The barn and exchange of their body heat kept them warm enough to get by and there was ample hay to feed but supplying water became a challenge. Ice on the pond got more than two feet thick and despite my efforts to keep a water hole open, nighttime temperatures quickly erased any gains made the previous day. Even the old trick of piling rotting boards and small logs over the hole failed. It was one thing to carry water to the barn and another to spend hours chopping out ice to obtain the life giving substance. Thank goodness parts of the stream below the pond stayed open even though it was a considerably longer and more difficult carry with pails of water.

Time passes quickly and memories blur when a man tussles alone with the land each day. This may seem odd to those who have never lived as a recluse. The tendency is to think of time "moving like molasses in January" and extreme loneliness being constant companions. The land for me, however, had become my mistress. I say mistress instead of wife because the land makes no promises or legal vows that could stand up in court if a marriage fails. Like a mistress the land remains faithful and loving as long as you pay the price with apt attention and due diligence. And, even then, she is subject to mood changes that can quickly swing from loving embrace to deadly opponent come storm or fire. As for female companionship, I found it safer and much less costly to make an occasional foray into a Piseco or Lake Pleasant hotel for drink and making merry.

Carlton's love of Brownsville spilled over onto his family. Soon it became a tradition for Ada and the girls to make an annual trip into the old hermit's headquarters on Fall Stream. After one disastrous May encounter with black flies they came in late July each year. Knowing I was going to have female company, their annual visit prompted a good cabin cleaning before their arrival – including a good bath for me, and Spook.

Ada, Marion, and Helen enjoyed rowing my old boat around the pond whether they caught fish or not. But, the girls' most favorite place was the waterfalls a short distance downstream. Their joy in escaping the summer heat of Gloversville was written all over their faces as they jumped, splashed, and frolicked in the deep cool pools. Time in the stream also included considerable learning about nature as they searched between the rocks for crayfish, minnows, and that elusive brook trout the girls "almost caught" a hundred times. And, of course, the boy in Carlton couldn't resist joining the children in their adventures. Showing off his best dive, Marion and Helen couldn't resist laughing when he came up sputtering from a little too much Fall Stream water in his throat. Ada and I were contented to serve as referees to the shenanigans taking a dip now and then or soaking our feet.

Often we would take a picnic lunch and linger at the waterfalls until the prospect of darkness prompted a return to camp. We three adults spent the afternoon talking about "everything under the sun" while the children explored the special world of Fall Stream and their secret mountain waterfalls.

Those days with the Banker family will forever be etched into my mind. I had never known a family vacation. Not that there was no love in the Owen and Catherine Brennan family but, serious work to survive each day on the farm inhibited getting to know one another as deeply as Carlton and his family did. Families that play together reveal the softer side of their personalities and bond in ways that work alone can't provide. And as Carlton liked to point out, Theodore Roosevelt said, "So it is in the life of the family, upon which in the last analysis the whole welfare of the nation rests."

While the passage of time can have healing effects, it is also the enemy of all mankind. Experts say we alone, of all the animals, can sense that each day marches us closer to a meeting with our mortality. That may or may not be true as an experience with Spook soon revealed. For some reason, on my fifty-third birthday, it occurred to me I had lived some 19, 345 days, give or take a few for leap years. Thinking if I only had another ten years, my account was down to about 3,650 days. That's not a whole lot of time. Keeping track of your life in terms of days may be a healthy exercise. It can make the mind focus on the value of each day. But, then again, a convenient or short memory can blur the pain of such consciousness. The burden of full consciousness may be what drives many men to the whiskey bottle.

Perhaps my preoccupation with time had been brought on by Spook. He had turned thirteen during late summer and showed symptoms of an aging dog. He had trouble getting up, standing in one spot for a long time, and needed more naps. I understood his behavior because some of the same conditions had begun to visit me. He sought out spots closer to the woodstove on cold nights and was content to stay there unless something really interesting occurred. Animals that live with you have an uncanny sense of what you are about to do. Spook knew if I was merely stepping outside to get some firewood or if I was going to spend extended time at the barn. I could put on the same boots, cap and jacket to pursue either chore and if it was the barn he was ready to go. Anyone who calls animals "dumb" is dumber than dumb.

Dogs, maybe cats too, seem to know when their time has come. For a while Spook needed more attention and looked to be petted more frequently sometimes to the point where he was underfoot. I tried hard to accommodate him by doing things like moving my bed closer to the stove and giving Spook a blanket on the floor next to me. That way, I could reach down to comfort him most anytime. Gradually, however, he lost interest in eating no matter how tasty a chunk of venison or other meat was in his dish. Then he began to have accidents with his bowels leaving a mess on the floor by the door and sometimes leaving a little trail between his bed and the door. I cleaned them up without scolding Spook, but the expression on his face said it all – "I'm not supposed to mess inside." He also began to have a constant worried look on his face and the sparkle that had always graced his eyes was gone. I thought, "Maybe he will just go in his sleep and I won't have to watch his agony." I thought he hoped so too. Even though I knew his passing was not far off it still caught me by surprise.

After breakfast a day or two later I decided to head for the barn. Spook was ready and waiting at the door. He had a renewed energy level that morning and wanted to chase a thrown stick as we had done for many years. I threw one three or four times but noted, despite his willingness to chase, he had a limp and even groaned once or twice when trying to run hard. So, I made him sit beside me on the porch. He couldn't get close enough and kept licking and mouthing my hand when I stopped petting him. I talked to him about getting old and needing to rest more frequently. He gazed at me as if every word was understood and occasionally made a little grunting or whining sound. The sparkle in his eyes was even there once again. Spook's vocalization wasn't painful in tone. It was like someone listening to you and murmuring "uh ha, got you" and shaking their head in agreement. We spent fifteen or twenty minutes doing this before he dozed off. The sun had reached a sufficient level to warm the porch and I left him to begin my chores. An hour later, I saw him look in at me through the open barn door. It would be the last time I ever saw Spook.

Lunch time came and I headed to the cabin noting Spook was not on the porch or anywhere within sight. I gave a shout expecting him to pop up from behind a tree or bush. Two more calls produced no results and I figured he had found one of those tasty morsels that meet a dog's fancy. I spent an hour eating dinner while looking over the gun section in a Sears catalog Carlton had hauled in.

Around 1:00 p.m. I headed outdoors to split some wood. I liked to do something physical outdoors after eating to avoid falling asleep on a full stomach. Nap time was usually around three or four in the afternoon. Spook was still nowhere to be seen and didn't respond to my calls. Sometimes the ring of the axe splitting a block of wood drew him close to the woodpile where he used to wait for me to pick up and toss a piece to fetch. A half face cord of wood later produced no Spook. This unnerved me and I decided to go look for him.

I always had my small Iver Johnson .32 caliber pistol in a pocket. However, my habit also was to always carry Cy Dunham's old shotgun whenever going any distance from the cabin. The best hunting opportunities often materialize when a man is in the woods for other reasons. I searched a quarter mile circle around the cabin until nearly dark with no luck. As darkness fell the cabin felt strangely empty and I realized it was the first night, except for my trip to Boston, in more than thirteen years that Spook had not slept near me. His scent still lingered on the old blanket near my bed. It and the hope he might be on the porch next morning were with me as I tossed and turned before falling asleep.

Sunrise brought the same disappointment to Brownsville as was here at sunset the night before. Spook was still out there somewhere and did not respond to my calls. I grabbed a quick breakfast and completed barn chores before 7:00 determined to find Spook that morning. I made a smaller circle of the cabin than the day before checking every nook and cranny that he might have crawled into. I began to accept the notion that Spook was probably dead, but it was important to find his body and at least bury him near the cabin. The thought of critters feeding on Spook and scattering his bones bothered me. He was my family not just another old dog.

I spent the rest of the morning making expanding circles around the cabin. By noon, I had climbed to the top of Willis Mountain and then descended along the trail leading to Vly Lake. I met a hunter out of the Abrams camp who promised to ask Bill Abrams to watch out for Spook. By midafternoon I had reached the Spruce Lake trail near the backside of Mud Mountain. My efforts had produced no sign of Spook and I went into Piseco to leave word with Bill Courtney and at the Abram's Sportsman House.

Dusk and a great weariness in me were settling in as I walked home. I had traveled more than twenty miles that day hoping to find Spook. Hope is soothing to the emotions, but reason told me my dog was gone. The forest had swallowed Spook up as it does most residents sooner or later. There would be no burial closure for Spook and me. I tried not to think about how his remains would return to the earth.

I was alone again and vowed not to get another dog. They say, "There is a price for everything." That may be truer for love than anything else. The cost of lost love is heartbreak and it exacts a price money can't touch. It's easier in many ways to live as a recluse and remain unattached to anyone or thing.

Cy and William Dunham (Joann Dunham Estes)

*Charlie, Julia (holding rifle) and Audrey Preston. (Courtesy
of Preston family)*

Conservation Commission Game Protector, circa1911. Officers were often brought in from other regions to apprehend persistent and difficult to catch local perpetrators. (C.Yaple)

11

Changing Times

The years following Spook's death disappeared much like water flow in Fall Stream – sometimes rapidly like an early spring snow melt and other times as a trickle during a dry Adirondack summer. I was caught in a cycle of farming and guiding – the seasons dictating my work causing one day, week, and month to roll into another. They say old farmers become similar to their horses or oxen. We get sort of comfortable in the harness or yoke and keep on pulling without thinking much about the labor – just letting it blur the passage of time without really focusing on the business at hand. For me that was good because thinking about the past and long term future wasn't to my liking. It was one reason why I began to dread winter.

Winter allowed more time for reflection when farm work slowed down. Longer days inside by the wood stove meant more napping and the dreaming that came along with it. Even though my troubles with George Murphy had been cleared up years ago, I still had recurring nightmares of being led up to the gallows – waking up with a start just as the hangman reached for the trip lever. It didn't help these dreams when news came about Henry Hartman over near Lake Pleasant murdering the old guide Willard Letson in May of 06. Seems Hartman thought Letson was carrying on with his wife. Then there was Chester Gillete murdering his girlfriend, Grace Brown, at Big Moose Lake later in July of the same year. Both Hartman and Gillette escaped the hangman, however. Letson got a life sentence and Gillete the electric chair. Neither option seemed good to me.

Death came to visit my old friend, William P. Courtney, on June 25, 1907. It wasn't a friendly meeting – he took William P. away and left only a gravestone and our memories. The funeral and burial were over at Lake Pleasant. Thanks to Tim Crowley, I learned about William's passing and got to attend his services. It was the least I could do for someone who had befriended a stranger named Foxey Brown, shaky reputation and all, back in 1890. A friend that looked out for me in ways I sometimes didn't know about.

Why is it that we humans often don't fully appreciate, and recognize, a family member or friend until they pass? William P. Courtney had a long and interesting life characterized mainly by good deeds – with the scales definitely tipped towards the good. He had married, raised a family, and been a guide, blacksmith, innkeeper, postmaster, town board trustee, and town Clerk. William even survived smallpox while working in Bill Lamkey's lumber camp. He used his seventy years as well as his unique and rascal like ways would dictate. My friend and benefactor were gone. Trips into Piseco Lake were noticeably poorer due to his absence.

Carlton was also saddened upon learning of William P.'s death. Reminiscing about Piseco Lake's loss, we shared our own wishes for a final resting place. Carlton, of course, had a Gloversville family history and wished to be buried near kin. For years I had thought it my desire to be buried here at Brownsville near the base of Witness Rock. But the prospect of not living out my days here, made going back home to Benedicta for burial, near my mother and father, seem a better choice.

Despite growing concerns about my ability to remain at Brownsville, there were many good times – especially when Carlton and guests came to visit. Carlton had continued to spread word about my guiding prowess back in Gloversville, so there was no shortage of men wanting to accompany him. It was a bit of an irony that I came to Fall Stream to hide in an obscure place and became a widely known guide.

One spring Carlton wrote saying his brother-in-law, Ira Wooster, no longer had sufficient health to make the trip. Therefore, he was bringing a good fellow named Fred Bagg who also worked for the F.J. & G. railroad. They were due in the first Saturday in May. Carlton had always been enthralled about the large brook trout fisherman supposedly caught on Fall Stream in the old days – legendary fish some two feet long weighing better than four pounds. Carlton had said Fred was also an avid fisherman so I decided to have a little fun with the two of them. I wrote back to Carlton telling him I had discovered a secret lure that really appealed to big trout and I wanted him to use it. The truth was I didn't have any such thing, but I thought the anticipation would get Carlton and Fred all charged up. I would think of some alibi when my secret (whatever it might be) lure didn't work.

As luck had it, Fall Stream flooded between the exchange of letters and Carlton and Fred's arrival. The high water had receded quickly and providence provided just the right situation to have great fun with my guests. Patrolling Fall Stream north of my pond, I discovered several small pools of floodwater off to the side of the main channel. Knowing that fish sometimes got stranded in these landlocked pools, I checked each one out. Usually I would find a few small fish, mainly minnows and a small trout or two. The last pool was no more than two feet deep. However, my intrusion caused a large fish to swim wildly back and forth. There was no trouble guessing its identity; before me was a brook trout easily measuring twenty inches long. It wasn't the legendary trout of Carlton's stories, but it would do. My trap was set. All I had to do was keep the fish alive, and hungry, until my guests arrived.

It didn't take long after Carlton and Fred reached Brownsville for them to bring up the subject of big trout and my secret lure. Playing dumb, I asked Carlton to remind me what I had said about a secret lure. He did so. Playing this to the hilt from the beginning, I paused, pretended to search all my pockets, and finally slid out a small "Carter's Little Liver Pills" tin container telling them the secret lure was inside. And it would, for sure, catch a large brook trout at least twenty inches long. Well, this was quite a boast – more than Carlton could tolerate. "Well Dave, tell us what it is," he exclaimed, almost dancing a little jig. Now the fun was about to begin.

I said, "Can't do that Carlton, the secret lure only works for whoever personally discovers it. French Louie learned about it from an old Indian who warned that the lure loses its power if it is merely given to someone else." I went on to swear the secret lure had worked for me once I discovered its power.

Well, Carlton and Fred were educated men and not easily persuaded about the "power of secret lures." It made me, so to speak, play another card. "Well, you know they laughed at old Floyd F. Lobb and his lake trout spoon at first. And, after a while almost every fisherman had to have one in his tackle box." This caused my friends to pause. "OK, how do we discover your secret lure," Carlton snickered? I replied that there were two ways. One, they could go out and try different lures until something worked on a big trout. Or, if they could correctly guess what I had in the tin, the lure's power would be theirs. And so, the game began.

Being pretty savvy fishermen, Carlton and Fred guessed all the typical brook trout baits – earth worms, red worms, insect larva, may flies, cadis flies, stone flies, minnows, crickets, frogs, grasshoppers, lures like Lobb's spoon... to all of which I said no. Pausing for a bit while we ate, the game continued up to bedtime. Stretching their imaginations about big trout the list shifted to non-traditional foods ranging from mice to small birds.

Now the secret of pulling off a good joke is to keep the intended victims interested. Sensing Carlton and Fred might be tiring of my game; I added another component. "Men, there is one more way to discover the power of my secret lure. That is, to actually see someone use it. Tomorrow, I'll do just that for you." Determined to have the last word, Carlton said, "Darn you Foxey Brown, if you can guarantee catching a twenty inch trout on the first cast, I'll eat my fedora." I asked if he would like salt and pepper. Smirking, Carlton replied he would eat it without seasoning. Fred chimed in saying he was a witness to the bet.

I think we all went to bed anticipating tomorrow's brook trout outing. Carlton had never called me Foxey before, so I knew he had "bit" on my story. And, of course, both he and Fred couldn't wait to call my bluff.

We began walking along Fall Stream above my pond. Putting on my best poker face I played the game to the hilt. Stopping every forty yards or so, I got down onto one knee and crept up on a pool. Of course, my guests had to do the same knowing brook trout in a stream had to be stalked as any little shadow on the water sent the fish seeking safety under a rock. Looking the pool over, I would shake my head and tell Carlton and Fred this wasn't the right pool today – the big one had moved upstream.

After inspecting several pools in the same fashion, we arrived farther upstream closer to my imprisoned trout. Looking over the stream, I told my buddies that sometimes really big brookies hide in strange places and we would have to bushwhack a little ways and their silence would be very important. As we crept along towards the flood pool, I thought it unfortunate no camera was capturing these three fishermen, all in a row, crawling through the Adirondack bush. Hearing Carlton and Fred mumble something about, "What the heck is he up to," I held back a giggle seeing our destination was just ahead.

Bringing our little safari to a halt, I motioned Carlton and Fred to come along beside me. Putting a finger to my lips to indicate the need for silence, I slowly parted the remaining weeds between the small pool and us. Seeing what lay ahead, I think both men thought I had gone completely crazy.

Motioning for Carlton to hold out his hand, I pulled the Carter's Liver Pill tin from my pocket and removed its top. Watching Carlton's face carefully, I poured its contents into his hand. He looked, incredulously, at the single fishing hook and snippet of red cloth. At this point, I suspected my friends were catching on to Foxey Brown's shenanigans. Fred patted Carlton on the back whispering "Good luck." Shaking his head and laughing, Carlton tied the "secret lure" to the fishing line and cast it over the weeds and into the pool.

It didn't take but a second or two for that very hungry fish to strike. After a two or three minute struggle we were admiring a weary but beautiful twenty-one inch brook trout. Carlton handed me his fedora saying, "Dave, I should have known an old poker player like you would have covered his bet. Cut that hat up into small pieces, will you? And, I will take the salt and pepper!" Handing me his fishing pole, Carlton turned with the gasping trout in hand, marched to Fall Stream, and gently released it. "There," he said in a joking fashion, "I hope it ends up in Brown's Pond and you choke if you ever catch and eat it! And, don't blame me when folks call you Foxey Brown!" Somehow, I sensed that was not the end of my little prank on Carlton.

Carlton visited two more times during the following months. Each time I warily waited for him to get revenge for my big trout escapade. He acted if nothing had ever happened, sometimes almost killing me with politeness. Like an old wolf Carlton was setting up his prey and before the next fall hunting season came around he struck.

Carlton loved guns and could afford the newest models available. I had already benefited when he "handed down" an older model Savage lever action rifle. This time he brought in a new Ithaca double barrel, twelve-gauge shotgun. It was a beauty with gold plated trigger guard and nameplate in the stock. He and Fred also brought in some clay targets, a hand held throwing device and a good supply of ammunition. Soon we were trying the new Ithaca out as the clay targets soared over the pond.

Carlton showed us how well the Ithaca performed by promptly breaking five targets. Fred was next and nicely broke four of the five targets thrown for him. Carlton handed the gun and two shotgun shells to me – showing no facial expressions that something might be up. I innocently accepted the gun, loaded it and called for the first target. My shot broke it nicely into a cloud of dust. Congratulating me, Carlton tossed the next target when I called for it – "click" went the gun as it misfired. "Must be a bad cartridge," said Carlton handing me two replacements.

I loaded and called for the next target. This time the gun produced a weak "pop" as it fired. Somehow the target broke in half as if hit by a single pellet. Shaking his head, Carlton said, "Darn another bad cartridge. Here take these two from a new box." Carlton, the wolf, was about to slaughter Foxey, the totally unsuspecting lamb. The stage was set, even the wind cooperated with Carlton as a slight breeze came across the pond towards us.

Accepting and loading the two new cartridges, I called for the target and quickly lined it up in the gun sights. "Poof," the Ithaca went upon firing and the target was lost in a cloud of dust – white dust that gently floated back from the gun muzzle slowly decorating me with flour. Carlton and Fred had carefully rehearsed filling the shotgun shell with flour because, as I turned, Fred was ready with camera to snap my picture. "Why Dave" said Carlton. "You look like one of those Japanese lady dancers with all that makeup. This picture will make some interesting advertising for your guiding business, you know, now you offer theater and dancing back at Brown's Pond."

I had been had! Wiping my face left a good coating of flour on my hand. Looking at Carlton and Fred enjoying convulsive laughter, I said, "Good one guys, guess I need to wash up in the pond." Pausing, I bent over into a runner's stance and said, "Guess who's going to join me" as I charged toward Carlton. Like many small men, Carlton was very quick on his feet and easily avoided my grasp. I made a lunge at Fred and soon three grown men were playing tag like schoolboys yelling and screaming while running here and there after each other. After several attempts, I managed to get Carlton trapped at the edge of the pond. Harnessing all of my energy, I leaped trying to tackle him. Agile as a mountain goat, Carlton ducked gracefully but slipped in the pond shore mud causing me to soar over him.

I did my best not to land face down in the pond managing to turn over, tuck my legs and end up in a sitting position a foot from shore. With that the chase ended as the three of us sat pointing at one another and laughing just like the kids we were just then. With all the dignity I could muster, I stood and began to wash some of the mud and flour off my face. Not one to let one last dig slip away, Carlton picked up my soaked cap, wrung it out ever so gently and handed it to me asking if I might want to summon up that big trout to help me clean up. I could stand no more! The chase was on again.

Even Fred thought Carlton had gone too far and he blocked his friend's escape allowing me to finally get my hands on my fleet-footed foe. Fred could see the pond was going to be Carlton's destination, and in the fun of it all, helped lift and throw Carlton a good six feet out into the pond. He made a nice splash. Not wanting Fred to be left out of a Brown's Pond baptism, I pushed him in and waded out splashing both of them relentlessly.

As our wet clothing dried near the woodstove that night, we retold the flour shotgun shell/pond story over and over again – each speaker telling his own version. It was one of the most joyful times in my life. The laughter had been so intense my chest actually got sore causing me to feel muscles not used in normal work around the farm. I wish that night could have been captured and put into a bottle to help remedy sadder times that were ahead.

Carlton, Fred, and I joked even after going to bed. When they dozed off, my mind kept replaying the day's events. I chuckled to myself about the flour drifting from the end of that Ithaca double barrel and the grin Carlton had on his face when wringing out my cap. Slowly, my chuckles turned to tears trickling out the sides of my eyes and down my face. Puzzled by this emotion taking over, I realized they were tears of joy. Hidden feelings that had been put far way, under lock and key, were unleashed. I had found a family who cared about me and me about them. Albeit, they were not an everyday, always present family. But, Carlton, Ada, Helen, Marion and friends like Fred were sharing the personal sides of my life. They would be there for me in time of need; and, I would now share in their joys, troubles, and sorrows. It was a good but scary feeling. The scary part was that I remembered, from past experience, there is a price for caring about someone other than you. The times with Carlton and family were changing me from a gruff mountain man who preferred to be alone most of the time to a more kindly uncle who had a great place to visit in the woods. Carlton told me I was mellowing in my old age.

The times were also changing old ways of life for everyone in the mountains – actually across the whole nation and President Roosevelt was leading the way. In 1908, he organized the first national conference of state governors in Washington, D.C. The whole theme of the conference was "conservation" – a word no one had used just a few years earlier. TR opened the conference by telling the governors conservation was the "Weightiest problem now before the Nation" and that "the natural resources of our Country are in danger of exhaustion" if we let exploitation of them continue. To underscore the seriousness of the conference, Roosevelt created a National Conservation Commission to inventory the nation's resources and thirty-eight governors returned home to establish their own state conservation commissions. Of course, since TR had already been governor of New York our conservation efforts were well underway.

There was good reason to be concerned about natural resources in New York. The subject became a "hot issue" later that summer and fall when forest fires broke out once more in the Adirondacks. Caused again, mainly by railroad locomotives, more than 368,000 acres of the forests were consumed by fire. Brownsville and the Piseco Lake area were spared actual fires but Saranac Lake village was nearly destroyed and communities just north of New York City received clouds of smoke as thick as fog. The days were tolerable at Brownsville, but sleeping at night necessitated lying on the bottom of my boat anchored in the middle of the pond.

1908 was also the same year "Sports" and other visitors began driving automobiles into the mountains as far as Blue Mountain Lake. Gasoline powered Caterpillar tractors worked the woods and boats with motors began appearing on the lakes. A paved macadam road all the way from Lake Pleasant to Speculator was constructed and a few years later (1912) an airplane flew into Raquette Lake. Carlton said Brown's Pond was too small for one to land here. Thank goodness! Chasing away unwanted foot travelers was bad enough without worrying about them descending from the sky. I didn't like the thought of people flying over and peeking into my business either.

The upshot of automobiles and airplanes coming to the mountains was not only something one could see. It could also be felt. The ease and speed of getting from downstate cities was changing both our mountain community and the visitor's experience. Instead of struggling by stagecoach and on foot for many hours, visitors could now arrive in hours instead of days. This meant more people, more demands for services and loss of adventure in getting to and staying at one's forest/lake destination. If a hunter or fisherman didn't penetrate the deepest reaches of the West Canada Lakes, the possibility of interruption by sounds of an airplane, motorboat, or doodlebug vehicle was quite likely. Winter was also no longer a barrier to motorized vehicles as snowmobiles became increasingly popular. I was witnessing the end of a special time in Adirondack history. Like the transition from bows and arrows to guns, harsher sounds now interrupted ages old forest symphonies.

Game laws and allowed uses of the forest were changing almost as fast as the new mechanical inventions. By 1908, licenses were required of all hunters and every county had a game protector or two. Bear populations were very low. No mountain lions or wolves roamed our woods; trout populations were dwindling despite stocking endeavors of the Conservation Commission; and efforts to reintroduce elk and moose had been abandoned. Thankfully, for guides, whitetail numbers were still very good and hunters could take a deer of either sex. However, the days of scaring off conservation officers were over as some of the less ethical guides learned the hard way. Convictions for poaching and taking more deer than bag limits allowed were more and more common as the Conservation Commission added new officers and learned not to try offenders in local courts. The increasing presence of Conservation officers and the Adirondack Guides Association support of State conservation regulations made many guides, members and non-members, reconsider how they conducted their business. It also made sense to try and work with local conservation officers instead of always trying to "stay one step ahead of them." Following that new philosophy is how I got to know Charlie Preston.

Charlie had visited my place a couple of times before 1914. On both instances I mistook him for some young Sport trying to sneak fish out of my pond. So, he got the standard welcome – two rifle shots from my

Winchester 351 auto loader and accompanying message, "Get out of here or I'll send you lead for sinkers." On the first visit he disappeared rather quickly. The second time he stood behind a tree and called out to hold fire saying he had no official business with me and was just checking for Sports fishing Fall Stream without a license. Appreciating his efforts to keep Sports away from Brownsville, I invited him up to the porch for a chat.

Charlie was a good-looking twenty-three year old man. He had recently married Julia Burton who became one of the first female licensed guides and quickly established a reputation for being one of the best in the business. Julia carried a 30-30 Winchester rifle and was darn good at using it when her Sports weren't successful getting a deer on their own. Word was that she was well worth her $10 a day fee. She could cook as well as anyone over an open fire and tell great stories to boot. In the end, Julia hunted and guided in these mountains for nearly fifty years – longer than any of the men then listed as guides.

Charlie, being a laid back sort of guy, didn't get too excited over things and understood the needs of folks living back in these woods. He didn't really like his conservation officer job and had only taken it because good paying work was difficult to find in the Adirondacks. Being a conservation officer still put him at odds with friends and neighbors who were accustomed to taking what they needed from the forest. Arresting a local person for shooting a deer out of season or cutting firewood on state land made living in the community difficult. Some officers were threatened and actually shot at when patrolling the woods and streams. They also had to work strange hours, sometimes deep in the forest, to catch poachers who made their forays at three or four o'clock in the morning.

I could tell Charlie had no need to watch every little thing I did at Brownsville. Besides, my farming efforts contributed to healthy deer populations by giving them some open grazing areas. And, I sure as heck didn't allow over hunting or fishing of any sort near my place because my livelihood depended on it. In a sense, both Charlie and I were conservation officers. He arrested law breakers and I shot at them – at least in their general direction.

Conservation officers enforcing hunting and fishing regulations caused me no great problems. However, they were also required to enforce new regulations related to squatters living on Forest Preserve lands. And,

I was a squatter for sure having no paperwork of any sort to claim owner-ship of Brownsville. Troubles for people like me began in 1910 when the Forest, Fish & Game Commission ordered camps torn down and squatters ejected. Fortunately, there were conflicting opinions about this among prominent politicians so the order was not carried out. However, as Carl-ton said, "The clock is ticking unless a case can be made to exempt a squatter from being removed." He talked to his representatives back in Gloversville about people like me who could help the State immensely by watching for, and helping to put out, forest fires. Carlton thought this might help my situation since a series of dry summers had made forest fires common consuming thousands of acres of forest most every year. The State had responded by constructing a network of fire towers on moun-taintops staffing them with rangers like Bill Dunham. The fire towers helped but the fires continued.

Another factor the State had to consider was the threat that some squatters might torch the forest if forced to abandon their homes. Carl-ton didn't think the State, however, would back down from threats. On the other hand, he pointed out that the Conservation Commission had a good deal of flexibility in where and how fast it enforced the eviction of squatters, especially squatters like me who were also guides. He fig-ured the Commission was smart enough to use guides to its advantage. Since it was in a guide's best long term interest to protect wildlife and fish from being overharvested in the areas where he worked, the Com-mission had unofficial, and unpaid, game wardens all over the Adiron-dacks. Carlton said this was one reason the Commission was cozy with the Adirondack Guides Association knowing it would, to some extent, police the actions of its members. I suggested to Carlton that I had been one of those unofficial game wardens going back to when I first moved into Fall Stream. The crazy recluse Foxey Brown up on Fall Stream had been monitoring who and how many hunted and fished around Browns-ville since 1890. We decided it wouldn't hurt to re-establish that repu-tation with a few well-placed rifle shots and shouts of "Get out of here or I'll send you lead for sinkers" the next time some uninvited Sports showed up!

To my good fortune, talk, and little action, seemed to characterize the squatter issue during the next four years as the State worked to strengthen its case in areas where there were significant numbers of squatters.

However, I got somewhat nervous when in 1915, the State evicted eighty-one year old guide Daniel Wadsworth over in the Town of Benson. I knew then that Carlton was right about the clock ticking. Unfortunately, it was ticking, in a different way, for him also.

Most folks live day to day focused on the business of making a living and issues in their immediate community leaving little time to reflect on bigger events. My way of life allowed time to read and think on things beyond Brownsville, Piseco, Hamilton County, the Adirondacks, and New York State. The concepts of conservation and preservation of wild places had become a national issue. A valley far across the nation in California was causing the controversy. The place in question was called Hetch Hetchy and lay in the Tuolumne River valley – part of Yosemite National Park. Being in the park it was, by statute, supposed to be kept forever wild. However, the nearby city of San Francisco had, since 1890, politicked to dam Hetch Hetchy canyon and create a much needed water reservoir. They were unsuccessful until an earthquake, in 1906, devastated the city. Sympathetic to the city's plight, the Department of Interior approved San Francisco's application to dam Hetch Hetchy. This ignited an intense public campaign pitting those wishing to preserve (The Preservationists) Hetch Hetchy against those seeking utilization (The Utilitarians or Conservationists) of the water resources. Poor President Roosevelt was caught between loves for both sides. Compounding TR's situation was his friendship with both leaders of the opposing sides. John Muir (TR's camping buddy) and the Sierra Club were championing the preservationist faction while Roosevelt's own head (Gifford Pinchot) of the U.S. Forest Service strongly supported using Hetch Hetchy as a dam site. Fortunately, or unfortunately, depending on one's view of Roosevelt, he lost the 1908 election and did not have to make a decision on the Hetch Hetchy situation.

Carlton and I followed these events closely during a five-year national battle heavily covered in newspapers and journals. I had mixed thoughts about the situation. One side of me favored protecting a pristine place like Hetch Hetchy, just as I would Fall Stream from development. On the other hand, the benefits of a dam for San Francisco or the one that created Brown's Pond were evident. If I cheered for saving Hetch Hetchy how could I not agree with the Adirondack Preserve's intent to remove squatters from within its interior? To support preservation efforts meant supporting my removal and the destruction of Brownsville – it would be similar to cheering at your own funeral. Someone said about baseball games, "You win some, you lose some, and some get rained out." Hetch Hetchy got dammed in 1923 and Brownsville would eventually return to the wild without me around.

Carlton came into Fall Stream on October 16, 1912 full of news about Theodore Roosevelt's latest adventure. As Carlton told it, TR had been in Milwaukee, Wisconsin to make a campaign speech when a crazy man in the crowd somehow managed to shoot him. The bullet hit TR squarely in the right breast and would have made a fatal wound except for three things: a folded copy of his speech and a steel spectacle case in the breast pocket of his coat and the massive muscle mass in his chest. The bullet hit the folded speech and spectacle case and slowed before entering his chest causing only a superficial wound. The surgeon who operated on TR called him "a physical marvel" and said he was one of the "most powerful men" he had ever seen on an operating table. Instead of penetrating into Roosevelt's lung the bullet lodged in his chest muscle and was later easily retrieved. At the time of the shooting Roosevelt paused, put a handkerchief over his wound, and demanded to see the assassin the crowd had apprehended. When the trembling assailant was brought forward, TR looked him over and said, "The poor creature... it is a natural thing that weak and vicious minds should be inflamed to acts of violence when the press prints every negative comment uttered by my political opponents." Always the hero type, Roosevelt refused immediate medical treatment, changed his shirt and went on with the planned speech saying, "I will make this speech or die. It is one thing or the other."

Listening to him speak about Roosevelt's behavior reinforced my understanding of Carlton Banker, the man. Similar to Roosevelt, Carlton was small and frail as a young man. Like many young men short on stature and muscle, they were blessed with great amounts of energy and used it and determination to build themselves up through rigorous exercise. Both had sought out the company of rugged working men and tested themselves in wild places and with wild animals. Unlike most men, however, Carlton and TR also worked hard to develop their minds through keen observation of the world and reading on a wide range of topics with passion. I sometimes thought it would be wonderful if Carlton could actually meet President Roosevelt. But, then it occurred to me their high energy levels and similar personalities might hinder them from really getting along. Often times it is best to admire a thing of beauty from a distance. Getting up close and personal can reveal blemishes otherwise unnoticeable. Many a lover has made that discovery the morning after an intoxicated affair from the evening before. I submit that last statement based on personal experience.

Later that fall Carlton and I began making plans for my retirement as "Mayor" of Brownsville. I had long been nervous about keeping my meager life savings hidden away in the barn. Besides, a few hundred dollars wouldn't take me far into retirement someplace else. Carlton suggested opening a bank account in Gloversville. In addition to earning some interest, he would look out for investments that could help my funds grow quickly. He had excellent connections as a railroad superintendent and had done very well investing for himself over the years. Carlton also believed he could find some part-time work for me with his branch of the F.J. &G. (Fulton, Johnstown, and Gloversville) railroad. The plan was to look for a place in the country near Northville where I could continue to fish and hunt, maybe even do some guiding. Reluctantly, I had to agree with the wisdom of such plans and took solace in the belief such a life change was still a few years off.

Carlton politely mentioned, however, that work as a representative of the F.J. &G. would require more of a refined look than that of an old, rough and tumble Adirondack Mountain guide. His comment caught me off guard, as my appearance was not something I thought about very often. I said, "What's the matter? Does your cook's appearance at Brownsville ruin your appetite?" Realizing that was a pretty defensive statement and Carlton was only trying to help I fumbled for a mirror and took a look at myself. He was right; I still did look a little wild and dangerous.

The next Saturday we went into the Piseco Hotel where a traveling photographer was in town. A bath, shave, and haircut along with a new suit, and one of Carlton's beloved fedoras, made me almost unrecognizable from old Foxey Brown the mountain man of Fall Stream.

I still wasn't sure how I would fare with lots of other people around all the time. Both Carlton and Fred understood my fears. We agreed to continue putting away money for my retirement and revisit the subject of moving again next year.

My twenty-fourth year (1914) in Brownsville was pleasant despite troubling times in the outside world. A World War had broken out in Europe and it appeared the USA was going to get pulled into the fighting. This was frightening because the news publications regularly reported on the carnage and deaths of tens of thousands of people. Roosevelt was no longer president and our armed forces were at a low point of preparedness. Young men like Charlie Preston were almost certain to be drafted.

Disturbing also was the rate at which the wild look of our mountains was disappearing. Dams were being built seemingly everywhere. Hinckley Dam on West Canada Creek made one of French Louie's favorite places (Jock's Lake) disappear under a much larger body of water. Other dams were built or reinforced at Eagle Falls, Taylorville, Hudson Falls, Brows Falls, and Butler Pond. West Canada Creek was even being diverted at Prospect Falls for electric power.

On the other hand, there was another engineer building dams in the mountains – one that had been long absent and didn't need a permit from the State. Beaver were non-existent when I moved to the Adirondacks in 1889. They had all been trapped out earlier in the century and only a few scattered colonies lived in New York State. Around 1904, the State decided to reintroduce the animals and released some breeding pairs in a few locations. Given complete protection from hunting, trapping, or disturbing them in any way, the beaver population began to increase rapidly – to the point that by 1911 the State Conservation Commission was providing woven wire to private landowners for the purpose of protecting trees from hungry beaver. Some estimates claimed there were nearly 15,000 animals in the Adirondacks by the end of 1914. Beaver became such a nuisance in one place that a man named William Barret sued the state for damages. Barret won the first round of court hearings, but eventually the State got its way to preserve wild animals without liability for any damages they caused. I had no problem with beaver at my end of Fall Stream, but nearer to Piseco the busy critters, like we human dam builders, were changing the looks of things. Places where the stream once had fast moving water and rapids now held placid pools. On the other hand, there were now more places for ducks and geese to nest.

Troubling news arrived early in 1915. In March, came a report about French Louie's death. Feeling weak, he had come out the woods to the

Brooks Hotel towards the end of February. Folks noticed his pack was considerably smaller than normal. He had only a few furs and some personal items. Strangely, however, he also had a mess of fish for Mrs. Brooks. Gratefully accepting the trout Mrs. Brooks offered to cook them up. But, Louie declined anything to eat and joined the men at the bar. He was soon "feeling good" and shouting his favorite phrase, "Ba da holy feesh. Louie, da boy!" Later that night he suddenly got sick and needed a doctor. Louie died the next day, Sunday, February 28th. As happens often in bars, there was much speculation on what had killed Louie. Pants Lawrence and the other old timers laid Louie's sickness to eating too much raw venison over the years causing his kidneys to fail.

Folks up in Speculator gave Louie a grand funeral. School was closed for the day and services were held at a packed Methodist Church. The many children who loved Louie sat in front row pews and, "before the casket was closed, they filed slowly past it and each laid a spray of fragrant green balsam on Louie's body. In the procession to the cemetery, about a third of a mile away, the children held branches of balsam in front of themselves as they walked." Louie had made his last earthly journey. I regretted living so far from town and current news. If I had known, nothing would have kept me from attending his funeral. I vowed to visit his grave in the spring and pay a last thanks to my friend and mentor. His passing, like mine when I left Fall Stream, would mark the end of an era where men lived year round in the forest and made their living directly from its bounties.

There most likely would never be another French Louie in these mountains. Death not only took a very unique man but a great deal of knowledge that might be permanently lost. I remembered being with Louie in the woods one day hunting deer. It was a very still day with no noticeable wind and we were discussing which way to travel so the deer wouldn't scent us. I blew my breath, tossed some grass in the air and thought maybe it was coming out of the east. Louie said it was coming out of the west. He said, "See de bird in de tree, he sit and lok to de wes, mak him fly goot wen he leave." Of course, he was right – birds take off into the wind. Men that observant of nature will always be few and far between.

While Louie's departure was a loss in many ways, it caused no shortage of men willing to follow in his footsteps. Each year there seemed to be more and more guides. The local census taker didn't miss me in 1915 and as we chatted I learned there were fifteen of us in the Arietta area alone. They included people I knew like Bill and Dimick Abrams, George Courtney, Tim Crowley, Tru Lawrence, Charlie Preston, and his wife Julia. And, since there was also no shortage of Sports, most guides got along with each other. I did, however, begin to hear rumors that some of the guides didn't like me. I was pretty free about expressing my opinions and there were men jealous about my relationship with Carlton and the special pay and favors he brought into Brownsville.

More dramatic events occurred later in the summer. Legislators, sympathetic to squatters, were unsuccessful in passing regulations to provide exemptions. The head of the Conservation Commission once again ordered the removal of squatters. This time 700 Forest Preserve sites were targeted and many people up near Raquette Lake were actually removed and their buildings torn down. Carlton said, "It was the first wave of removals." For now, my area didn't seem to be a target but it was pretty certain the state would "get around to me." My location being so far inside the Forest Preserve boundary made it unlikely an exemption could be obtained. He believed "we had a year or two but that would be about it." Neither of us at that time understood how tragically prophetic his words would become.

That fall bestowed a bumper crop hunting season upon us. The deer were fat and heavily antlered. The men I guided took several large bucks and female deer. The talk of the woods, however, was about a 268 pound, thirteen-point whitetail taken by Stephen Harris over near Lake George. Knowing deer of that stature were around kept hunters enthused until the end of season.

The season had nearly ended, Carlton and friends had returned to Gloversville, and I had no other guiding parties booked. It occurred to me that I had not taken a deer of my own. There was a good deal of canned venison stored away, but one more animal would tide me over the winter nicely.

I had noticed an unusually large buck rub north of the vly and no one had taken a deer from that area. The rub was on a five inch maple sapling and extended from four inches off the ground upwards a distance of four feet – definitely not the work of a small antlered deer. I made my way into the rub area before dawn the next day. Four deer immediately bolted out to my right and a single deer loped off to the left. The semi-darkness prevented seeing anything other than their white tails. The signs of a wasted morning hunt were all over this venture – but when deer hunting "you just never know."

I didn't linger at the rub and continued at a steady pace about fifty yards into the forest taking a stand behind three trees – two ashes and a beech, growing in a clump. A swampy area, with some standing water, was at my back and I could still almost see the rub tree. The wind was gently blowing from the rub toward me. My choice of a ground stand felt good with the trees concealing my presence and providing protection from the wind. I felt snug in my little hidden part of the forest floor. My privacy, however, was soon to be interrupted.

First, several squirrels began doing what squirrels do on a cool fall morning – chatter constantly, chase each other and scurry up, down, and around trees. Soon the booming noise of beating wings upstaged their antics as first one, two, then three and finally five ruffed grouse came down out of a hemlock tree. Some strutted, others scratched the ground, and one hopped up on a log, not five feet behind me. It fluffed up its feathers and took on the oddest shape I had ever seen. The bird began to resemble a round ball. Only the top of its head and eyes were visible as it drifted off to sleep. One by one the other grouse melted away into the forest. The squirrels took a break leaving the grouse and me to watch for deer – although I didn't think my sleepy bird friend would let its slumber be interrupted by much of anything.

An hour passed, my grouse companion woke from its nap, and walked away in search of its companions. I was finally alone to watch for my winter meat supply to come along. Another half hour went by. Needing to stretch, I cautiously and slowly crept forty yards away, looked things over and returned to my stand. I had now spent close to three hours in this spot and felt hungry. Checking carefully for any signs of movement out front in my shooting zone, I reached into my pocket for a biscuit. Looking again for deer, I took a bite of the heavily buttered treat, relishing its sweet and salty taste. Having spent only fifteen or twenty seconds getting the biscuit in my mouth, I looked up.

As if somehow materializing from nowhere, a large, heavily antlered deer was moving directly parallel to me not twenty yards away. There I was, a half biscuit in one hand and my rifle propped against a tree.

Fortunately the wind was still in my favor and the three trees provided enough cover so I could put the biscuit down and lift my rifle. The large buck was now so close that the trees blocked both him and me from seeing each other. I couldn't move and was forced to wait, and hope, he would continue in the same direction of travel. After what seemed like many minutes, he came out from behind a tree and slowly moved away. Lifting my rifle, ever so cautiously, I got the area just behind his front shoulder in my sights and prepared to pull the trigger. Time stood still, as this gray-muzzled senior citizen of the forest stopped. He appeared to be looking directly at me but gave no indication actually seeing me. Unsure of what was happening between us, I hesitated momentarily before succumbing to hunting instinct and pulling the trigger.

Somehow, the muzzle blast didn't distort my sight picture and I had a sense of seeing the bullet make initial impact on its intended target. There was a slight pause before the old deer leaped and then bounded away up a slight incline toward a thick stand of trees. I was left with a glimpse of its rear disappearing out of view. Had I missed? The next part of our encounter will forever be in my mind.

The buck turned after disappearing into the forest. Suddenly, it came back into view running and bounding, at full speed, directly towards me. It gave no sign of being wounded but appeared intently focused on coming at me. I remember no thought of shooting again only having a fleeting notion of maybe having to hide behind my three trees. Like the deer, I was totally focused on his movement. In an instant he was within twenty yards of me. He leaped, fully airborne, over a large log. I was hypnotized by the majesty of it all – his head held high, large spread of antlers, graceful leaping ability, muscled body, all picture like before me. I imagined him saying, "See me in my full life form, and always remember me this way – for like you are now, I was once a prince of this forest."

He fell into a depression behind a log just out of my sight. An eerie silence prevailed in the forest as if the audience couldn't decide to boo or applaud what had just happened. The whole episode had occurred in less than a minute even though my sense of time would have counted it as much longer. The buck had died quickly after being shot and making one last run about his kingdom.

At this point in my life, I had killed more than a hundred deer. I had prided myself remembering every one of them believing that a life taken ought to be worth remembering. But there had never been one like this animal. Never had a wounded deer run away and come back in such a fashion. It was as if this creature, in all his magnificence, had presented himself to me in an unforgettable way. As if to say, "It's my time to go, do your part, don't forget me." I could get my mind around this notion. But, why did the old buck charge directly back towards me before dying? Did he merely tire when running up hill from the mortal wound I inflicted, instinctively turn and run back downhill? Or, was it some sort of message about a precious thing in my life that I might lose – something that might die directly in, or by, my hands. That hunting experience was dream-like leaving me confused as to its meaning and significance. It haunted me then, and off and on, the rest of my days.

*Foxey Brown/David Brennan, circa 1916 (Hamilton
County Historian collection)*

*Carlton Banker (Used with permission of
Fulton-Montgomery Community College Evans Library)*

Adirondack guide, William B. Abrams
circa 1905. (Joann Dunham Estes)

Fire Ranger, William Dunham (Joann Dunham Estes)

*Piseco Logging Crew. William Dunham standing on Frank Parslow.
William B. Abrams: tall man, center rear.
(Joann Dunham Estes)*

12
Brownsville's Demise

Nearing age 62, I thought I had gotten away from believing in dreams and possible omens. Too many unpredictable and sudden occurrences had happened in my life that didn't fit my dreams. But, then again, who is to say with certainty what significance lies in a man's dreams? Do they contain grains of reality swirling in our brain among uncountable numbers of past and present experiences? Maybe, this is why the Bible says, "Old men will dream dreams." Alas, if only we could interpret those dreams accurately might they steer us away from disaster? Wherever the truth lies, an omen seeker paying attention to world events at the beginning of 1916 might have predicted a bad year was coming.

To start, an earthquake struck Lake George on January 5th. While the quake sent only minor tremors throughout the Adirondacks, it made many residents very nervous. We had grown somewhat accustomed to the perils of drought, fire, and flood. People can fight those things to some degree, but when mother earth begins to tremble without warning you can only go along with the ride hoping luck will provide a safe landing. Like January's unexpected earthquake, the fall hunting season was going to bring an unforeseen, unbelievable, and nearly unbearable shock to Brownsville.

Winter began in earnest in late January, destined to break all previous records for snowfall before it was over. Early in March, lumbermen had already reported snow depths of five feet with drifts up to twenty feet high. Then, on March 9th, a blizzard of incredible strength pelted the Hamilton County area with eight more feet of snow and by the end of March total snow depth in the Piseco Lake area had reached 122 inches.

The March 9th storm delivered itself with stinging snow particles in gusty and intense sheets like two gravediggers trying to finish a burial before dark. It came so hard and fast at Brownsville I feared the snow would entomb my cabin and me. I shoveled snow away from the door and lee-side window off and on throughout the night to make sure the cabin remained my shelter and not a coffin. For several entire days my life consisted of shoveling, doing chores, and shoveling more. Fearful the roofs on the cabin, barn, ice house, and storage shed might collapse from heavy snow loads; many hours were spent in the cold trying to reduce chances of a larger disaster. Some days the weariness from all the shoveling found me skipping supper and merely flopping into bed. Was my resolve to remain at Brownsville as long as possible being tested by nature? I thought only superstitious fools think such thoughts – nature just is; it has no need to be concerned about human endeavors.

More bad news filtered into Piseco Lake and Brownsville as the year progressed. The world war in Europe was intensifying and gobbling up human beings in unbelievably large batches. The Battle of Somme commenced in July and by early September had consumed more than a million soldiers. The armies had become increasingly sophisticated in ways to kill each other and short on any sense of compassion for people. Technology had given them chlorine gas, machine guns, tanks, and airplanes to indiscriminately decimate each other. It appeared the strategy was to keep throwing soldiers into the trenches until one side ran out of fodder.

The United States was not immune to the global aspects of this war but our leaders chose to remain neutral despite ample reason to take up arms against the Germans. In 1915, RMS Lusitania, a luxurious British ship, left New York carrying nearly two thousand people, 159 of who were Americans. Unfortunately, the Lusitania fell into the sights of a German submarine that promptly sunk her in a matter of eighteen minutes. Nearly 1200 people died including 100 children. There was a good deal of public outrage toward the Germans, but little other action except to get a pledge stating they would not sink passenger ships thereafter. The pledge was not often honored as many subsequent passenger ships learned the hard way.

To make matters worse German submarines began appearing off our Atlantic coast. Spies and agents had also come ashore for destructive purposes. Their intentions became evident on the night of July 30,

1916. Black Tom Island in New York harbor had long been a storage area for munitions intended to aid unofficial allies Great Britain and France. Around 2:00 a.m. a large explosion sent bomb fragments into the Statue of Liberty and the clock tower of the Jersey Journal building over a mile away. Windows broke in Manhattan twenty-five miles away and the blast was felt in Philadelphia – some estimates calculated the explosion as being equivalent to a moderate earthquake. Seven people were killed and hundreds injured.

Carlton was livid over this attack on American soil as were many of his friends in Gloversville. Despite ample evidence that a German agent had been behind the dastardly deed, President Woodrow Wilson did nothing. It was an election year and Wilson was running for a second term on an anti-war platform. Great suspicion fell on Wilson and his failure to acknowledge the Black Tom Island explosion as an act of sabotage. Many politicians said he feared such an admission might cost him the election since he was running for office on a "no war for America" campaign.

Characteristically, our hero and former president, Theodore Roosevelt made his views plain on the Black Tom Island incident by "bellowing" for American entry into the war. We heartily agreed. It's wise to negotiate first when trying to settle disagreements. However, as Roosevelt proclaimed, sometimes a bully understands nothing except a good beating.

A good 1916 summer growing season promised excellent hunting for October and November. The deer herd was very healthy and bucks were showing off sleek bodies and sizable antlers. I hadn't seen anything like the monster 268 pound, 13 point whitetail shot near Lake George in 1915, but there were some similar to the mysterious buck I had taken last year. For some reason, I had never told Carlton the whole story about the mortally wounded deer charging me. I wasn't sure why. Perhaps it was related to a dream that came to me one night shortly afterwards.

In my dream, I had wandered a short way out into the mud flats of a large river. The mud was deeper than I anticipated causing me to become stuck up to my waist. I wasn't sinking deeper but could barely move my legs. Carlton and Ada were on the shore dressed like they were going to church – suit and tie for Carlton and nice dress for Ada. Carlton, suit and all, began to wade out to help me. I yelled for him not to do so, but instead to get a long stick or downed sapling from shore and use it to pull me out. He didn't listen and continued wading towards me. The mud flat swallowed him in an instant, like a trout taking a floating insect! He was just gone. Only a little swirl on top of the mud, for a few seconds, marked where Carlton went down. Surely, he would struggle and surface. Paralyzed by the mud and fear I waited for him to come up – but he didn't. Nothing but a few bubbles on the water marked his submerged whereabouts.

I struggled to free myself and find Carlton. My efforts, like in many dreams, were useless. I was a prisoner forced to watch a loved one be executed. Ada began walking into the mud, beautiful dress and all. I yelled for her to get the sapling. She stopped, ankle deep near the shore edge, just looking at me.

The nightmare ended there as I woke shaking in a cold sweat even though the woodstove was burning hard. Analyzing the dream, my emotions ranged from a foreboding fear to extreme anger that I could, even in a dream, imagine such a thing happening to my friend. Was it an omen? I didn't believe in omens. Perhaps I should tell Carlton about the dream. Maybe its grip on me would loosen if I did so. But, how do you tell a friend about a dream where he dies and you and his wife stand helplessly by and watch? I kept the dream to myself. And, I sure as hell wasn't ever going to take Carlton anywhere near deep water or mud.

Wednesday & Thursday, November 8-9, 1916

Carlton came to Piseco with a party of other F.J. & G. Railroad executives and friends from the Gloversville area. They stayed at Tru Lawrence's camp the first night. After unsuccessfully hunting the deer runways there on Thursday morning, Carlton, Fred Bagg and the others headed for my camp at Brownsville. While there was no snow on the ground, the day had gotten steadily colder and damper. When they arrived around 5 o'clock I was surprised to see so many men. Accompanying Carlton and Fred was Fred's brother Harry, Charles Newnham, Henry McLean, and Andrew Swart. Carlton apologized for not notifying me about such large numbers, but quickly indicated that only he and Fred were going to stay on for a few days as we had planned. The others were going back to Tru Lawrence's camp the next morning. They had hauled in plenty of food so feeding the group wasn't a problem.

Carlton was not feeling well. He had been struggling with a sore knee and the hike in had exhausted him. I also knew a doctor back in Gloversville was treating him for high blood pressure – something Carlton didn't like to talk about much. I always thought to do so was, in his mind, a sign of weakness; that he couldn't handle the pressures of being a railroad executive. Carlton took great pride in being a strong man. That can be a good thing but pride can sometimes push a man towards valor when discretion is the best path.

The conversation, before and after supper, was about the presidential election that had occurred on November 7th. Everyone had been rooting for the Republican candidate, Charles Hughes. After all, Hughes was a New Yorker and TR had strongly supported him to the extent of withdrawing his own Progressive Party candidacy. Roosevelt disliked incumbent president Woodrow Wilson immensely believing him to be weak for allowing Germany to "bully" the United States out of entering the war.

No one in our hunting group knew the outcome of the presidential election. Hughes had gone to bed election night believing he had a comfortable lead and surely would be the new president on November 8th. However, Wilson gained many electoral votes, from the western part of the nation during the night, making election results uncertain. The outcome was still unknown when Carlton, Fred and the others came into Brownsville that Thursday afternoon.

Carlton and the others took this situation seriously because they greatly distrusted the "liberal leaning" Woodrow Wilson. One joke was that Wilson would probably lick German Kaiser Wilhelm's boots if it kept us out of war. They were all puzzled as to why, "in this day and age," with telegraphs and telephones, it took so long to tally up votes and declare a winner. Carlton agreed, saying most of the daily newspapers weren't worth the two or three cents it cost to buy one. Someone piped in saying, "Yep, the papers do best with advertisements. Well, at least maybe all those Bell-Ans indigestion pills they promote will help settle some stomachs if Wilson ends up the winner." I ended the conversation by announcing supper was ready and if they had to use any Bell-Ans afterwards to do so in secret as my feelings were easily hurt!

We were all in bed by 8 o'clock. For November, it was a very cold night and the wood stove, despite being loaded every few hours, had trouble keeping the whole cabin comfortable and my supply of heavy blankets was stretched thin with seven men spending the night. Some of the most difficult times to keep the cabin comfortable were when there was no snow cover and a moist wind blew out of the east.

Reloading the stove around midnight I noticed Carlton was shivering despite having two heavy blankets. I pulled a blanket from my bed and covered him. In so doing, I accidently woke Carlton and he, of course, protested my action. This woke up Fred who offered one of his blankets. After a brief discussion, I convinced them I was having trouble sleeping. And, since they were all in bunk beds, it might be easier to just pull my single bed closer to the stove.

Friday, November 10, 1916

Carlton seemed markedly better the next morning and was eager to begin hunting. After the others left for Tru Lawrence's place, I took Carlton and Fred out to hunt at our favorite deer runs back of the pond. By 9 o'clock Carlton had shot a small deer just the right size for camp meat. We dressed the animal and hung it to fully bleed out.

After an early dinner we headed up the Spruce Lake trail about a mile or so near the Fall Stream/Spruce Lake Trail crossing. By this time, Carlton's knee problem had resurfaced so Fred and I put him on watch near a good deer run just off the main trail. The plan was for Fred and me to walk up the mountain a ways and then slowly hunt back down with each of us making a sweep that might push deer back to Carlton. The three of us would then go back to camp with any deer taken. I kidded Carlton about not shooting too large a deer and make me go back to camp for Ox and the wagon.

According to plan, I hunted back down the mountain seeing plenty of deer sign but no actual animals. From the absence of gunfire, it was certain Fred and Carlton were also having no luck. Around 4:30 I arrived at the spot where we had left Carlton. To my mild surprise, he wasn't there. I made our favorite crow call knowing he would recognize it and respond in similar fashion. Despite repeated calls there was no response. I waited a few minutes for Fred but he didn't appear either. After loudly calling Carlton and Fred by name a few times, I decided to go back to camp confident we were all familiar with this hunting area and everyone was on their way to the cabin.

Approaching the cabin, I found Fred walking towards me. At first, I thought Carlton was in the cabin. But the look on Fred's face quickly dismissed that notion. Somehow, we had both missed connecting with Carlton. While the situation was a little discomforting, we knew Carlton was an experienced woodsman and had hunted this area for nearly twenty-five years. To be sure, Fred fired a signal shot and we heard what seemed to be a faint return shot from the direction where Carlton had been posted earlier in the day. Reassured, we headed for the cabin and began making supper.

By 6:00 p.m. Carlton still hadn't arrived so we ate and rested some. Around 7 o'clock we became concerned and grabbed lanterns to start a search for our tardy friend. Retracing our steps to the spot where Carlton had been on deer watch, we yelled his name and let out a single gunshot every twenty minutes or so. Five hours went by and we had found no sign of Carlton other than where he had sat while on watch. Exhausted, we returned to camp still somewhat confident that Carlton's woodsman experience led him to do what he always said to do if a man got lost – make a fire and stay put until someone finds you. I slept in fitful spurts, waking sometimes thinking I had heard Carlton calling. At the same time, I was trying to fight off remembering my earlier dream about Carlton, Ada and the river mud.

Saturday, November 11, 1916

At first light, Fred and I left a note for Carlton and renewed our search over a wider area. We found footprints, but they were much too large for Carlton's small feet. Noon came and went with no sign of Carlton. He had to be in serious trouble and we needed help. We agreed Fred should go to Piseco, report the situation, and get more searchers. I planned to go up Fall Stream checking one side and then the other on my return thinking Carlton might have followed it back toward camp. If I came up empty I would return to camp and wait for Fred and the search party.

Frantically, I rushed to Witness Rock thinking a perch there could let me see a great deal of the surrounding forest and spot any campfires or hear faint rifle shots in the distance. Firing my rifle from an elevated position might increase chances of Carlton hearing the blasts and making a response. But, silence was to be my companion that afternoon. The damp, cloud covered day made the forest seem lifeless – its somber mood interrupted only by the occasional murmurs of chickadees. It seemed odd even the crows and blue jays were silent. I fought off thoughts about the forest mourning Carlton's death. An hour passed and I headed up Fall Stream.

I found no clues until beginning my return trip on the Willis Mountain side of Fall Stream. There, on a sand bar, less than a half-mile from our camp was Carlton's unmistakably small footprint! In the center of the sand bar were the remains of a small campfire not more than a few hours old. It was strange that Carlton had made a fire out in the open where he wasn't sheltered from the wind. Even more puzzling was that he had apparently tried to burn green sticks broken off nearby bushes. This couldn't have been the practice of a normally functioning Carlton Banker. Something was hindering his thinking. Knowing he had high blood pressure, a stroke entered my mind. Then there was weather – the cold starting to take its toll by numbing Carlton's already stroke infirmed mind. My dear friend was in deadly serious peril and my lack of attention to signs of his illness had put him there!

Checking to determine Carlton's direction of departure from his campsite, I found no trail. Did he cross the stream, walk a ways up or down the other side? I hurried across the stream to the other bank certain his footprints would be there. Finding none, I carefully searched upstream several hundred yards and got the same results – nothing. Returning to my stream crossing spot, I checked downstream a good distance to find not one footprint or clue of human presence. Had Carlton waded up or down the stream exiting beyond my area of search?

I was stumped and frustrated. I thought, "If only French Louie were around. Damn, we have to get some dogs on Carlton's trail." Snow was sure to come soon and then even dogs would have trouble following a trail. I rushed back to camp hoping Carlton might be there or, at the very least, find Fred had returned with more searchers.

Fred must have run most of the way to Piseco Lake because he was back just before dark with two hastily organized search parties made up of local guides and others staying at Piseco Lake hotels. The group consisted of men I knew like the Abrams' (Bill, George, and David), Herb Aird, the Lawrences (Frank, Harry, and Truman), Will Dunham, Dick Kempster, Peter Judway and William N. Courtney. Tim Crowley also showed up, along with Carlton's Gloversville hunting party and some other men unfamiliar to me. A teenage boy was sent back to Piseco to see what could be done about getting some tracking dogs into Brownsville.

Sunday, November 12, 1916

On Sunday morning the rest of us went back to my foot track discovery at Fall Stream, spread out, fifteen to twenty feet apart, and hunted throughout the day only to end up totally frustrated, tired and hungry. Word came into camp that fifty men or more were scouring a fifty-mile area of forest. Various stories also had begun to come into the search headquarters at Piseco. Supposedly, someone else had found small footprints, but they too disappeared in a stream; a hunter found a dead deer with part of the hindquarters missing; and yet, another man had found what appeared to be a quickly prepared and abandoned camp.

Most discomforting were stories that two separate hunting parties near Cherry Lake, north of Piseco had heard shots and shouts from a lost man. One group heard the shots late on Friday night and the other on Saturday night. They said the shots were fired in rapid order. In both instances the hunting groups headed out to help the lost person, but their efforts were stymied, as the man seemed to move away as they tried, in vain, to reach him. It was as if the man was disoriented and couldn't focus on the direction of hunting party shouts and rifle shots. Heeding these stories, searchers were sent to scour the areas only to find the remains of some old campfires here and there.

By Sunday night Fred and I had gone more than thirty hours without sleep. Knowing rest was necessary if we were going to continue helping with the search, we fell into bed praying that rumors of nearly 200 men (the largest manhunt in Adirondack history) due to arrive Monday morning would come true. A full night's sleep did not come to either Fred or me. We tossed, turned, and got up several times to sit by the fire and talk about where Carlton might be headed. It was pretty evident he was wandering and not staying put. Both of us avoided any mention of Carlton being dead. There was an unspoken understanding that such talk might somehow jinx or influence the outcome of Carlton's ordeal. I later thought how strange it is that superstition can influence the minds of reasonable men during trying times.

Monday, November 13, 1916

Sure enough, several carloads of Carlton's friends and co-workers from the F.J. & G. Railroad did reach Piseco on Monday. And, like Adirondack folk always reacted to emergencies, dozens more came from Lake Pleasant, Spy Lake, Scandia, Speculator, and other nearby communities. The large gathering of more than 150 men, determined to find Carlton, caused spirits to soar and optimism to run high. Predictions flowed freely that Carlton would be found that day. That optimism soon got tempered, however, when the realities of searching for a missing man in the Adirondack wilds set in.

With all good intentions, the F.J. & G. released as many personnel as possible under the direction of General Passenger Agent, Robert Colt to conduct their own search. In the end, matters got complicated with too many bosses and having to use our best guides to bring inexperienced volunteers themselves out of the woods. It was a wonder some of the normally desk-bound office workers didn't suffer heart attacks or strokes. Many of the men were not physically fit enough to tramp hours on end in the woods. Thankfully, it was only a matter of them getting temporarily lost.

Monday morning also brought colder temperatures, heavy cloud cover, and the growing threat of snow. Instincts, and experience living in these mountains, told me we had only a short time to find Carlton. Such dark thoughts flew away when word came in that a fresh trail, consisting of small footprints, had been found near Mossy Vly southwest of the Perkins Camp over towards Speculator. A large search party using dogs was following the trail. The guides in charge were confident they would find Carlton "by noon."

Another report arrived saying a fairly fresh campfire and small footprints had been found close to where Fall Stream approaches Vly Lake. Once again, the camper had tried to burn green twigs and branches. This news alarmed me greatly because I knew how wet and swampy it always was in that area. Like Mossy Vly and Willis Vly, the swampy land between Vly Lake and Mud Lake was extremely dangerous. I had hunted and trapped there many times and could recall pushing an eight foot pole into the wet earth and watch it quickly disappear beneath my feet making only a slurp sound like a frog who had just swallowed a fly. It didn't take much imagination to picture a small man like Carlton, in weakened condition, being pulled into a hidden watery grave. Was my mud flats dream about Carlton going to be prophetic? Should I have told him about it? Who would now believe such a tale? Might I be suspected of fabricating a story to hide my guilt in losing Carlton? Fred and I, with thirty or so men, immediately headed for Mud Lake. Accusations and stories would have to come later.

My stomach churned and gurgled all the way to Mud Lake. Too many hurried meals and lack of sleep were taking its toll on all of us. The first few flakes of an approaching snowstorm added to my fear and anxiety. Seeing them filled me with an uncontrollable fear and my already queasy stomach rumbled. I stopped, bent forward, and promptly threw up the contents of a grossly large breakfast. Weird ideas entered my head – perhaps there really was a Wendigo, a forest god that grabbed on to weakened humans and didn't let go. Shaking these thoughts off, I wondered what I would do if in Carlton's predicament. Even if not fully coherent, I would follow the stream sensing eventually it would lead to Piseco. The problem was that once a man reached the Vly/Mud Lake area he had to encounter the swampy terrain we were now approaching.

On our arrival, several men from the Abrams' hunting camp greeted us including two who had discovered the most recent abandoned campfire. Sure enough, there were signs of someone having tried to burn green twigs and small footprints partially covered by a faint dusting of newly fallen snow. The snow would soon obliterate the tracks. Only dogs, and only for short time, could track down Carlton. A runner was sent out to headquarters with hopes of getting some dogs in here.

After thoroughly scouring the area for an hour or so, we agreed if Carlton hadn't fallen victim to the vly, he most likely headed up Mud Mountain in hopes of finding the trail into Piseco – that is if he was able to think at all by now. With no tracks to follow, we were forced to use the remaining daylight in hope of finding Carlton between the main trail and us. With more than thirty men we were able to spread out, maintain visibility with each other, and sweep a good-sized chunk of forest. At least that was the plan. The snow had its own agenda.

By 4:00 p.m. the gloom of cloud cover, shadows of large trees, and heavier snowfall created conditions forcing the men to spend most of their concentration and energy keeping track of one another lest they get lost. Concerned for the welfare of the search crew, we grouped together at the

Spruce Lake trail about three miles from Piseco considering ourselves fortunate to have lost no one in the group. We had planned to fan men out
on both sides of the trail to search for Carlton on the way back to Piseco.
However, the snow and pending darkness made it seem wisest to quickly
return to search headquarters. Perhaps the Perkins Clearing search party,
and dogs, had found Carlton near Mossy Vly.

In my college literature class we read some of William Shakespeare's
writing. It wasn't my favorite subject, but I remembered that he wrote
something about timing "being everything." Many years later our decision to quit searching along the Piseco to Spruce Lake trail, would sadly
underscore Shakespeare's wisdom. But on that late snowy afternoon in
November of 1916, our best hope seemed to lie in finding out the results
of the Perkins Clearing search.

A large group of men was stomping snow off their boots as we
approached search headquarters. Spotting Bill Abrams, I ran ahead to get
the news. Seeing me, Bill dropped his eyes towards the ground, and softly
said, "Sorry Dave, we've been on a wild goose chase. The dogs did their job
but led us right to a man and his wife." They had been out on a hike up near
Mossy Vly. The small tracks were the woman's. She kept getting tired and
cold, so her husband built a series of small fires as they went along." There
was real pain in Bill's eyes and voice as he told me the news. Of all the men,
he understood what it was like to lose a loved one in the forest. In a sad way,
we were bonded because of similar tragedies – his with his brother. I sensed
that is what drove him to search so hard for Carlton.

As the bad news spread among the men only muffled voices could
occasionally be heard above the steady whisper of falling snow. We ate and
rested knowing the odds of finding Carlton alive were not good.

By then there had been an all-out, three-day hunt for Carlton. Many
of his friends and co-workers from Gloversville and surrounding areas had
to return for work. Considering the eight-inch snowfall it was also agreed
that search work was growing too dangerous except for those men very
familiar with the woods in winter. Even those of us expert in woods ways
would have to rely on the wonderful smelling abilities of dog noses knowing full well they too would become clueless in a day or so as snow cover
grew deeper. Armed and alarmed by these facts, guides and permanent
residents vowed not to stop looking for Carlton. Motivations to do so, I
suspected, were mixed.

It didn't hurt Carlton's cause when the newspapers announced on Tuesday that the reward for his safe return, or recovery of body, had been raised from $250 to $1,000. That handsome sum surely motivated many men to keep searching for a long time. At the time most guides were still working for ten dollars or so per day and railroad workers back in Gloversville labored away for twenty-eight cents an hour. However, the money was a pittance compared to what I had at stake. Carlton was my best friend and had made me part of his family. Some said we were "soul mates" and our friendship was only overshadowed by the love Carlton held for his wife and daughters. Mountain recluses don't have many close friends, much less soul mates. We had spent nearly fifteen years hunting, fishing, and hiking together and countless nights under the stars or by my wood stove sharing conversations about most anything imaginable – life, death, God, politics, women.... Carlton had kept my interest in learning alive with a constant supply of good reading and challenging discussions. And, he was the key figure in making my retirement some-what comfortable. Few men ever have a friend like Carlton Banker. I had to find him and make sure he got a proper burial. The thought of wild animals devouring his remains like they probably had Spook's, sickened and infuriated me.

My anger and frustrations were further incensed by newspaper reports coming into Piseco. Carlton's station in life, concerns of family and friends, the reward, and human gossiping fueled all sorts of stories regarding his whereabouts. Most devastating was one newspaper headline claiming I had murdered Carlton, hid the body, and was pretending to be frantically searching for him.

Even those who didn't particularly like me were not supportive of the murder theory arguing I hadn't had the time or motivation to commit such an evil deed. Thank goodness, Fred Bagg was with me throughout the whole ordeal. He quickly squelched talk of me murdering Carlton pointing out there were no shots the afternoon of our hunt, no blood or body drag marks near Carlton's deer watch station, and that Fred, along with other searchers, had carefully looked all around the site finding no evidence of foul play. And, then there were the reports about campfires, Carlton's small footprints, and searchers near T Lake hearing a man, still alive, calling for help. Fred also told how he had seen me, in the cold cabin, covering Carlton with my own blanket the night before his disappearance.

His testimony convinced officers of the F.J. & G. that I couldn't have harmed Carlton. And, like you would suspect, the end of the murder angle sent the newspapers scurrying for more theories to satisfy their readers. I sure as hell wasn't going to talk to the news hungry bastards.

The notion of someone murdering or killing Carlton swirled through my mind. It was certain that didn't happen while he was at the deer watch stand last Friday. I had found his foot tracks along Fall Stream on Saturday. But, what if someone had found him wandering around, weak and defenseless? But what motive would there be to finish him off? Finding Carlton would make a man a hero and bring a reward. Could Fred Bagg have done such an evil deed hoping to get Carlton's position with the F.J. & G. railroad company? That made no sense; I had seen them happily hunting and fishing together for too many years. You get good opportunities to judge a man's character when you hunt, fish, and work together in mountains.

Had a guide or Sport, fearful of reporting the incident, accidentally shot Carlton as he blundered deliriously along through some thick brush? We knew from prior experience that hunting accidents happen even to good and experienced men like Bill Abrams.

Subsequent newspaper stories suggested outlandish things about Carlton. One had him running away with a secretary from F.J. & G. headquarters. Another claimed a witness had seen Carlton in Toronto, Canada and yet another said he was spotted in New York City. And the *New York Times* carried a story brought in from Gloversville claiming "Banker's ammunition was low and bears and panthers are more numerous than usual this year..." That reporter probably never got outdoors farther than Central Park. There hadn't been a panther around for two decades and bears pretty much denned up by mid-November! Some people back in Gloversville even consulted a clairvoyant who predicted Carlton would be found lying face down in the woods. Some help that was considering how many thousand acres were hiding Carlton.

The most outlandish story was that Carlton had committed suicide. This was a pathetically, almost laughable, theory. Anyone who met Carlton encountered an energetic, thoughtful, and full of life person. How would a man contemplating suicide, after suffering a knee injury and exhausting hike the day before, get up the next morning raring to go hunting, shoot and dress a deer, and go on another hunt the same afternoon?

Suicidal people also don't crack jokes just before taking their lives. The night before his disappearance, Carlton had not only kidded about the presidential election but picked on himself saying in his haste to come hunting he had neglected to take cash out of the bank. He said for a wealthy railroad executive it was kind of embarrassing to only have twenty-five cents (two dimes and a nickel) in his pocket. Of course, none of us lost the chance to chide him, indicating he could pass his fedora around and we would help him out!

Then there was the story that Carlton had business problems with the F.J. & G. railroad back in Gloversville. The truth was just the opposite because the F.J. & G. had recently released its quarterly financial report showing a fifty percent gain in net income for 1916. As Superintendent of the F.J. & G. Electric Division, Carlton was proud of this accomplishment and excitedly shared it with everyone the night before he disappeared.

Reporters even found their way into my camp while I was off searching for Carlton. Pictures of my cabin and interviews with local folk, who supposedly knew me, soon found their way into newspapers across the region including Amsterdam, Johnstown, Gloversville and Utica. Hungry for any details they could muster, reporters wrote about my dugout barn, pond, cow, and pet snake – any detail to round out a story. While all this surely sold more newspapers, none of it helped the search or eased the pain being experienced by Ada Banker and her daughters Helen and Marian.

With all these things floating around in my head, I joined the other guides to begin Tuesday's search for Carlton. Perhaps it was my imagination, but I noticed some of the guides were talking in hushed tones especially when I was approaching them. Sometimes it seemed that conversations were abruptly terminated, or the subject changed to Woodrow Wilson's come from behind presidential victory. The absence of Fred, Carlton's other friends, and his original hunting party, was probably opening the door for more speculation and gossip as to the cause of his disappearance. A guide losing a member of his hunting party was serious business in these woods and I would later learn that few people were ever going to let me forget it.

The snow had stopped and the sun was making an occasional appearance between low-lying clouds on Tuesday morning. The storm had done its damage depositing nearly eight inches of light flaky snow – enough to mark the outline of fallen trees, stumps and mounds on the ground. Below freezing temperatures predicted for the day offered no hope of melting snow to assist our search. Convinced Carlton had been trying to find his way along Fall Stream, we agreed it best to use the dogs to search the Vly Lake/Mud Lake area again. If that failed, we would then head back up Fall Stream toward my camp. Perhaps Carlton had reversed his direction of travel in an attempt to get back to Brownsville.

Moving water and wind are two of the great shapers of this world. This is especially true when they are challenged only by thin soils. These forces, overharvesting of trees, and the thin Adirondack Mountain soils, had set the stage for huge expanses of tangled, blown down trees that made travel difficult along Fall Stream. The slippery snow added to our woes. Even the dogs struggled and avoided the blow downs – places we should have searched in case Carlton had crawled into one seeking shelter. The only advantage given by the snow was that there would be tracks if he were still alive and moving. Otherwise, Carlton could be buried most anywhere under it.

We reached Brownsville late in the afternoon, fatigued and discouraged by the lack of any sign. The dog handlers had brought adequate food for their animals and we bedded them down in my barn. A sizable number of our search party had already headed back to Piseco via the main trail. The remaining twelve of us crowded together in my cabin for the night. Fortunately there was little wind and the men had all packed in warm blankets and food. We ate pretty much in silence knowing chances of finding Carlton alive, or dead, were slim. We were determined, however, to continue searching.

Wednesday, November 15, 1916 marked a week since Carlton Banker had arrived at Tru Lawrence's camp. What started out as a joyful annual hunting and reconnection with wild country experience had transformed into his funeral procession. Only, we couldn't even proudly carry him to a final resting place where family and friends could visit from time to time. The forest and the mountains were most likely going to keep Carlton at least for the winter. At two o'clock or so our search party gave up after patrolling Fall Stream above Brownsville. Thinking he might have wandered in a large circle; we revisited the deer run area where Fred and I had left Carlton to watch for deer on Friday. Once again, the mountains continued to hide Carlton.

Our search was over for the day. Dogs had to be returned downstate, men were exhausted, and more snow was on the way. Small groups of local guides and individuals would continue searching for Carlton, but barring a miracle, his death was now certain. No one volunteered to spend the night at Brownsville and I didn't encourage it. Once again, I was a mountain recluse left alone to contemplate the errors of my ways. I cried, uncorked a bottle left by the search party, cried some more, and drank myself into a mind wrenching stupor with reoccurring dreams of Carlton calling for help as he wandered along Fall Stream. Each time I got near him, he would slip just beyond my reach in the blowing snow.

The whiskey provided one benefit in that I slept late into the next morning – right through the bellowing of my hungry cow. Thanks to the lingering effects of the alcohol, at first I almost convinced myself that what had happened was a dream. That notion quickly disappeared as I saw the evidence of many men having eaten in my cabin over the past few days and, of course, there was the empty whiskey bottle by my bed. Still fully dressed from the night before, I struggled with dizziness and aching muscles to get out of bed before stumbling my way to the barn.

While returning to the cabin I stopped to suck some fresh air into my lungs. It struck me that I was totally alone for the first time in a week. Aside from the muffled "dee-dee-dee" of Chickadees working here and there, the forest was mum – even the Blue Jays were keeping their presence to themselves. At first, I relished the silence but it soon overwhelmed me and painfully drove home the reality of having lost Carlton. Resisting temptation to open another bottle of whiskey, I filled the coffee pot and fixed some food. The nights would provide ample time to mourn and second guess my mistakes. Daylight hours had to be used to try and do something. I stuck some biscuits in my pocket, grabbed the snowshoes, and a rifle. I was going to the section of Lunkazoo Mountain where Fred and I had left Carlton nearly a week ago. I thought maybe alone, I could find or sense something that might help find my dear friend. At least the exercise would clear the pounding in my head.

False hope is a painful thing. No hope at all is worse. I got the no hope side of things after arriving and poking around at Lunkazoo Mountain.

The snow had totally covered any visible signs of anyone ever having been there. As for sensing something about Carlton's whereabouts, I also came up empty.

I searched a different section of Fall Stream every day and traveled to Piseco twice a week during the course of the next few weeks hoping against hope that someone had found Carlton. However, the news was all bad despite the efforts of many guides who had continued searching alone or in small groups. Then on December 8th we all got a portion of false hope from an unusual twist of nature.

Over Thanksgiving week temperatures rose well above freezing and a driving rainstorm settled into the Adirondacks causing the snow cover to entirely disappear. Small search groups quickly formed enticing men from many parts of northern and central New York to join in and try their luck – a $1,000 reward to find a missing man's body being a good incentive. Sadly, the renewed search also failed to produce any evidence of my old friend's whereabouts. Winter weather returned and as snow depths got large again the searches petered out. Many guides vowed to start again in the spring.

During the absence of snow newspaper reporters continued to visit Piseco and interview guides about Carlton's disappearance. The generally held theory among guides was that Carlton Banker had fallen into one of the "bottomless" bog holes common in the Mud and Vly lake area. One unnamed guide provided a demonstration of bog depth for a news reporter by tying a long rope of "six lengths" to an iron wheel. After playing out the rope, the wheel was thrown onto a bog soft spot where it immediately began to sink. In less than a minute, the end of the rope disappeared below the surface. The subsequent *Utica Press* story on November 24, 1916 ended with the statement, "The quagmires of the north tell no tales." After reading this my dream about Carlton, Ada and the mud flats reoccurred on a frequent basis. Had I somehow been warned about Carlton's death? The absence of his body lent a lot of credibility to the bog soft spot theory.

Not being able to find Carlton's body had other consequences that bothered me terribly. I had written to Ada and the children expressing my grief and apologies for what had happened to Carlton. She returned a short letter stating she didn't blame me for his disappearance. I learned from Fred Bagg that Ada was convinced Carlton was still alive and would return "most any day." The family was worried about Ada because she continued to grieve heavily and showed signs of declining health.

To make matters worse Ada was left in financial difficulty because Carlton's life insurance company refused to pay without "proof" of his demise. "No body, no money" was the company's position. Ada was forced to live off their savings and help provided by Carlton's mother. Guilt nagged me frequently that long winter at Fall Stream causing me to ask over and over again; "What if I had only done this or what if I had done that?"

There were other consequences for having lost Carlton. For nearly two decades I had been a highly regarded guide in the southern Adirondacks and had taken hundreds of sportsmen on hunting and fishing trips. I had enjoyed my work and reputation immensely but my heart could never again rejoice in such activity. The loss of Carlton haunted me and I knew it would taint relations with any new clients. And which of Carlton's friends and associates in Gloversville would want me to guide them? There would also always be unpleasant memories and questions.

My reputation was ruined by losing Carlton and there were some guides quite pleased to see Foxey Brown humbled. I had known for some time there was jealousy over the type of clients I had enjoyed serving over the years. And Carlton's practice of bringing gifts and helping with my retirement were also known. One unnamed guide was quoted in a newspaper story as stating, 'To take a man out and not bring him back again is a pretty serious thing." Of course, he claimed not to be accusing me of anything. But the damage was done.

The rumors also continued to circulate that I had killed Carlton. Bill Gallagher told me that such talk was still going around Piseco. Fully frustrated one day, I asked Charlie Preston, in front of others, "You don't think I killed Banker, do you Charlie? No one should. He's always done things for me, always took care of my money." Without hesitation, Charlie told the group he was convinced that I wouldn't have harmed Carlton under any circumstances. That statement coming from the local State Conservation Commission officer shut the mouths of many gossipers. Others like Bill Gallagher, William Dunham, and the Courtney and Abrams families also stuck by me. But the rumors of murder persisted then and well after my days of living at Fall Stream and Piseco ended.

13
NO REST FOR THE WEARY

I spent the next four years (1917-1920) at Fall Stream living more and more like a recluse and hermit. Fred Bagg and other former clients from Gloversville tried to stay in touch. We talked about doing some hunting and fishing, but never did. Memories of Carlton, and the unspoken but shared belief that he (like anyone lost and presumed dead in those days) might not be at rest, cast a shadow that would have darkened any get-togethers. I referred hunting and fishing inquires to other guides, seldom went to town, and relied on my little farm and some trapping to get by. Anyone trying to serve as a fishing guide was out of luck anyway. The years of overfishing the streams in our portion of Hamilton County caused severe declines in brook trout populations leading the Conservation Commission on July 1, 1919 to prohibit fishing for three years. The regulations included "Fall Stream and all its tributaries, known as Dave Brown's 'dam' and up Cold Stream and all its tributaries from Abrams crossing." The long list went on and on to include all the tributaries from Piseco Lake up toward Raquette Lake. I was no longer legally allowed to fish in my own pond – one where I had diligently tried to protect trout from being overfished.

A similar situation developed for those trying to make a living as deer hunting guides. By 1920 the legal take for deer was down to one of either sex per hunter for the whole season. This discouraged sport hunters and local residents who depended on venison to help feed their families. The upshot was that fewer law abiding hunters came and poaching increased greatly. The decrease in numbers of deer and trout and smaller bag limits pretty much ended the guiding business as we had known it since the

1880's and the list of men available to work as common laborers grew quickly.

In a twist of fate the shortage of trout and deer presented another way, at least temporarily, for local folks to earn money. In 1919, the Conservation Commission, encouraged by the rapid growth of the protected beaver populations, declared lynx, bobcat, red and grey fox, weasel, otter, porcupines, pine martin, and fisher as enemies of wildlife. More or less any predator of fish, game, or trees, except beaver, was now considered a varmint and the state deemed it good business to reduce their numbers so there would be more game species. I wondered why the coyote had not made the Commission's list. They had returned to the mountains recently in small numbers to prey on other critters – especially any tasty beaver that came their way. Many former guides became trappers and established long trap lines to take advantage of the new Conservation Commission philosophy. Some made good money especially when fur prices rose to the point where one pine marten skin put as much as $200 in a man's pocket. Of course, by then, there weren't many pine marten around and, with the farm to maintain, I could only manage a short trap line.

Some men found good jobs with the State as the Conservation Commission added game protectors, forest rangers and fire rangers. Fire, or the threat of it, also provided jobs for local men. Since the State couldn't totally stop fires from springing up, it decided to minimize the damage they caused. After the great fires of 1903 and 1908, the Commission began erecting steel observation stations or towers and paid rangers to watch for fires on a daily basis. The stations were built on the high spots so the watchers/fire rangers could observe as much of the forest as possible. Equipped with powerful field glasses, range finders, good maps and special telephones, the fire rangers could immediately report any fires spotted and allow the nearest fire-fighting teams to quickly get going. By 1918, there were fifty-two towers scattered across the mountains. Bill Dunham was the fire ranger at T-Lake for many years and Floyd W. Abrams served as the local fire warden responsible for assembling men to put out any reported fires near Piseco.

One thing I never gave up was searching for Carlton's body. I tried to convince myself that my dream of Carlton sinking in the mud had foretold of him being devoured by the Vly Lake swamp and therefore, there was no chance of finding him. But part of me sensed, or at least hoped, he had avoided death by drowning; that somehow his woods savvy and determination steered him away from the vly. My state of mind was thus one of hope and distraction. Hope that I could find him and at least help Ada and the children find some peace of mind. Distraction, in that everywhere I went in the woods or along Fall Stream caused me to stop and explore any odd looking mound on the ground, behind downed trees, on the backside of big rocks and, of course, in any crevice or hole.

One early spring day, on the way to Piseco, I stepped off the trail to relieve myself behind a large boulder. Doing so, I noticed a crevice under the boulder leading to what could be a cave. The opening was large enough for a man, or a bear, to make its way through. I thought surely some of the searchers had known about this boulder and investigated it when the search for Carlton was actively taking place. But, what if everyone had made the same assumption? No one had kept a record of who had searched where. I had to investigate this place where Carlton might have crawled into or worse yet was dragged into.

However, I carried no lantern and discretion suggested a newly awakened bear might just be exiting as I entered its lair. There had to be some way of investigating what was under the rock without going in. I looked around for something to poke with and found a pole nearly twenty feet long. Lying on my belly, with my revolver nearby, I slowly worked the pole into the crevice. From time to time, I had to wiggle and joust it about to get over and around small rocks on the cave floor. The numerous thrusts of the pole suggested the cave was considerably larger than its entrance. Having pushed almost the entire length of the pole into the cave, I bumped into something soft that wouldn't give way like a pile of leaves. The feel of it suggested a body of substantial size, like a deer or small bear. I made several hard thrusts and received no response that a living thing was being disturbed. Then slowly, the stench of decaying flesh began drifting toward me.

Not wanting to repeat the folly of being trapped again as with my log experience years ago, I made a hasty trip back to Brownsville to fetch a lantern. All kinds of possibilities as to what the cave held ran through my mind. Had Carlton crawled into the cave and died? Had a bear found his body and dragged it into the cave? If so, wouldn't Carlton have long since been devoured leaving nothing to rot and give off a scent? Had someone killed Carlton and secretively hid his body in the cave? What would I do if it was Carlton? If I was the one to find him, would that again open suspicions that he died at my hands? Consequences be dammed, I had to find out what the cave was hiding.

It was mid-afternoon when I got back to the cave but a clear blue sky and sunshine promised ample daylight to begin my cave exploration. Just in case a critter of any sort had entered during my absence, I inserted the pole once again, prodded here and there, and listened carefully. It appeared the cave was mine to explore. I opened the lantern, scratched a match and put it to the mantle. After waiting for the lantern to burn clear, I gently pushed it into the cave as far as my arm would reach and poked my head through the entrance. I could see that some belly crawling was in order as the entrance shaft was less than three feet in height. After crawling only ten feet or so there was room to get on my knees and move ahead into a chamber nearly five foot high. By now the smell of something rotten was quite evident and, to my surprise, there was a small shaft of light coming from the ceiling and striking the cave floor just ahead of me. As I moved the lantern towards the portion of illuminated floor a circle of stones came into focus. Someone had once built a small fire using the slit in the cave ceiling as a chimney. My heart pounded as I thought Carlton might have sought shelter here before he died.

However, my new found hope was quickly extinguished as I could then see the fire pit had not been used in many years, maybe decades. Before I could investigate further, I felt and heard the presence of something alive in the cave with me. At first, it was the sound of something shifting its weight perhaps crouching getting ready to spring. Pushing the lantern toward the sound, I growled at the top of my lungs hoping whatever lay out of sight would think I was the bigger predator. There was a rustle of disturbed leaves and feet digging for traction before two large wood rats flushed and ran directly between my legs and out the cave entrance.

Silence returned to the cave with the departure of my four footed companions and after my heart ceased to thump like it was coming out of my chest. Another ten feet past some rusty tin cans took me to the back of the cave and what I had once thought might be Carlton's body. In the lantern's light I could see a large mound of black hair and then a leg and foot with claws. Thank goodness I had seen them first because next into view came a bear's head with an open mouth exposing fang-filled jaws. Its eyes were gone probably to satisfy the appetite of the hungry rats. Judging from the size of the bear's head it had once been a large animal and many broken teeth suggested it was old when it died. Defeated once again, I turned the lantern off and slowly crawled back to the cave entrance.

Outside in the fresh air and sunlight, I sat to collect my thoughts. It came to me that the bear had probably died during its winter slumber never knowing it was ill or suffering the consequences of a long sickness and lingering death. It would have helped if I could have believed Carlton died in similar fashion. But all evidence during the large manhunt suggested he had spent several days and nights trying to find help. Even in a deranged state Carlton must have known hunger, fear, panic and the pain of frozen fingers and toes. And, perhaps worst of all, knowing he would never see Ada, the children, his mother or home again. I wondered that if, wherever dead people go, his father had somehow been able to guide and comfort him into the next world. In the game of baseball a player comes to bat and gets three strikes before being declared out. For me, and Carlton's death, it seemed there would never be an out. Staying at Fall Stream I would forever be at bat flailing away at false hopes of finding my lost friend.

I tried to busy myself with work and reading at Brownsville. I kept up on the adventures of Theodore Roosevelt somehow feeling it kept me connected to Carlton in a small way. TR had remained critical of President Wilson's attempts to keep us out of war with Germany. He believed Germany was a great evil and that Wilson was acting cowardly while the leadership of someone like Washington or Lincoln was needed. Even though he had turned age 58, when war with Germany actually did come, TR asked permission to raise a brigade of infantry and mounted infantry soldiers. But he had made an enemy of Wilson and his request was turned down a day after it was made. I thought Carlton would have raised quite a fuss about the treatment Roosevelt had received. I could almost hear him saying that TR deserved better in light of all the good he had done in America.

Roosevelt got more bad news in July 1918 when his son, Quentin, was shot down and killed in France. Less than six months later, Theodore Roosevelt died on January 6, 1919. His was one of those gentle deaths as Roosevelt simply passed on during his sleep. I lost interest in politics after that. There was no one left to hash over ideas with or living great

men to read about. I think old age was beginning to settle into my body
and mind. My body reminded me with aching muscles and joints – which
usually disappeared once I got moving – but my mind increasingly ques-
tioned the point of living much longer. I had had my day, done many
things, and thought there wasn't a lot new to see or do. I went to bed
many nights thinking maybe I too might get a quiet death bestowed
upon me.

The poor deer hunting situation in 1921 was more or less the final
straw in deciding to leave my place on Fall Stream. I could still find
deer but being allowed to take only one buck or one doe for a whole
year severely limited my meat supply. I had reached age sixty-five on
March 24th and tired more easily from the constant farm chores, cutting of firewood, gardening, shoveling snow and other daily tasks necessary to live off the land. I also no longer tolerated the cold like I did as
a younger man. And living alone, especially in winter, got tougher to
deal with. I found myself drinking more and reading less. With Carlton's passing and the end of guiding groups of hunters and fishermen, I
had fewer opportunities to take part in good conversations lessening the
need to keep up on world events. And, then there was the question of
how much longer the State would overlook that fact that Foxey Brown
was a squatter living on Forest Preserve lands. With the decline of forest fires, and rangers in towers to watch for those that did get started,
and fewer hunters and fisherman after deer and trout, the Conservation
Commission no longer needed me as some sort of unpaid game warden at
Brownsville.

In February of 1920, I learned that Ada Banker had died in January.
According to the news story, death had come about in part due to her
"unrelenting grief" related to Carlton's death. The obituary said she was
"a woman of fine character with broad and generous principles" and that
her "chief aim in life was to make her home and loved ones happy and so
attractive did she make it, that it was the haven they all sought." Reading those words caused my knees to buckle. A vision flashed through
my mind of Carlton struggling, perhaps even crawling, to nearly his last
breath as he tried to get home to Ada. I prayed that night, that somehow,
somewhere, they were together in a peaceful place.

I had been doing better staying away from alcohol. But the report
about Ada's passing made my sense of guilt raw again and I went on a

drinking binge. After a few days my body wouldn't take any more booze and I slowly came to my senses. It was time to go and do something different. I sold off my animals, equipment, and as many household articles as possible in late summer 1921. My plan was to work for Bill Gallagher around his farm and at a new lumber business he was starting near Oxbow Lake. Bill also had a small cabin on his property large enough to accommodate a single man.

I spent a night on Witness Rock before leaving. Memories, mostly happy ones, from nearly thirty years of living at Fall Stream flowed forth under that late August star-filled sky. Peering into my campfire, I pictured the many nights Carlton and others had shared one with me. The stories, tall tales, and jokes from those days filled my mind and I chuckled recalling the big trout and flour-filled shot gun shell episodes. Then there were all those years Spook had been my constant companion. The pain of having lost Carlton was still with me and I remained puzzled how the mountains had hid him so completely despite the hundreds of days I had spent trying to find him. But that is the way of wild places. They have their own way of organizing things without consulting the needs or advice of humans. I fell asleep knowing I had lived an extraordinary life here – one filled with adventures and freedoms most men only dreamed about. I vowed to make return visits to Fall Stream every year. But I never did. Wounds can't heal if you reopen them all the time.

My last night in the cabin was a sleepless one. I kept wondering if I had made the right decision. I thought maybe there was someone who might come and share the place with me. But I had no idea who that person might be and I knew my habits and interests wouldn't match up easily with someone else. And then there was the State and enforcement of its squatter law to deal with. All things considered it was best to go and not look back.

As I lay pondering those things late that night, the howling of a lone and faraway coyote drifted through the cool still air. Like most men, I didn't understand coyote language. I did, however, respect their ability to survive most any situation. Smart and resourceful, they continued to exist in spite of attempts to wipe them out by hunting, trapping, poisoning, and killing by any means possible any time of the year.

The coyote calling was persistent and continued his solo concert for a long time. Pondering his reasons for doing so, I thought perhaps somehow there was a message being sent to me. Was it meant for me to be like the coyote – adaptable, flexible, willing and able to make a living in most any surroundings? Like the coyote it would mean keeping my eyes open for new opportunities wherever I wandered. I took his long and final hopeful notes as a stamp of agreement that I should move on. He would take care of new business at Fall Stream from now on.

I closed my cabin door the next morning knowing other men would visit once my departure became public knowledge. I guessed some would respect this special spot in the Adirondacks and others would trash what had been my home. It crossed my mind to torch the farm, barn and all. But too much of me had gone into building the place to do such a thing, although I had heard the State had no such compassion when it evicted squatters elsewhere. Fighting back tears, I turned and walked up the hill and into the woods. My chest was heavy and heart tense the first mile or so. But, as always, the exercise gained from walking and the forest air filling my lungs soothed me. Soon I was into my walking gait and the trail gave way to a new life that lay ahead.

Working for Bill Gallagher lasted only a short time. He was a kind and patient man and, out of compassion, never said anything about Carlton. I sensed he understood the burden I was carrying. Lacking the routines of life on Fall Stream, and forgetting to be like the coyote, I more or less stumbled my way, working and drinking, through the fall season before leaving Bill. After a particularly heavy drunken spree, I had had enough and resolved once again to change my ways. To do so, it seemed best to make a new start somewhere else – someplace where no one had heard of Foxey Brown or the Carlton Banker case.

I had recently made contact with my older brother James who was back from his prospecting adventures in Oregon. James had opened a small wood business in Gardiner near Augusta, Maine and invited me to move up and work with him. I turned down his offer preferring to try living in a warmer state for a change. I chose Maryland after learning from James that we had cousins down there. So, later that fall of 1921, I visited Charlie Preston and gave him a gun he had always liked. The gun had originally belonged to Cy Dunham who Charlie had admired. I asked Bill to "hold my blankets" and a few other things. The plan was for me to write and provide an address once I got settled in Maryland.

I went over to Wells and stayed for a short while. If I was going to visit relatives in Maryland, I decided it best to clean myself up with a bath, shave, and haircut and to get some new clothes. Dressed up in a new suit, I took advantage of a traveling photographer that had set up in the lobby of the Hosley Hotel and had some pictures taken of the new David Brennan. No one needed to know about Foxey Brown in Maryland or that I had been an Adirondack mountain man for many years. I thought I looked the part of a business man and headed for Northville to catch the next train south – and I went first class.

It's strange how events can yank a man away from even the best of plans. I had been in Maryland less than a year before a letter from Bill called me back to New York. The letter came with a newspaper story about Carlton. On Friday, November 10, 1922 – *six years to the day Carlton Banker disappeared in 1916* – Bill Abrams, while doing some scouting for deer, stepped off the Spruce Lake trail about three miles from Piseco. His attention was drawn to a beam of sunlight reflecting off an old tobacco can. Pushing aside some leaves with his foot, Abrams was startled to see human bones and a skull with a set of false teeth. He also noticed a small pair of women's boots and a very rusty rifle. Having been part of the original search party in 1916, he investigated no further – everyone knew Carlton Banker had very small feet! Bill quickly hiked back to Piseco and telephoned authorities.

Coroner J.D. Head of Wells and other officers accompanied Abrams back into the forest and brought out what remained of Carlton and his possessions. Confident Carlton Banker had been found, Coroner Head telephoned authorities in Gloversville to break the news. Because Ada Banker had died, the grim task of identifying Carlton was forced upon his children, Helen and Marion, and the family dentist.

All personal items (watch, diamond ring, engraved knife, rusty rifle) were with Carlton's remains including the meager three coins (two dimes and a nickel) he had joked about in my cabin the evening before he was lost. Carlton had died about three miles from Piseco Village and approximately five miles from where Fred Bagg and I had left him to watch for deer in 1916. How many times had our search parties walked past him? Tantalizingly close on the afternoon of Tuesday, November 14, 1916 when, instead of fanning out to search that section of trail, we marched quickly back to Piseco Lake due to snow and the lateness of the day. And how many times did I, his best friend, travel hauntingly close to Carlton during my numerous trips from Brownsville to Piseco between 1917 and 1921? Why didn't I sense his presence? Perhaps my dream of Carlton drowning in the vly, along with the newspaper stories about the "bogs of the north," had clouded my thinking.

Even if Bill Gallagher could have reached me by telephone, I wouldn't have attended the services Helen and Marian arranged for Carlton. My presence would have only made their grieving more difficult to bear. The few bones and skull left by forest scavengers had to be disturbing for the girls to see as they imagined their father's body being devoured by the gnashing and chewing jaws of forest critters. I knew full well the burden of such images. It was best to leave Helen and Marian alone with family and friends as they brought closure to Carlton's tragic death.

I visited Carlton's and Ada's graves in Johnstown cemetery the next spring. It was a warm and sunny April day with a wind coming gently out of the south. Robins and other migrating birds were already getting into their mating rituals with songs and calls filling the air. I thought the time for tears had passed. But sadness and melancholy set in as the notion of death and disappointment filled my consciousness. But, like all things, this passed as I sat in the grass next to Carlton's stone and began to recall our days together at Fall Stream. Visions of him excitedly talking about Teddy Roosevelt and telling of his conversation with some deer came to mind as did his glee when getting even with me for the big trout trick I had pulled on him and Fred Bagg. I could almost hear Spook barking that night in my cabin when we nearly laughed ourselves unconscious about my gold mine at Fall Stream. It came to me that we had had only one bad time together – that being the night Carlton was lost to the mountains. A poker player would love to win and lose at that rate. In the end, a man can't ask much more out of life than to attain some success pursuing his passions. So many people never find a life-long passion. For Carlton and me it had been a love affair with Adirondack wild places and things. And, for Carlton, there had been an added bonus in his love for Ada, Helen, and Marion.

I lingered there a long time enjoying memories of my times with Carlton. Reflecting more on our days together, it struck me that life comes in episodes. Some we get to choose and others just happen. I thought that is sort of a definition for adventure – things we get into that test us and where the outcome is in doubt. Perhaps that's also why so many men love hunting and fishing. It helped explain what bonded Carlton and me so strongly.

A chickadee landed ever so lightly on Carlton's stone, looked around, ruffled and soothed it feathers like a music conductor might straighten his suit before beginning a concert, and gave forth its spring song, "Fee-bee, fee-bee-ee." In an eerie way, there was a pause in the songs of other birds and the lone chickadee on Carlton's stone had the stage to itself like it had that day when we gave up the search for Carlton. My hearing may have got it wrong, but the bird's repetitive song came to me as "free-free, free-free-ee." I started repeating "free-free" thinking somehow Carlton had found a way to send a message that he was doing fine and I should go on with my life. An image of Carlton with a large smile on his face entered my mind for the first time since he disappeared.

Perhaps my brain was only making itself comfortable but I felt lighter when the chickadee finished singing and took flight. Somehow it was taking a great weight off my spirit. Was the chickadee carrying away my burden of guilt and shame? I recalled the chickadee's song the rest of my days in Maryland and even eight years later as I lay dying at brother James' house in Maine.

The Catholic priest back in my boyhood days used to say St. Peter up in heaven was keeping a book of life where everything we did got recorded. At the time I didn't much care what got written down because I had no plans of leaving my earthly home. But, when a man grows old he knows more time has lapsed then lies ahead and there's no option coming except to leave. In a way, I was looking forward to what I hoped was another life after death. It was just the trip that scared me most.

Based on what I had seen in nature, I figured the odds were pretty good there was another life coming after this one passed. It just seemed that nature didn't waste much and was in the business of creating and recreating life most everywhere. I thought what a waste it would be for a man to live a long life, make mistakes, learn from them and only have all that experience just go to no good. I was betting the Creator had a better plan – one where the circumstances leading to the man's mistakes were taken into consideration before deciding what to do with him. After all, most humans don't get to set the stage here on earth but have to play out the parts handed to us as best we can. In the end, I was at peace believing while I had messed up here and there in my roles as David Brennan, the troubled Maine farm boy, and as Foxey Brown, one-time outlaw and Adirondack guide, I had done some good things too.

Foxey Brown/David Brennan, circa 1921. (Joanne Buyce)

EPILOGUE

David A. Brennan/David "Foxey" Brown died on July 19, 1930 at age seventy-six in Pittston, Maine. At the time he had been living for two years with his older brother James on Spring Hill Street. David was buried shortly afterwards in the family burial lot in his home town of Benedicta, Maine. The death record lists Owen Brennan as his father and Katherine Brennan as his mother. Survivors mentioned in David's obituary include brothers James and John plus two sisters, Mrs. Bridget Roach and Mrs. Mary Cummings. David suffered from angina and died from an unspecified "chronic heart" problem. His previous residence is listed as Maryland.

David Brennan probably died believing history would not remember Foxey Brown and his days as a well-known, almost legendary, Adirondack guide – much less that, today, his name might be printed on regularly purchased maps of the West Canada Lake Wilderness Area. He may even have tried to disassociate himself from his Foxey Brown days and involvement with the disappearance of Carlton Banker.

An article in the *Amsterdam Evening Recorder* (December 7, 1920) is headlined, "Banker's Last Guide Lands in Montgomery County Jail." As the story goes, Foxey was very intoxicated and caused a disturbance on a train headed eastbound out of Fonda. In his possession was a long bladed hunting knife. When police officers arrived, Foxey claimed his name was Collins and that a Mr. Carey of Rome, NY had given the knife to him. The police checked with Mr. Carey who stated that he had, indeed, once given the knife to a friend and guide named Foxey Brown. Confronted with that fact, Foxey stated, according to the newspaper, that his real name was "Edward" Brennan and he was the guide last with Carlton Banker. Brennan then related the story of Banker's disappearance and proclaimed his innocence of any wrongdoing. Why he tried to mislead police with the first name, Edward, is unknown. Perhaps, Brennan was still under the influence of alcohol or he was trying to close the Foxey Brown portion of his life. No charges were pressed other than public intoxication and Brennan/Brown was released after a few days in jail.

At first glance the tale of Foxey Brown appears to be a sad one – a mismanaged life coupled with some unfortunate luck. His story is filled with premature losses of those he loved – brothers and sisters in their childhoods, his father at age sixteen, two brothers before they were forty, and his best friend, Carlton Banker. There were also tangled relationships with people in his hometown and the brawl in a Boston barroom that caused David Brennan to flee to the Adirondacks and become Foxey Brown. And then, after all those years of solitary living in the mountains – dealing with blizzards, sub-zero temperatures, droughts, and forest fires – his last years were spent as an ailing poor man having to live with his brother.

However, as described in the preceding pages, Foxey Brown enjoyed many happy days on Fall Stream. Reflecting on his life may reveal important messages for those of us currently inhabiting the planet. What could twenty-first century people learn from the life of an Adirondack recluse/guide who lived a hundred years ago?

An obvious lesson from the Foxey Brown story involves how to survive in a wilderness setting. While it is very likely Carlton Banker suffered from a stroke and didn't have fully functioning faculties, he did violate the cardinal rule of being rescued when lost – Stay put! Busy yourself preparing signal devices, build a fire and some sort of shelter. Secure drinking water and food if you can. Then, let searchers find you! Mr. Banker's demise was most likely a case of hypothermia doing its devious and deadly business. However, it is somewhat puzzling why so many possessions (boots, rifle, knife, watch, compass, coins, and a pair of opera glasses) were found with his body. Often a person in the later stages of hypothermia will discard personal items – even their clothing – just as the Wendigo story involving Gideon Prince graphically illustrates. Did Carlton Banker stave off hypothermia only to succumb to a final stroke or heart attack?

It is possible that Mr. Banker actually died from a series of strokes. If so, he broke another good rule to honor before undertaking rigorous exercise – be sure the body is ready to handle it. Carlton was known to have high blood pressure and may have been on medication. Whatever the case, the lesson is to take wilderness, even backcountry, excursions seriously and plan accordingly. Wild places can reinvigorate the mind and spirit but they can also be unkind hosts for the old, weak and infirmed.

Foxey Brown and Carlton Banker both loved the Adirondack wilderness. Carlton had been visiting the mountains starting as a young man in 1893, when he returned to Gloversville with "as fine a catch of trout" as anyone could remember. He and Foxey had hunted and fished the Fall Stream region for decades and were very familiar with its general features and its nooks and crannies. However, familiarity can lead to comfort, comfort to carelessness, and carelessness to danger. Being a mistress, and not a wife, nature is free to run off, or turn against the visitor on short notice – or with no warning of any sort! Many a human traveler has learned this lesson the hard way in the realms of wilderness travel and human relationships. One day a snow bridge may be a welcome winter short cut across a stream and the next, a trap door plunging the unwary traveler into frigid water and a deadly date with hypothermia. It is safest to remember that nature brings people into this world, bears us for a while, and is always ready to reclaim its work. Life is a dance. However, in wilderness settings, nature chooses what, when, where and how the music is played.

Another lesson from Foxey Brown's experience lies in the realm of living a simple life filled with plenty of outdoor exercise. As close as their friendship was, Carlton Banker and Foxey Brown had markedly different lifestyles. As a railroad executive Carlton lived in a city filled with the foulness (smoke from railroad engines, factories, and thousands of wood/coal heated homes) cities were known for at the time. His work put him behind a desk most days and Carlton had to shoulder the stresses all business executives must bear. We don't know his eating habits, but Banker's wealth would have allowed consumption of most anything he wanted, when he wanted it.

Foxey, on the other hand, lived an exercise-filled outdoor lifestyle. The daily routines of farm work using axes, saws, shovels, pitchforks, scythes and other hand tools kept muscles toned and provided an outlet for mental pressures. His diet consisted mainly of basic fare, fresh and devoid of contamination found in factory foods. Foxey also endured none of the foul air Carlton breathed day after day near the railroad yards.

Whether Foxey consciously knew it or not, he was enjoying a special kind of air only the forest provides.

In her 2007 book, *Teaching the Trees: Lessons from the Forest*, biologist Joan Maloof discusses the possible benefits of the "sweet, rich, earthy smell" of forest air. According to Maloof there may be many medicinal benefits from breathing forest air. The Japanese even have a name for it, *shinrin-yoku*, or wood-air bathing. Researchers in Japan claim diabetic patients experience blood sugar drops to healthier levels after a walk in the forest. Research with autistic children also suggests they become more responsive after a walk in a natural area. And, even city office workers are more productive after returning to work from a walk in a park. But what is it that makes people feel better being in the forest?

California researchers working the Sierra Nevada forests found 120 chemical compounds in the air – fifty of which couldn't be identified. There is no question that we are product of what we eat. We may also be heavily influenced by what we breathe. Do the molecules in forest air alter perceptions and physical health when entering our nasal passages and become fully absorbed into the body? Aroma therapists have believed so for centuries. Could Thoreau have been on to something when he wrote about the "tonics of forest air" in 1854? Did Foxey Brown choose, in part, to stay at Fall Stream instead of returning to Boston because of conditioning by forest air? Perhaps it was a combination of environmental imprinting and philosophical choice.

Literature of the day was replete with claims about the healthfulness of Adirondack living. Prominent physicians of the 1890's, for example, extolled the benefits tuberculosis (consumption) patients could gain from time spent in the mountains. Dr. E.L. Trudeau, famous for his sanatorium in Saranac Lake, professed that "Twenty-five per cent of the patients sent to the Adirondacks suffering from incipient consumption come back cured…" Dr. Alfred Loomis, "an eminent authority," wrote profusely about the "evergreen forests" having "a powerful purifying effect upon the surrounding atmosphere, and that it is rendered antiseptic by the chemical combinations which are constantly going on in them…" namely "the product of atmospheric oxidization of turpentine."

Known to be an avid reader, Foxey Brown would have been aware of the highly publicized health benefits of living in the Adirondacks.

Whatever the case, Foxey Brown died at age seventy-six well beyond (eighteen years) a man's life expectancy of fifty-eight years in 1930. And, he was a smoker and possibly a tobacco chewer.

Precisely how David Brennan Brown gained the nickname "Foxey" may be lost to history. In telling Foxey's story, the author has attributed it to Brown's poker playing skills and expressions of wit. Wherever the truth lies, Brown/Brennan certainly didn't come to be called "Foxey" because he lacked intelligence. Records state David Brennan had college studies to his credit and, "It was evident to many who knew him that he was a man of some culture and learning by his discussions of affairs and books." Whether David Brennan got his nickname from a poker game, from his wit, or because he successfully avoided officers trying to catch him breaking hunting/fishing regulations, his intelligence and craftiness is legendary.

Knowing Foxey Brown was a man of considerable intellect raises one last question. Did he write? Are there diaries somewhere filled with Foxey's thoughts about the many and varied events of his life? Usually people who read voraciously also put pen to paper. It is difficult to imagine David Brennan/Foxey Brown spending all those nights alone in the Adirondack wilds of Fall Stream without trying to record some of his thoughts. Someday, somewhere in an old second hand shop, maybe a lucky visitor will stumble upon the writings of Foxey Brown/David Brennan. Then perhaps we can learn, from Brennan's own words, why he chose to live wild and free.

For now, we are left with the saga of an Adirondack mountain man who lived through the beginnings of the American Conservation movement as it unfolded, between 1885 and 1920, in New York State's "North Woods." He came to the southern Adirondacks when a laissez-faire way of using wild things and places was on the wane. Brown witnessed the State's hit and miss starts at conservation and preservation of the Adirondack Park and Forest Preserve. As a guide and resident he also experienced the impact of increasingly strict regulations designed to save wildlife, streams and forests – regulations that often overlooked traditional ways of life and the needs of year-round Adirondack residents. Caught in the conflict of needing to hunt and kill wildlife and yet ensure their continuance, Adirondack guides played a significant role in discussion of issues and influencing decision makers in government and business circles.

As a group, sometimes knowingly and sometimes unknowingly, they helped the State advance its conservation agenda.

Unfortunately, current Adirondack residents still face problems similar to those encountered by working class people of Foxey Brown's time. Perhaps most frustrating is that people have difficulty finding private sector employment opportunities that pay above minimum wage rates. Most often they must work for a local, state, or federal government agency to earn salary and benefits of sufficient size to own, maintain, and pay taxes on property. Those jobs are small in number and have long waiting lists once an opening does occur. The net result, in the words of the Common Ground Alliance of the Adirondacks (CGA), is seen in "loss of main streets, out-migration of youth, lack of business development and markets and inadequate and aging infrastructure."

In short, the dilemma facing leaders in the Adirondack Park is how to enhance the economic well-being of their communities without destroying the natural attributes of the mountains. To use the parlance of "common ground," leaders may find a guiding principle written by American naturalist Henry David Thoreau in 1854 useful: "in Wildness is the preservation of the world...From the forest and wilderness come the tonics and barks which brace mankind." The Adirondacks are fortunate to have both wild places (backcountry) and designated wilderness areas. Indeed, wildness in its various forms is the unique feature that makes the Adirondacks special. If marketed creatively in our rapidly urbanizing world, wildness can help generate a sustainable and unending supply of economic well-being for Adirondack residents.

Foxey Brown's story may enlighten and inspire those who would live close to nature and stop marching to the dictates of machines and the maddening pulse of modern life. Brown's life suggests he understood what prompted Henry David Thoreau to live on Walden Pond – the belief that "The mass of men lead lives of quiet desperation and go to the grave with the song still in them." Settling for small comforts they become "serfs of the soil" and, in so doing, never fully live at all.

The next time someone opens a West Canada Lakes Wilderness Area map, reads the words "Foxey Brown Hermitage," and does a "Google" Internet search, there will be an additional website to explore – one that doesn't feature a rap singer. Instead, the Internet searcher will find a story offering a different and very ancient formula for well-being.

You belong outside with the wind blowing strong through your hair.
It seems only right; it's so natural to see you running there.
Spread your wings to fly, go without a care
Through the cloudless sky, the wind'll take you there.
There's a chance you might live forever as you breathe the free air.

– B. Matthews, 1974

THE BALLAD OF CARLTON BANKER

COME ALL YOU ADIRONDACK FOLK, A STORY I WILL TELL
THE TALE OF CARLTON BANKER, WHO KNEW THE WOODS QUITE WELL
IN THE FALL OF 1916, HE DID DECIDE TO GO
TO HUNT PISECO'S FOREST, BEYOND THE MOOSE LAKE ROAD

YOUNG BANKER LIVED IN GLOVERSVILLE, HE WAS A WELL-KNOWN MAN
A HUSBAND AND A FATHER, A DEER-HUNT WAS HIS PLAN
HE WAS THE SUPERINTENDENT, OF THE CAYUDUTTA LINE
HIS LIFE WAS ALL IN ORDER, AND THINGS WERE GOING FINE

FOR HUNTING AND FOR FISHING, IN THE ADIRONDACK RANGE
RICH SPORTSMEN ALL DEPENDED, ON GUIDES WHO COULD ARRANGE
TO TAKE THEM THRU THE FOREST, MAKE CAMP AND FIND THEIR GAME
TO KEEP THEM SAFE WITHIN THE WOODS, AND BRING THEM OUT AGAIN

CARLTON BANKER LOVED THE FOREST, TO HUNT THERE AND TO FISH
FOXEY BROWN WAS ALWAYS WITH HIM, FOR THAT WAS CARLTON'S WISH
FOXEY KNEW THE ADIRONDACKS, HE WAS A WELL-KNOWN GUIDE
AND WHENEVER CARLTON HUNTED, FOXEY BROWN WAS BY HIS SIDE

NOW CARLTON HAD AN INJURED KNEE, AND NOT LONG ON THE TRAIL,
THE WEATHER TURNED MUCH COLDER, AND HIS KNEE BEGAN TO FAIL
FOXEY BROWN & FREDDY BAGG AGREED, TO SCOUT THE MOUNTAIN 'ROUND
TO DRIVE THE DEER TO CARLTON, SO HE COULD BRING IT DOWN

THE MEN WENT ROUND THE MOUNTAIN, AND TRIED TO TURN A DEER
DARKNESS GATHERED SLOWLY, BUT FOR THEM IT HELD NO FEAR
THEY FOUND NO DEER FOR CARLTON, THEY RETURNED WITHOUT A CARE
BUT WHEN THEY GOT BACK TO BANKER'S STAND, THEY FOUND HE WASN'T THERE

NOW IT DIDN'T REALLY BOTHER THEM, NO, THEY DIDN'T THINK IT STRANGE
FOR FOXEY KNEW THAT CARLTON, WAS FAMILIAR WITH THAT RANGE
THEY WENT BACK TO THE CAMP SITE, THINKING SOON HE WOULD APPEAR
BUT WHEN HE DIDN'T FOLLOW, IT GAVE THEM CAUSE TO FEAR

THEY SEARCHED THE SNOWY DARKNESS, WITH THE LANTERNS AT THE CAMP
THEY YELLED AND FIRED GUNSHOTS, BUT NO ONE ANSWERED BACK
FOXEY BECAME FRANTIC, LEST CARLTON COME TO HARM
THEY TREKED BACK TO PISECO, AND ISSUED AN ALARM

ONE HUNDRED FOREST GUIDES CAME IN, TO THE TRUMAN LAWRENCE CAMP
ED GLAVIN CAME FROM SYRACUSE WITH HIS TRACKHOUNDS, DUKE AND PEG
THEY SEARCHED UP JESSUP'S RIVER, WHERE SOME SAID TRACKS WERE FOUND
BUT DUKE AND PEG FOUND NOTHING, AND THE SNOW KEPT COMING DOWN

CLIFF VROOMAN AND THE SLACK BROTHERS, PACKED IN THRU MOSSY VLAIE
THRU THE WILLIS MOUNTAIN COUNTRY, MOOSELAKE THEY THOU'T THEY'D TRY
THESE WERE HARDENED WOODSMEN, WHO KNEW EACH ROCK AND LEDGE
BUT IN SEVEN DAYS THEY REAPPEARED, AND ONLY SHOOK THEIR HEADS

EXACTLY SIX YEARS TO THE DAY, WHEN CARLTON DISAPPEARED
BILL ABRAMS FOUND A SKELETON, DEEP IN A MOUNTAIN WIER
THREE MILES NORTH OF PISECO, A RING AND WATCH HE FOUND
THEY BROUGHT OUT CARLETON BANKER, AND LAID HIM IN THE GROUND

NOW MANY GUIDES BLAMED FOXEY BROWN, THEY FELT HE SHOULD ATONE
FOR ALL AGREED IT WAS UNWISE, TO LEAVE YOUR MAN ALONE
THE IRON LAW OF GUIDING, IS NOT HARD TO EXPLAIN
WHEN YOU TAKE A MAN INTO THOSE WOODS, YOU MUST BRING HIM OUT AGAIN

WHEN BANKER WAS DISCOVERED, FOXEY BROWN WAS FAR AWAY
HE'D LEFT THE ADIRONDACKS, HE COULD NO LONGER STAY
GUIDES AND SPORTSMEN SHUNNED HIM, THEY DID NOT COMPREHEND
CARLTON BANKER WAS NOT JUST HIS MAN, HE ALSO WAS HIS FRIEND

– PETER BETZ, 2/14/2011

Author's Note and Acknowledgements

In the beginning of this book I alluded to the notion that instead of my finding Foxey Brown perhaps he found me. Being a professor trained in the scientific method, I am not prone to crediting supernatural powers for fortuitous/unfortunate things that happen to me. However, I must share some things that occurred for which I have no concrete explanation.

Looking back on the five year quest for information on Foxey Brown, I remain amazed at the generosity and spirit of cooperation people demonstrated. In most cases, I was contacting complete strangers asking for information on a long deceased and relatively unknown Adirondack Mountain man.

Time after time, after a brief explanation of my project, busy people promptly found information I was seeking and expected/wanted no compensation. "Just happy to help tell Foxey Brown's story" was a common response to my "Thank you" and other expressions of gratitude. What is it that resonates with people about the adventures of Foxey Brown? Perhaps, in part, it is because they can relate to hiding in the mountains and living a simple outdoor life. And most of us can relate to tragedies we know might occur most any time in the course of living.

People were also willing to share personal stories with me – a stranger on the telephone or the writer of an email. Stories that entailed trusting the listener (me) would not think them a kook. One great grandchild of Carlton Banker told of a Gloversville experience that occurred when he was a young man in the early 1960's. On a late spring day that year, he stood nearby as demolition experts were taking down some of the old F. J. & G. railroad buildings including one that had housed Superintendent Carlton Banker's office in 1916. As the workers proceeded to push the buildings down with heavy equipment and make piles of debris, a breeze sprung up and blew dust and light-weight materials around. Some papers landed at the grandchild's feet. Reaching down he picked up a November, 1916 F.J. & G. railroad ticket to Northville. The exact ride Carlton Banker had taken on his way to Piseco and Foxey Brown's camp in November of 1916.

Another individual who had lived in Ada and Carlton Banker's Gloversville home spoke of "the presence of past family members being felt in the house." Evidently, the previous owner related having the same sensation. Who knows what things happen in realms beyond our temporary earthly experience? Is Ada Banker still waiting for Carlton to return "most any day" as newspapers reported in 1916? I hope not. To think of Ada being trapped in that manner is very sad.

Other less supernatural and debatable experiences occurred during the research phase of this book. Trying to "leave no stone unturned," I placed an advertisement in the *Hamilton County Express* newspaper requesting information/photographs on Foxey Brown or Brown's Pond. Adirondack writer, Don Williams, saw the advertisement and telephoned to say there might be a photograph of Foxey Brown in the Wells Historical Society museum although no one had ever verified it to be Brown. Don didn't know at the time that his simple act of kindness would later lead to reading and endorsing my manuscript.

A telephone call to the historical society revealed they had recently sold the photograph at a garage sale because no one knew anything about it. And, it had "hung around too long." Fortunately, Wells is still a small community, and unlike many places in American today, people know each other and I soon had a name and telephone number to call.

That evening I was chatting with Joanne Buyce. Joanne, not knowing anything about the man in the photograph, purchased it because she likes old things and was attracted to the large, heavy wooden, twenty by fourteen inch, frame that protects the photograph. Joanne described the man in the photograph as being late middle to early senior aged and was dressed in a suit of some sort. She had seen Foxey Brown's image in *The History of Hamilton County*, thought there was a resemblance to her photograph, but couldn't promise they were the same man. I was "welcome to come and see" for myself. The next Saturday I began my three hour drive to Wells, NY.

News had spread that some downstate fellow writing a book about an early 1900's Adirondack character, named Foxey Brown, was coming to visit the Historical Society and Joanne Buyce. While I can't say, "the whole town turned out," six or seven members of the society, along with Joanne and her husband Ken, greeted me. Everyone agreed there was a striking resemblance to the images of Foxey Brown I had brought along. Ever so carefully, Joanne removed the frame and backing from her photograph hoping some notes or writing of any sort might verify the man was Foxey Brown. We were not that fortunate, but all witnesses to date agree Don Williams was correct. The image is, indeed, a very distinguished looking Foxey Brown/David Brennan attired in a tuxedo type coat and bow tie. Why and how the photograph got left in Wells, NY when Foxey departed the area around 1921, remains a mystery. The formality of the image, however, suggests something about the underlying refinement and tastes of the old Adirondack guide. Could it have been a Christmas gift Carlton Banker was preparing to surprise Foxey Brown? The route from the Northville F.J. & G. railroad station to Piseco took travelers through Wells. Questions about the life of Foxey Brown continued to enter my consciousness as I tried to bring his story to an end. I sometimes suspect Foxey Brown may not be done with me yet. I say this not in the sense (but who knows) that Foxey Brown is somehow directly guiding me from the beyond but that story once told and recorded never dies. The story then carries a life and force of its own.

Acknowledging those who helped put Foxey Brown's story into print is no easy task. As a lover, but non-resident of the Adirondacks, it was with some trepidation that I began asking natives about Foxey Brown for he was their folklore character and here was some downstate professor trying to tell the story. Perhaps my determination to find exactly where Foxey lived and uncover unknown particulars of his story helped bring about a sense of shared adventure. Wherever the truth lies, I am indebted to many people.

In rough chronological order, they include: Paul Wilber long time Hamilton County Historian, for acquainting me with Fred Aber and Stella King's, *The History of Hamilton County*; Historian James Morrison, Gloversville, NY for finding death records regarding Carlton Banker; Judy Marcoux, for her collaboration and search of archived newspaper accounts regarding the disappearance of Carlton Banker; Paul Larner at the Fonda, Johnstown, and Gloversville Railroad Museum, for providing newspaper clippings and chasing down elusive images of Carlton Banker; Mary Donohue at Fulton Montgomery Community College Evans Library for gaining access to, and approving use of, Carlton Banker images; Robert Maider for searching his law office records regarding the Carlton Banker case; and to T. Samuel Hoye for sharing of a photograph of Ada Banker and her children at the Gloversville home they shared with Carlton Banker circa 1916. A very special thank you goes to Peter Betz, Fulton County historian, song writer and singer for composing and sharing his *Ballad of Carlton Banker*. Peter also lent his expertise in checking Banker family burial records and retrieving photographs.

Thanks also: to Lynn Billingham and the Piseco Lake Historical Society for opening its archives and sharing every tidbit of information she could find and to Annie Weaver, Town of Lake Pleasant historian. A special salute goes to Bill Abrams (Floyd William Abrams, 1927-2009) and Don Courtney of Piseco for allowing me to visit and interview them about Foxey Brown and relatives who knew him in the early 1900's. Tom Preston was also generous in discussing family memories and stories about his grandparents, Charlie and Julia Preston.

Without the assistance of Gardiner, Maine Public Library volunteers, Rob Whittier and GariLu Weeks I may have never found Foxey Brown/ David Brennan's death certificate, obituaries, and census records. GariLu's exhaustive efforts at the Maine State Library revealed much about Foxey's life after he left Piseco. I am indebted also to Richard Kelly, Jr. for the gracious sharing of his book, *Requiescant in Pace, 1839-1991* detailing burial records in Benedicta, Maine cemeteries.

Some good luck is indispensable when one tries to describe life in an earlier period of history. Written records are, of course, very helpful. But, as the saying goes: "A picture is worth a thousand words." My incredibly good luck came from Cindy and Fred Adcock when they published their book, *Images of America: Piseco Lake and Arietta* in 2008. It is a treasure trove of images and information about the life and times where Foxey Brown lived. There is no way to adequately express how invaluable the Adcock publication has been. And, to boot, both Cindy and Fred generously shared their images and advice throughout the duration of my project.

I also had the good fortune to discover Joann Dunham and her tremendous work assembling an Abrams, Courtney, Dunham, and Judway family tree on Ancestry.com. Joann's commitment to preserving her family Piseco Lake history is inspiring and very representative of good genealogical research and record preservation. Thanks also go to Don Williams for reading my manuscript and sharing his writing and Adirondack history expertise.

Much love and appreciation go to my daughter Jessica for her support and assistance formatting photographs and conceiving cover designs. Time spent working together on a project of shared passion is always a good thing.

Recognition is also due to Angel Bovee. Despite carrying a heavy load of graduate studies and working many hours per week; Angel graciously, and with genuine interest, supported my attempts to "make images of Foxey look good." Her work and that of good friend Jerome Natoli contributed greatly in preparing an interesting book cover.

Storytelling and outdoor adventures are best when shared with people of kindred spirit. In this vein, I give much credit to my brother Jerry Yaple for introducing me to Piseco Lake and Fall Stream. Without him, I may never have learned about Foxey Brown and been able to make initial forays into Fall Stream.

A good portion of the Foxey Brown story may not have been written without the assistance of Dr. David Miller my college colleague, hiking and hunting partner, and friend who used his GPS expertise to locate Foxey Brown's home on Fall Stream. Many more apple pies at the Yaple family home are due to Dave for sharing my quest and all those bushwhacking hikes into, and cold nights camping at, the remains of Foxey's homestead. I will always joyfully recall our many campfire talks and collaborations about the life of Foxey Brown. And, I agree it is best to keep those map coordinates secret lest too many hikers visit and disturb Foxey's hideout on Fall Stream.

One test of a real friendship involves having someone who never tires of hearing about your passions – enter Jerry Marsh my boyhood friend of nearly sixty years. Thanks for listening, discussing, encouraging and helping evaluate my endless theories and progress with Foxey Brown – and, after all that, for carefully copyediting my manuscript. I remain deeply regretful about subjecting you to that biting insect filled night without a tent at Foxey's place!

A salute also goes to Dale Weston my other boyhood friend who after more than sixty years continues to share my love for wild things and places – a passion shaped by our countless childhood explorations of streams and forests and the construction of secret hideouts.

Sincere appreciation goes to those who assisted my Foxey Brown writing endeavor. Another test of a good friendship is when someone takes time out from a heavy work schedule to read and constructively comment on your manuscript. I am indebted to Bruce Matthews my outdoor loving, fishing, hunting, hiking and camping buddy of more than thirty years, for his honest evaluation and suggestions regarding the various drafts of Foxey Brown. They were insightful and critical to whatever success comes from the book's publication. A special thanks goes to Bruce for sharing so many good outdoor books over the years and for the song (*You Belong Outside*) he wrote and gave to me in 1974. It still hangs prominently on my office wall and I reflect on it regularly.

Likewise, many thanks are due to my colleague and friend John Hoeschele for sharing his professional writing, editing and graphic design skills as he carefully read the last drafts of the manuscript and tried to keep me focused as to how Foxey Brown might have told his story. A large pat on the back also goes to John for patiently helping me settle on a final title for the book.

Last, but certainly not least, I would be greatly remiss in not recognizing Sharon, my wife of forty years, for understanding and sharing my love of the outdoors and wild places. Together, we have created a homestead on Hermit Hill surrounded by wild landscapes and creatures. Like Foxey Brown, I have been able to breathe forest air every day and be re-energized by the rhythms of the natural world. Unlike Foxey Brown, I have also been surrounded by a loving wife and children!

– Charles H. Yaple II

SOURCE NOTES

The German scholar, philosopher and cultural critic, Friedrich Nietzsche, postulated that "There are no facts, only interpretations." The attempt to tell the life story of an Adirondack guide and recluse who died eighty years ago required considerable allegiance to Nietzsche's words. Other than three images of Brown, a brief description of Carlton Banker's disappearance in a history book and related newspaper articles; there are few written records pertaining specifically to Foxey Brown's (David Brennan's) life. That being said, the author has diligently tried to interpret his life in a fashion consistent with what has been recorded about the place and times that influenced him. The notes that follow include a conscientious attempt to clearly identify fictitious characters and actual people who interacted with Foxey Brown.

ABBREVIATIONS USED

ADCOCK: Adcock, Frederick and Cynthia. *Images of America: Piseco Lake and Arietta*. Portsmouth, NH: Arcadia Publishing. 2008.

AD CHRON: Chilson, Gary (ed). *An Adirondack Chronology*. The Adirondack Research Library of the Association for the Protection of the Adirondacks Chronology Management Team. 2010. Available as a pdf.on line at www.protect ads.org. An excellent timeline resource for anyone wishing to understand Adirondack history and the rise of conservation in the United States.

AD TALES: Aber, Ted and King, Stella. *Tales from an Adirondack County*. Prospect, NY. Prospect Books. 1961.

CENSUS: United States Federal Census.

DUNHAM: Dunham, Harvey. *Adirondack French Louie: Early Life in the North Woods.* Utica, NY. Thomas Griffiths Sons. 1952.

CRIMES: Jacoby, Karl. *Crimes Against Nature: Squatters, Poachers, Thieves, and the Hidden History of American Conservation.* Los Angeles: University of California Press. 2001

DUNHAM: Dunham, Harvey. *Adirondack French Louie: Early Life in the North Woods.* Utica, NY. Thomas Griffiths Sons. 1952.

HAMHIS: Aber, Ted and King Stella. *The History of Hamilton County.* Lake Pleasant, NY. Great Wilderness Books. Lake Pleasant, NY. 1965.

HERALD: *The Gloversville and Johnstown New York Morning Herald.*

DEDICATION

Nature deficit disorder: Louv, Richard. *Last Child in the Woods: Saving Our Children from Nature Deficit Disorder.* Algonquin Books. 2005.

PROLOUGE

Adirondack map – Foxey Brown Hermitage: The Adirondacks Central Mountains. Plinth Quion & Cornice Associates. Keene Valley, New York. 1984. Available at various retail outlets in the Adirondacks.

Foxey Brown basic facts – HAMHIS, pp. 345-347 and AD TALES, pp. 195-199. Other than newspaper stories covering the disappearance of Carlton Banker, little written record exists concerning Foxey Brown. This is puzzling considering there are numerous references stating he was "the region's most legendary hermit" (AD TALES, p. 195) and "Brown is one of the well known guides and characters of the lower Adirondacks" (Gloversville Morning Herald, November 15, 1916). The Adirondack Museum at Blue Mountain Lake had no record of Foxey Brown in its Adirondack Guides files.

Brown educated man: "Remains of Hunter Long Missing Found in Woods." *Amsterdam Evening Record.* Saturday, November 11, 1922, pp. 1-2. Brown "had at one time been a student in one of the eastern colleges…" "It was evident to many who knew him that he was a man of some culture and learning by his discussions of affairs and books."

SUNY Cortland: State University of New York College at Cortland, Cortland, New York.

West Canada Lakes Wilderness Area: See: Map of *The Adirondacks Central Mountains.* Plinth Quion & Cornice Associates. Keene Valley, New York. 1984.

"Get out of here…send lead for sinkers:" statement used by Foxey Brown on a regular basis when he chased intruders from Brown's Pond. HAMHIS, p. 345

1. RUN FOR THE HILLS

David A. Brennan: Born March 24, 1854 in Benedicta, Maine. Father: Owen Brennan, Mother: Catherine Brown Brennan. Vital Records of State of Maine, 1923-1936, Microfilm Roll 7. 1860 US CENSUS: David Brennan, age five. Parents: Owen and Catherine Brennan

George Murphy: The actual name of David Brennan/Foxey Brown's barroom fight opponent is unknown. Other character names in this chapter are also fictitious.

Barroom fight: HAMHISTORY, pp. 344-47.

Owen Brennan: Died January 17, 1870. Requiescant in Pace 1839-1991. *St. Benedict's Roman Catholic Cemetery.* Richard Kelly Jr. Augusta, Maine: O'Ceallaigh Publications. 1994.

Making a living in the mountains: There are numerous books available that depict the lives of Adirondack guides, hermits, and lumberjacks. Three of particular value are: *Tales from an Adirondack County* by Aber and King, *French Louie* by Harvey Dunham and *Adirondack Characters and Campfire Yarns* by William J. O'Hern

Logging camp jobs: Good descriptions can be found in DUNHAM, HAMHIS, and Paul Schneider's, *The Adirondacks: A History of America's First Wilderness.* Road Monkeys were men responsible for keeping logging roads level. In the winter sprinkler wagons were used to fill road ruts with water in an effort to smooth things over once the water froze. Woodstoves under the water tanks sometimes were necessary to prevent the water from freezing prematurely.

Log Drivers had the most dangerous of jobs and also the most prestigious. Their job was to keep logs flowing down the river. This often required riding the logs with cant hook and pike poles to push, pull and do whatever necessary to untangle log jams. Such work required great leg strength and balance. Only a very few men remained Log Drivers for long as injuries and, fairly frequently, death claimed them.

Lumberjack pay: Wages paid to lumberjacks/choppers in 1889 varied between ninety cents and one dollar per day plus room and board, DUNHAM p. 126. The *History of Hamilton County* indicates tree "choppers" were earning $26.00 per month (plus room and board) in 1915, p.146.

2.   LUMBERJACK DAYS

Wells, New York and the HOSLEY HOTEL: A popular stopping stop for stagecoaches after leaving the Northville Train station. Wells was a busy little community and Foxey Brown was known to have spent time there. HAMHIS, P. 692, Amsterdam Evening Record, Nov 11, 1922, p. 1. An interesting incident occurred during the research phase for this book. Trying to "leave no stone unturned," I placed an advertisement in the *Hamilton County Express* newspaper requesting information/photographs on Foxey Brown or Brown's Pond. Adirondack resident and author Don

Williams saw the advertisement and telephoned to say there might be a photograph of Foxey Brown in the Wells Historical Society museum. A telephone call to the Historical Society revealed that they had recently sold the photograph at a garage sale because "it had hung on a wall for many years and no one knew who it was." Fortunately, a local history buff named Joanne Buyce was the purchaser and responded to my telephone call. If I was willing to come to Wells, she would make the "large, heavily wooden framed, twenty by fourteen inch photograph available." I agreed to make the trip the following weekend.

Several Wells Historical Society members along with Joanne and her husband greeted me upon my arrival. Sure enough, it was Foxey Brown as his image compared very favorably with the two other photographs I had brought along. The professionally prepared image in Joann's possession shows a very distinguished looking Foxey Brown/David Brennan attired in a tuxedo type coat and bow tie (see illustrations section). The cost of having the photograph prepared must have been substantial in Foxey's day and suggests something about the tastes of the legendary Adirondack guide. Why and how it got left in Wells, NY when Foxey departed, is an unsolved mystery.

Clint Neff: Clint is a fictional character created to help transition Foxey Brown into logging camp life and life on Fall Stream.

Asa Aird: It is not known for certain that Foxey Brown worked for Asa Aird. Aird, however, was a well-known Sageville/Lake Pleasant lumber dealer of the time period who lived and operated a saw mill "west of Lake Pleasant." HAMHIS, pp. 7, 97, 99, 101, 127.

Willis Mountain: May or may not be the lumber camp location where Foxey Brown worked for a short while prior to homesteading at Fall Stream. He, however, had to be very familiar with the mountain as it looms over the abandoned Fall Stream lumber camp he occupied for twenty-five years.

Pat Whalen: Considered to be the best chopper in the West Canada Lakes area. Also known as the best bar-room "kicker" because of the ability to leave footprints on dance floor ceilings. DUNHAM, p.121.

Pants on bedpost: Story (with names altered) taken from DUNHAM, p. 139.

Foxey Brown's Gloria: There is no record of Foxey Brown/David Brennan having had a female relationship or of his attitude toward women.

Brooks Hotel - Speculator: The Brooks Hotel was a village landmark for many years in what was known as Newton's Corners or the Four Corners. The village is known today as Speculator, NY. AD TALES, HAMHIS.

French Louie: Louis Seymour (French Louie) was an Adirondack hermit, woodsman, and guide circa 1875-1915 in the West Canada Lakes Wilderness area. Known for his woods wisdom, self-reliant skills and generous nature, Seymour was beloved by area residents of his time. After his death, school children and admirers raised funds to erect a gravestone (Speculator cemetery) in his honor. The dialect attributed to French Louie was adapted from that used in Harvey Dunham's book: *French Louie.* See also HAMHIS, AD TALES, AD CHARACTERS.

Handguns in poker game/Billy the Kid: Wikipedia.org/wiki/Colt_Model_1877.

3. SHORT TERM LOGGER

Logging camp song: Bethe, Robert D. *Adirondack Voices: Woodsmen and Woods Lore.* Urbana, Illinois: University of Illinois Press. 1981, p.120.

Driving trees: Schneider, Paul. *The Adirondacks: A History of America's First Wilderness.* New York: Holt & Company. 1997, p. 205.

French Louie and Foxey Brown relationship: There is no definitive proof that Foxey Brown and French Louie were friends. However, they did live approximately eight or nine miles apart between 1889–1915. That distance was an easy walk for Adirondack mountain men in those days. As wonderfully described by Harvey Dunham (DUNHAM), French

Louie wandered widely and spent time in Piseco. He surely would have known about Foxey Brown and the abandoned logging camp and large pond at "Brownsville." Given that Foxey Brown raised cattle, it is likely French Louie visited to obtain milk and butter from time to time. It is also interesting that Foxey Brown kept a pet snake as had been French Louie's practice for many years.

4. FALL STREAM

Fall Stream abandoned logging camp: As described in the Prologue, Foxey Brown did inhabit an abandoned logging camp and large pond on the upper reaches of Fall Stream. There he created his camp and small farm described in various written records (HAMHIS, AD TALES, 1916 newspaper accounts of Carlton Banker's disappearance). Hikers visiting the area today can view remains of Foxey's barn, pond dam, and artifacts scattered around the site. It is also obvious from examination of sheets of plastic and modern debris that hunters and fishermen visited Brown's Pond for many years after Foxey left his "Hermitage."

Logging camp characters: With the exception of Asa Aird, and French Louie, Foxey Brown's logging camp mate names were invented. The men Foxey Brown actually worked with could have been any of dozens pictured in Fred and Cindy Adcock's collection of period photographs. See ADCOCK, Days of Industry and Agriculture, pp. 117-126.

Killing of panther, mapping by State Forest Commission: Chilson, Gary (ed). *An Adirondack Chronology*. The Adirondack Research Library of the Association for the Protection of the Adirondacks Chronology Management Team. 2010. Available as a pdf.on line at www.protect ads.org. An excellent timeline resource for anyone wishing to understand Adirondack history and the rise of conservation in the United States.

Firewood rhyme: There is no definitive source as to the exact origin of the "Beechwood fires are bright and clear if the logs are kept a year..." rhyme. There are numerous versions of the mnemonic device. Numerous websites provide versions and list no authors.

Wadsworth gang: The Wadsworth family evidently had a long-standing reputation of being outlaws. French Louie had his encounters with them as did residents of Wells where several misdeeds occurred. Charles Wadsworth and his sons apparently patterned themselves after the Jesse James gang for several years before authorities ended their careers. HAMHIS p.242-243.

William P. Courtney: A genuine legendary Piseco character, Courtney had varied and definite relationships with Foxey Brown (see "Shooting hat off head story," HAMHIS p.346). In addition to operating the Piseco Hotel for many years, Courtney worked as a farmer, guide, and postmaster.

Floyd Lobb stories: Lobb was a long time Piseco resident and gained fame for inventing the "Lobb Fishing Spoon." HAMHIS, pp.322-323. AD TALES, p.43-44.

5.   FEARSOME FOXEY

Sending lead for sinkers: "Get out of here or I'll send lead for sinkers!" is a statement attributed to Foxey Brown when he chased hunters and fisherman away from his camp. HAMHIS, p. 346. AD TALES, p. 196.

Tim Crowley and spruce gum: Tim Crowley lived for many years at Spruce Lake approximately four miles up the Piseco trail from Foxey Brown. Crowley was one of the most successful spruce gum pickers in the region. The gum was usually picked from the tree in cold weather when it was hard and firm on the trees. Using a long pole with a sharp file on the end, a good man could scrape sixty or more pounds per day and receive between $1.00 and $1.50 per pound. When most laborers were working for $1.00 per day spruce gum pikers were making great wages. The Indian John Leaf, and the Abrams family (Floyd, George and Bill) were known to assist Crowley from time to time. HAMHIS, pp. 136-137.

Crowley also bought spruce gum from French Louie at West Canada Lake for $.50 per pound. DUNHAM, p. 48.

Saloons and bars: The tanning industry, lumber camps, and sawmills of 1890, apparently created substantial numbers of "hard working and drinking" men. As Aber and King point out (HAMHIS, p. 321): "It was a rip-roaring era with a full twelve saloons lining the road from Piseco to the Lake Pleasant line, and all well patronized on Saturday nights."

Piseco Hotels: Unlike more lavish hotels at Lake Placid or Lake George, Piseco Lake facilities "were simple, comfortable, and affordable." The charm that Piseco offered resided in its seclusion and rustic setting close to what was still considered wilderness. Only the Irondequoit Club Inn remains from many that existed in Foxey Brown's time (1890-1920). Gone, often due to fire, are the Piseco Lake Hotel, Abrams family Sportsman's Home, and the Truman Lawrence boardinghouse. HAMHIS, p. 340. ADCOCK, pp. 39-47.

Abrams Family: The Abrams family was well established in the Piseco Lake area when David Brennan/Foxey Brown arrived around 1889. Most prominent was Floyd W. Abrams who owned and operated the Sports-man's Home. Floyd W. was a man of many talents and interests. Over the course of his lifetime he worked as a farmer, guide, fire warden, hunting camp and hotel proprietor. ADCOCK, p.46; HAMHIS, pp. 139, 322, 325-327, 334, 338, 342, 343, 352, 356.

Family tradition (personal interview with William F. Abrams, August 21, 2007) relates that "Floyd W. Abrams, on more than one occasion, took in Foxey Brown when he came to town, got drunk, and shot off his pistols."

All Abrams' family members referred to in the Foxey Brown story are authentic individuals.

Foxey's reading materials: All publications listed were available via U.S. mail during Foxey's tenure at Fall Stream. Which publications Brown actually subscribed to are subject to debate – that he was a reader is not. *Amsterdam Evening Record.* Saturday, November 11, 1922, pp. 1-2.

Wolf, dog story: Adapted from Aesop's Fables: Wolf & Dog. Retrieved from: http. Ancient history.about.com/library/bl/bl-aesop_dog_wolf.

6.   MOUNTAIN LIFE

French Louie & Courtney's dog: DUNHAM, pp. 42-43.

Shooting Courtney's hat: "Shooting a hole in Old Man Courtney's hat while on his head" was something Foxey Brown kidded about. Whether he did so in anger, by accident, or by design with Courtney's collusion is subject to interpretation of the historical record. HAMHIS p. 346

French Louie nearly drowns: DUNHAM, p. 112.

French Louie and snakes: DUNHAM, pp. 32-33 images, p. 101.

French Louie's place: DUNHAM, pp. 91-95.

French Louie and boats and many camps: DUNHAM, p. 95 and 177.

Forest Preserve and conservation law begins 1885: DUNHAM, p. 89. HAMHIS, p.212.

Private parks: CRIMES, pp. 39-41.

French Louie & John Leaf fined for poaching: *First Annual Report of the NY State Commissioners of Fish, Game and Forests, 1895.* New York State Library, p. 51.

Local juries were initially inclined to acquit residents charged with poaching. However, persistent game protectors eventually "got their man." In French Louie's case, game protectors got convictions of $35.00 on August 6, 1895, $40.00 on November 8th, and $10.00 on November 20th. Members of the Dunham and Anibal families (first names not listed) in Piseco were also fined for game violations on May 1st and June 15th in the amounts of $50.00 and $44.50 respectively. A search of FG&F and Conservation Commission reports from 1895-1915 revealed no instances of Foxey Brown/David Brennan/David Brown having been convicted of breaking conservation law.

William Dunham "Firewood" letter of 1899: *Fish, Game and Forest Commission Report, 1899*. NYS Library, pp. 94-95.

Crosscut saw, first use: HAMHIS, p. 146.

7. CARLTON BANKER

"Sports": Nickname local residents bestowed upon well-to-do sportsmen who came to the Adirondacks to hunt and fish. Local residents willing to guide Sports could triple the wages (one dollar per day) laborers normally earned in the 1890's. CRIMES, pp. 26-27.

Carlton Banker: Banker had started hunting and fishing in the Adirondacks as a young man. An 1893 article in the *Gloversville Daily Leader* mentions him returning from Hamilton County "with as fine a catch of trout as anyone claims to have seen." His signature, and that of his brother-in-law Ira Wooster, appears in Tim Crowley's Spruce Lake Lodge guest register on September 21, 1901 and on October 16, 1902. Piseco Historical Society, Piseco, NY.

Aubrey Eneas solar power: Environmental History Timeline, www. radford.edu_wkorvarick/envhist. Renewablebook.com.

Banker family and Piseco: HAMHIS, pp. 343-344. 1900 U.S. Census

Wildlife discussion: AD CHRON, 1890-1902.

Blizzard of 1900: AD CHRON, 1900.

Man and Nature: Marsh, George Perkins. *The Earth as Modified by Human Action: A New Edition of Man and Nature*. Rev. ed. New York: Charles Scribner's and Sons, 1874. Pp. 29-30, 36.

Theodore Roosevelt's Adirondack journey: It is not commonly known that Roosevelt was in the Adirondack Mountains when word arrived about President McKinley's assassination. One account even places him as being in the wilds of Maine. Carlton's rendition of TR's ride out of the mountains is based on an article by: Engel, Robert and Watson, Judith. "TR's Midnight Dash." *The Conservationist*. October 1, 1999. Pp. 10-11.

TR and the strenuous life: Quote is from a speech given at the Hamilton Club in Chicago, Illinois on April 10, 1899. Retrieved from www. Bartleby.com/58/1.html. See also: Roosevelt, Theodore. The *Strenuous Life: Essays and Addresses*. NY: Century Company. 1900.

TR exercise story: Retrieved from www.legacee.com/Info/Leadership/Leader_Jokes.html.

Belden brother's gold mine: HAMHIS, pp. 128-129.

Fulton County Marble Company: HAM HIS p. 129.

Death of Fred Abrams: Latest Adirondack Tragedy. *Amsterdam Evening Recorder*. Nov. 5, 1902. P. 6.

William B. (Bill) Abrams: HAM HIS. Pp. 137, 346, 348. ADCOCK. Pp. 38,63, 68, 126.

Floyd W. Abrams: HAM HIS. Pp. 322, 325, 326, 327. ADCOCK. Pp. 58,126. New York Forest, Fish and Game Commission. *Annual Report,1899*. Albany, NY: James B. Lyon. 1900. P. 333.

8.   WITNESS ROCK

Origin of Piseco Lake name: The name "Piseco" appears to have been taken from an old Indian named "Pezeeko" found living on the lake in the early 1800's. HAMHIS, p. 6. "Pezeeko" was derived from a Native American word "pisco" that referred to fish. Hence, Pisceo Lake was known by Native Americans as Fish Lake. ADCOCK, p. 10.

Adirondack Park, Verplanck Colvin, Blue Line: HAMHIS, pp. 212-213. AD CHRON, 1892.

Gas driven automobile and telephone line: AD CHRON, 1898.

State purchase of land: Donaldson, Alfred L. *A History of the Adirondacks*. New York: Century, 1921, p. 178.

Theodore Roosevelt – "A corporation is..." Given at his May 9, 1899 address to the City Club of New York. The address may or may not have appeared in *Collier's Weekly*. Retrieved from TR Timeline at: graywolf/corp.com/trcalendar.php.

Martha Place execution: Retrieved from www.wordiq.com/definition/Martha_Place.

Theodore Roosevelt – "There is a time to be just..." Retrieved from TR Timeline at: www.graywolf/corp.com/trcalendar.php.

9.   SECOND CHANCES

1903 spring drought: AD CHRON, 1903.

William P. Courtney postmaster: The postmaster position was coveted by local residents probably due to the steady employment and good wages it offered. For forty years (1881-1921) four Piseco residents alternated in the position. They were: William P. Courtney, Lucy Abrams, William Dunham, and David Judway. Foxey Brown was certainly known by all of them.

Gold in Adirondacks: There is gold in the Adirondack Mountains. However, it apparently exists only in trace amounts. See HAMHIS, pp. 127, 129, 130 and 372-373 for descriptions of various temporary efforts to operate gold mines.

Elkins Anti-Rebate Act: Elkins Anti-Rebate Bill, *New York Times*. March 1, 1903, p. 10.

John Burroughs: pulse of old mother mountain: Burroughs, John. *Works of John Burroughs, Wake Robin.* Boston and New York: Houghton, Mifflin & Company. 1904. P. 102.

Pelican Island: AD CHRON, 1903. www.fws.gov/pelicanisland/

Brook Trout Limits: HAM HIS, p. 135. DUNHAM, p. 89.

10.   ADIRONDACK GUIDE

Boone and Crocket Club: Founded in 1887, by Theodore Roosevelt and George Bird Grinnell, AD CHRON, 1885. Named in honor of American hunters and outdoorsmen Daniel Boone and Davey Crockett, the Club was originally established to champion "fair chase" ethics – "the ethical, sportsmanlike, and lawful pursuit and taking of free-ranging wild game animals in a manner that does not give the hunter an improper or unfair advantage over the animal." The Club evolved, under the leadership of men such as Gifford Pinchot and Aldo Leopold, to lay the groundwork for wildlife conservation in the USA. Its mission today includes promoting "outdoor ethics for all people, emphasizing shared use of natural resources to protect options for future generations. Protecting wildlife population habitat on public and private lands, and associated outdoor recreational experiences is a major focus." Retrieved from: www.boone-crockett.org/about_overview. December 1, 2010.

Books by Theodore Roosevelt: Roosevelt was a prolific author. A visit to: www.theodoreroosevelt.org/research/biblioworks.htm will reveal the extent of his lifelong passion for writing.

Sheriff Ned James: Sheriff James is a fictitious character as is (fiction) the story of how Foxey Brown learned his Boston barroom opponent had not died.

1903 Forest Fires: AD CHRON, 1903. HAM HIS, p. 213. www.adkmuseum.org/about_us/adirondack_journal/?id

Foxey goes to Boston: Remains of Hunter Long Missing Found in Woods. *Amsterdam Evening Recorder.* Nov. 11, 1922. P.1.

Foxey Brown/David Brennan's family 1903: Requiescant in Pace 1839-1991. *St. Benedict's Roman Catholic Cemetery.* Richard Kelly Jr. Augusta, Maine: O'Ceallaigh Publications. 1994. David Brennan obituary, The Gardiner Journal, Gardiner, Maine, July 24, 1930. Vital Records, Maine State Library, 1923-1936, Microfilm Roll: 7.

Ruffed Grouse and Woodcock: Elman, Robert. *The Hunter's Field Guide to the Game Birds and Animals of North America.* New York: Alfred A. Knopf. 1974. Pp. 15-26 and 112-118.

Cy Dunham: HAM HIS, pp. 346, 326, 327. Dunham family history at Ancestry.com. I am deeply indebted to Joann Dunham Estes for generously allowing access to her rich collection of family (Abrams, Dunham, Courtney, Judway) tree records housed on Ancestry.com.

Bill Gallagher: HAM HIS, pp. 346, 350. CENSUS, 1910, 1920.

Wendigo: The notion of a "Wendigo" or spirit of lonely places can be traced to Algonquian mythology and to other sources. In Native American mythology it is often a spirit, just out of sight, that tracks the unwary forest traveler ready to strike if mistakes are made. Perhaps it was an early way of describing the outcome of hypothermia. The Internet is full of sources for those wishing to learn more about Wendigo.

Orrando P. Dexter (incorrectly listed as "Orlando" in many sources): Orlando P. Dexter Shot Dead By Hidden Enemy. *New York Times,* September 20, 1903, p.2. Murder of Orlando Dexter, *St. Lawrence Herald.* September 25, 1903, p. 1. Says He Knows Who Killed O.P. Dexter. *Watertown Daily Times.* November 6, 1908, p. 1. Calculating Woodsman Evidently the Murderer. *The Syracuse Journal.* September 21, 1903. P. 2. CRIMES, pp. 41-42. AD CHRON 1903.

Lodging for the Night: Original unpublished poem by William David Dunham (1873-1940) courtesy (August 1, 2010) of Joann Dunham Estes. Date of poem authorship unknown.

Skeeter Creek: William David Dunham (1873-1940) courtesy (August 1, 2010) of Joann Dunham Estes.

Roosevelt's Syracuse "Square Deal" Speech: Retrieved from www. memorablequotations.com/SquareDeal.htm. August 20, 2010.

William P. Courtney's Moose: AD TALES, pp. 46-47.

Forty-seven degrees below zero: AD CHRON, 1904.

Frank Baker and the alarm clocks: DUNHAM, pp. 154-155.

11.   CHANGING TIMES

Hartman, Letson murder case: HAM HIS, pp. 248-251.

Gillette, Brown murder case: HAM HIS, pp. 572-573. *See An American Tragedy* by Theodore Dreiser for a full length novel about the Chester Gillette and Grace Brown story.

Passing of William P. Courtney: Ancestry.com. website. Joann Dunham Estes family tree.

Roosevelt's 1908 White House Governors Conference: AD CHRON, May 13-15, 1908. Yaple, Charles H. Historical Turning Points in American Environmentalism: The White House Conference. *Journal of Nature Study*. February, 1991. Volume 44, No. 2-3, pp. 33-34, 40.

1908 Adirondack forest fires: AD CHRON, 1908. HAM HIS, p. 378. Retrieved from www.adkmuseum.org/about_us/adirondack_journal/?id=108. July 8 2010.

"Sports" and their machines: AD CHRON, 1908-1915.

Fish and game conditions circa 1915: AD CHRON, 1911-1915.

Julia Preston, guide: ADCOCK, p12. Williams, Donald R. *The Adiron-dacks, 1830 -1930*. Portsmouth, NH: Arcadia Publishing. 2004, p. 94.

Squatters: HAM HISTORY, pp. 216-217, 378-379. CRIMES, pp. 33-34. New York Forest, Fish and Game Commission. *Annual Report for 1910*. Albany, NY: James B. Lyon, pp. 8-9.

Hetch Hetchy: Nash, Roderick. *Wilderness and the American Mind*. New Haven: Yale University Press. Fourth edition,1967. Pp. 161-168.

Attempted assassination of Roosevelt: Lorant, Stefan. *The Life and Times of Theodore Roosevelt*. New York: Doubleday & Company. 1959. Pp. 572-573.

Dam Construction: AD CHRON, 1910 -1914.

Beaver in the Adirondacks: Gotie, R.F. and D.L. Jenks. Assessment of the Use of Wetland Inventory Maps for Determining Potential Beaver Habitat. *NY Fish & Game Journal*. Vol. 31, pp. 55-62.

French Louie's death: DUNHAM, pp. 194-199. HAM HIS, p. 331.

Squatters ejected: AD CHRON, 1915.

Stephen Harris large deer: AD CHRON, November 11, 1915.

12.   BROWNSVILLE'S DEMISE

Adirondack earthquake: AD CHRON, January 5, 1916.

Winter snow records 1915-16: HAM HIS, p. 942. ADCOCK, p. 35.

World War I history: Retrieved from www.worldwar1-history.com/ World-War-1-Timeline.aspx. November 20, 2009. Lusitania sinking: www.historylearning.co.uk/lusitania,htm. Black Tom Island: www. en.wikipedia.org/wiki/Black Tom explosion. www.new world encyclope-dia.org/entry/theodore_roosevelt.

The day by day search for Carlton Banker as reported in daily newspapers:

November 8-9, 1916. Banker arrives in Piseco and travels to Foxey Brown's camp: Supt. Carleton Banker is Lost in Wilds of Hamilton County. *The Morning Herald: Gloversville and Johnstown, NY.* Nov. 14, 1916. Pp. 1-2. Bloodhounds on Trail of Banker. *Amsterdam Evening Recorder.* Nov. 14, 1916. Pp. 2-3. AD TALES, pp. 195-196.

Carlton Banker's high blood pressure: Banker Found; Daughters Identify Remains of Father, Missing Six Years. HERALD, Nov. 13, 1922. P.1.

Politics discussion, Wilson vs. Hughes Presidential election of 1916: Retrieved from www.u-s-history.com/pages/h888.html. www.absoluteastronomy.com/topicsCharles_Evans-Hughes. August 1, 2010.

November 10-11, 1916: Lost in Wilds of Hamilton County: Search Parties Are Out Looking for Carleton Banker. HERALD, Nov. 13, 1916. Pp. 2-3. AD TALES, pp. 196-197.

November 12, 1916: HERALD, Nov. 14, 1916. Pp. 1-2. Bloodhounds on Trail of Banker. *Amsterdam Evening Recorder.* Nov. 14, 1916. Pp. 2-4. AD TALES, p. 197.

November 13, 1916: Probability of Survival of F.J.& G. Official is Slight: Eight Inch Fall of Snow in Piseco... *Amsterdam Evening Recorder, November 15, 1916.* Bloodhounds Will Today Take Up Fresh Trail Leading to Banker. *Amsterdam Evening Recorder.* Nov. 15, 1916. P. 2-3.

November 14, 1916: Lost in Adirondack Wilds: Railroad Man is Sought by 136 Men Night and Day. *The New York Times,* Nov. 13, 1916. P. 13.

Reward for finding Carlton Banker's remains: $250 Reward For Missing Hunter. HERALD. Nov. 18, 1916, P. 1. Remains of Hunter Long Missing Found in Woods. *Amsterdam Evening Recorder.* Nov. 11, 1922. P. 1.

Labor wages in 1916: Cease, D.L. (ed). *The Railroad Trainman*. January 1922. Vol. 39, No. 1, p. 177.

Murder and other theories: Friends Now Believe Banker Was Murdered. HERALD, Nov. 16, 1916. P. 1. Foxey Brown Was Banker's Friend. HERALD, Nov. 17,1916. P. 1.

F.J. &. G. quarterly report: F.J. & G. Railroad. *Amsterdam Evening Recorder*. Nov. 24, 1916. P. 2.

News story, with Photographs, about Foxey: Foxy Brown Was Banker's Friend: For Many Years Piseco Guide and Gloversville Man Had Been Joined by the Tie That Binds. HERALD, Nov. 17, 1916. P. 1-2.

December 8, 1916 rain storm and winter thaw & reference to Lunkazoo Mountain: In Central New York. *Cooperstown Otsego Farmer*. Dec. 8, 1916. P. 1.

Bog theory tested: Is Body in a Bottomless Pit? *Utica Press*. Nov. 24, 1916. P. 1.

Insurance company refuses to pay: Daughters Identify Remains of Father, Missing Six Years. HERALD. Nov. 13, 1922. Pp. 1-2.

Foxey's reputation ruined: Tru Lawrence Still Hopeful. HERALD. Nov. 17, 1916. P. 1.

Is Body in a Bottomless Pit? *Utica Press*. Nov. 24, 1916. P.1.

Conversation with Charlie Preston: HAMHIS. P. 346.

13.   NO REST FOR THE WEARY

Trout fishing season closed: HAMHIS, Pp. 332-333.

Deer take limited to one: AD CHRON. 1919.

Coyote expands range into Adirondacks: AD CHRON. 1920.

Conservation Commission lists "enemies of wildlife:" AD CHRON. 1919.

Fire Towers: ADCOCK. P. 103. HAM HIS. P. 215. CRIMES. Pp.77-78. New York Forest, Fish, Game Commission. *Annual Reports 1899 and 1903*. Albany: James B. Lyon. Pp. 333 and 127. William David Dunham (1873-1940) courtesy (August 1, 2010) of Joann Dunham Estes.

Theodore Roosevelt's last days: Theodore Roosevelt Timeline. Retrieved from: www.theodoreroosevelt.org/life/timeline.htm January 30, 2011.

Foxey leaves Fall Stream/Piseco: Remains of Hunter Long Missing Found in Woods. *Amsterdam Evening Recorder*. Nov. 11, 1922. P. 2. HAM-HIS, P. 346.

Ada Banker's grief and death: Obituary. *Amsterdam Evening Recorder*, Nov. 3, 1921. P.3.

Skeleton May Be Glove City Hunter's; Missing Six Years. *Utica Observer-Dispatch*. Nov. 18,
1922. P. 1.

Carlton Banker's body found: Banker Found. HERALD. Nov. 13,1922. Pp. 1-2. Remains of Hunter Long Missing. Amsterdam Evening Recorder. Nov. 11, 1922. Pp. 1-2. HAMHIS, P. 346.

14. EPILOGUE

Foxey Brown/David Brennan's death: Vital Records of State of Maine, 1923-1936, Microfilm Roll:7, 1923-1936. Obituary. *The Gardiner Journal*. Gardiner, Maine. July 24, 1930. P. 2.

Carlton Banker 1893 fish catch: Carleton Banker: The Man Who Never Came Back. Gloversville, NY: *The Leader Herald*. Nov. 10, 2008. Based on story in *The Daily Leader*, 1893.

Forest air: Maloof, Joan. *Teaching the Trees: Lessons from the Forest*. Athens: University of Georgia Press. 2007. Pp. 3-6. See also: Soaking in Nature. *AMC Outdoors*. Nov. Dec. 2010. P. 13.

Take a Dip in the Forest Air. *Psychology Today*. Retrieved from: www.psychologytoday.com/print/46828. Nov. 11, 2010.

Thoreau and tonic of wildness: Thoreau, Henry David. *Walden: An Annotated Edition*. Edited by Walter Harding. Boston: Houghton Mifflin. 1995. P. 308.

Dr. Trudeau, Adirondack evergreen forest air 1890's: Annual Report, 1891. *New York Forest Commission*. Albany: James B. Lyon, 1892. Pp. 137-138.

Foxey Brown smoker: David Brown tobacco sale. Judway store sales ledger 1910. Courtesy of Piseco Historical Society.

David Brennan, man of learning: "Remains of Hunter Long Missing Found in Woods." *Amsterdam Evening Record*. Saturday, November 11, 1922, pp. 1-2.

Common Ground Alliance: See www.adkcommonground.org/index.

Thoreau, "Wildness" quote: Retrieved from: Thoreau's essays on line at: www.thoreau-online.org/major-essays-by-thoreau.htm. November 10, 2010. P.10. "The West of which I speak is but another name for the Wild; and what I have been preparing to say is, that in Wildness is the preservation of the world. Every tree sends its fibres forth in search of the Wild"

Thoreau, "Lives of quiet desperation": Thoreau, Henry David. *Walden: An Annotated Edition*. Edited by Walter Harding. Boston: Houghton Mifflin. 1995. P. 6.

"You belong outside..." poem: Original poem created by Bruce E. Matthews, circa 1974 as a gift for the author.

ABOUT THE AUTHOR

Charles Yaple is Professor Emeritus of Recreation, Parks and Leisure Studies at State University of New York College at Cortland where, after thirty-five years, he continues to teach environmental and outdoor education courses. Dr. Yaple is also Director of the Coalition for Education in the Outdoors and editor of *Taproot*, the organization's journal of outdoor education.

Charles was the co-founder, first Board president and long-time director of the Lime Hollow Center for Environment & Culture in Cortland, New York. It has been his great pleasure during a forty-four year teaching career to help students see, understand, and love the land.